My Mother Bids Me

A Novel of Jane Austen's England on the Eve of
Waterloo

Rosy Cole

ISBN 978-0-9556877-5-4

New Eve Publishing
Great Britain

Echoes of a strange past haunted Kate. She dimly knew her destiny lay far beyond the South Downs rectory where she had been so strictly reared. Manoeuvred into an uninspiring marriage, she escaped to make her own way in a society overshadowed by the Napoleonic Wars where values were a stark contrast to those at home.

She was to meet La Belle Madeleine whose brilliant establishment was not what it seemed; the stormy baronet whose young daughter was dying of consumption and whose half-mad sister had eloped with a penniless lord; the Brighton soldier who won her heart one enchanted evening, and as swiftly broke it.

It was through a dramatic sequence of events that she was lured inexorably back to her roots in the wilds of Cumberland, to Silvercragg Castle and the baneful spectre of Meg McCullough, the blacksmith's daughter crossed in love.

There the mystery began to unfold, but it was not until months later, on the battlefield of Waterloo, that Kate's future was finally sealed.

My Mother Bids Me Bind My Hair

My mother bids me bind my hair
With bands of rosy hue;
Tie up my sleeves with ribbons rare,
And lace my bodice blue!

"For why," she cries, "sit still and weep,
While others dance and play?"
Alas! I scarce can go or creep.
While Lubin is away!

'Tis sad to think those days are gone
When those we love were near!
I sit upon this mossy stone,
And sigh when none can hear:

And while I spin my flaxen thread,
And sing my simple lay,
The village seems asleep, or dead,
Now Lubin is away!

Anne Hunter (1742-1821)

The Legend...

In a cloud of dust the London stage went spanking along the road which snaked through the valley between mountain and moor. At Carlisle, the last port of call, the merchant in broadcloth was pleased to see confirmation from the jubilant pages of *The Times* of Napoleon's imprisonment on the island of Elba. The prospect of resuming trade with the Continent was long overdue.

It had been a mild spring day. Dizzying columns of insects were hanging over the horizon. Away to the right, the grey steeps of Helvellyn closed with the oncoming darkness. A bloated amber moon loomed up behind Raven's Ghyll. Vagrant sheep were nosing over lichen-covered outcrops and dry tussocks of heath grass, their plaintive bleating echoing around the fells like lost souls in search of their tribe. Low on a hill crowned with firs, the towers of Silvercragg Castle stood proud behind a fretwork of larches, mirrored in the placid gloom of Lake Mereswater and possessed of a desolate air. Built in the Gothic style, it intrigued the traveller and exerted a mysterious influence over the humble homesteads scattered throughout Wrydale.

On such a night the White Lady was said to appear, lamenting her lost child, the daughter whose heritage had been denied her. There were tales of bold, bad lords who feared neither God nor men, and tales of ghostly revelry by night when visions of the past startled ordinary mortals out of their wits. There were rumours of sorcery and dark deeds performed to keep strangers at bay. Folk wagged their heads ominously and harked back to the winter of '95, that fateful Christmas Eve when disaster struck. But none knew of the psychic forces that bound living to dead.

All was deserted now, all still. The coach had shaken off the dust of the place and gone thundering south. Ere long, wise folk would be taking to their beds. A curlew's thin cry cut through the silence emphasised by the timeless purling of the beck which knew all things and kept its own counsel. Save for a few retainers who went about their business with one eye on the clock, nothing stirred in the Castle.

It was on the South Downs, far beyond that road linking Silvercragg with civilisation, that the shades preyed on the finely-tuned mind of the dale's errant daughter...

One

Kate closed the volume of sermons. Blood rushed into the pinched fingers clasping it so tightly. "May I go now, Papa?"

The Reverend James Hanslope heard her plea with a grave smile, and nodded. His whole demeanour wilted as though the sun itself had withdrawn from him. He loved to listen to Kate's voice which had a quality of sympathy mingled with passion. This, he realised, was the closest he would ever draw to her, for in most ways she managed to elude him. But God had granted this precious time each day when Kate would read the appropriate passages from the lectionary, or take dictation for his sermons.

During recent months, his eyesight had weakened. The mists at the outer edges of his vision were encroaching. It was like seeing through a clear patch in frost dispersed by warm breath on a pane of glass. Soon the ice would weave its hard pattern all over the surface, the light would grow dim and he would retreat into darkness and the landscape of memory. Already his other senses had become more acute and he sensed sharply now Kate's longing for freedom. Yes, God had so afflicted him that he could establish this habit with her, this shared hour when the day was fresh and orient light splintered the church windows which could be seen from the library. "Yes, you may go, Kate. Don't neglect your visits after breakfast, will you?"

"But Papa," she protested, "it's Sarah's turn today. Why, yesterday, I took clothes and provisions to Mother Jarman's brood, I collected the book you lent Mr Phillips and called in to see Tom Wakefield, too."

"My dear, Tom is very sick and may not live to see the summer. He's prodigiously fond of you. Tis not pleasant, I own, seeing him retch and cough blood, but if you knew how much pleasure you gave, you could not begrudge him."

Kate dealt her father a look of one prepared to survive injustice and with a swish of her skirts, left the room. He noted, not for the first time, how the forget-me-not hue of that gown complimented her eyes. If inclined to be wanton, she seldom disobeyed him. But those eyes could wound him to the core. At times, they shone with an almost palpable defiance. Poor Kate! Day in, day out, she sat darning stockings or copying verses into an album. She clear-starched linen, patched sheets and made over old garments for the poor. She was a clever needlewoman, a consequence more of practice than enjoyment. Like lightning her needle would pierce the cloth, and sometimes her fingers, and her eyes would brim with tears of frustration. The blood, hot and vital, would well up and stain the article. She dreamt about those stains. How hard they were to remove! Those blots told against her, like sins.

Hanslope had kept a tight rein upon her. She was his adopted daughter, the middle child, and he meant that she should not fall victim to that wild strain she had inherited. Luckily for her, she did not know the power of her own charm. In many respects he would be glad to see her wed. With a husband and children, her energies would find a healthy outlet. When Ruth, his eldest, had married young Dr Taplow and flown the nest, well, then they would see. Meanwhile, out of a deep regard, he chastened Kate, but could not expect her to understand that.

She, of course, did not understand. It often seemed that her father was unfair. She assumed that she stood in greater need of discipline than Ruth and Sarah. They were never caught racing their ponies in the paddock and making bets with the wheelwright's game apprentice! They were not seen talking to strangers outside The Shoulder of Mutton Inn, whose well-sprung chariots might bear a bright lozenge on the panel. They were never discovered reading exciting romances from the Minerva Press, books Kate purchased in secret and smuggled under the bedclothes or escaped to the orchard to read. Her Reverend father had seized them and thrown them into the fire before her very eyes. "Better that they should burn than your soul in the fires of damnation!" he had cried in self-righteous indignation. She saw her whole world disintegrate among those flames, for the world of her imagination was vivid and life a mere shadow. The characters in those stories were more real than her prissy sisters who seemed to have no trouble being good.

Whenever despair overwhelmed her, as it frequently did, she stole away to her room and took her favourite childhood toy from the cupboard. This was a clockwork doll, dressed in peasant costume who sat at a spinning wheel performing her toil to the strains of *My Mother Bids Me Bind My Hair,* the poignant little song made famous by Franz Joseph Haydn's melody around the time of her birth. Kate would rest her head in her cupped hands, mesmerised, while the automaton rotated jerkily over and over again.

The sound of the glockenspiel moved her profoundly. It made her blood tingle. She yearned for a former time and place, she knew not when or where, only that she was haunted by an irrational urge to seek it.

Released from her Papa, Kate ran out of the house. Outside, the air was crisp and bright. The wallflowers were dazzling, shell pink and wine velvet. In the orchard, the grass was long and ragged and thin. Her kid shoes were saturated. She bent down and ran her hands through the grass, pressing cool palms to her burning cheeks. She opened the wicket gate and ran into the lane, scattering dust and brown and white hens who clucked irritably. Oh, if only something exciting would happen! Merrowdene was the nether end of nowhere!

"Top o' the mornin', Miss Kate," called a roguish voice.

Kate span round to be confronted by a grinning youth with

freckles and a thatch of sandy hair. It was Jem Potter, Farmer Staples' stepson who dallied with Polly Pringle, a maidservant in the Hanslope household. Twice each day, he took his dog-cart to meet the Mail Coach at Lewes, returned with the village post and saw it delivered. Very early on a still morning, the shrill blast of the post-horns could be heard in the distance as the team thundered towards the town. Since Mr Palmer's system had been adopted a decade or two ago, the speed of the British mails was the pride of all Europe.

"Oh, Jem, what a turn you gave me! Has Papa any letters?"

He shook his head, his eyes glinting with mischief. In his capacity as bearer of tidings, he had a self-important air and a way of drawing himself up to his full height. He made a pretence of sifting through the bundle of mail wedged between his thumb and forefinger. "Well, darned if I ant mistook!" His fist struck at the empty air. "No, t'ant for Parson. Tis for ee, Miss. From London, too, by the looks of un!"

"Oh, do let me see!"

Jem held a pale primrose letter aloft so that the tormented recipient had to jump up to reach it. "I'll lay my blunt there's some Corinthian back in the Wen with more'n half an eye to ee!"

"What nonsense! Papa does not let us go abroad. We haven't even been to Brighton!"

"Tis a reg'lar town of vice, that! What with this new-fangled waltzing and sea-bathing and gambling! And Prinny no better than he should be. The goings-on at the Pavilion!" Jem spoke with authority. He had connections with Royalty. His married sister, Alice, lived in Brighton and had once served in the Prince Regent's household below stairs.

"How I wish I could have a peep at it all!"

"There be foreigners, too," Jem went on, "folks as fled from the Terror. And, o' course, in the summer the place fair swarms with city bloods racing their gigs on the Downs, and fancy folk parading back and forth on the Steyne. Just now, they've got a travelling fair!"

"A fair! I should like of all things to go to a fair, Jem."

"T'ant for the likes of ee, Miss Kate. Best stay at home where tis safe and do as his Reverence bids."

Kate scampered off down the lane and sat in a niche on the packhorse bridge to read her letter. Water sparkled and chuckled over the pebbles way below, giving expression to her own abounding joy. She had recognised the handwriting at once as that of Anne Vernon, a young lady who had befriended the Hanslope girls the previous year when her brother, Robert, acquired Piers Hall, a Jacobean Mansion on the sylvan outskirts of Lewes. Kate, in particular, was attached to Anne. In fact, if she had any confidante at all, other than the stalwart Polly Pringle, vicarage housemaid, it was Anne Vernon. This last winter had seemed an eternity without her. She had invited Kate to spend Christmas in London under the chaperonage of Mrs Cornwallis, her aunt, but Mr Hanslope had refused to sanction it. He was appalled at the idea of his daughter's exposure to the false city life at so tender an age and instructed his wife to decline politely on the grounds that Kate could not be spared during the season properly associated with hearth and home.

"But my dear Mr Hanslope," his lady protested, "is that wise? Mrs Cornwallis is a very good sort of person and the Vernons themselves most respectable. Why, Mr Vernon is an Honourable and keeps more than one carriage! If events were to er...develop," said she, pouncing cosily upon the word. "I'll not say how, but you know how vastly taken Mr Vernon was with our Kate..." She clasped her hands together at her bosom. "Just think of it! Such a brilliant establishment!"

"You're building castles in the air. A pastime of the foolish. The wise man, you may recall, builds his humble abode upon rock. It's young Anthony March you'll have for a son-in-law, mark my words, madam. He has a distinct predilection for Kate and, what's more, she likes him. I fancy she does not share your partiality for Mr Vernon."

"Then she ought to be ashamed! Casting her chances to the winds. Our girls make few acquaintances. And I don't see why you should deem it so improbable that Mr Vernon has serious intentions. Kate may not be my own flesh and blood, but I'm sure she has more brains and beauty than many a frippery Miss of the *ton*."

"Be that as it may, my dear, I personally would favour Mr March's suit. He's a steady, reliable fellow. He won't go putting dangerous notions into her head."

Thus Mrs Hanslope yielded peevishly to her better half and Kate was spared her first glimpse of the *Beau Monde* cavorting along the Broad Winding path to Destruction.

Kate quickly absorbed Anne's latest epistle. "And now, my dearest friend," it ended, "I am so longing to see you and your sisters. Robert feared we might be delayed in Town over some tedious business matters, but, happily, it is not to be. Soon, soon, we shall meet again! Already some of our servants have been despatched to Piers Hall to prepare for our arrival next month. *À bientôt!* Your most affectionate, Anne." Along the side of the page, in minuscule writing, a postscript apologised that Anne had neglected to commit the letter to the mail for several days.

Kate jumped from her perch with a whoop of delight and ran home to tell them the news.

"Ruth! Sarah! Mama! Such news!" she cried, colliding with all three at the door of the breakfast parlour.

"Just look at you, child! Your gown is stained with green!" chided Mrs Hanslope, who had a rare scale of values in Kate's book.

"Listen, I've had a letter..."

"Come to the table, Kate," ordered Mr Hanslope in sober mood. He was standing at the head awaiting his womenfolk. "Where have you been?"

The joy flew from Kate's heart. "Out for a breath of air, Papa.

I was not aware that time had gone on so."

"When we have given thanks, you may proceed to tell us your news."

The Grace piously offered, Kate told them of the Vernons' return.

"Goodness gracious!" exclaimed Mrs Hanslope. All the girlish salt-and-pepper curls peeping from her mob-cap quaked. Life was prosaic: she rejoiced in a crisis. "That's less than four weeks away!"

"And you will need all of that to repair the ravages of winter, my dear," sympathised her spouse.

"You delight in taunting me, Mr Hanslope," said she. "We cannot afford to make light of it. If Kate were not such a silly Miss, she'd see the wisdom of giving Mr Vernon every assistance! Obstinate gel!"

"Perhaps he will transfer his affections to me, Mama," suggested Sarah. There was no coquetry in either Ruth or Sarah, but both took delight in siding with their father to tease their more worldly parent. "I'm sure I should not be so heartless."

"You were ever a considerate child," observed her mother. "Kate is not blessed with your sweet disposition, alas! It would be quite wonderful to see her mistress of Piers Hall and to know that she would be close to us, at least for part of the year."

"Quite wonderful," agreed Mr Hanslope, "if you are not averse to large draughty rooms and a kitchen barely within posting distance of the dining-hall!"

"Pray, take no heed of your father, Kate. With several thousand a year to line your pockets, you'll not take a chill!"

"No, Mama." It was useless to argue. Far better to let her mother's mind run riot. It amused Mrs Hanslope, this game of constructing her daughters' destinies. For it must be a game.

"I wonder why the servants have been sent down so early," mused Ruth. "A month in advance?"

Kate decided that she had no appetite and was staring

gloomily into a willow pattern world when she was jolted into a recollection of Anne Vernon's postscript. "She forgot to post the letter. She did, Ruth. Anne forgot! It was written days ago, in April! They must mean to come down this month, not next. Suppose they have arrived!"

"Merciful heavens!" shrieked her Mama. "How shall we contrive? The larder is empty and cook's ordered no birds to be killed this week. My wig needs crimping and the Van Dyck is in pawn! How could Mr Vernon do anything so ill-advised! Kate, what are we going to do with you? To misinterpret such a thing! How you vex me! Your head is so full of fancies!"

There were errands to run. No time to dream. Kate must take a basket of victuals to the Wakefields' cottage in Paradise Lane. She pressed a jaunty poke bonnet over her ringlets and pulled the ribbons into a taut bow with an impatient gesture. How she hated this old bonnet! These fussy curls! She longed for the gamine hairstyle that young and fashionable French women favoured. With Napoleon under lock and key on the Isle of Elba, she fancied it could no longer be considered unpatriotic to emulate them.

Clouds were gathering. The day had promised brilliance too soon. The distant woods were clear and tinged with blue. A heavy drop of rain landed on Kate's cheek and she opted for a short cut across the meadow. A breeze gleamed over the grass and set buttercups dancing like a silent concourse of people and broke the spheres of seeding dandelions. Swifts dived about the hedgerows and snatched at insects. Rain began to fall in earnest and she quickened her pace. The fluster of breezes which had frivolled away the best hours joined forces. Rain fell with a purpose, pattering on leaves and tattooing the ground. Minutes later, it came in a torrent mingled with hailstones as hard as dried beans. Kate broke into a run but the tangled grass checked her feet. In a corner of the field there was a chestnut whose broad foliage would afford shelter from the worst of the downpour. A horse and rider had already taken refuge there, but Kate, with her head bent down and the limp brim of her hat fending off the rain, did not notice them. She summoned all her strength to run faster. A stitch pain thrust itself into her ribs and, before she realised what had happened, she found herself sprawled headlong with her hand in a clump of nettles and her foot jammed in a rabbit hole concealed by matted clover. Most of the basket's contents were intact, but a yellowish slime oozed over her clothes from the shattered eggshells. She winced as her foot twisted free of its snare. And not a dock leaf in sight! A sob of despair shook her.

"If it isn't Miss Kate, by all that's famous!"

"Anthony! What are *you* doing here? Oh, that you should see me so! I'll never forgive you! Never!" In a vain attempt to salvage her dignity, she looked him sternly in the eye, much to his amusement. Flicking out a neatly laundered handkerchief, he proceeded to wipe the broken mess from her skirts. Then he untied the ribbon of her sandal, glancing at her once or twice, gauging her reaction. His familiar face, lit by sherry-brown eyes, was touched with a softened humanity. Anthony March, the young squire of Merrowdene Manor, who loved the simple pleasures of life: his rare books, a good madeira or claret, his collection of rare Britannia silver, a ruminative pipe of tobacco after supper. These things, with the occasional diversion of a little sport, a card or dinner party, were his chief delight. His cover was frequently laid at the Hanslope table and the girls tended to regard him as a brother.

Kate had never taken his attentions seriously. She had too little vanity to think them earnest. Besides, he was not the sort of fellow you mooned over, whose lock of hair you kept under your pillow.

The sole of her foot was now in his grasp. "Your ankle is

already a trifle swollen. Can you move it without discomfort?"

Kate rubbed the prickling white rash on her palm and wriggled her toes, blushing stupidly. He helped her to her feet, the miscreant he had rescued from scores of scrapes and she scarcely knew why she should be so put about by this one!

She placed all her weight on the tender foot. "I can manage perfectly. I am obliged to you, Anthony. Pray, don't let me keep you."

"Come, Kate, don't be so missish. Give me your basket. I'd not dream of deserting you and, in any case, I am on my way to the vicarage to invite you all to dinner on Thursday."

"Oh!" Kate said, duly put down. "How exceedingly civil! Was your recent stay in Bath pleasant?"

"Tolerable, I thank you. I missed you," he ventured.

"Yes, I presume your grandmother does not go much into society nowadays."

"My dear," Anthony began exasperatedly, "you are superb at the art of evasion." He took the liberty of kissing her without more ado. He had not kissed her before, nor had anyone else, except in the way of affection. She resisted at first, not as a token, out of genuine fright. But then her lips opened. A wave of emotion swept through her body and she surrendered to this keen new pleasure. "Well, well," Anthony approved with suppressed satisfaction. "An earthquake beneath the ice! Tell me," he said gently, "why were you in such despair when I found you? It was more than a tumble's worth."

"Papa is so *unrelenting*," Kate told him dolefully. "And Mama has taken a pet because of a misunderstanding. Mr Vernon is coming down to Piers Hall sooner than anticipated and she fancies herself his Mama-in-law one way or another!"

So that was the lie of the land! Anthony should have guessed. Well, then, he would make the most of his chances.

"It is all so simple, really," he said.

"What is?"

"To solve your problems at a stroke."

"I don't understand."

"Don't expect me to go down on one knee in this mud! I mean, deuce take it, Kate, it's not very romantic, is it, with us looking like a couple of drowned rats and you with your bonnet askew! My pockets aren't exactly to let and I know I don't snore and you may do as you please in respect of the house...!"

Swayed by these considerations, Miss Hanslope flung her arms about Mr March's neck in a most intemperate manner, crying: "Oh, Anthony, yes, please...!" and wondering why the glorious solution had not presented itself before. From which Mr March understood that his proposal had not been rejected out of hand. The warmth of her response surpassed his wildest fancy and he expressed himself with demonstrable gratitude, saying he would speak with her father when the family came to dine at the Manor.

A pale sun beamed through the clouds. A rainbow shimmered on a distant hill. The air smelled clean, of earth and blossom and hope revived. Life was packed with magical surprises. You could never tell what was around the corner.

"Mercy me!" cried Mrs Hanslope, refusing to believe her eyes. "Who can this be?"

The girls threw down their embroidery and clamoured around her. An emerald barouche drawn by two frisky greys had turned into the drive and was pulling up outside. A footman in green and black livery jumped down, opened the door and assisted a young lady in a white bonnet and pelisse trimmed with swansdown to descend. She was followed by a dark gentleman, of medium height, with brooding Roman features. The doorbell jangled vigorously. The residents of Piers Hall had returned.

"Well, did you ever...? What an imposition! Not a word of

warning!" Mrs Hanslope whisked her sewing and a stray newspaper under the sofa cushions and ran to the mirror to adjust her lace cap. She licked the tips of her forefingers to smooth her troubled eyebrows and generally rendered herself as glamorous a Mama-in-law as she hoped Mr Vernon would find anywhere.

"Mr Vernon and Miss Vernon is in the hall, madam," Polly announced. "Shall I show them in?"

"At once! At once! The wings are no place for nine thousand a year! Bring them on to the stage! And tell Mr Hanslope they're here, child."

"Very good, madam."

"Now Kate, pinch your cheeks and be sweet to the gentleman."

"Yes, Mama."

"And you, Sarah, might as well do the same," said the matron, fortifying herself against disaster.

Anne Vernon sailed in on a wave of gardenia, each gesture wafting the downy edges of her trim figure. Ruth and Sarah could admire, but Kate immediately felt drab.

Miss Vernon cooed how she had missed her dear friends and how she trusted she found them in health and spirits. How disappointing it had been that Kate could not join her at Christmas. "Such a winter it's been, though! Do you know, the Thames was frozen solid from Blackfriars to London Bridge. It was dammed by huge ice-floes. You never saw anything to equal it. Everyone went skating. And for weeks there was a Fair. There were braziers roaring away and sides of mutton being roasted. They held dances and acrobatic shows and firework displays. Why, it was like Vauxhall on ice!"

Mr Hanslope entered the room and cordially welcomed the visitors. "Will you take a little wine?" he enquired, peering from Miss Vernon to her brother. Smiling, they declined.

"Oh, then tea?" said his wife. "I insist you take some

refreshment. It is so long since we had the pleasure of seeing you. Kate, for one, has quite *pined* for your society." She glanced directly at Mr Vernon, spent a fluttering sigh and averted herself with a neat twirl so that her hand alighted on the silver bell which summoned Polly.

The gathering sat down, a somewhat odd expression crossing Mr Vernon's countenance. He realised that the lacy article poking out from beneath his cushion was not in fact a lady's fichu, but a half-stitched pair of the unmentionables belatedly in vogue. Intriguing speculations flitted through his mind only to be squashed by the recollection that this was, after all, a rectory. The room was sombre and shadowy, the blackened beams riddled with woodworm. Overgrown shrubs crowded close to the windows, hunching their backs against the prevailing wind. He imagined the profound silence of the dark winter afternoons, relieved only by the sound of female chatter and the chiming of the Tompion clock. The girls had resumed their sewing, plying their needles in unison.

Hanslope sank into his favourite buttoned leather chair as if life was overtaking him. "I see the Allies are to come and shake us by the hand."

"Early in June, I gather," Robert Vernon said. "The city has fairly buzzed with excitement since Boney's captivity."

"And well it might," sighed the vicar. "Heaven knows, we've waited twenty years for it."

"The Czar is the people's hero," Anne said, "almost as much as Wellington himself."

"Doubtless it will irk Prinny's pride," her brother added. "He's a devil of a fellow for the limelight and rather covets military glory. He'd have joined the campaigns had not the King raised a dust."

"As it is," Anne said, "he has had to content himself with designing uniforms for the Tenth Hussars."

"Heir Apparent or no," averred the Reverend, "he'd have

done better to have spent his life in an honest cause than in his present reprobate fashion. He has made himself most unpopular over his treatment of the Princess Caroline."

"Oh, but my dear, consider!" his spouse reminded him. "She is hardly beyond reproach herself. A keeper of low company. They say she loves nothing more than to go to a Fair!"

"The Regent has driven her to desperation," said Hanslope calmly. "He stops at nothing to hurt her. They lock up Charlotte with the Queen at Windsor and refuse her mother admission... Ah, lubrication!"

Mrs Hanslope was relieved that Polly had had the good sense to lay out the best white china, dainty scalloped pieces edged with gold.

"The Prince was furious," Vernon was saying, "when he learnt that Charlotte and her mother had contrived to meet in the Park. He's behind her engagement to the Prince of Orange, you may rely. He'll see her whisked off to Holland at the first opportunity. Her mother violently objects to the match."

The Reverend stirred his tea. "I dare say she'll deal well enough with the 'Orange'. Convenient matches stand to be as successful as any others. What say you, Kate? And you, Ruth and Sarah? You are very quiet and industrious this afternoon."

Kate was separating strands of coloured silk. These snippets of news were absorbing enough to take all the drudgery out of needlework. She had rapidly covered a sizable area of the cloth, as if translating her excitement into stitches. "If I were Charlotte, Papa, I'd marry the Prince of Orange just to escape. Her present life is so restricted."

"Ah, but it's good to have Boney right where we want him," Vernon said, demolishing a small cucumber sandwich and sucking his fingertips. "The whole nation is ringing with anthems and ablaze with bonfires."

"We've such plans for the summer, have we not, Robert? Picnics, musical evenings, a strawberry party and a Midsummer

Ball…"

"Which I hope to have the honour of opening with Miss Kate." Vernon inclined his head graciously.

Kate smiled an acknowledgement, but said nothing. As a humble guest, she did not underrate this compliment. Her mother, picturing her as the belle of that dazzling occasion, fêted, courted, flirted with and finally led to some twilight arbour to be proposed to, could have wished for a more affirmative response.

Kate tossed and turned on her bed that night. Fractured dreams floated up through a feverish haze. She began to surface from sleep and some emotion pierced her psyche so sharply that she sat up with a jerk.

She could have sworn she heard the music box playing, that bewitching sound which so tormented her, she almost ceased to exist.

"Lawks, Miss, the price of silver lace now!" Polly gingerly wrapped a silk frock in tissue and replaced the lid of the bandbox.

The return of those good folk at Piers Hall had prompted Mrs Hanslope to order that Kate's wardrobe be overhauled without delay. Her spouse, overhearing these instructions, did not scruple to add: "And while you're about it, start planning her trousseau and a layette in time for the happy event!" Which advice shocked his lady into silence and was retailed in the scullery with great relish.

Polly began to enumerate upon her fingers. "You've made over your poke bonnet. I've put new braid on the silk and stitched the frayed buttonhole on your merino. Now what about the sprigged muslin? The ruffle's torn if I'm not mistaken. Shall I be doing that for you next?"

"What? Oh yes, if you please."

"Maybe you'll be wanting to wear it to the Manor tomorrow

night, Miss?"

Kate seemed distant today. She had in her hands a pair of satin slippers stained with dust and perspiration, worn to a ball at Piers Hall last summer. It had not been worthwhile to replace them. "Would it be very wrong of me to feign sickness and not go?"

"Not go to the Manor, Miss. Why ever not? You'd as lief dine with Mr Anthony as anyone."

"Listen, Polly, I've a plan… Promise not to breathe a word!"

Polly glanced nervously over her shoulder toward the unlatched door. She was fiercely loyal and would sooner have suffered the pillory than break one of Kate's confidences. "Cross my heart."

"Tomorrow evening, we could slip away to Brighton Fair. I'll pretend I've a headache – nothing too serious or Mama will be in a taking and wish to put off the visit. Oh, do say you'll come, Poll. It's the chance of a lifetime!"

For Polly, much as she enjoyed Heathfield Cuckoo Fair, there was not the illicit attraction pulling Kate. The poor, sweet maid, shut up like a princess in a tower! "If the Reverend finds out, there'll be such ructions. He'll turn me off without a character, sure as fate."

Mutiny kindled in Kate's eyes. "He won't find out! I don't wish to deceive him, but what harm can there be in a Fair? Mama said only yesterday that the Princess of Wales loves nothing better!"

Realising they would need a mode of transport, Jem Potter's services were soon enlisted in the conspiracy. Females and their hare-brained schemes! "If your Papa gets wind of it, you'll swing, and so will I!"

"Then let's drink to it, sir! A toast to our pending connection!" Anthony March was in high good humour. He tilted his chair, swivelled it deftly, bringing its wheel-back flush with the table, and then sat astride it. Mellow port trickled from the decanter into his companion's glass. His offer for Kate's hand had been received with unabated delight. The only thing to mar his contentment was that Kate herself was not there to share it. "It's most singular," Hanslope had said in apology. "Kate's rarely out of sorts. Even robust, one might say."

Anthony was all solicitude. "I do hope she hasn't taken a chill from her soaking the other day."

It was a cold evening for May. A damp wind with a tang of brine blew off the Channel and bore drifts of seagulls inshore. Their curved lines, dissolving and reforming, were like the interaction of waves on a swelling tide. So eager had Anthony been to sue for Kate when the ladies had withdrawn that he had omitted to have the curtains drawn and the lamps lit. A few candles were burning in wall brackets. The flames shuddered in the draught and slightly distorted the sallow features of the two gentlemen facing each other across the table. The light blaze of underbrush cleared from the thickets of the Manor estate, crackled in the grate and hardened the shadows. From the drawing room, the harpsichord spun melancholy airs as Sarah's fingers plunged into the keyboard.

Abruptly, the atmosphere had altered. A shadow passed across the cosiness, the camaraderie, the best laid plans. James Hanslope was not yet elderly, but seemed to have put on a kind of veteran wisdom, shrinking wearily into himself. His sober clothes hung limply about him. He drew the glass across the surface of the table with an enigmatic expression and caressed the knotted stem. His awareness of the tactile had increased.

He touched his glass to his host's. "I wish you joy of each other. The alliance has all my blessing. But before it takes place, there are certain things, concerning Kate, I must apprise you of."

The younger man raised his brows in quizzical amusement. "Indeed? Don't say she's a lady with a past."

"You're not so wide of the mark, though it's none of her making." Hanslope sipped his port and came straight to the point. "You may have noticed, at one time or another, a lack of resemblance between Kate and the rest of the family. She is not our daughter. We adopted her in rather distressing circumstances."

To Anthony, the dissimilarity was plain enough, but it had not crossed his mind that she was any other than Hanslope's child. "She... She is aware of this?"

"No. No, she is not. There has been no pressing reason to tell her. She is to us as much a daughter as Ruth and Sarah. We have made no distinction. She has received all the affection it was in our power to give."

"That I don't doubt," Anthony said in some alarm, "but is it wise to keep the matter dark? If she happens to find out, think what a shattering blow it could be."

Hanslope rubbed his wrinkled brow. It had been the cause of endless debate, sleepless nights. For years he had persuaded himself that Kate would not chance upon the truth. Had he kept quiet for her good or his own?

"Kate has been a great joy to us. Her love of life is contagious. Yet, sometimes, I feel we scarcely know her at all. There's no telling what goes on inside that pretty head of hers. I am put in mind of that Shakespearian phrase: *'Fathers trust not your daughter's minds by what you see them act.'* She has a hint of the seductress which, I confess, sometimes disturbs me."

"Oh come! You cannot confuse high spirits with waywardness! Tis part of her charm. A pleasant relief from the dull converse of most young women."

A draught whined under the door, lifting the edges of the carpet a little and adding to the atmosphere of unease. The tap, tap, tap of lithe young branches became more insistent as the wind arose. Hanslope gazed into the muted glimmer of his port. "They say that blood is thicker than water. The whole story would undoubtedly shock her. To have given a modified version, well, who knows where that would lead? If I'm any judge, her romantic turn of mind would make a meal of it…"

"Go on, sir."

Slowly the clergyman launched into his exposition, having kept the truth under lock and key for nearly twenty years. "As you know, Anthony, we are not native to this part of the country, my good lady and I. We used to live in Cumberland. It was where we were both brought up. My father was the incumbent of a living on the Penrose estates and when he died, it passed to me. The following year, I married Priscilla and in due course Ruth arrived. She was a placid baby, easily amused. I remember she had reached the toddling stage when the tragedy occurred…"

"The tragedy?"

"There was a certain blacksmith's daughter in Wrydale called Meg McCullough, a flighty young woman. Her own background was obscure. Some whispered that the blacksmith had been cuckolded and that Meg was the offspring of an eccentric peer whose custom it was to put up at the inn where her mother was a serving maid. As to that, I cannot say. What I do know is that Zac McCullough worshipped the girl. She lost her mother at an early age and was hopelessly spoiled by him. He worked all the hours God made, not merely to keep body and soul together, but so that she should have her heart's desires. What a dance she led him! She would parade up and down the street in a most affected manner and in apparel quite out of keeping with her station. Once she plagued her father for a parasol and, indulgent as he was, he saw she had one. A parasol for a blacksmith's daughter! We all feared she'd meet with a corrupt fate. But McCullough paid no heed to the warnings. 'Bah! She'll take no harm, my Princess won't,' he'd say. 'She's a canny head on her shoulders and her feet are fast to the ground!' I can see him now, poor fellow, with his rope-like veins, brushing the sweat from his soiled face. He was one of life's optimists. He had a perpetual grin."

"I suspect you are about to reveal that this creature you describe was Kate's mother?" Anthony said, visibly on tenterhooks.

Hanslope nodded. "Would that it had been a simple case of illegitimacy. That would have been a veritable blessing!" He swallowed some port without enjoyment and went on: "One thing that could be said of Meg was that she was comely. Too many heads were turned from the path of rectitude by her wiles. At barely fifteen, she could be seen hanging on the arms of excise officers and looking down her nose at the local youths. She grew up too quickly and acquired an aura of worldly sophistication. She saw to it that she came to the notice of Mark Penrose, the young Viscount, a quixotic fellow with an eye to the fair sex and a considerable fortune burning a hole in his pocket. They were birds of a feather. Within two or three years, he'd pretty well run through his legacy. However, his late father had wisely taken the precaution of making the greater part of his bequest inaccessible until Mark should marry. Though he was quick to perceive Meg's attractions, she was no candidate for marriage. Under cover of going into service, she went to live at Silvercragg Castle, but the other servants vouched for it that she never did a stroke of work. They declared her time was spent in his lordship's apartments, giving commands with all the aplomb of a lady born and bred. The pair gained notoriety and were spoken of throughout Cumberland. In his selfish way, Penrose was dotingly fond and showered gifts on Meg, jewels, trinkets, silks and satins, anything to delight the heart of a foolish girl. His lust was only matched by her avarice. A vain creature who despised the low born estate, she now set her sights on nothing less than a title and fortune. The taste of power and of opulence was heady indeed! I do not wonder it is easier for a camel to go through the eye of a needle than for a rich man to enter the Kingdom of God."

Hanslope was totally engrossed in his narrative by now. He

told his tale with such unaccustomed verve that it was impossible not to feel part and parcel of the events.

Translucent wax dripped down the candles and solidified in the draught. Anthony got up and threw another heap of sticks into the rapacious flames, arranging them with a pair of tongs. The sticks spat and protested, then burst into a blaze, making a phantom beacon of polished oak surfaces.

"Fire and water," Hanslope mused, "opposing elements."

"Forgive me, I don't follow."

"Meg's nature, Meg's fate. Her burning desires drove her into the lake where she drowned."

"She took her own life?"

Hanslope winced. A hideous business. There may have been a streak of madness in her, but I would not take an oath upon it. Passion and greed can warp the human mind more dangerously than mental weakness. Meg was with child and Mark had no intention of making an honest woman of her. He meant to make the match his family expected of him, the bride that was destined for him from childhood. What's more, by then, he was in financial straits. He had promised Meg an establishment of her own. She would want for nothing and their relationship could continue in a less flagrant style. Meg refused to understand that, in his world, this was the way of things. She would not be treated in that offhand manner. Meg McCullough would play second fiddle to no one! Her son would be the Penrose heir! She threatened to do away with herself if Mark did not wed her. The Viscount could, if he chose, have written her off without so much as a halfpenny piece and risked the consequences. I prefer to believe that a needled conscience made him hesitate to wash his hands of her." The cleric huffed a heartfelt sigh at the fecklessness of mankind. "Mark gambled and sank deep into debt as the months passed. It was imperative that he obtain some funds. He disappeared without a word to Meg. He must have guessed that the servants would prove hostile in his absence.

Most of them were honest village folk she'd grown up with."

"I fear rural communities can be less forgiving than townspeople."

"Her lying-in approached and she returned to the forge where she gave birth to her child…"

"A daughter. An unlikely heir, even had they been wed."

"Yes, *our* Kate. About a fortnight later, Mark arrived from London with his bride, Thomasine. It was just before Christmas, I recall. There was a thick rime on the trees and the peasants had strung lanterns between them on the Green where they sang carols. Up at the castle, a ball was planned for Christmas Eve. A momentous affair, it promised to be. Gossip went the rounds that there was to be a hamper of victuals and slivers of wedding cake for every family in the dale. What a hustle and bustle there was as they made ready for it! Guests came from all over the county, indeed further afield. The villagers blew into hands that were purple with cold and they huddled together to watch the fine carriages bowl into the drive. How pinched and chilblained their toes must have been. It would have taken me a week to thaw."

Anthony's gaze settled gratefully on the fire. "And Meg? What of Meg?"

"Mark had hoodwinked her, hadn't he? This usurper, Thomasine, had robbed her child of its inheritance. A grim future lay ahead, barbed with scoffing tongues. Treachery never gleamed so fierce in a woman's eye as it did in Meg's then! She was consumed with a craving for revenge. Like a bad coin, she turned up on the night of the ball. By all accounts, the Viscount was out on the terrace taking a breath of air when he surprised a figure crossing the lawns and realised it was Meg. He knew in his bones that she boded no good. There was some kind of altercation, for two or three guests, hearing raised voices, came out of the ballroom to see what was amiss. "You'll rue your wedding day before this night is over!" screamed Meg, and they said she looked insane. Mark was ashen-faced as she forced her way past him and entered the castle. That instant, a servant came rushing into the ballroom. 'My lord! My lady! Fire! Fire!' The orchestra ceased. Women screamed and fainted. A tremendous panic broke out. A fire had started in the stables and was rapidly communicating to the main building. Meg's hysterical laughter could heard above the din as she overthrew candle stands and set fire to the drapes with a torch. In a couple of winks, she'd wrought Armageddon! She fled from the blazing castle into the night. They found her body next day washed up among some reeds in a creek."

"How macabre," Anthony grimaced. "And how lucky for Kate that she was removed from it all and sheltered in a loving home."

"As for old McCullough, he could get no trade after that. No one would go near him. Mrs Hanslope and I went down to see the poor fellow, thinking to set an example and to try to console him. But the spirit had gone out of him. We saw how ill-cared for the baby was. It was upsetting beyond anything. Those motherly souls who'd have taken in the infant fought shy of doing so. You know the sort of superstition ignorance breeds. We had no recourse but to take her under our wing. McCullough was immensely relieved. Eventually he packed up and left."

"And Kate became Ruth's adopted sister."

"Naturally, Ruth was too young to understand. Kate entered her life much as she would have done had she been born to us. But we decided for Kate's sake to leave the district. Indeed, living down the past would have placed an insupportable burden upon all of us. A year later, by the intervention of the Almighty, I managed to obtain a living in this parish. We moved south and began our new life. By that time, Sarah was on her way. We looked upon her as God's house-warming gift."

After an uneasy silence, Anthony said: "It makes no difference, sir, to the way I feel about your daughter, be sure of that." He picked up his pipe. "Do you mind?"

From the drawing room, a hoot of mirth he recognised as his wife's brought Hanslope back to the land of the living. He was glad to have the matter off his chest. Airing the story had helped to dispel some of the misgivings about Kate's upbringing. Had he been too harsh with her? Might he have told her the truth had there been a stronger bond between them? Was he as concerned with her spiritual welfare as he was loath to risk losing her loyalty? Would he even have won her confidence had he allowed her more freedom? He did not know. The older he got, the more uncertain he was. Sometimes, his breast ached with life's uphill struggle. Already he was beginning to feel out of touch with daily reality. Well, Kate's future was secure at least.

Anthony March had paced over to the mantelpiece for his tobacco and was tamping it down in the bowl of his pipe. He took a paper spill from the nearby cupboard and thrust the end into a candle flame. "Tell me," he said, igniting the blend, "what became of the castle and the Penrose family?"

"One wing was destroyed, rased to the ground. Many lives were lost that night, including the Viscount and his bride."

"They'd have no heirs, of course."

"No. The title passed to Mark's younger brother, Adam. He was made of quite different clay, an almost ascetic nature compared to the elder son. He couldn't sell the estate fast enough. Folk used to say that when hoar-frost glistened and the moon was high, Meg's footprints could be seen on the Silvercragg lawns." The parson clutched his chin. "If memory serves, it was bought by a Scottish baronet and restored. Stewart, I believe the name was."

"Silvercragg," Anthony mused. "That's a name evocative of shades."

Jem Potter, with two fair passengers in his charge, was keen to demonstrate his prowess with the ribbons. His modest chariot was of the boneshaker variety and his driving at the best of times in true hell-for-leather style.

"Have a care for our supper, Jem," Polly complained, half-choking on a mouthful of pastry. Kate rocked with laughter at her apoplectic face. They were eating pasties and apples smuggled from the larder. Polly had to allow that Mr Anthony's table could not have offered so tempting a feast.

The girls had raided a black-bolted wainscot chest in the uppermost regions of the house where Mrs Hanslope stored cast-off garments, donated for the poor and destitute and awaiting repair. The cache had yielded a homespun shawl and a nankeen mantle, pregnant with smells of old timber, mould and stale lavender bags. In these, the girls slipped incognito down a back twitten from the rectory and through a sycamore grove where Jem's dog-cart awaited them in a lane on the outskirts of the village.

It was a dismal evening, though a forceful breeze kept the rain at bay. All about them was the wide perspective of the Downs and far behind, the road threading into a dark and light wood. The assorted roofs and Saxon tower of Merrowdene Church diminished, already remoter in imagination than distance.

On the way, Jem described how the Brighthelmstone of former days, a sleepy hamlet nestling at the foot of chalk hills, had mushroomed into Brighton town. There had been a cluster of cottages, a church and a couple of inns. Bearded fishermen with skins as coarse as their sweaters could be seen mending nets or dragging boats ashore. Seagulls pecked between the canes of the lobster creels. The only link with the world of commerce was the fish wagons that went pitching and rolling up to Billingsgate bearing slithery cargoes of herrings and shellfish. Life ambled along peacefully until Dr Richard Russell, a mildly eccentric fellow, published his *Dissertation on the Use of Sea Water* in which he recommended the therapeutic properties of a dunking. Folk were chary of trying it out to begin with, but a few respectable persons came in dribs and drabs to douse themselves and to drink it. Whether the cures they reported were due to the new panacea or to the coastal air was for conjecture, but they came back regular as clockwork, bringing with them a fillip to trade. The locals grumbled but were glad to see the colour of their money. By and by, concessions were made to their wants. A library opened and a room for dancing at one of the inns. Brighthelmstone was absorbed into Brighton and seemed little the worse.

And then, all of a sudden, as was his wont, the young Prince of Wales took it into his head to come down, throwing the town into a whirl of excitement. Things changed overnight. In his wake sailed the *Beau Monde* with a swish of fine silk and a snort of fine horseflesh. A summer palace appeared; crescents with Grecian façades spread their tentacles. Bucolic reels gave way to minuets. Everyone who was anyone and many who weren't flocked to Brighton to air their *toilettes* on Marine Parade.

In The Lanes, the tiny shops had put up their shutters when the companions arrived. The butcher's, baker's, fishmonger's, tallow chandler's, the candy store and print shop displaying the cartoons of Mr Gillray, Mr Cruikshank and Mr Rowlandson. With the influx of high life, Brighton folk could well appreciate a satirical comment upon their betters and the political questions of the day. Mr Cruikshank was fond of burgeoning bosoms and Mr Rowlandson of billowing skirts and naked bottoms tumbling down staircases. They spared the Royal family no mercy. Prinny's follies figured in many a caricature.

Jem deposited his passengers within a furlong of the Fair. They had calculated that they could not safely spend longer than an hour in Brighton and he promised to pick them up in the same spot. Jem reckoned they'd come to no harm if they didn't look for it and drove off without a qualm to visit Alice.

"Just look at the folks, Miss!" Polly exclaimed. As they wove in and out of the throng, rounded vowels of King's English mingled with Sussex drawl and raw, Romany cant. Against the rhythmic percussion of the surf and the squalling of gulls, the cries of competing stallholders rang out loud and clear. *"Crabs, crabs, any crabs!" "Mackerel, three for sixpence, mackerel." "Sugar plums and brandy balls!" "Hot chestnuts!"* Old men with winter in their bones stretched out gnarled hands to the braziers.

"Come, dearie, ye've a lucky smile," cajoled a fat goodwife at the Wheel of Fortune. She touched Kate's cheek. "Won't ee spin the wheel, then?"

Polly nudged her. "Well, go on, Miss Kate. That cameo brooch is 'andsome piece if ever I saw one."

"Pretty maids, won't you favour me with a stake in your fortune?" interjected a stranger. The girls found themselves looking into the merry bright eyes of a raffish blade of about five and twenty. Upon each arm, he sported a raddle-cheeked female who giggled at his exploits. He was well-spoken, but his clothes, though of the finest quality, had long lost their pristine cut and finish. His name was Johnny Jarvis, he said, introducing his companions. There was Emma, trailing a pink feather boa, impatient of the distraction, and Eliza Jane, a dusky beauty, shier than her plaintive friend. He asked whose acquaintance he had the pleasure of making.

Kate relaxed at this easy manners. Clearly he meant no harm. "I am Kate Hanslope," she owned, "and this is Polly, our faithful maid." Lies did not come readily to her tongue and perhaps she did not need to conceal her identity miles from home.

"Ah, I divine a bold stratagem here," Jarvis concluded gaily. "May your romp be a memorable one!"

He scattered some coins over the board. Chuckling, Kate span the wheel. How scandalised her father would be if he could see her now! The scarlet ball rattled madly for several seconds, then slithered to a halt.

"Oh!" cried Polly. "Not the brooch, but you've won a prize."

From the array of more modest prizes, Kate selected a pinchbeck button hook. "A souvenir of our adventure," she said to Jarvis. "Thank you, kind sir."

The servant could not share Kate's sublime trust of the stranger and chose to forego her turn. She was on her guard for hands that might snatch Kate's reticule, or accomplices that might be summoned out of nowhere to abduct the pair. How susceptible her young mistress was! It was a relief when, swayed by Emma's entreaties to come away and see the buffoons, Jarvis doffed his buckled hat and was gone. "Goodnight, sweet maids! Trip lightly!"

Soon he was lost in the sea of bobbing heads. Polly's apprehensions had been groundless and Kate's willingness to accept her fellow creatures at face value, endorsed. The blithe countenance of Johnny Jarvis was not quickly forgotten and Kate couldn't help comparing it to advantage with that of Anthony March.

Daylight was fast waning. It was colder. After they had spent a little time shivering among the spectators at the Archery Contest, Kate glanced at the pendant watch, borrowed from her mother's jewellery box, and admitted they ought to turn back.

As they passed The Castle Tavern, music could be heard. A minuet was in progress. They could see the courtly dancers posturing like figurines behind glass and Kate was vexed to be on the outside looking in.

"Oh, Miss! Did you ever see anything so beautiful?" Polly lingered in covetous awe before a confection of white tiffany in a dressmaker's window. A notice in neat copperplate script read: *Madame Matthieu has a vacancy for an intelligent young woman in her sewing-room. She must be able to sew a neat seam, hem, buttonhole, smockstitch and ruche.*

"Shall I sit on a cushion and sew a fine seam, Polly, as it says in the rhyme?"

"Indeed you won't. You've done enough sewing to last a lifetime and that's the truth," Polly declared. "Now do come, Miss. Jem'll be waiting and he won't take kindly to that. He always did say when a female says seven of the clock, she means eight!"

Polly, when she vouched for Jem's punctuality, quite forgot the occasion his father had hauled him, inebriate, by the ear from under a table in The Shoulder of Mutton whither he had collapsed during a game of dominoes. These measures were entirely warranted since Jem had promised to plough the 'top acre' before sunset. Polly wrathfully called it to mind.

"My, I'd like to tie a jumping-cracker to the seat of his breeks, that I would!"

Dusk was falling. Under the lamps, Kate looked pinched and distressed. They'd have to race back to Merrowdene and in the dark! Jem's driving was hair-raising enough in daylight. She pictured herself arriving on the doorstep of the vicarage simultaneously with her Papa. She began to feel lost and a little afraid. Drunkards tottered out of taverns and whispered obscenities she did not understand as they went by. Once a carriage drew alongside and then moved slowly on. If only Jem would come!

"Hark, he's a-coming!" Polly cocked an ear. "I'd know the creak of that rattle-trap anywhere!"

Dear heaven, let her be right! Kate thought, repenting of her deception.

"A pretty coil you've gotten us into, Jem Potter!" Polly accosted him. "Tis mortal cold on this corner." The girls clambered aboard the cart.

"Now, Poll, doan ee start champing the bit," Jem ground his teeth, setting the cart in motion with a mighty jolt. "Twere one of Alice's tackers, been took of an ague he has – and Jake down at the tavern an' all – Jem, her says, run and knock up the 'pothecary afore the poor mite fails."

"Just like a man to shift the blame, so it is!"

"Tis true what I'm telling ee. And didn't I have to fetch Jake from The Ship afterwards?"

Kate preserved a tactful silence, deeply thankful to have been rescued from that corner. Now the whole of her being urged the vehicle towards Merrowdene through the black, blustery moonless night and only the glow-worm light of Jem's lantern swinging and bobbing over the uneven road ahead. Trees loomed tall and weird, sheathed in ghostly green moss.

Those colloquial lovers were still at it, hammer and tongs, when the cart gave an ominous lurch and precipitated Polly into Jem's lap. "You clumsy oaf! Now look what you've done! We're stuck!"

He tossed her the reins, sprang down and unhooked the lantern to inspect the damage. One wheel-rim had sunk several inches into the sodden verge and fibrous outgrowths of oak had somehow become entangled with the spokes. "We'll be here till Kingdom Come," Polly wailed.

Half an hour slipped away before Jem succeeded in digging out the mire, bare-handed, and extricating the wheel, obstinately refusing all offers of assistance. Improvising with some sacks, a smooth ramp was made and the cart launched cautiously back on to the highway.

In despair, Kate clung to her one shred of hope: that her family had lingered at the Manor.

When at last they trundled into Merrowdene, an irascible Jem saw his passengers delivered to the vicarage and bade them a sullen goodnight. He watched the double silhouette disappear among the bushes but failed to notice the freshly-scored drive made by Anthony March's barouche in which his guests had been delivered home.

"Lawks, Miss, they're back!" Polly squeaked. All storeys

were a blaze of candles and the front door was ajar.

"Brace yourself for Papa's wrath," Kate said with fatalistic calm. "I am sorry for your sake, Polly, dear, but don't fret. I shall leave him in no doubt that I am to blame."

It seemed to Kate as she pushed open the door and walked into the light, blenching, that the chrysalis of childhood, with all its fetters and restrictions, fell away. Irrespective of her soiled and slovenly appearance, she drew herself up to her full stature and met the onslaught bravely.

"Merciful heavens!" cried Mrs Hanslope. "Where have you been, child! What on earth have you got on? No message, nothing! The whole village is alerted!"

The Reverend, hearing this outburst, hastened to the scene before Kate could speak. "What in the name of heaven have you been doing?" he demanded.

"We have been to Brighton Fair, Papa. I persuaded Polly to accompany me against her will."

"Go into the library, *daughter*," he ordered. "Polly, you are dismissed. You may look for a new post in the morning."

The poor harried servant erupted into a flood of tears and disappeared below stairs. Ruth and Sarah were gaping over the banister above at this unprecedented display of passion.

"That's grossly unjust, Papa. If Polly leaves this house, then so do I!"

"Kate!" shrieked her Mama. "You're rambling! You have taken a fever!"

"I repeat: Go into the library, Kate!" The vicar's partial vision lent a touch of ruthlessness to his anger and she obeyed him.

He closed the door and they came face to face. Kate was baffled by the uprush of pity she felt for the hurt expressed there. He did not invite her to sit down. She was shaking.

"Now perhaps you will render an account of your doings and explain why you are dressed in that outlandish garb."

She told him everything with a fluency he could only

admire. Nevertheless, she was careful not to implicate Jem, though she feared her Papa must perceive who had been drafted into the plot. He was touched by her appeal on Polly's behalf. As the tale lost momentum, Kate showed disarming signs of contrition, yet Hanslope was sorely troubled by their nature. "I am sorry to cause you pain, Papa, I am truly, but you never allowed us to engage in such harmless pursuits."

"That you should wish to, Kate..." He spoke in accents of defeat, dropping into a chair and looking in her direction with a curious intensity. The evening had enervated him. To be confronted by this slattern aroused in him a ferment of emotions and he could find no suitable response. A juvenile escapade, perhaps, but symbolic. She was no longer a child. He could not punish a young woman about to be married. Indeed, he could not have borne to do so, yet he feared for her soul. It was ironic coming upon the heels of his discussion with Anthony. Maybe the love of a good husband would tame and mature her. He said: "I was delighted by Anthony's news this evening."

"Oh?" She lowered her gaze.

"I cannot say it altogether surprised me, though I must own it occurred sooner than anticipated. You're a dark horse, Kate."

"Papa, I..." She fiddled with her bonnet strings, binding them around her fingers. Her voice trembled and was full of tears. "I cannot hold to it. I know that now. It would hardly be fair to Anthony."

The axe dealt another blow to all Hanslope had sought to establish. "What nonsense! An early attack of wedding nerves, nothing more! I do not doubt that is what prompted tonight's folly."

"You must understand, Papa, I accepted in haste. The heat of a moment... You must see..."

Kate began to flounder but was so remarkably clear-headed, Hanslope felt chilled. "You cannot retract now. You have given your word of honour to a truly worthy gentleman. Does that mean nothing to you? He is someone for whom we all have a deep affection. Almost a member of the family, not a comparative stranger."

"Heaven knows, I don't wish to injure him… I am fond of him…"

"It is the best basis for marriage, my dear. That's something the young seldom appreciate."

"Don't press me, Papa. You make me so unhappy. Surely it is better to break one's word at this stage than spoil two lives. The engagement is still unofficial. I just know in my heart that this is the wrong course to take. Don't ask me to explain."

He got up and went to her, gently taking her by the shoulders. Her lips quivered and a tear ran down her cheek when she blinked. He said with an uncommon degree of tenderness: "Take heed, Kate, when we run counter to God's will, he sometimes allows us the very thing we want. Try to understand that it is because I love you dearly I shall insist upon your marriage to Mr March. You will not reproach me for long."

The room lined with dreary volumes of theology closed in upon her. With a convulsive sob, she made for the door which had slipped open. Her mother was still there, distraughtly dabbing a handkerchief to her eyes, and beside her was Anthony in riding gear, an air of purpose about him, like a whirlwind caught in an alley. She could not bear his longing gaze. She had made and broken his happiness within so short a space. Blindly, she gathered up her skirts and ran up the staircase. "Kate!" he pleaded. "Kate, let me speak with you…" But to no avail. She heard nothing save the clink of padlock and chains, knew nothing but the dire urge to escape.

She slammed the door and leaned against it, panting. At Mrs Hanslope's request, Polly and cook had lit a fire and prepared a hip bath. They had drawn the tapestry screens around it to shield her from the draught. She turned the key in the door. A sense of crisis curled off her soul like a volatile liquid. I must get away, she thought. It is clear Papa wants to have done with me. And if I do not have Anthony, Mama will strive to bring about a union with Robert Vernon. I am trapped!

Poised for flight, she ran to the chest of drawers and tossed out stockings and chemises. She sifted through the linen-press, drew out two gowns and found her best pair of shoes. On top of the wardrobe was a valise. She climbed on to a chair to reach it, brushing dust from her fingers. One by one, articles were haphazardly folded and flung into it, followed by a brush, a comb, her pinchbeck button hook.

Someone knocked on the door. The handle twisted futilely. "Tis Polly, Miss. May I come in? I've brought you some soap and a clean towel."

In a flurry of agitation, Kate let her in. The maid had brightened. She had suffered a homily from Hanslope, but he was on the point of relenting about her dismissal. He said he knew her devotion to Kate had been the guiding principle in her wicked deception and that he would re-appraise the situation next day. "He'll be right as ninepence in the morning, Miss, you see. All forgiven and forgotten like a true Christian."

The news elicited no rejoicing from Kate. "Polly… I cannot stay here. Not now. Papa distresses me so. I am a thorn in his flesh and always have been. It is better that I go."

The yawning travel case and its random contents impinged on Polly's eye. "Oh Miss! No!"

"I will scribble a note to Mama and Papa and try to convince them that I am in possession of my wits and shall come to no harm. It is in all our interests that I seek a position in another household. I shall creep out before dawn and walk to Lewes. Once there, I can board the Brighton coach. Keep my secret, Polly, do that for me, and wish me well. Don't, I beseech you, inform them of my whereabouts."

"But, Miss, where *are* you going?"

"Why, to seek my fortune in the world. I am going to

Brighton, to Madame Matthieu!"

Two

She was ushered over the threshold and abandoned in opulent wastes of reflected light, all gilt and pastel green in the rococo style, with a chandelier that would have graced a palace. The room reverberated to the rumble of wheels and the clatter of hooves on the stone setts outside. She paced up and down, her heart beating wildly. What now?

Presently, the door at the far end of the room opened to admit a pleasant-looking lady of middle age, small and silver-dark and neatly built: Madeleine Matthieu. The lady was a positive dynamo of energy and something of a *femme fatale* in the least obtrusive sense. She was not at all pretty – her face did not bely her years – but a brilliance of eye and a youthful outline conspired to give the impression that she was younger. Men would happily recall her with a bemused glint of nostalgia.

She took to Kate at once. Oh, the girl was obviously country born and bred. Her clothes and her posture lacked finesse, but her looks were out of the common way. Madame was intrigued. This was not the sort of applicant she expected for her sewing-room. Most of them came to her from the outlying rural areas, but were of a coarser class altogether and sometimes undernourished. In the spring, they flocked to Brighton hoping for employment in the mansions of the rich. There were fewer vacancies than the number of girls to fill them and those who found work with Madame considered themselves fortunate indeed. She was very particular in her choice and liked them to be literate. She worked them hard, but they were prepared for that. They lived in comfort and were given beautiful clothes to wear. The food was superior to anything they'd ever known and it did not occur to them to cavil at the meagre portions. At home they'd subsisted on diets of oatmeal and water in many cases. A lively eye and trim figure were of as much moment as nimble fingers.

For Madame's stake in the fashionable world extended beyond the bounds of *haute couture*.

Entertaining was done on a lavish scale. Not a week passed without its quota of dinners and card parties, musical evenings and dress shows. The widow, by the sheer force of her charm and personality, had gained an enviable reputation as a hostess. *Chez Madeleine*, as it was known, was a temple to a goddess who plucked fruit from life's choicest trees. Culture went hand in hand with couture, probity embraced carnalism. Madeleine offered something to tempt all palates and guests thronged to her banquets. She had created a code, a fashion, and all who entered her Grecian portals fell under her spell.

In Madeleine's house, nothing was vulgar, nothing questionable, nothing obtruded. All was elegance, good taste and discretion. No ordinary mantuamaker, hers was no disreputable house of assignation. With the frequent migrations of the *ton*, she was as conveniently situated in Brighton as in Bond Street. Better so, since she had no rivals, although her trade was inclined to be seasonal. Princes, poets and politicians set foot in her salons. Whigs and Tories pitted their wits in the gamest of spirits. Many a famous raconteur flourished in the convivial haze of port and cigars after one of her dinners. Good repartee was as important as the quality of her table. And Madame would circulate among them with an air of light-hearted grace, chiding, teasing, commiserating, laughing her tinkling laugh with its tarnished overtones. She had a wonderful knack of seeing all sides of an issue and agreeing with all of them, ingeniously switching her view to the prevailing one.

But now, confronted by Kate, she was curious and amused. She indicated a plush sofa. "Please to be seated, Miss...er..."

"Hanslope," Kate prompted, obeying her with a little curtsy.

"Kate Hanslope."

"Will you take a glass of madeira? But no, it is too early. Perhaps you would care for some *café noir!*"

"Yes, if you please, I should prefer the coffee, though with a little milk."

Madeleine rang her handbell and gave instructions. "*Maintenant,* Mademoiselle Kate," said she, settling back into plump cushions, "you 'ave come to me for employment. Why is it that you are wishing to work in my showrooms?"

Kate coloured. "I believe I am proficient with a needle, Madame."

"Ah, so." Madeleine cast her eyes up to the cornices for inspiration. A direct answer, though not the one she sought. "Forgive me if I am a leetle impertinent, but your parents – you have the parents, yes? – do they find themselves in – 'ow do you say? – in Queer Street?"

"Indeed no, Madame. I am here because I wish for a life of my own."

Strength of character! Independence! A rational way of thinking! Madame's own success was founded on the boldness to take from life exactly what she wanted, to mould circumstances to her own advantage. The girl might be a trifle misguided, but she was young. Such exuberance must be profitably channelled.

She had certain reservations, however. "And your parents approve of these measures you are taking?"

Kate hesitated, mentally tracing the design on the carpet. Then her eyes met the older woman's. "They are not aware of them, Madame. I have run away from home!"

"I see. And why did you do this thing, Miss Kate?"

Kate lowered her lids and said calmly, as a statement of fact: "My father would constrain me to marry where I do not choose. He is a clergyman, Madame, and we lead a cloistered life. My sisters are well content with their lot, and so please Papa. I fear my worldling tendencies have been a source of great concern to him."

"Mon Dieu!" cried Madeleine on the verge of incredulous laughter. "You do not look like a worldling to me, *ma petite!"*

The girl was saying in wistful confusion: "I am but eighteen and know little of life. I am not ready for matrimony yet. Some day, perhaps I will fall in love...and if not, Papa will have no cause to repine if I am not dependent upon him."

The girl plainly saw her predicament in such uncluttered terms that Madeleine could only feel touched and as eager to protect as to exploit. She wanted to help, but there were aspects of the situation she did not relish. Kate was a minor. She was no starving waif turned out to fend for herself. And yet, Madeleine saw that Kate's flight had not simply been one of panic and rebellion that would soon be regretted. It was a thirst for adventure which life in a parsonage could never assuage.

Her thoughts were interrupted by Travers, prim and starched, who entered with a chased silver coffee pot and some dainty Limoges cups and saucers. She gave Kate an appraising glance and enquired pertly whether she took cream. This was not common procedure for sewing-room interviews, but for those young ladies who had just stepped out of the seminary and had been entrusted to Madame to make their entrance into society by the back door. They were often half-castes, the by-blows of noble folk, and came to her pleasingly possessed of large dowries. Two of the girls under her wing, the twins Charmaine and Celeste, were *emigrées* like herself, of good birth but penniless. They were orphaned and had been brought up in Brighton by their grandmother who, in order to buy bread and lodgings, had had to resort to baptising the Quality when they coyly emerged from their bathing machines. It was a healthy life and the gratuities plump. Madeleine had long known the family and was glad to do what she could for her fellow exiles, but her services were generally of a more lucrative nature. She was being handsomely paid by Bronwen's mother, and in truth, Madeleine felt she had earned it. Bronwen was a wild-eyed bawd, quite devoid of modesty and manners. Madeleine despaired of her. Late in life, her mother, a coarse woman outlawed from Polite Society but the toast of Prinny's table, had married a baronet. Formerly, she had been the mistress of Sixteen String Jack who ended his days on Tyburn gallows. Her daughter was the outcome of that liaison.

Rachel, on the other hand, another of Madame's girls, was fey and demure, with the eyes of a startled fawn. In her case, it was her father's lineage she would choose to recall. He was a gentle Marquis who preferred country life to the bright lights of London. His wife, however, a mercurial beauty, was of a different turn of mind. She spurned his advances and played him false again and again so that the poor fellow was driven to seek comfort in the arms of a compassionate maid. Thus Rachel entered the world.

They were all birds of passage in Madame's house. They stayed while the climate suited them.

Kate watched thick cream slither over the back of the spoon Travers was holding. (Madame taught her staff to be punctilious in the execution of their duties.) How lucky this dressmaker was to live in sumptuous surroundings and enjoy such elegant catering to the finer things in life!

"Will there be anything further, Madame?"

Madame replied in the negative. She began to ponder the advantages of taking on this *jeune fille*. There would be no profits, of course, at least not directly, though Kate would certainly be an asset to the establishment. Not for long would she be confined to the sewing-room. She was of finer clay than that. It would not do to work her pretty fingers to the bone and it would not be ethical to require of her the kind of service those needlewomen rendered. All her girls modelled her gowns and graced her soirées but those barely educated females from the back room who received no tuition in charm, deportment and current affairs, could soon be singled out for other purposes. The more cosmopolitan of her refined young ladies had their delicate intrigues but that was another matter. Madame turned a blind eye. She always advised these girls to preserve their virtue, but the affairs of those who paid no heed did not always end in disillusion. A creditable marriage was their aim and Madame did all she could to promote that end, for it meant extra guineas in her pocket. This often warred with her Gallic heart which preferred natural romance. However, those who won both love and a position were not rare blooms in Madame's garden. It would be interesting, she mused, sipping coffee, to see what became of this engaging creature with her slightly impudent air. The gentlemen became so quickly bored with sophistication.

"*Bien!*" she said resolutely. "You wish for a position. You wish to see life, *Katrine*. I am persuaded you will not be disappointed with what I offer you."

"Oh Madame! I am indebted to you. I am so glad to be able to be of service."

From that moment on, Kate did not look back. She was under a spell. It was as if an unseen hand beckoned her on. Soon she was caught up in a whirl of excitement, headier than arrack punch. Miss Hanslope from Merrowdene might never have existed.

Madame was enchanted with her progress. Few of her girls had combined so much intelligence and beauty with so little affectation and a willingness to be taught. Day by day, Kate gathered poise, pacing the crimson strip of carpet under a volume of Shakespeare. In the afternoons, she sat in the workroom and sewed pearls and Mechlin lace on to ball gowns. If the clothes were urgently needed, the girls had to work at tremendous speed into the night under small lamps which had glass chambers filled with water to magnify the light.

During Kate's third week in Brighton, the sewing team was particularly hard pressed. Summer was Madame's busiest season and all her clients seemed to want their gowns at once. Each night, the girls sat up late and stifled yawns in the tense atmosphere. Their lively chatter petered out and tempers frayed as readily as the clipped satin. Daphne's hand was numb and calloused from cutting. Chloris's fingers were taut from tailor's chalk, Beth and Jenny complained of pricked fingers which snagged the shiny fabric, and Kate gritted her teeth and tried yet again to fit a tacked bodice on to a wicker dummy. Madame came to inspect each stage of the work and sometimes poked her head around the door to see what progress had been made. *"Depêchez-vous, mes filles! Vous devez finir ce soir!* Katrine! Those darts!"

"Lordie, we've run out of yellow thread," wailed Jenny when Madame had gone. "I hope there's some more in the mercery cupboard."

"I'll go and see," Kate offered. She needed a breathing space. The top of her spine was stiff with cramp.

"Bring another box of pins, will you, lovie?" Chloris piped up.

Kate escaped to the haberdashery room and rummaged through drawers billowing with lace, insertion, ribbon, thread of every hue but the one she sought. She took a deep breath. Tucks and gathers pulsed in her brain. The side street door jangled and brought her to herself. She flexed her lids, chose the nearest shade of gold and snatched up a box of pins. Slightly dazed, she hastened from the room into the hall, into echoes of voices and rapid footsteps, into the soft angles of a Kerseymere coat. The impact was like waves crashing together and falling away. "Oh!"

The pins dropped on the chequered tiles in a tangled heap, splaying out in all directions.

"Oh, the deuce! I do beg your pardon! Allow me…" said a man's voice. It was gentle, solicitous, intimate.

They both stooped down to retrieve the pins, Kate fighting back last straw tears. When she glanced at him, she saw that he regarded her with an expression of startled whimsy. He looked as though he had lost sixpence and found a sovereign. He caught her gaze and held it fast. His eyes were the warmest hazel and his hair the colour of sun-bleached tobacco.

"Leo! I ask you! What is it that you are doing, please?" Madame appeared on the balcony above. "Essie, she paces up and down, up and down. Already you are twenty minutes late for the theatre!"

"Damn it all, Madeleine, it's barely eight o' clock."

"I do not ask you what is the time. I tell you you will miss half the performance!"

"Nonsense," Leo returned good-naturedly. There was a good deal of complicity in the glance he exchanged with Kate. "As you see, we have had a slight collision. Or perhaps I should say a pointed encounter!"

Madame threw up her hands with a gesture of despair. *"Agh! Son humour est aussi mauvais que sa courtoisie!"* She disappeared into a room above.

"Oh dear, I am sorry to get you in such bad books," Kate said in dismay as he tipped the last pins into the box. "Thank you for your kind assistance, sir."

"Not at all," he replied, sketching a bow. "The pleasure was all mine."

With an air of injured dignity, Madame's sloe-eyed daughter, Estelle, sailed down the stairs in her opera cloak, linked her arm through her escort's and suffered him to bear her out to the waiting carriage, leaving Kate to stare after them, idly wondering who he was.

It was dark and the thick June heat shimmering off the Parade all afternoon had abated. On the Steyne, the blind windows of Prinny's summer palace advertised that he had cut short his stay and had taken himself off to Town where he was to receive the Allies and set in motion his grandiose plans for celebrating the

Peace. Half Brighton had followed him and the streets were quieter than usual for the season.

The Honourable Leo Quinn settled back against the shabby upholstery of the hackney cab and made a vain bid to suppress a yawn. Stuffing, he noticed, was bursting from a gash in the leather. Propriety obliged him to make use of such anonymous means of transport when escorting Essie and her kind, though he might not disdain to be seen with her in public. Another yawn escaped him. Even Mr Sheridan's trenchant wit had failed to divert him tonight.

"I am quite out of patience with you," Essie fretted, working her fan nineteen to the dozen. He caught sight of her pouting mouth in the wavering torchlight. He knew that look well and all that went with it: the wounded cajoling that sought consolation from soft words and kisses. "You have been perfectly disagreeable this evening. You scarcely said a word at supper and you know how I dislike to be bored. To say little of the fact that you were late, very, very late, Leo."

"Sweetheart, I apologise, indeed I do. The truth is, I'm exhausted. We danced well after dawn at the Stewarts' ball. Cassandra was splendidly launched into her majority!"

Since last winter, a friendship had developed between Leo and Sir George Stewart, brother of the lady mentioned. The death of their father the year before, had conferred upon him the guardianship of his inscrutable and well-dowered sister which had proved quite a headache. Each May, he rented a house in Royal Crescent and spent several weeks there with his family and a handful of guests. This year, Leo, who had suffered some grave reversals at the faro tables and was glad of the hospitality, was among them.

"So Miss Stewart is free to choose a husband for herself. By all accounts, her brother has turned away several suitors. And did you dance with her and pay her pretty compliments?"

"Oh, prodigiously!"

"Do you suppose she has some swain in mind?"

"If she has, I am not privy to it."

"A fortune hunter, perhaps?"

"*Has* she a fortune?" Leo parried the innuendo.

"You must know she has, Leo. Her father was vastly rich. Why, I have heard it said that she is to inherit one of his estates in the North of England."

As they passed The Castle Tavern, an oblique patch of light slid over the interior of the carriage. Leo shrank further into the shadows. The warmth rose beneath the high points of his collar. "You are exceedingly well-informed," he said in a reined tone.

"Lady Diana, the baronet's wife, is one of our clients and sometimes whispers little confidences to Mama."

"Then you must also be aware that the old baronet was a true Scot and quick to stamp on a slippery coin. He was a firm believer in consolidating the family wealth."

"I don't follow."

"My dear Essie, it is of no consequence what Miss Stewart's portion is since she is promised to her cousin, Eugene McBride."

"Oh! I had no notion…"

"*Chez Madeleine* is not the repository of everyone's secrets, though it may sometimes seem that way!"

"Then it is already settled?"

"They were to marry this summer, but with the advent of Peace, McBride decided to take the Grand Tour before putting his head in the noose. He is expected to be away for a year or so, I believe. The Stewarts are rather put out of countenance by the whole thing. To spare Cassandra's feelings, they judged it best not to announce the betrothal until he returns."

"I see. Trust me, I won't breathe a word."

"It is said," Leo enlarged in careful phrases, "that under the terms of her father's will, Cassandra may bid farewell to her expectations if she refuses her cousin's hand."

"Well, I do think he might have taken her with him as his

wife, Leo. It is not very pretty in him to abandon her in so callous a fashion. Not very wise, either." With a flick of her hand, Essie closed her fan.

Essie was a sad romp. In her dealings with Leo, she had been unable to bring a proper detachment to bear. He was fond of her, but his affections were well in hand. An evening such as this would culminate in the rollicking wastes of her bed with its gilded posts and drapes of white Chantilly lace. Murals of Venus presided while they tumbled into one another's arms with a kind of pagan innocence. But circumstances had foisted upon Essie a way of life that was alien to her nature. Unlike Kate, she was not deceived by her mother's world. Whilst it gave her a chance to mingle with the best society, she knew she could not be accepted on that plane in her own right. In her lovers, Essie sought an identity, a place to belong, and, so far, had been bitterly disappointed.

Tonight they crept into the house, signalling silence to Voltaire, Madeleine's phlegmatic old butler who was accustomed to taking everything in this irregular establishment in his stooping stride. They tiptoed, giggling, past the salon where Madeleine still held court with a bunch of her seasoned admirers, pausing to indulge in an extravagant embrace on the threshold of Essie's chamber.

Later, despite the excesses of the last twenty-four hours, Leo lay awake. He reached out and turned down the lamp burning low behind a haze of white filigree. Smouldering wisps rose from the wicks and briefly submerged the odour of stale perfume. He sighed heavily. This aimless way of life was beginning to cloy. His problems were pressing in on him. And something new. He could not forget the lass he had run into downstairs. Throughout the evening the image of her face had haunted him. Who was she? Surely not one of Madeleine's country wenches, thankful for their modest comforts and willing to perform any service that would spare them destitution. The thought of her as prey to some of the old roués who darkened these doors filled him with repugnance.

Earlier, when he had tentatively enquired, Essie, sharp to scent danger, had been evasive. "She's just one of Mama's little maidens," said she. "Why?"

"Maiden or grisette?" he asked pointedly.

"Really, Leo!" Essie averted her face, curling a ringlet around her finger in a travesty of confusion. "There are times when I think you are quite the crudest man of my acquaintance!"

He let the matter drop. He was becoming alarmed by Essie's possessiveness. Poor girl, he felt vaguely responsible for her and had no wish to give her pain.

Leo's thoughts churned like a millwheel. At length, he got out of bed and went to the window. Between a gap in the pale terraces, he caught the steely glint of the sea. A Channel's width between himself and a new beginning! The war had ended. Ought he to make a clean break? Escape his creditors? Would he respect himself if he did? Could he afford the luxury of such fine feelings?

The moon emerged from cloud to throw a shaft of bluish light over the slumbering Essie, over the carpet where her clothes were strewn in a trail from the door to the bed. Essie exiled, longing to go back to the land of her birth. It was not a fate he wished to share. He had to get away, clear the cobwebs from his brain. He dressed hastily. With his coat under his arm and his shoes hooked over his fingers, he made to leave the house quietly.

Essie stirred at the turn of the door handle. She jumped up. "Leo, what is it? Where are you going?"

"For a ride on the Downs."

"At this hour? You're mad!"

Leo saddled Paloma and rode the chestnut stallion, softly

whinnying, out of the courtyard at Royal Crescent and along the beach to a track that led upwards to the Downs. He galloped at speed, steering perilously close to the cliff edge, the wind rumbling in his ears. Way below, the sea slapped and frothed in a perpetual rhythm.

As dawn broke in pale streaks over the horizon and both sky and water were awash with flamingo pink, he knew what he must do. He must swallow his pride and return like the prodigal to his father to plead for aid. Surely Viscount Penrose would not refuse him a loan to recover the deeds of Angell Place. The Richmond property had belonged to the Quinns for two centuries. It had passed into Leo's possession at his coming of age, although Julian, his younger brother, had done rather better. A large estate in the Vale of Evesham had been his portion. Julian was his father's favourite, always had been. The fact that he, Leo, having obtained a Captain's commission three years ago, had been out in the Peninsula fighting for his country and had returned in January from Bayonne with shoulder injuries from which he still suffered searing spasms of pain, buttered no parsnips with the Viscount. More than anything else, Leo felt his reappearance had been a source of embarrassment. His lordship had at the outset raised no objections to his heir putting himself in the firing line whilst Julian stayed behind to marry, beget a brood of offspring and live off the fat of the land.

If only his mother were alive. The peculiar redolence of grief at her death which had driven him to enlist in the cavalry, came back to him. The blood and squalor, the hardships of the Spanish climate and terrain, had blotted out all personal feeling. He had been glad of it and had enjoyed the camaraderie of army life. It owned a quality he had been unable to find among the patrons of Brooks's and Boodle's. For Leo had lost a true ally when Elizabeth Penrose passed away, unforgiven by the husband who had made her life so difficult to bear.

By heaven, it was more than flesh and blood could endure,

to have to humiliate oneself before such a man! But he must do it. He did not dare involve himself any deeper with Jews and moneylenders. And it wouldn't make much of a hole in the old man's funds.

Had Leo only known what Madeleine Matthieu knew about that sanctimonious peer, he would have been better equipped to get his own way.

Rain was gently falling in the leafy byways of Warwickshire when Fernleigh Manor came into view. The leaded windows of the wisteria-clad south face winked like facets of a jewel between the trees. A Tudor mansion built of timber and rose-red brick, it was situated on the edge of a conifer forest where, in childhood, Leo had often gone beating for Old Stokes, the gamekeeper, alert for the sudden whirr of pheasant or partridge, or the wild, intelligent eye of a fox creeping through the undergrowth.

Smoke curled from the chimneys at one corner of the house when Leo turned in at the main gates. The Viscount was unlikely to be out. He was not a sporting man and rarely bestirred himself to visit his neighbours, preferring his books and occasional strolls in the park, the pair of lean-faced greyhounds he so much resembled trotting at his heels.

Meaker, Lord Penrose's aged gentleman's gentleman, was somewhat taken aback by the intrusion and took Leo's hat and gloves, bidding him wait in the parlour. Leo sniffed disapprovingly at the odour of curing hams. In his mother's day, there had been flowers everywhere and delicate Minton pot-pourri bowls. The Viscount, he was told was engaged in the library with Mr Seagrave, his attorney. "I will inform his lordship at once. Had we anticipated your arrival, Mr Leo... Will you take a glass of wine, sir, while you wait?"

"Thank you, no, Meaker," Leo declined, thinking he would not corrode his innards with the cheap ratafia Lord Penrose inflicted on uninvited callers. "Pray don't put yourself into a taking on my account, cursed fellow that I am, dropping in unannounced."

"Will you be dining with his lordship today? Am I to instruct Robson to prepare your old room?"

"Good lord, no! I shall be away well before noon!"

"Very good, Mr Leo." Meaker shuffled off, scratching his pate through a shock of white hair. It was not in the way of things, on a quiet Monday morning, to have a young man of fashion, all tousled hair and glazed boots, breeze in to parade up and down in the parlour.

Indeed, Leo did feel out of his element in that dark-panelled room with its discoloured chintzes and threadbare window seats. How distant and unreal his childhood seemed, as though it belonged to someone else. In happy mood, and at a long remove, he was able to believe the best of the Viscount, that he was well-intentioned, but misled. But on returning to Fernleigh, the chill began to set in. The weight of past bitterness and strife pressed down upon him so that his breathing came uneasily. How could he for one moment have imagined that there would be any charity, any indulgence here? The coal scuttle was empty and the grate even emptier in this room. Everything bore witness to the Viscount's needless parsimony.

A door opened. Leo's muscles tensed. Voices carried from the hall. The outer door groaned upon its hinges and Mr Seagrave's footsteps could be heard descending the steps outside.

Lord Penrose appeared in the parlour doorway wearing a brocaded waistcoat spotted with grease. He was hollow-cheeked and haggard, his thinning hair raked loosely behind and tied with a ribbon. If he had been a truculent spouse, widowhood did not sit easily upon him. He had not aged well. He had developed the hunch of a clerk much preoccupied with ledgers. His complexion was grey and the misanthropic turn of his mouth more pronounced. The hard bright eyes took Leo in.

"I hope I find you in health and spirits, my lord," Leo ventured.

The Viscount ignored this courtesy. He ushered his visitor into the library where a cone fire crackled and intermittently puffed palls of pungent smoke out into the room. "So you are come hotfoot from the metropolis…"

"From Brighton, sir."

"Brighton, eh?" Penrose eyed him oddly. A staleness came up from the pair of used glasses on the small pie-crust table. "So that is where you have been taking refuge from all this tomfoolery going on in the capital at the nation's expense."

"Ah, the Allies' visit."

"Our first gentleman of Europe has been making a consummate ass of himself with all the pomp and display. Anyone would think it was he who had led the country to victory. And Wellington does not come."

"He is expected soon."

"I dare say he is waiting for the hullabaloo to subside. He knows the price of war. He will not make a spectacle of himself seeking the people's adulation."

"Wellington has no need. The Prince has made himself thoroughly unpopular by driving a wedge between his wife and daughter. Apparently, the Princess Caroline was cheered at the Opera several nights ago and her husband, bold as you please, bowed and took the acclaim himself.

"He did well to put that German wife of his away at Blackheath, coarse and unprincipled baggage that she is!"

Leo sensed hostility springing from deeper sources than royal misconduct. Already they were heading for a feud! "Come, sir, you are too harsh upon the lady. The common view is that he has provoked her."

"Lady! I'd as soon call the lowest scullery wench a lady! Pah women! A pox on all of 'em!"

On this strident note, the Viscount moved with a slight limp towards his escritoire and produced from an inner compartment a soapstone snuff box, sniffing a pinch or two of its contents in a most inelegant manner. He sneezed explosively into a stained handkerchief and waved his arm impatiently towards a chair. "For pity's sake, sit down, boy! I imagine you are not come to listen to my strictures on the state of the nation!"

Leo was finding it hard to judge his lordship's mood. He suspected a certain grudging relief in the old man at having the tenor of his dull existence interrupted. He was about to speak but Penrose forestalled him: "Pray tell me," he said, sinking into a Queen Anne chair and there was that same shrewd narrowing of the eyes Leo had earlier perceived at the mention of Brighton, "pray tell me what you are about down in Brighton. I fancy you do not go merely for the salubrious air, but the society must be pretty thin on the ground at present."

"Not everyone has forsaken the coast for Town. I am staying with George and Diana Stewart."

"Stewart!" The name came from Penrose's lips like a whip crack. "Old Angus Stewart's son?"

"The same."

"By God, it must be a twelvemonth since they buried the old skinflint. Had some dealings with him years ago. Twas he who took that accursed property of my brother's off my hands."

"Silvercragg? Yes, I remember."

"Got it for a song, mark you. But I was glad to be rid of it. He called in Wyatt, had the place renovated in the Gothic style, towers and so forth."

This reminiscent strain did not bode well. It was most unlike Penrose. Perhaps loneliness had mellowed him, given him time and space to reflect. For years, the subject of his brother, Mark, had been taboo. Leo vividly recalled Papa storming into the town house in Hanover Square long ago, after that fateful Christmas in Cumberland when tragedy struck, and the deeper than usual gloom which had swept in with him and laid all their spirits low for the rest of the winter. Papa had gone there alone. Mama had been unwell and unable to travel and he and Julian had stayed behind with her. But when their father returned to fill the house with his brooding presence and impose his jarring silences at table, Mama had given them to understand that Uncle Mark was never to be mentioned again. Leo thought this grossly unjust. He had been deeply attached to his Uncle Mark, a winsome fellow who made Mama laugh so that stars shone in her sombre brown eyes.

"When some of the builder's men met with misfortune," Penrose went on, "it was rumoured that Silvercragg was haunted. Sheer fustian, of course!"

Leo noticed the shudder which belied the old man's words. "Oh? How so?"

"All manner of injuries. Some lethal. Falling masonry. Insecure scaffolding. Due to negligence, you may rely. But the tenants must have it that supernatural forces were abroad. Caledonian or not, Stewart didn't believe it." The Viscount gave a hoot of false laughter. "It cost him a tidy penny in extra wages, getting men to work on the site, particularly the West Wing where the fire broke out. He caught a cold there, I can tell you!"

"Were you never tempted to restore the family seat yourself?"

"Not I, boy! I wanted nothing pertaining to that profligate brother of mine. Whatever he touched turned ill. Never cared for the place anyway." Penrose seized the andirons and wedged a lead-streaked lump of coal into the incendiary cones. "I'm not a sentimental man. One can't afford to be in this life. Now George Stewart's a sharp fellow if I'm not deceived. Like as not he'll sell up and invest elsewhere."

Leo rose and moved towards the window. The lawns were a flossy green under the wind-shaken limes. "George cannot do that, however," he said quietly. "The estate belongs to Miss Cassandra. That is to say," he amended, "it will belong to her when she marries."

"The daughter inherits, does she? A singular arrangement."

"She is expected to make a match with her cousin, Eugene McBride. Those were her father's terms… which brings me," Leo hazarded, "to the purpose of my visit."

"Ah, your purpose…" The words were stiff with sarcasm. Leo wondered whether the Viscount had been stringing him along, enjoying his advantage.

"I'll not beat about the bush, sir. I have come to impose upon your good nature. The fact is, I'm badly dipped and need funds rather urgently."

The Viscount's countenance turned livid with rage. "Do my ears play me false, boy? I'm persuaded they do! You wish me to rescue you from your embarrassments?"

"I had hoped… a loan, sir. A purely temporary measure."

"You have the temerity to seek my assistance? You give your life up to idle dissipation and expect me to condone it?"

Leo stood his ground with dignity. There was more at issue than the matter of debts, imperative though that had become. "Yes, you may fairly accuse me of improvidence since my return from Spain, but that is all over. I am not proud of it and wish to start again."

"Then you may have the prospect of the sponging-house hanging over you for a while and we shall see how deedily you acquit yourself. Raise a mortgage on your house if you are minded to reform."

"Unfortunately, the deeds of Angell Place are no longer in my possession."

"What!" thundered his lordship. "And where are they now, pray?"

"At Hoare's Bank. I played deep at Watier's a few weeks ago."

"The devil you did! Do you dare to stand there and tell me that the fortunes of this family are imperilled by the turn of a card, the throw of a dice! Are you so bereft of sanity? May I remind you, boy, that you are my heir!"

A coal tumbled from the hearth, glimmering with white heat. Leo tapped it smartly with his boot. "I am the successor to your title," he revised with soft emphasis. "Half London is alive with speculation as to why it is Julian you indulge at my expense."

At this Penrose turned pale and began to flounder. "Then half London is stupider than I gave credit for. Julian leads a sober life. He is industrious, a man of principle. He upholds the good name of the Quinns. Julian owes no man a farthing. He is worth ten of you!"

"Julian," Leo added pointedly, fixing the Viscount's eye, "is his father's son."

"Aye, and you are of my brother's mould. Have I not always said so? Have I not always said how much you resemble him?"

"You lie in your teeth!" Leo rasped, goaded now to speak his mind. "Don't gammon me with that. I know the truth. There's not a drop of Penrose blood in my veins and I'm glad of it!"

A profound and dreadful silence ensued. "And where did you glean that notion?" his lordship asked at length with menacing calm.

"I have long had my suspicions."

"Where, boy, where!" Penrose banged his fist down the arm of the chair so hard that the floor shook.

"Oh, you may rest easy. From the closest of sources. Your secret is safe with me, I give you my word."

"Your... your mother told you?"

Leo marked the progress of little runnels of rain driven against the mullioned windows. The park was a blur, the watered greens, dark and bright, running together. "She told me when she was dying. She begged me to forgive her for what I'd endured on her account. How could I not forgive her? Who, knowing the truth, could level blame?"

"But this is beyond everything! Had she no shame?"

"Shame! What had she to be ashamed of? Of having the ill-luck to fall in love with one man when her marriage had been arranged to another? She loved my father deeply. He wanted her to elope with him. But she would not. She told him she must abide by her vows. And you were implacable in your resolve to punish her when her one indiscretion came to light. You let her die grieving. You could have made her forget Dieter Neumann in time had you buried your wretched pride!"

There was a time when Leo would have done anything to win the Viscount's approval and keep the peace between his parents, for he had sensed at an early age that the contention between them was in some incomprehensible way linked with his own existence. But long years of callous rejection had hardened him. Now, he would not, at any cost, allow his mother's integrity to be impugned.

Penrose was breathing rapidly, a hand clamped to his ribs. "I gave her security. A position," he protested weakly. "What was she but the daughter of a grasping wine-merchant with ideas above his station?"

"She was beautiful."

"Aye," Penrose said, seeming to wrench the admission from low in his throat, his wrinkled eyes hooded with regret. "She could have been a duchess any day."

How hard it must have been for Penrose to have had his image of the lovely Betsy Chadwyck shattered when he would have moved heaven and earth for her had she but cast herself upon his bosom. He had paid Dieter Neumann a large sum of money to take himself back to Hanover where he had been a musician at Court. Chadwyck had engaged him to teach his daughter the violin. But neither Adam nor his reluctant bride knew then of the lifelong legacy that was to mark her fall from grace. Leo, her firstborn. How could Adam forgive her? It was as if his own morals mocked him. Even brother Mark with his penchant for pretty women was no fool for them.

"Why, in all those years were you never reconciled?"

"Your mother," Penrose spat, expanding with the force of his own venom, "was no better than a harlot!"

Leo swore through gritted teeth, his chin jutting dangerously. He made a grab for the Viscount by the armholes of his waistcoat and hauled him from the chair. "You're despicable!"

A terrible fear kindled in his victim's eyes. His breathing was shallow and rapid. "Unhand me, you ruffian! Let me go this instant! Meaker! My drops, Meaker! Some brandy!"

Leo let him go and shoved him backwards. The old man, for all his belligerence, felt pitifully feeble and sparrow-like beneath his grasp. The wine-table tilted and skittered over the varnished floorboards in a shower of glass whose glinting atoms became lodged in the pile of the hearthrug to wreak their destruction long after the event. Penrose lay splayed in his chair, consumed by each wheezing breath. His pebble eyes were slightly protuberant and glazed with panic.

"For the love of God...! Loosen his neckcloth, Mr Leo, I adjure you!" Meaker came rushing in, his usual mask of resignation abandoned, and while Leo struggled with the obstinate knot, tipped brandy down his employer's throat. Penrose gulped and choked. There was a curious roll to his eyes and for a few chilling moments Leo was numb with fear at what he had done. But when the brandy had taken effect and some drops of laudanum in water had been administered, his lordship sufficiently recovered to direct a gaze hollow and dark with hatred towards him.

Leo straightened up and said with all the presence he could command: "Meaker, be so good as to see that my phaeton is brought round to the door."

"Aye," Penrose snarled, refusing to be beaten. His cramped fingers were like claws around the tumbler. "Aye, take yourself off, you misbegotten sinner! You have eaten at my table and slept under my roof. I have paid for your education. Go, prey at fortune elsewhere and never cross my path again!"

Three

When Madeleine Matthieu looked down from the balcony to see the damsel in distress and the young paladin retrieving pins with such alacrity, she did indeed think that her own days of 'preying at fortune' might be nearing their end.

The height gave her a sense of detachment, of watching actors on a stage. There was an indefinable magnetism between Leo and Katrine, so what harm could there be, she reasoned, in giving nature a helping hand? It would conveniently divert his attention from Essie. For she had other plans for her daughter.

On June 23rd, Madeleine was to hold one of her musical evenings. That same day, Prinny's guests were due to leave London and head for Petworth. They were to spend the night there before returning to Dover where they would set sail for France. One or two were reluctant to leave the land of the free and stayed behind to dance with the ladies renowned for their beauty and to savour the mutton which was second to none. Old Blücher, the fleecy-haired Chancellor of Prussia and veteran of battle, always drunk as a lord, was so impressed with England that he was heard to exclaim on first beholding its capital: *"Himmel!* What a wonderful city to sack!"

The Stewarts, who were distantly related to Lord Egremont of Petworth and had been invited to dine with him on this grand occasion, could not be present at Madeleine's entertainment. She made sure, however, that Leo was possessed of a ticket and that Katrine was breathtakingly turned out, duly sending Monsieur André, her own coiffeur, to wait upon her. Swiftly, he conjured for her a classical topknot with corkscrew tendrils escaping just below the temples. A dress of silver gauze over sarsnet trimmed with rose velvet ribbon completed the look. Décolleté was strongly in vogue but Madeleine knew it would have been a mistake to robe Katrine thus.

Essie, her sour puss of a daughter, cocked her head on one side and appraised the new recruit. "The India muslin would have been more becoming. Do you not think so, Mama?"

She herself was attired in purple crape and had shamelessly gone to the lengths of dampening her petticoat so that her gown clung to her thighs and pert bosom.

The salon doors were flung wide and the portentous tones of Voltaire announcing the guests could be heard above the orchestra which plucked and piped and boomed tunelessly as it quickly prepared to enthral.

"Come, Katrine, permit me to introduce you to Mr Moore," Essie said dutifully. "He will no doubt favour us with a ballad or two later on."

"That I will, lady, to be sure," beamed the playful rogue, affecting a hoarse whisper, "though me t'roats tinder dry for want o' refreshment!" He bowed over Kate's hand. "Katrine, is it? Ah, twinkling as crystal."

"I'll fetch you a glass of wine, you old scapegrace," Essie chaffed him. "We've none of your cursed Irish whiskey here."

"Ah, the saints bless you! But, be easy, me dear, the Scottish will do!" He received a scowl for his sauce and turned to Kate. "Tis a mortal struggle to stay in fine tune without a drap o' good liquor to tone up me cords." It was all a pose, his air of a mischievous simpleton, for Tom Moore was a highly articulate fellow and wrote shrewd accounts in his journals of his patrons' doings, the most celebrated of whom was the Prince Regent himself. He told Kate he'd a wide repertoire of ditties and ballads. He was sure they were good ones, he'd composed them himself!

No sooner had Essie plied the minstrel with wine than her society was claimed by a blubber-faced gentleman past his prime. He spoke with ingratiating solicitude and Kate fleetingly saw him caress the gap of bare flesh between Essie's puffed sleeve and her glove. His manner was altogether repellent and it was plain that Essie found it so. And yet, it was as if an understanding existed between the two of them.

Presently the players challenged the air with a few chords. Gossip ebbed and everyone took the cue to be seated.

He was late again. Many a hostess, remarking his tardiness, had been surprised by the glowing reports of his abilities as a cavalry officer. He blundered into the sparkling and orderly world of Mozart, tripping over a spindly chair in an effort to be unobtrusive. Frowns of annoyance were turned upon him, but Essie's jet ringlets bobbed up and down as she repressed the urge to burst into laughter. He cast a contrite glance towards Madeleine whose gaze had wavered between the ormolu clock and the closed door.

And then he saw her.

Kate was sitting just a few feet away from him. The rows of chairs formed a semi-circle and he was able to see her pensive expression. Leo willed her to look his way. After a moment, she obeyed, her gaze captive to his. He tried to read her, unaware of the mute appeal upon his own countenance. Her pin-gatherer! Dear heaven! she thought. She felt instantly helpless, as though she were falling into a chasm. She did not dare venture so much as a glance in his direction again, but was aware of his scrutiny burning into her.

When the music was over and Mr Moore had given an emotional rendition of some songs from his native land, supper was announced and the guests passed into the Athenian Salon where an elaborate cold collation had been spread upon tables swathed in Brussels Lace. It was a palatial room in gold and aquamarine, lined with mirrors.

Kate was swept into supper by the Second Baron Alvanley.

He was a genial fellow, something of a wag, and not versed in the arts of flirtation, for which she was thankful. Essie was steering the pin-gatherer across the room and it was clear that she did not intend to relinquish him. Madeleine was aware of her daughter's air of rebellion. There was a suggestion of despair, even hysteria, in it. Had she not warned the silly goose a thousand times not to lose her heart to the same lover two evenings together!

The Marquis of Radstock, that hardened debauchee whose advances Essie took pleasure in rebuffing, had his attention trained on the dark-eyed demoiselle and was aware of her strange mood. His hands itched to lay the sweet creature across his knee and give her a good spanking. As for that fellow, Quinn, it was as well that his bank balance didn't cut such a fine figure as he did!

Quinn was merely dallying, Radstock did not doubt, but he chose not to underrate the wiles of Estelle. Tonight the flame of coquetry burned bright within her. How he longed to enjoy those ripe curves, that uncertain temper, to the full! He licked his flaccid lips and sank his teeth into a leg of capon, smothering his chin with grease. What a pity it would be, he thought, gloating over the sumptuous fare, if straitened circumstances forced *Madame La Patronne* to dispense with her elegant soirées. What a genius she had for extravagance! He said to her in a steely, caressing voice: "Do I detect, dear lady, an unwholesome regard in your daughter for that Adonis yonder? I trust you will not suffer her to make a fool of herself."

Madeleine flung the punch ladle daintily back into the bowl so that it sank like a wrecked galleon. "They trifle with each other, they are young," she shrugged. "Your jealousy, it is blinding you, *peut-être?* I fancy there is something fresh in the wind."

Following the direction of his hostess' gaze, Radstock's eyes alighted upon Kate. He lifted his quizzing-glass. "A perfect peach!" he declared with all the subtle emphasis of a dedicated epicurean pronouncing upon his favourite dish. "More than a trifle piquant, I don't doubt. Tell me, how came you by her?"

"Tonight I launch her, that is enough!"

Radstock added under his breath: "Lucky fellow who has rapture of her. I'll lay my blunt it's going to be Quinn."

Madeleine's brows arched expressively whilst her lips pursed into a faint smile. "The fates are at work unless I mistake the matter. But we give them a helping hand – no?"

"This apricot tart is delicious," Alvanley told Kate. He was avidly sucking his pastry fork as though he could not bear to miss a morsel. "Have some, madam, I entreat you. No better not. I apprehend there are only two portions left and I shall need those!"

The Baron's fondness for cold apricot tart was a legend. He had instructed his cook to leave one on the sideboard every day and appeared to be in no danger of growing tired of this fare. His companion, Captain Fitzwilliam of the South Gloucesters still encamped on the Downs, pointed out that in spite of his popularity, Alvanley could keep few close friends. This was due to the hazards contingent upon having a guest under one's roof whose habit it was to snuff out his bedside candle by stuffing it under his pillow or by hurling it against the wall! Exhausted maids, yawning their heads off, had to be posted outside his room into the small hours to make sure that nothing went amiss.

Kate's imagination took fire. She was instantly caught up in the aura of another time and place, more potent than nostalgia, more elusive than memory. She felt faint with anxiety, poised on the threshold of recollection. How easy it would be to set the whole house alight in a moment of rashness!

Footsteps were approaching on the mosaic-tiled floor and all other sounds blurred. She knew whose they were. "Will you excuse me, my lord, Captain Fitzwilliam," she said and was gone.

"Katrine!" called Madeleine. "Something is amiss? You are unwell?"

Kate pressed fingertips to her forehead. "A trifle giddy, Madame. A breath of air and I shall recover myself."

It was almost dark outside. In the fading avenues of light thrown from the salons, Kate glimpsed the gleam of gold epaulettes and a whiff of perfume she associated with Beth, but her mind was so closely preoccupied that it did not fully register. Madame was following her, exuding concern, ushering her into the house via the tradesmen's door and up the secondary staircase to her own apartments. She would soon persuade her charge into circulation again!

Upstairs, Madame bade her lie on the couch. She came into her own as an angel of mercy and sailed away to fetch hartshorn and water. Kate adopted the line of least resistance and downed the loathsome stuff obediently. "Perhaps," said she, "I might carry a vinaigrette against such a turn. Miss Daphne, I know, has one to spare, a pretty thing in silver and crystal she said I might have should the need arise. I will go at once and beg it since I am quite resolved to fulfil my duties tonight."

Madeleine held up her hands to curb the impulse and tactfully eased Kate back into supine mode. "I find you one, *ma petite*. Miss Daphne, she 'as retired for the night."

Meanwhile, Leo, on the cusp of a promised introduction, was left chafing with impatience.

"A dashed pretty girl, by Jove," Alvanley averred, revealing jaws crammed with pulped pastry. "I'll wager a monkey I dance a waltz with her before you do, sir!"

"Done! And if the lady is not indisposed, we'll settle the matter tonight."

"Is there to be dancing, then?" His lordship's eyes jerked off his food. He was beginning to regret stuffing himself.

"An impromptu affair, I gather. Not to be recommended as an aid to digestion!"

The Baron snorted and got on with the matter in hand. He was determined to go down a hero at all events.

Lord Radstock, when he got wind of the wager, could hardly suppress his satisfaction. It appeared that fate was indeed taking the situation into her own hands, now intervening in the unlikely and amplitudinous shape of the Second Baron Alvanley. With what triumph he casually imparted the news to Estelle, savouring the electric silence which followed and the fiery flash of her eyes. She went to Leo and slipped her arm through his. "But we have arranged to play whist with Mr Sheridan and Mrs Coutts," she wheedled, donning her injured look. "You can't have forgotten."

"That you agreed to do so on my behalf is more to the point," Leo detached himself, needled by her persistence. He eyed the Marquis who was near enough to hear. "I am sorry to inconvenience you, but there are others no doubt who would be most willing to step into the breach."

"I for one," Radstock neatly jumped to the cue, "would be only too honoured to oblige, my dear."

Essie was trembling with fury, but controlled herself enough to say: "You are very considerate, my lord, but I do not release Mr Quinn. A promise is a promise."

Thunder brooded over Leo's genial features. He was damned if he would humour the little baggage!

When Madeleine returned to the salon, he and Alvanley were solicitous of the welfare of Kate in a way which was gratifying to behold. "She is quite restored and will come down directly," she told them. "The night is too warm for her, I think."

In the Music Room, servants were scurrying about to shift the chairs aside with all the unassuming efficiency of stage hands. The orchestra struck up a vivacious cotillion.

"Ah, *la petite fleur* approaches," Radstock nudged Leo as Kate descended the staircase. "I believe she is engaged to dance the first waltz with me."

"You cunning dog, Radstock!" Leo exclaimed, quick to perceive how the various intrigues of the evening might be turned to good effect.

The Marquis let out a guffaw. "Enchanting as she is, it was not one of my wiser moves, I fear. A liberal quantity of cider punch accords ill with the gentle paces of the waltz. I would not wish to embarrass the lady."

"You would perhaps prefer a quiet game of cards? I, on the other hand, am committed to an evening of whist I do not at all relish."

"Why, sir, then you must make my apologies and I shall make yours!"

There were no bounds to Essie's chagrin when she learned of their stratagem and that her mother, moreover, was smiling benevolently upon the whole affair. She looked a little pathetic in her defeat, standing there, briefly-clad, with her gilded toe-nails exposed by Grecian sandals.

"Ye gods!" Alvanley was heard to expostulate when the first waltz struck up. "Quinn has the bun and the penny too!"

Kate stood unclaimed among the forming couples. The Marquis of Radstock was nowhere in sight. Unprepossessing as he was, the ivory tablet attached to her wrist clearly stated that she was promised to him for this dance.

But a partner emerged in another shape altogether. He came so intently towards her that she was powerless to do anything but give herself up to an earnest dialogue of the eyes. His arm encircled her and she was carried off into the sweep and lilt of the music. The stress of his proximity heightened her senses.

"You are very quiet," Leo said at length.

"I have never danced the waltz."

"You dance like a sylph."

"It has always been thought improper."

"Almack's have sanctioned it, however, and we need no longer fear to compromise our virtue!"

She smiled up at him, aware that she was being teased. He felt her relax. If the conduct of the Polite World was largely governed by that patrician institution, Almack's Assemblies, Leo wanted to believe that it was his own reassurance which had set her at ease.

"Did you enjoy the performance of Mozart and Purcell?" he asked, hoping to draw her out.

"Oh yes, indeed! The music of Mozart is like diamonds, but I believe I am so fond of it because it takes measured strides. I like to feel safe. And you?"

"I admire the Austrian's music, but to me it speaks of an age already gone. They call Herr Beethoven a madman, and so he seems at times, but his are the sounds of the Modern World."

"He is sadly afflicted for a composer."

"His deafness? His music is the finer for it."

"How can it be so?" Kate glanced into her partner's face, but at that moment he was looking ahead. There was about him the blind heroism of one who has known constant disappointment in transactions of the heart and who pledges himself to a cause as a refuge from bitterness.

He regarded her with a kind of sad and tender reflectiveness. "Have you not heard how they pierce with hot needles the eyes of those linnets trapped in gilded cages they sell on street corners, in order to make them sing more sweetly?"

"How barbaric!" Kate was appalled "The poor creatures! I did not know that."

A vision of her father sprang to Kate's mind. She saw his chair in the library at Merrowdene, the scraped leather hollowed by his weary frame. Had he not grown more sensitive and aware since his sight had faded? She swallowed hard and resolved to forget him. The music had taken command of her limbs. She was at one with her partner. She danced recklessly on.

"Katrine... I could not banish you from my thoughts last night..."

"Pray, don't. You are Essie's young man."

His expression kindled with startled disbelief. "Are you so innocent?" he queried, though more to himself. "Now I have offended you. Forgive me. Katrine...? Is your name really Katrine, when you are the soul of the English rose?"

"*Je m'appelle Katrine.* To speak truth, I am Kate. Single syllable, sir. I have lived nowhere but Sussex, though my parents are from the Border country. A visitor observed that my father sounds a little like Mr Wordsworth, the poet."

"Kate. *My* Kate."

"You take liberties with the possessive case, sir," she countered gently.

"Oh Kate, where have you come from? What are you doing in this house?"

"Why, I sew seams. Is it so disreputable to earn one's keep by plying an honest skill?" Kate was well aware that those who moved in the best circles looked down their noses at people engaged in trade, however successful.

He could have sworn, as she spoke, that she knew nothing of the business of this house. Yet how could that be? If Madeleine's needlewomen were referred to in whispers, it was no secret what they were.

"And am I to have the privilege of knowing who addresses me thus?"

"I stand chastised for the omission! Leo Quinn, ma'am, late of His Majesty's Dragoon Guards." He did not divulge his aristocratic connections. He had no reason to be proud of them.

"Then you've resigned the military life, Mr Quinn?"

"I sold out when the War ended, but had been out of action for some time prior to that owing to an injury. Sometimes I think

I was too precipitate. My regiment was not one of those shipped off to America when hostilities ceased in France."

"Were you not anxious to return to your homeland?"

"I love my homeland with all my heart, but there is no one here to care whether I do or die."

This was said without rancour, and Kate smarted with an uprush of sympathy. As the dance drew to a close and the final configurations resolved into bows and curtsies, her eyes were bright with unshed tears.

"Congratulations!" Essie burst upon them. "That was neatly contrived." She turned to the ingénue with treacherous charm. "Did you know that you have been the object of a wager between these two?" Her closed fan swung like an upturned pendulum between Leo and Lord Alvanley. That gentleman was keeping a diplomatic distance from the trio. He had gathered that there were more delicate matters at stake than a sum of money. Fighting a duel or riding to hounds he could stomach, but entanglements with the fair sex took the iron out of a fellow.

"That is unworthy of you, Estelle," Leo snapped.

"I?" Kate asked.

"His lordship bet Mr Quinn five hundred pounds that he would be the first to dance a waltz with you. What a good thing Leo is the winner because he has had such bad luck of late, poor lamb. He is by no means as warm as he was used."

Kate stared at Leo reproachfully, with a kind of disillusioned wonder. "Excuse me, I must go to my room."

"No, please don't go..." He was intensely conscious of her diminishing form among the concourse of guests. "Confound you, you shameless jade!" he rounded upon Essie. "Why could you not hold your tongue! Upon my oath, if you were a man I'd call you out for that!"

Leo shoved off the hand which fiddled seductively with his waistcoat button and stormed off through the anterooms, taking a curt leave of his hostess as he passed her. A footman gave him his hat and cape and he ran down the marble steps to the Square and made off into the night.

He was glad he had gone to Vanbrugh Square on foot and was now free to work off his anger. It seemed to be the pattern of late, he reflected wryly, to be quitting scenes of battle in a hurry. But that house! That temple of vice and vanity! He could not endure the thought of Kate there, though he could not bring himself to believe that Madeleine would be as unscrupulous as to take lovers for her. Her bearing was decidedly not that of seamstress. Nor yet of one accustomed to the ways of society. Whichever way he viewed it, he could not make her fit.

But none of these considerations hung so heavily upon his heart as the remembrance of a pair of speedwell blue eyes full of soft reproach. He had felt, as they danced, entrusted with a whole fragile, precious world. It was something entirely new to him and in some half-obscure way he had betrayed it. All he wanted to do was to go back, explain. He gasped at a sharp twinge of pain from that other wound when he had lain, a casualty of war, watching his own blood incarnadine the Pyrenean mire until the young Bayonnaise had come to his aid, her hair plastered down by the relentless winter rain.

Leo stopped in his tracks. The street was deserted. A carriage rattled along the Parade behind him. The echo of hooves died away. He must see her. He turned back. His pace quickened. In no time he had tossed off his outer clothes and scaled the garden wall at the back of 7, Vanbrugh Square, getting a purchase on the knapped flints by means of some elderberry bushes. With barely a sound he dropped down into a patch of wild garlic. The crushed stalks released a pungent vapour into the darkness.

He was able to learn Kate's location when, having discreetly entered by a side door, he ran into Travers on the servants' staircase. She, supposing his intentions were not as impeccable as they were and knowing that he was a respected patron, was not unforthcoming and skipped off to purvey this tasty snippet of news elsewhere.

He came out on the main landing at the rear of the house, the plush oyster-pink carpet a sharp contrast to the scrubbed boards of the stairs. Further along the corridor, a maid bearing a tray with cognac and glasses disappeared into a room. He tapped on Kate's door, a soft but insistent tap. There was a moment's hesitation before a small voice answered: "Who is it?" He burst across the threshold, closing the door by leaning his full weight against it.

She looked up, startled, her head tilted in the course of brushing her hair which fell in ripples of spun gold down her back. She had on a sprigged cotton nightshift drawn up at the neck. A single candle created an island of misty light about her and crowded the wall with fitful shadows. There was not a shred of evidence to suggest the venue for a seduction. He was relieved and triumphant.

"Kate! Kate, I had to come…" he floundered. "It was not quite as Estelle would have you believe. Only say I am forgiven."

"You certainly don't deserve to be, forcing an entry into a lady's bedchamber!"

She invited him to sit beside her on the counterpane. She smelled delightfully of lavender soap which helped to counteract the faint scent of garlic flowers clinging about him. His shoes looked incongruous beside her small bare feet. "Oh the deuce, Leo, you should not be here," Kate giggled, wondering what to do now. "You are Essie's dear friend. Shall you marry her?"

"Marry her!"

"Kate…" he began with tender exasperation, taking possession of her hand. He was exceedingly perplexed and strongly inclined to believe her modesty was genuine. "Do you truly not understand?"

"Understand what?"

Leo almost wished he had not come. "Tell me, how did you come to be here?"

"Well, to tell the truth, I ran away from home," she confided. "Madame took me in. She has been the soul of kindness."

He fought hard to keep his countenance as he digested this. "And why did you do that?"

"Because they said I must marry Anthony and settle down and not get into scrapes! I don't think they quite liked to be responsible for the consequences!"

A bellow of laughter escaped him. In some alarm, Kate put up her hand to cover his mouth. "Ssh! Someone will hear you!" she warned in a stage whisper. "Madame would be outraged at such goings on!"

"I think," said Leo with rueful amusement, "that Madame might take it in very good part." All the same he thought it imprudent to delay. He was anxious not to jeopardise Kate's honour, especially in the light of her disconcerting confession. Neither did he desire to risk inflaming Essie's jealousy. She could be a formidable foe. He stood up. "Kate, come for a ride on the Downs tomorrow afternoon," he said suddenly. "Can you ride?"

"Tolerably well, I fancy. But I have no horse."

"That can be remedied."

"But, sir, I have work to do. Madame would not take kindly to malingering."

"I suspect, my dear, you will find her all compliance. I shall take it upon myself to intercede for you."

"Oh, I think I ought not..." wailed Kate. Something felt wrong: she wasn't exactly sure what.

"Do come. I engage to take good care of you," he said earnestly.

"Well, then..."

"Tomorrow, then?"

"Tomorrow."

Leo quit the house even more discreetly than he had entered. His mind churned. The future was no longer clear.

"But it is true, Mama! The servants are talking. And this is his own."

Essie toyed with the mother-of-pearl waistcoat button belonging to her wayward lover. Travers had pounced upon it outside Kate's door and lost no time in bringing it to Essie's attention. The maid had never been overfond of Madame's haughty daughter.

Madeleine refused to become agitated. A half-ironic smile played upon her lips. She was sitting back in bed over a breakfast tray, dipping macaroons into a dish of tea as if testing the temperature. It was a beautiful bed with a carved shell for its headboard, but the gilt was peeling. She reclined in it like a voluptuous mermaid, a box of *marrons glacés* to hand. Overhead and around the walls, many mirrors gleamed. The atmosphere in her boudoir was frowsty and craved the benison of an open window. Scented powder decayed between the threads of the carpet, mingled with subtler odours.

"So," she concluded, "our little Katrine has a loveur."

"Is that all you have to say, Mama?"

Madeleine removed the lid from her buttered eggs and banged it down on the tray. "Essie, what is it that you wish me to do, please? You are becoming an over-scrupulous Miss."

"I wish you will send her away. I don't know what you were thinking of to engage her. She doesn't belong here. Suppose her parents succeed in tracing her, as they must surely try to do? Depend upon it, they will not be as ill-informed as she. Pray, don't forget that she is not of age."

"Listen. She comes to me wanting work as a seamstress. I take her in. She 'as done nothing against her will. She will vouch for that herself. Come, you silly creature, you forget we 'ave the weight of influence upon our side. No one wants our cosy salons to end. No, we keep Katrine."

"I know full well what you're about. There's no use in denying it."

"And what is that, please?"

"You are glad, glad she has stolen Leo! It is what you wanted. Well, I'll tell you this, Mama, if you think I'll be mated with that repugnant Lord Radstock, you are vastly mistaken. I would sooner go to the guillotine!"

"C'est folie! Be sensible. Be calm. You know we 'ave the difficulties. If we are to entertain high society, we must pay the price. 'Ow do you think we are earning our name. By frugality? The War sends up the price of everything! Candles! Silks! Food! Our house, already it is mortgaged to Radstock and what hope have we of redeeming it? But he promises to release us if you become his wife. He will foreclose, Essie, if you do not. And then we shall be ruined, turned out on the street to beg crusts. Twice in one lifetime!"

Matthieu had been a well-to-do silk merchant with noble connections. The pair resided in Paris in the Faubourg Saint-Antoine where Madeleine held a salon for artists and writers. He had grown rich running cargoes of cloth across the Channel. British silk was inferior and the government had placed an embargo on the foreign import to protect the industry at home. They lived in style, Matthieu and his bride, that was until Boney's men plundered and ransacked their home. Madeleine told how her husband had bled to death in a Paris street after being involved in a skirmish. She had bundled her baby under her arm and fled across the sea one stormy night in a boat full of singing and weeping nuns in blue habits. "Essie, I shall never forget it! *Ton pauvre père mort.* Our house in ruins! We had not a centime to bless our name! *Rien!*" They came ashore at Brighton where the local folk turned over inns and stables to accommodate them. Madeleine and her baby were welcomed into the bosom of a linen-draper's family. Mrs Bates adored the gurgling, dark-eyed baby with ruddy complexion and dimpled limbs.

Madeleine's optimism seemed to wither at these sombre memories. When serious, she had a wide, uncompromising mouth like the Queen who had many afflictions to bear with her demented husband.

"But, why," Essie railed, "if we were compelled to mortgage the house, did you allow yourself to be in Radstock's pocket?"

Madeleine heaved a sigh. "One night I am troubled. He asks what is the matter. I weep on his shoulder and tell him the bills are climbing!"

"But you knew he had designs upon me and that I had made it clear that his advances were unwelcome. Why, he is old enough to be my grandpapa!"

"So – you are free of him the sooner! Pander to him, wear him out, and you will be a rich woman."

The crystal ring tree on the dressing-table glinted and flashed in the morning sun. "I don't want marriage on those terms!"

Her mother let drop her fork on to the plate and pushed aside the tray with a gesture of distaste. "Now you spoil my breakfast. Essie, I do not understand you. It is marriage he offers you. A title! A place in society! What does it matter that you dislike him? When you have a roof over your head, a name, then you can enjoy your little intrigues. You are lucky to have the chance of such a match. You, *ma fille,* are a Fashionable Impure, a daughter of the shade."

"Oh Mama, I wish we could return home. Why can't we? It is safe now, in France. Half England is flocking to Paris to see the new fashions and the Emperor's treasures."

"My child, my child, what can you know? Do you suppose, after twenty years of Revolution, that France will be as it once was? The old France is gone, vanished for ever."

"But the Bourbons are back. Our king is restored."

"Heem! *Louis le Gros!* And who will give allegiance to that laggard, that numbskull, whose only concern is for his own thick skin? Who? The peasants have tasted blood. They want a champion, a man of vigour and imagination. *Ah, mon pauvre pays! Ma belle patrie!* I shall never see you again."

Such a heartfelt cry! Essie was not accustomed to hear her mother speak of the old country in this vein. Usually, she was evasive about the past, eager to blot France and its horrors out of her mind. In contrast she would speak with such verve of the English and appeared to have found in Brighton the fulfilment of her dreams. With a youthful want of wisdom, Essie accepted it at face value, but in her present highly-strung state, a nerve was touched. She had grown up believing that life was a stage: its players were there to be manipulated to one's own advantage. Madeleine's success had demonstrated the truth of it again and again. What reason had her daughter to doubt that with a little guile she would get what she desired? Now, she realised what a grave misapprehension this had been. It was as if the walls were closing in upon her. She flung herself on to the bed, clutching at the damask cover, and wept fit to break her heart. "But I love Leo so!"

"There, there," soothed Madeleine, tousling the cluster of ringlets escaping their ribbon. "You must learn to give a small portion of your heart and keep the rest for yourself. Now come, dry up your tears. No one wants to look at a lobster-face!"

"But he was fond of me, Mama. I believed he would... might... offer..."

"Even so, he is not solving our problems!"

Essie brushed away her tears with the back of her hand. "Leo will come about, I am sure. I cannot think the old Viscount would see his heir starve in the debtors' jail. Mama? You're not listening."

Her mother started from intense meditation. "Please?"

"You were far away."

"What a dimwit I am! Why does it not occur to me before? Now, I begin to see... It is not Kate who is your rival..."

"What can you mean?"

"Oh Essie," Madeleine's voice seemed to plunge an octave, "he is a cunning young man, your Leo. Unless I am greatly deceived it is Cassandra Stewart who will wear his ring."

"Cassandra! You're mad!" Essie's brittle laugh was followed by unease. A conversation she had had with Leo in the carriage returning from *The Rivals* came to her mind.

Her mother reached for the tea-kettle and replenished her cup, chasing the silver sugar-tongs which went slithering across the tray. The assay marks were wearing thin, she noted irrelevantly. The silver was foreign. Nevada or German, she could not recall. The soft white gleam of sterling had been sacrificed to a faintly leaden tinge. She drew in her chin; her nostrils had a slightly pugnacious flare. "There are things you do not know about my past…"

"What? What are you saying?"

"They signified nothing, until this moment." Madeleine gave a defensive shrug and went on: "When you wair small, when we flee the Terror and the good Bates' give us shelter, I find work as a governess with a family in Lewes and meet the man who becomes my loveur. Soon I am dismissed from my post."

"Not Mr Justice Jessop, your employer?"

"Non! Non, encore!" Madeleine recoiled from a ludicrous image of herself swamped by the bristling jowls of the barrel-bellied Judge. She was beginning to enjoy the situation. "The gentleman concerned was named Adam Quinn, plain Mr Quinn in those days."

"The Viscount? Leo's Papa? Then did you know Leo when he was a boy?"

"Quoi! Do you imagine he introduces me to his wife and sons? A man keeps his mistress in a separate apartment!" (Essie smirked at this specious inexactitude.) "All I know is that his marriage is a façade, but I make him forget his troubles. Eventually, he buys this house, this *petite pièce d'Angleterre,"* she

said with a melodramatic sweep of her hand, "and installs me as its châtelaine."

"Lord Penrose bought this house," repeated Essie, nonplussed. "He is reputed to be such a puritan."

"They are the worst," Madeleine said darkly. "When they go to the devil, they don't spare the horses!"

"Were you deeply attached to him? Or shouldn't I ask?"

"Of course! I adore all my loveurs. But after a while we quarrel. I like to live my own life. I tell him I am not a possession to be stored away and taken out at whim. It piques me that he is so jealous of his own reputation. Discretion is one thing, incarceration another. A lady alone must consider the future… so he signs the deeds over to me."

"He bought you off?"

"*Oui.* Not that I threaten him; it is not in me to do anything so dishonourable. But he thinks discretion is the better part of valour and I tell him I believe it is! I guess he does not want the world to know he makes love with his bedstockings on!"

"Mama, you're incorrigible! And Leo has no knowledge of this?"

"No! And you, mademoiselle, will not make mischief, please."

Essie was struggling to come to terms with these startling disclosures. "It is a strange coincidence, is it not, that you should become involved with the father and I with the son?"

"I would swear it was due to some perverse strain in the blood, except that Leo is no relation of Penrose's."

"Not…?" Essie focused again. It seemed Madeleine was hell-bent on piling one confusion upon another. "Not his son? Not his heir? Then who…?"

"That," Madeleine interjected, "is precisely my point, *chérie.* And that is why I tell you Cassandra Stewart will become his wife."

A dull pain, like a cold stone, lodged below Essie's

breastbone. "I don't understand..."

Madeleine confessed that she was unacquainted with all the circumstances of the Viscount's past, but he was an embittered man. His wife's heart was as faithless as her beauty was devastating. She had come bearing another man's child to the wedding feast. She claimed that she was ignorant of her condition at the time of the ceremony. There had been no joyful bridal night. She had shied from him and, putting it down to a very becoming maidenly modesty, he had not forced himself upon her, preferring that they come together by mutual consent. In the event, he had not touched her until after Leo's birth when their partnership was on quite another footing . The child was named for Elizabeth's mother's family. The Leonards, as the old lady was fond of reminding anyone courteous enough to lend half an ear, had been yeoman farmers in the county of Suffolk whose parlour had boasted a fine broadloom carpet and a clavichord in burr walnut. Adam had always discriminated against the child. Madeleine had serious doubts about Leo's expectations. It was the younger son who would inherit. Not the title, of course, because that would entail a complicated and invidious lawsuit, even if it could be proved. What Penrose would do, Madeleine said, her gaze narrowing astutely, would be to hive off the greater part of his estate and leave it to Julian. Folk would infer that it was his disenchantment with Leo's way of life which had driven him to do so.

"So if he is to settle his debts and hold his own, he must entrap an heiress?"

"What else can he do?"

Essie was ready to fly to Leo's defence, for had he not given her to understand that Cassandra would not come into her inheritance unless she married her cousin? Besides, he wouldn't saddle himself with a plain-featured wife who had so many freckles she looked contagious. If he must hook an heiress, he'd do it in style and would find someone who'd set the town by the ears. Wouldn't he?

"Such duplicity isn't in him," she said after a moment's reflection.

"Where is the duplicity? He promises you nothing."

"It is pure conjecture, nothing more."

"Informed conjecture." Madeleine pressed bunched fingertips to her forehead, her eyes wide awake. "What I am forgetting until now is that Silvercragg once belonged to the Penrose family."

"Silvercragg?"

"The North Country castle Miss Cassandra inherits!"

Silence prevailed.

"Don't you see," Madeleine pursued, "what a fine ploy it is for cocking a snook *à son vieil homme?* Leo acquires the ancestral seat of the Penroses and begets a successor to the title!"

On the chime of six that very morning, Essie had awoken with a sense of impending doom.

The contorted images of a nightmare were still vivid in her mind. Its aura suffused her waking hours, underlining all her actions with a predatory menace. She had been on the scaffold, out in some wild, desolate place, not even a crowd to jeer at her, like the miller of Falmer's son, strung up on a gibbet at Devil's Dyke last year for stealing a sheep. She had come across it one winter's day, the icicles hanging in glassy fangs from its spars and the body in an advanced state of decomposition. Flesh was flaking away like bits of charred leather and the bones rattled together in the moaning wind. In her dream, Leo had ridden along with his bride and had passed by on the other side, anxious not to delay over so offensive a sight. The bride's face was Katrine's, but then it resolved into some other unknown face and finally blurred into a nondescript presence. She had started awake in panic, seconds before the unseen hands of the executioner had brought the axe remorselessly down.

The servants hated her, she was convinced, though they loved Madeleine. What a to-do Travers had made about discovering the button. There was furtive enjoyment in the girl's small spiteful eyes, close-set like a pair of currants in a Bath bun. Oh, how she detested the English, all of them, with their insolent references to 'damned frogs' and their presumptuous attitude to victory!

She was in no frame of mind to woo the salon's clients that day. When, later, Cassandra Stewart's sister-in-law, Lady Diana, descended upon Vanbrugh Square, fresh from Petworth, to regale them with gossip and collect the promenade dress she had ordered, Essie received her with brittle politeness.

Lady Diana Stewart was small and fine-boned with a mass of hair the colour of beech leaves in autumn tucked under her saucy Wellington bonnet, and twinkling eyes more green than blue. She prattled and twittered gaily and seemed to fear the imminent cessation of life upon the planet when silence prevailed.

"Only fancy!" said she, speaking of the young Princess Charlotte. "No sooner had Prinny sent her her wedding guest list, than she returned it with her own name struck out!"

"Mon Dieu!" cried Madeleine, affecting outrage at this lack of filial co-operation and casting her daughter a meaningful glance.

"She won't have 'The Orange' at any price."

"Good for her," Essie muttered. She brought out the gown, a creation of turquoise and ivory striped bombazine.

Her ladyship retired behind the Chinese screens and, with a little help, divested herself of her outer garments and flung them over the ebony framework. "Of course, they say it was because her mother's name was omitted, but there is more to it than that, you may rely. The Grand Duchess, Catherine, the Czar's sister, you know, has been at pains to impress Charlotte with the Prussian princes. She hates Prinny and sought every opportunity during the visit to put him down. My dears, I quite blush to remember how she cut the poor man dead."

"And Miss Princess listens to her?"

"It is remarkable, I own," Lady Diana babbled on, "but the woman has a forceful character and Charlotte was ready to be led. Dear George, my own George, that is, is of the opinion that she was also influenced by that wily lawyer, Mr Brougham of the Opposition, who has always taken Caroline's part. He says that the fellow planted the notion in Charlotte's head that once her father had packed her off to Holland, he would divorce her mother, marry again and deprive the child of the Succession."

"Surely, dear ma'am, he would not do that," said Essie aghast.

"Indeed, I don't know. But George says it had the most striking effect upon her. She'll not do her father's bidding now."

Essie shot a look of triumph towards her mother. "Such flagrant disobedience! I think she should be chastised, this Charlotte, until she learns what is good for her!" Madeleine cried.

"Well, I don't doubt she needs a firm hand, Madame. Her speech is full of cant terms that would disgrace a stable boy. She gets that from her mother. The Queen is adamantly set against receiving Caroline at her Drawing Rooms. Heigh-ho! Charlotte will have her way, I dare swear." Lady Diana broke off to prink and preen and twirl before the cheval glass like a young girl preparing for her first ball. "It is divine! Charming! I am greatly taken with the trimmings, Estelle."

"Those colours do become you, ma'am. Won't you try the reticule we have made to match?"

"Of course, you 'ave the so-sylph-like figure," endorsed *Madame La Patronne*.

Essie helped the client to remove the gown, deftly slipping the buttons through their fabric loops. Lady Diana emerged in her camisole and unselfconsciously adjusted her georgette pantaloons edged, Madeleine perceived, with French lace of a quality that could only be come by, so far as she knew, in the middle of a crisp French loaf baked by an enterprising boulanger on the Promenade who dealt in the distribution of smuggled goods. "I only wish that poor Cassandra's affairs were settled as Charlotte's. I vow and declare it is the most worrisome thing having an eligible ward on one's hands, though in truth, she is no longer our ward since her birthday."

"Is there no suitor on the horizon?" Essie asked lightly.

"My dear, George is turning them away at the door. She won't look at any of them. Prefers to wait for her cousin to return from his travels. But I own one cannot be quite comfortable with Eugene away for so long."

"They are betrothed then, she and Eugene?"

"Indeed, no, not *exactly*. That is the devil of it." Lady Diana hesitated, uncertain how much she ought to divulge, but her gossipmonger's habits were quick to assert themselves. "It is all a result of her father having arranged his bequests so confoundedly when he knew he hadn't long to live," she said as she stepped into the well of her old dress and shrugged herself into its sleeves. "You see, he was deeply attached to his sister, Eugene's mother, whose husband was not the most prudent of investors. It was his dying hope that their respective offspring be united. He left Silvercragg to Cassandra on the strength of it, but he would not force her hand."

"I don't follow," frowned Essie. She noted her mother was listening intently at this point.

"Well, she was to inherit Silvercragg upon her marriage to Eugene, or upon her coming of age, whichever was the sooner."

"But if your sister-in-law desires to wed her cousin, what can it signify?"

"I am not at all sure, Estelle," answered the client, "that he is of a mind to wed her, despite the inducements. Recollect, they are not actually betrothed. She is in an ambiguous position with her cousin gone off in that cavalier manner and there's no telling when he'll be back, for all he's living on a shoestring and the goodwill of his friends. It is too shocking of him! He might be in Paris or Persia by now! In the meantime, Cassandra herself could suffer a change of heart."

The sardonic lift of Madeleine's brow did not elude Essie.

Lady Diana swept out from behind the screens and sat down at the Hepplewhite dressing-table where she availed herself of the facilities provided for clients, inspecting either side of her profile in the looking-glass. She dipped a hare's paw into the powder-bowl and dusted it over the curves and crevices of her tautened countenance, then set her bonnet neatly over her curls, stuffing away the wispy side-locks with an air of finality. "If I were Cassandra," she averred wickedly, "I'd accept the first well-endowed male who came my way and the devil take Eugene!"

"No doubt," Essie submitted, "she cares more deeply for her cousin than she dares to show when he treats her so."

"She really is the oddest girl at times," frowned Lady Diana. "One cannot fathom her."

At this juncture, the conversation took a new turn. Watching Madeleine wrap the gown in tissue and lower it into a bandbox, Lady Diana mentioned her difficulties in finding a suitable governess for her daughter, Fiona. The child was twelve and handicapped by consumption. She needed a companion as much as someone to supervise her education. "She has such a sweet and sociable nature. It is heartbreaking to see her so confined. She loves to have George's friends about her. They tease her mercilessly, but she thrives upon it. Mr Quinn is her favourite. So patient! He thinks nothing of spending a whole afternoon reading to her or whittling animals out of a piece of wood with a pocket knife, a skill he acquired in Spain."

"He is every inch a gentleman," Madeleine agreed, tailoring her view to suit her company.

"I do hope his fortunes may soon take a turn for the better. The poor fellow is punting on tick, George says."

"Won't you take a dish of tea, Lady Stewart, before you go?"

Essie interjected wildly. "Some cordial? A glass of apricot brandy?"

Lady Diana turned and, squinting, drew back from a shaft of sunlight. She was rather abashed by the outburst of hospitality. "Dear me, no, Estelle. I am obliged to you, but my carriage awaits. I must away and see how Fee does. Mr Cosway is come to take her likeness for a miniature and the baronet is shut away with his lawyer. But I shall return soon, for I hanker after one of those saucy frogged riding-habits. In bottle-green velvet, I think. No, on second thoughts, it shall be burgundy."

"As your ladyship chooses," smiled Madeleine.

"We shall be leaving for London shortly. We have promised that Fee shall not miss the Peace Celebrations. The Prince proposes to return here afterwards and I dare say we shall follow suit if the weather holds. The warm sea air has improved Fee out of all recognition. Oh, how I dread the onset of winter! I wish I could persuade my husband to take us to Italy for the whole of the winter."

So saying, she snatched up her purchases, bade the women 'good day' and, breaking a sunbeam, whisked herself off in a flurry of dust-motes.

"If wishes were horses," Essie whispered, "beggars would ride!"

Moodily, Essie wondered about the empty workroom, examining seams and buttonholes with a critical eye. The girls were in the kitchen at their midday meal. Pincushions, shears, chalk, caskets of buttons, a shimmering length of Florentine silk and fragments of lace were spread about the workbenches as though, on the stroke of noon, the crew had abandoned ship in great haste, clamouring to appease the pangs of hunger.

Charmaine and Celeste passed by the door in peals of laughter, deep in discussion of their morning's exploits. During the day, Madeleine permitted her well-bred young ladies to go out unchaperoned provided they went in pairs. The twins had been out to drink coffee on the piazza outside Thomas's Circulating Library. Inside, they were ogled by the young bloods, and some not so young, who lounged around on the pretext of catching up on the London newspapers, several days old. In his prime, long before the War, Mr Thomas himself used to bellow the news to his customers, causing a stir of amusement at his mispronunciation of any French words in the text.

"There you are, Essie," Madeleine accosted her. "What do you think? Your philanderer 'as the impudence to request the pleasure of Miss Kate's company this afternoon. He desires to take her riding on the Downs, if you please."

"Katrine! What did you say?"

"I send the footman away with a note and a flea in his ear! I tell Leo, no, not today, she cannot be spared. Tomorrow, per'aps. Please don't look at me so. We must humour him. First I speak with the girl and learn the lie of the land."

Leo! Essie froze. But Kate should not have him! No one should have him! He was hers! Anyway, who was this milk-and-water Miss from the backwoods who had chanced upon their world and was carrying off all the prizes while she, Essie, was left the easy prey of the likes of Radstock? "I hate her!" she vowed through her teeth and her black eyes glittered.

It was unfortunate that at this moment footsteps and a murmur of voices should announce the approach of the girls. Entering the workroom to find Madame and her daughter in fractious mood, they fell silent and quickly dispersed to perch themselves on the benches, fully expecting a tirade about their slovenly ways. Kate was last to come in and, seeing Essie, lowered her gaze uneasily. Essie grabbed her by the sleeve. "You!" she hissed. "Why did you have to come? I was happy before you came here!"

"Please, Essie," her mother sharply reproved. "Restrain

yourself."

But Essie closed her ears, her mind to all reason, giving herself up to an insensate desire for revenge. On Kate. On Leo. On life! "We don't want you," she fumed. "We don't want your sort here!"

Kate paled and back away in alarm, feeling behind her for the wall. Its touch was cold as steel to her back. "I think… I think you are not yourself…"

"I am never myself!" Essie cried. "I am not required to be myself in this house! Isn't that so, Mama? Tell her! Tell her how we really exist! Don't imagine, greenhorn, that you're here to sew and sell clothes. Not for long! It's yourself you must sell, to any rakehell who'll pay for you!" Anger in full spate, she seized Kate by the shoulders and shook her so viciously that her teeth rattled. She wanted the stark truth to dawn: to shatter the blessed dream of innocence which had never been hers. Since the age of fourteen, Essie had been a courtesan, and long before that her gaze had been blighted by a precocious awareness. "Don't you know what it is, this place? It's a stew! A glorified bawdy-house for the high and mighty who care to indulge their vices in style and can afford to protect their own interests! You're here to ply a new trade, my sweeting, so swallow your precious ideals and be a good little drab!"

A shiver of terror ran up Kate's spine. More acutely than the assault on body and mind, she felt exposed to incommunicable powers of evil. Madame, eyes blazing, stood by and issued ineffectual commands. "*Arrêtez! Silence! Je vous en supplie!*" Kate held back her head and made a valiant endeavour to keep her assailant at bay, jerking back her arms by gripping them at the wrist. Essie's hands, robbed of strength, spread out and clawed at space, straining to grasp Kate's hair. For a split second she gained the ascendancy and lunged forward to drag her nails across her victim's neck. Tiny red beads sprang up in the scraped flesh.

Without further hesitation, Madeleine lifted her hand and

fetched her daughter a resounding blow across the jaw. *"Imbécile!"* she raged from the shuddering depths of her voice. *"Que faites-vous? Votre chambre, tout de suite!"*

Essie's eyes watered. Pain thudded inside her skull. Nursing her stinging cheek, she fled from the room to fall at the foot of the staircase, passion spent, sobbing wildly.

Kate's vision blurred. She was trembling and more profoundly enervated than she would have thought possible. The room and its effect, the gaping girls, pinch-faced over their seams, the dominating form of Madame, swam together in a senseless kaleidoscope and whirled about her head to vanish in an enveloping darkness.

She came to, bewildered, in her own blue and white bedchamber. The curtains were drawn. On the ceiling above the window, the ragged fringe of deflected light was fading. She could hear the sound of muffled laughter in the garden below and, in the distance, the soughing of the sea.

Why was she here? Had she been dreaming? Every nerve and fibre tingled with an urge to escape. Then the sorry memory of what had happened came rushing back. Touching her smarting neck, Kate realised that her scars had been anointed with salve smelling of herbs and country hedgerows.

She had been blind to the true character of this house! She had seen what she wanted to see. She had been hoodwinked by its reigning principle of *laissez-faire*. What a relief it had been after the constraints of Merrowdene! Yet this, too, was a prison. Here she was, her fingers pricked and sore, spending hour after wearisome hour at toil she hated at home. Home! How Papa had betrayed her, feeding her books to the flames! When she might have imbibed, by the gentlest of means, a knowledge of the ways of society, he had put a brace on her mind. He had even gone so far as to forbid her access to his library lest she be exposed to the dubious influences of Fielding, Defoe and the Journals of Boswell. That it was to protect her, she didn't doubt. But what purpose did it serve if one didn't emerge fitted to understand the human race? Ignorance had made her vulnerable. She would never have sought her present post if she'd known the dangers.

So where was she to go? She could not remain in this abode of dark secrets with its nauseous goings-on behind closed doors. Dear life, she could not bear to think of it! Why, at this moment… "Do you really not understand?" Leo Quinn had probed. Leo! She wanted to weep when she thought of what he was to Essie. The girl had good reason to fear that someone might supplant her in his affections if all that bound them together was a business arrangement. And had he been grooming her, Kate, to bestow the same favours? What a fool she had been! How led astray by the magical atmosphere of the music room the other night! She had believed in Leo implicitly. Even now, hurt to the quick, she could not reconcile the man who was so gentle, considerate and curiously sad, with one whose designs were more primitive.

At length, she came to a decision. She dare not go home. Her flight would only increase her father's desire to see her safely wed to the first stuffy squireen he deemed suitable. She would go to London. The opportunities for work as a companion or governess must be legion. Papa had given her a good grounding in the classics and arithmetic, in geography and the use of the globes. At least she could thank him for that. Tonight she would pack and at first light creep away to await the opening of the stage coach office in Castle Square.

She started upright and clasped a hand to her forehead with a sudden spasm of pain. Had they given her a sleeping draught? She dragged herself off the bed and fumbled to light candles, replacing the glass chimneys carefully. Then she groped under the feather mattress for the little bead box where she kept the money she had brought with her from Merrowdene. There had been no need of it here. She counted out a whole sovereign and a number of florins, shillings and pennies. She was in funds!

Yes, she would leave Brighton behind and board the first coach to the capital!

"God's truth, I reckon ye're not roasting me!" exclaimed the booking clerk, gruff and sibilant, when Kate presented herself at the Spread Eagle office early the following day and requested a seat on Mr Chaplin's Comet. A sense of purpose heightened her colour and added brilliancy to her eye. She had on a pelisse of sober grey merino, accounted very smart in her vicarage days, she calculated ought best to recommend her to the new station she sought. "Pretty bit o' fluff, ain't ye, Miss Prim? Not afeared for your virtue, then?" The man leered at Kate, exhibiting a single long tooth, like a blunted spur, protruding from his upper gums. His face was afforested with a growth of steely stubble from his ears down to his scrawny neck wound in a grimy red kerchief. The bloodshot eyes molested her.

"Be so good as to answer my question," Kate demanded.

He roared with laughter. Kate ducked aside from his spittle and clenched her teeth. "And I s'pose my fine lady'll be wanting a seat wi' the gentry, like?"

"I should prefer to travel in the open air, if you please."

"Travel wi' the rabble, will ye? And ready to pay for the privilege!"

"Can you or can you not accommodate me, sir?"

"I can 'commodate the likes o' you at any time, my little lovebird. That'll be nine shillings and sixpence wi' the rest o' the baggage!" He peered over the counter at her luggage.

Kate glared at him and drew the coins from her reticule, scattering them under his strawberry nose. He was hugely enjoying her humiliation and she was aware that one or two other passengers were watching.

"Coach leaves the tavern at half past the hour, sharp." The clock on the wall behind him indicated that it was two minutes past seven.

She sat down, overcome with the magnitude of her undertaking. Where would she go when she arrived at the terminal? Lodgings would have to be found before nightfall. Then there was the problem of persuading someone to engage her when she had neither references nor a letter of introduction. It would be necessary to supply a plausible explanation.

"All alone," a voice intruded, "and unaccustomed to travelling, I'd hazard."

Collecting herself, Kate looked up into the face of a young man of pleasant appearance. He was tall and slightly angular with well-defined features and slate-blue eyes that dilated with warmth. He made a gesture that was half-bow, half-query. His clothes were elegant, but as plain as her own. Kate's immediate impression was of one destined for the Church, or perhaps one of the professions.

"Edward Grey, at your service, ma'am." He bent with some grace over the hand she absently extended. His manner had no trace of affectation.

"Mr Grey… I…" Kate faltered, managing to subdue the flush rising under the brim of her bonnet. Events were proceeding apace and she had the unnerving sensation that they were overtaking her.

"Have you a long journey to make?"

"I'm going to Town.

"And will you be travelling inside or out?"

"Outside."

"Good. Maybe you will not object if I join you, for I, too, have no travelling companion."

Kate was not ungrateful for his kind intervention at a moment when her courage was failing. He was blessed with an honest countenance and the bearing of a man of integrity.

Flicking aside his coat-tails, he perched on the edge of the bench beside her.

"Oh, forgive me, sir. My name is Kate Hanslope and I am from Merrowdene, a little village tucked away on the Downs. Do you know it?"

Mr Grey confessed that he did not. A Londoner born and bred, he had no opportunity to explore the byways of his native land and was unfamiliar with these parts. He was articled to a firm of lawyers and had come down from the offices of Messrs Sperry, Odell and Attwood in Lincoln's Inn Fields at the request of a client. The firm administered the affairs of many notable people.

"I had you down for a lawyer," Kate smiled.

"Did you now? Well, do you know, Miss Hanslope, I rather think I am glad to be what I seem to be."

"Yes," she replied pointedly. She smoothed the creases of her kid gloves and then looked away.

"You said that with feeling."

"Did I? Pray, don't refine upon it, Mr Grey. Listen! Is that the coach?"

A scarlet and black equipage fit to rival a mail coach was drawing rein in front of The Castle Tavern. Kate stood on tiptoe and craned to see between the shoulders of folk bulking the exit. Mr Grey took charge of her valise along with his own carpet bag and called for the 'boots' to see them safely stowed in the luggage box. The vehicle creaked and swayed on its springs as the passengers scrambled aboard, four inside, seven on top. At least there was a Guard to protect them from highwaymen!

"Come, sit down, Miss Hanslope and tell me what takes you to the city."

Kate resisted this invitation to enlarge upon her predicament and asked if his business in Brighton had been successful.

"My time was well spent. Several matters were resolved. I think it would be no breach of confidence to say that what

102

concerns my principal most at present is that we find a governess-companion for his daughter."

Kate's attention was instantly caught.

"It may not be easy to find someone in whom all the qualities needed are united," Grey went on. "The young lady in question is but twelve years old and in failing health. Her doctors fear she may not survive into womanhood."

"Poor, unfortunate child!"

"'Tis touching to see her. She has the sweetest temperament imaginable and a great deal of spirit, but she cannot go about unless the weather is fine and warm, and then quite often only in a Bath chair."

"And she lives here in Brighton?"

Grey shook his head. "She is merely taking a vacation. The family have a town house is South Audley Street and estates in Cumberland and Argyllshire."

Harnesses jingled: horses tossed their dark manes and pawed at the ground, anxious to be off. The coachman gulped down his negus and thrust the tankard towards the aproned innkeeper. "Thank ee, good Squire," he cried, wiping his mouth on his sleeve. "That'll keep us on the straight and narrow, so it will!" The Comet lurched forward and burst into motion, skidding through dust and stones. In no time, it was on the turnpike, gathering speed, the breeze rushing past everyone's ears and every milestone pointing to London and the promise of a new chapter.

"Ours is indeed a fortuitous encounter," Kate said.

"Why so?"

"Because, Mr Grey, I am looking for a post such as you describe."

"You are? Well, then, Miss Hanslope, I shall take you directly to my office when we arrive at our destination. I am sure Mr Attwood would be most happy to interview you!"

What Kate did not know, what she would never have dreamt while the coach charged along the highway full tilt for London, putting space between herself and the years of childhood, was that Anthony March, whip in hand, was striding up to hammer furiously upon Madeleine's yellow front door.

Polly had finally broken down and blurted out the truth to her master.

Four

Sunlight gilded the capital when Kate caught her first breathtaking glimpse of it. The coach breasted a rise and there it was, diminutive in the distance and invested with a strange ethereal quality against the dark thunder clouds brooding behind it.

They crossed Clapham Common without incident and were soon rumbling over Battersea toll-bridge, the brown, sluggish Thames glistening below. On the far bank, willows trailed branches into the water and the lowing of cattle carried from the Chelsea meadows. At the approach to each village, the Guard gave a blast on his 'yard of tin'.

Before long, they were in the heart of London, part of the noise and bustle and teeming life. Here, the miniature peal of a clock carillon: there, chimes from a church tower. And everywhere, the vendors' cries rising in a shrill counterpoint and subtly changing en route.

Fine felt hats! Spectacles to read!
Pretty pins, pretty women!
Rosemary and lavender! Buy my sweet-briar!
Old shoes for some brooms!
Old satin! Old taffety! Any old cloaks!
Lily-white vinegar!
Any work for John Cooper?
Oranges, fair oranges and citrons!
Strawberries ripe and cherries in the rise!
Hot peascod! Many a pie!
Ripe cowcumbers! Ripe young beans!
Buy my dish of oysters!

And so to Gracechurch Street and the Spread Eagle Inn where the Comet set down its sore and cramped passengers and the driver swiftly disappeared in pursuit of something to appease hunger and thirst.

"Some refreshment would be welcome, do you not think, Miss Hanslope? Then we'll see if we can rouse Mr Attwood from his afternoon nap."

Josiah Attwood removed the gold-rimmed spectacles which did little to improve his myopia but a good deal to enhance his prune-like features, and rubbed his red, bleary eyes. It was manifestly clear that he suffered from hayfever and had, like the late Mr Pitt, a permanent drip at the end of his nose. Having conducted Kate to the inner sanctum, he bade her be seated and then took out his handkerchief to polish his glasses and blow his nose with uninhibited vigour. He was a fossil of a man who in youth must have been gangling, but whom age and decrepitude had given the posture of an ungainly stork. He would have retired long ago had not his devoted spouse preceded him to the grave. For nearly half a century he had managed the affairs of the same old-established families, watching sons and grandsons come into their inheritance, reaping an obscure personal satisfaction from the continuity. Now he was obliged to delegate many of his tasks. The summons from his client in Sussex was a case in point. He could no more contemplate an excursion of some fifty-odd miles, by public transport at that, than stand on his head. Best send the stripling, Grey, he'd decided. The lad had a good head on his shoulders and was eager to make his mark. Having conferred with him in private just now, Mr Attwood owned he was amazed by the expediency with which the young fellow had not only carried out his orders but had produced an applicant for the new vacancy! Mr Attwood applied his spectacles as if donning a mask and peered at Kate.

"Your pardon, Miss… er…"

"Hanslope, sir. Kate Hanslope." She hesitated for a moment and then leaned forward earnestly. "If I may be so bold, Mr Attwood, may I suggest that you try an infusion of chamomile for your affliction. I know those who have found it most efficacious."

What an engaging way she had with her! The elderly lawyer was quite bowled over. Few people noticed him nowadays. A very fetching and lively young woman to boot, not at all the kind one desired to see banished to that limbo between drawing room and servants' hall. He had installed many a prim custodian of rectitude in his time.

"Thank you, I will bear your advice in mind." He cleared his throat. "Miss Hanslope, you are seeking employment as a governess? Why?"

"I am well educated, sir, and have several accomplishments and should like of all things to work with children."

"You have experience of them?" he challenged from under strongly contracted brows.

"Oh yes! A little, that is. I have organised entertainments for the village children on several occasions."

"I see. Miss Hanslope, forgive me, but you bear no letter of recommendation. You have held no previous position?"

The heat was oppressive. The mighty legal tomes arranged all along one wall, from floor to ceiling, dark and smelling of mildewed leather, bore down upon her. Her thoughts flashed back to the vicarage library. She fought back her discomposure and answered with a steadiness which surprised her. "My father is a clergyman and a classical scholar. He saw to it that my time was profitably spent and my instruction thorough."

"Then might he not have written some communication to that effect? Might he not himself have contrived to see you suitably placed, hmm?"

"Mr Attwood," Kate said, directing candid blue eyes upon him which disturbed his equanimity, "Mr Attwood, my father does not entirely approve of what I am doing."

"Indeed?"

"He hoped to see me married to a gentleman I did not... could not... sufficiently care for," she foundered with a blush. "Since I cannot do what he wishes, I am resolved not to be a drag upon him."

"I think we may safely conclude that you are not, as they say, on the shelf yet," the lawyer chortled. "And you are not one of those whom penury has obliged to seek an occupation. Might you not regret your hasty decision?"

"No, sir, I shall not regret it."

"And what of your mother? What does she have to say?"

"Her opinions are much in accord with my father's."

"So you are quite set upon independence?"

"I am, sir."

"Tell me, Miss Hanslope," said he, leaning back and putting the tips of his fingers together with the air of a man forming his own conclusions, "tell me why, when were I to advertise this post I should have a string of competent ladies all eager to fill it and better qualified than you are, should I offer it to you?"

Kate raised her eyes which had been demurely downcast. "Because Mr Attwood, I should endeavour most earnestly not to disappoint you."

"Very well, then, madam, you shall have your chance and we shall see how you acquit yourself. And may I say how much I applaud your spirit!"

Mr Attwood went on to outline the terms of her employment. "I believe Mr Grey has already acquainted you with the circumstances of the Stewart family. Your charge, Miss Fiona, is a taking little thing, but because she is an invalid, you may find your duties onerous at first. Intelligent companionship is what she stands most in need of. For her part, I doubt not that she would prefer someone youthful like yourself." How delighted Sir George would be that his commission had been so speedily despatched. Mr Attwood drew a sheet of parchment towards him and, dipping his quill in the standish, began to scratch out an explanatory letter to Mrs Butterfield, the housekeeper in South Audley Street. He assured Kate that this lady would make her quite comfortable until the Stewarts returned from the coast. Kate saw his disciplined script gliding over the page, hardly able to suppress her intense relief.

The lawyer sanded his handiwork, folded it with studious precision and sealed it with a red wafer. He rose and, opening the door to the outer chamber where a row of tallow-faced clerks sat, nose to quill, over their sloping desks, bellowed for Grey. As he did so, that familiar peppery twitch started again and with a sharp intake of breath he was just in time to stifle a Leviathan sneeze in one of the many handkerchieves secreted about his person.

"Grey, be good enough to escort this young lady to South Audley Street."

"Indeed, I will, sir. Congratulations, Miss Hanslope."

"You have both been exceedingly kind," she said, smiling appreciatively from one to the other. "How can I thank you?"

"My pleasure," responded Mr Attwood, feeling the germ of some long-buried chivalry stir within his battered old frame. He bent awkwardly over her hand. "I bid you 'good day', Miss Hanslope, and wish you well."

"Goodbye, Mr Attwood. And pray, do give the chamomile a try, won't you?"

Josiah Attwood returned to his desk feeling that a ray of sunshine had penetrated the overcast sky.

Down in Warwickshire, Penrose lay in his fourposter bed, staring out from sunken eyes at a colourwash landscape. It was evening and the sky was tinged with coral and flame, the first brightness for over a week. He had lain watching the silver rain come slanting down. It had rained the day Leo turned up, out of nowhere, to scourge him with memories of the past and he had been unwell since then. That was a month ago, or near enough. Twice his chest had been gripped by a vice-like pain which shot down his arm and made his eyes roll upwards so that only the bloodshot whites were visible. It was worse when it smote in the dead of night. But he would allow no one to keep vigil over him. It was mortifying to let others see him helpless and at the mercy of his own defective body. Meaker had placed a handbell by his bedside, but Penrose doubted of its being any use: he had told Meaker so. He had made his cross of loneliness and he would endure it. His lower limbs were hideously misshapen from swelling. Dr McGillivray had ridden over from Warwick in a thunderstorm to bleed him. Repelled, Penrose watched the leeches grow fat and dark as garnets on his own lifeblood, and cursed himself if he was going to pay the mincing little Scot several guineas for the privilege. Moreover, he did not require a homily upon his addiction to grape and grain which was the only pleasure left nowadays. Nor did he need the offices of a prating clergyman as some had dared to suggest.

The subtle tints overhead were starting to fade; there was a strange valedictory mood about it. Day was sinking into darkness and soon he would be shut in with the shadows and his own menacing thoughts. They brought him opiates, the staff, and some bitter decoction of foxgloves which was supposed to strengthen the heart. The tester above him was an atlas of damp, the plasterwork on the ceiling, cracked. Incorporated into the design was a Tudor Rose dating from the reign of King Henry VIII with which a prudent ancestor, respectful of his own head, had sought to keep the good opinion of that fickle monarch. King Hal had favoured Fernleigh with a visit and slept in this room, in this very bed, in 1541, the year before Catherine Howard put her

110

pretty neck on the block. Faithless whore!

Images of death. They were all about him. The dark time was the worst; the long, shrouded silent time before dawn when grotesque faces loomed out of the blackness inside his brain.

The soft hues had gone. Ashen cloud was rolling across the sky. Something was causing a stir among the rooks in the elm-tops who, in the spring, had wrangled so bitterly over the tenure of last year's nests. They burst upwards in a raucous flurry, resembling scraps of charred paper as they wheeled about the air. Perhaps Shem Stokes' boy had taken a potshot at them. He needed a firm hand, that young scullion; he was wild to a fault, ungovernable as Leo had been, with the same good-humoured demeanour while he plunged in the knife. Leo! He'd made the wretch squirm at all events, sent him packing with his tail between his legs. Yes, there it was! The report of a fowling-piece, loud and clear, clattering around the stable walls. Why hadn't he heard it before? Blasted fool! What did the boy think he was about?

The pain lanced, white-hot, between the Viscount's shoulder-blades. His jaw dropped open in agony. He groped for the handbell and sent it flying off the side-table on to the carpet. The muffled tintinnabulation mocked him. Penrose clutched his throat and fought for air.

A quarter of an hour later, Meaker knocked timorously on his master's door and entered. In sickness the old man had become more crusty and foul-tempered than ever and the servants were apprehensive of their reception. "Does your lordship wish me to close the curtains now?" he enquired.

No answer came.

Rain trickled in steady rivulets down the window-panes in South Audley Street and a greenish gloom filled the sitting-room where Kate curled up on the rug before an empty hearth. The drama of the last twenty-four hours had played itself out and dejection had set in. All ties with the past were well and truly severed.

Impatiently, she wiped her cheeks on her sleeve and chided herself for giving way to despair. Fortune had smiled upon her. But for Edward Grey she would have been out in the storm roaming the streets in search of lodgings. The welcome she had received from Mr and Mrs Butterfield could not have been warmer.

In addition to this elderly couple, there was a little maidservant whose face was ravaged by smallpox. The child's ankles were thin as sticks. She looked pale and undernourished and Kate learned that she had only recently come to the house. Pru was a relative of the Butterfields. Her mother, a war widow, had fallen on hard times. She had been hired by a silk-winder in Spitalfields market and thought herself lucky. Pru's infant brother had also been taken on. From dawn to dusk the tiny mite filled quills from the weaver's shuttle and was beaten for falling into an exhausted heap before his work was done. It was no use his mother protesting: they had to eat bread and one such employer was no worse than another. When Harry grew bigger he would become a 'draw-boy', Pru told Kate, and earn a few shillings of his own. "They have to pull up the threads making the pattern when there's brocade in the loom," she explained. "It's tiring work, even for a hefty lad with meat in his belly. But there's not much else for the likes of us, Miss. We're better off than some, and that's the truth. I'm glad Aunt Butterfield found me this job. It's what I'd set my heart on, Miss. A real chance to make something of my life."

Kate listened with an interest which flattered the girl. Her education was expanding as it could never have done in Merrowdene. Out of loneliness, she encouraged Pru to linger and talk and the maid would have expatiated at great length had not her Aunt Butterfield, faithful retainer of the well-heeled baronet, taken her to task.

The governess' accommodation was at the top of the house, next to Fiona's room and across the landing from the nursery and schoolroom. Kate had a sitting-room to herself, although Mrs Butterfield assured her that her ladyship was not a stickler for keeping to one's own apartments and she could expect to be invited regularly to join the family downstairs. She wondered what her new employers would be like. Mrs Butterfield had intimated that the mistress was of a sunny disposition but inclined to be scatterbrained. The master was a rugged Scot, as dour as they came when his temper was high, but his wife could twist him around her little finger. As for Miss Fiona, she was a brave wee lassie.

The days passed. Kate explored the grand Squares and gardens of Mayfair. In the schoolroom, she browsed through Fiona's exercise books of copied verse, dates of the reigns of Kings and Queens, maps, painstakingly traced of lands the child would never see. In a drawer, she discovered a delightful portfolio of botanical drawings. Miss Stewart was obviously a keen draughtswoman. Kate found herself gazing into the sculptured curves of an arum lily, or the striped petticoats of a Gallica rose. She spent hours watching the comings and goings along the street. Hardly anyone rapped on the door, except Mr Grey. He was becoming quite devoted to her and she looked forward to his visits. Mrs Butterfield did not demur when she wanted to entertain him in the drawing room and sent Pru up with roast beef and horseradish sandwiches, shortbread and Darjeeling tea. He was a respectable fellow, known to the family, and his conduct was of the most seemly.

One hot Sunday afternoon, late in July, Edward took Kate on a tour of the Parks in a hired chaise. He wanted to show her the elaborate preparations for the peace festivities on August 1st. Wellington had come home at last to a resounding welcome. There had been a fête in his honour at Carlton House that went on until breakfast, in a hall specially built for the purpose by Mr.

Nash.

In St James's Park, lanterns were strung up; there was a Chinese bridge surmounted by a pagoda arching over the canal and suspended upon its own reflection like a Cotman painting. In the Green Park, a Castle of Discord and a Temple of Concord had been erected to depict Britain's victory in allegorical terms. Fireworks and a battery of Sir William Congreve's rockets were to feature in the extravaganza. On the Serpentine, a fleet of model frigates had been launched. Edward said that there was to be a reconstruction of the Battle of the Nile. Most folk, he said, had no notion what had taken place in defence of their heritage. For two decades there had been wars and rumours of wars, but little of it had registered at home save for the absence of loved ones and the soaring price of bread.

"His Royal Highness has gone to great lengths to win the good opinion of the people, has he not?"

"It's like a fable land," Kate said, entranced. "How much labour and ingenuity have gone into it! What it must have cost!"

"And the Prince deep in debt! There are many in high places who murmur against him."

Yes, the Prince was anxious to recommend himself to the people. Nothing was to interfere with this last ditch attempt to make himself popular. August 1st marked the centenary of George 1's accession to the throne and the Regent was in a fever to remind his subjects that the Hanoverian dynasty which earlier had put the Stuart rabblerousers to rout had, under his helmsmanship, wrested a still more glorious victory. He was also desperate to distract the people from their troubles. The war machine was being dismantled, turning thousands of soldiers loose upon the streets. You could see them loafing around tavern doors, the expendable dregs of humanity. Many were maimed and wounded and thought themselves lucky to have escaped the yellow fever raging among the regiments awaiting transport from abroad. A good number had resorted to begging their way home. War had delivered them from crime and privation: now they were being returned to it, their sole objective the price of strong liquor to stave off the pangs of hunger and the prospect of unemployment.

Now that time had elapsed, weeks of unwonted inactivity in which Kate had been alone with her thoughts, her heart was troubled. She was concerned about her parents and sisters. Nothing would have induced her to go back, but she did not like to think of them grieving, wondering. And what of poor faithful Polly? Kate hoped that her father had relented.

Then there was Leo. He disturbed her dreams of late. She awoke at dawn to a raking sense of loss. Brief though the encounter had been, she could not ride roughshod over her feelings for him. She had acted like an immature child, taking fright and running away. Yet she could not have stayed under Madame's roof, knowing what the house was, any more than go home to Merrowdene. As for Leo, she no longer cared what he had done, or what he had hoped for of her.

"You're very pensive," Edward ventured. He had been studying her covertly during a supper of oysters and whipped syllabubs, light as air, in a booth at Vauxhall. It had been a good day, but as evening closed in a mood of irrational disappointment overtook his companion. The scent of firs, mildly damp, was unspeakably sad. Lamps festooned between the colonnades of the Grove twinkled crimson and gold through the quivering plane trees. Strains of Handel's *Water Music* careered and darted into the night above the resonant play of silvery fountains.

Kate dipped her long-handled spoon into the glass cornet and scooped up the remains of her syllabub. "There is much to absorb!"

He called for a waiter to set a taper to the candles. The flames flared up and brought to life the rollicking scenes of Hogarth about the walls.

"Edward, I have so enjoyed this afternoon…" She touched his hand and instantly withdrew it as though it had been scorched. "You have been kindness itself at a time when I needed a friend."

"And it has been my utmost endeavour not to take advantage of that. But Kate…"

"Please…" she entreated him.

"…won't you come home with me one day soon and see my mother? It's a solitary life for her out at Highgate with my father away on long voyages at sea. I know she will warm to you…as I have," he said, glancing at a near empty wine bottle. "She will bake apple cakes and gingerbread from her native Yorkshire. She will show you her collection of treasures brought back by my father from foreign lands. He is captain of an East Indiaman and beyond a peradventure the most intrepid of them all! He boasts of hand to hand fights with pirates in the China Seas."

"Were you never tempted to follow him?"

"I'm no Jack Tar, Kate. Besides, someone has to take care of my mother. Our family is sadly depleted since my sisters died, all in the same winter, of an ague they say was borne on the East wind from Russia. There were five of us once. I'm the only one left."

"Edward, how tragic! That is unspeakably harsh." Kate began to perceive him in an entirely fresh light. His was a lean, bony face, pleasing in its fashion and evincing sincerity. But it was the wrong face. Her vision trembled and cleared and to her dismay hot tears dripped down her cheeks. She muttered an incoherent apology. "You don't make it simple, do you?"

"I don't mean that it shall be simple, my dear," he replied pointedly and added, after a tactful pause: "Mr Attwood did mention that you had set out on your own to avoid an arranged marriage. Perhaps you were too impulsive? Perhaps you judge matters differently now?"

"Oh no! I have no regrets upon that score!"

"Then I must assume your affections are fixed elsewhere."

There was an awkward hiatus. "I shall never see him again," Kate said quietly.

A flourish of trumpets brought the stately music to an end. "Come, drink up. Tis a sin to waste good champagne!"

In the carriage, on the way back to South Audley Street, he folded her against him and she did not resist, nor the sweet pressure of his mouth when he kissed her, at first with a delicious trepidation and then with mounting urgency. In desperation, she returned his kiss, but it was the imprint of other lips she imagined and the image of another face she recalled with breathtaking lucidity. She broke away on a dry, anguished sob.

"Whoever he is," Edward vowed, turning her face towards him in the chequered darkness, "I mean to make you forget him."

The very next day, Sir George Stewart came charging up to Town with his wife and daughter in tow and the house was roused from its lethargy. A great ox of a man with curly red hair, the ornaments rattled as he paced about. Kate gathered that there had been some kind of family crisis and he was seething with wrath as a result of it. After a cursory interview, in which he seemed ready to be satisfied with her, he wanted nothing but that she and his daughter be left to their own devices.

"Well, I wish her joy of him! Hell's teeth," roared the baronet, "I'd break every bone in his body if he were here!"

His vivacious little wife, poised on the edge of the sofa, reached to prod a slice of lemon and immersed it in her tea with superlative unconcern. It was politic to ride out her husband's tirades. Presently, he would be over his ridiculous posturing and she could have her say. If his Scots accent had been tamed by an

117

education south of the Border, there was more than a touch of Gaelic fire in his veins and no tutor, no birch-brandishing dominie, had ever been able to quell that.

"He comes hell-for-leather from his pater's funeral to take my sister to the altar without so much as a 'by your leave', capers off to Paris for the honeymoon – Paris, if you please! – and then calmly informs me in the same random style that they propose to set up house in Silvercragg, snug as mice in a wainscot!" He struck the offending missive which hailed from the land of Frogs and anarchists. That it was courteously worded, he could not deny, but his brother-in-law's hand conveyed a strong dash of brio, a careless disregard of society's censure.

Lady Diana exploded with laughter, but quickly assumed control of herself under his stern gaze. "You must confess," said she, "that it is all very neatly contrived!"

"What!"

"Do but be reasonable, George. Cassandra is no oil-painting and Eugene has not come up to scratch. You may fairly rest much of the blame upon him. Leo is a better catch than she is likely to find anywhere."

"Do you defend him, madam? He is a cad! A bounder!"

"Oh, come. Think how wonderfully patient he has been with Fee. She will not hear him maligned in the slightest."

"It is all part of his strategy, all to ingratiate himself."

"I think not," said her ladyship with soft emphasis. "You can spare some of your recriminations for your sister. What a sly-boots she is! Setting her cap at him under our very noses. We took his interest in her for the same brotherly affection he showed Fee. Of course, now I quite see how it was between them. I only wonder we did not tumble to it sooner."

"The deceitful hussy! Leading us to believe she was content to bide her time until Eugene's return."

"For my part, George," sighed his wife, crushing a meringue shell under her pastry fork and compounding it to a mulch with a clot of cream, "I can't find it in my heart to condemn them for presenting us with a *fait accompli* and making a discreet exit until the dust has settled. Really, my love, you can be so mulish at times. It's enough to stiffen anyone's resolve to head in the opposite direction! Where would be the sense in arousing your ire? What would it achieve? They were going to marry and marry they did. Cassandra is not some chit fresh out of the schoolroom when all's said and done."

"He might have had the goodness to seek my blessing," growled the baronet.

"Ah, I see you are piqued. Have a meringue, dearest, it might sweeten your temper."

"Enough of your havering, woman!" The veins of Sir George's temples bulged like cords. "The fellow is lately bereaved. To say nought of his being a guest in my house. Are you lost to all sense of decency?"

"Decency? Fiddlesticks! I'll tell you this, George: he is no hypocrite. It is general knowledge how things stood between him and his father."

"Then you'll maybe appreciate," he responded, scornfully teasing out his words, "why I'm more than a wee bit concerned for Cassandra's welfare. When old Penrose's will is proved, tis my belief there'll be next to nought in the coffers for Leo. He'll be lucky to redeem his vowels out of his own pocket. He had an eye to the main chance."

"Who has not in this world? He is no ruthless gold-digger. And eminently respectable. He will do his best by Cassandra."

"He's a womaniser."

"He needs a wife, poor lamb. He will soon settle down. And I shall teach Cassandra how to take him in hand!" Lady Diana cocked her head on one side and glanced up at her spouse archly. Her eyes danced with mischief.

"She's not right for him, I tell you. She's too introspective, too solemn."

"That will change now that she's wedded and doubtless blissfully bedded! It can transform a woman, you know, George."

"There's no knowing what goes on inside her head," he persisted darkly. "Hell and the devil, Di, they've been deuced close about this!"

"And that is what rankles, admit it! Now come and sit down and stop pacing around like a bear in captivity – do! Let me pour you some tea. Or shall I have the girl bring your madeira? Butterfield has made a heavenly saffron cake." She patted the sofa but he ignored the invitation and leaned his elbow against the mantelpiece where a fine clock of patinated bronze muses whirred and heralded the hour close to his ear. He winced and gave the brass fender a pettish kick with the toe of his boot.

"She acted in a fit of pique, I'd stake my life on it."

"No! It was no such thing, George. She held her aces in reserve, I see that now. Her inheritance was her principal attraction and she used it to advantage."

"It is not what my father desired."

"Clearly, my dear, she does not give a fig what your father desired. And who shall blame her? He is dead and in his grave. She has her whole life ahead."

"Silvercragg was to stay in the family."

"Why, there is such a to-do about a pile of stones in some backwood beyond the reaches of civilisation, I cannot comprehend! The wretched castle forms no part of the Stewart tradition."

"Why? Why?" rasped the baronet. "Because for one thing my father spent a king's ransom setting the place to rights…"

"I cannot help thinking," mused her ladyship, "that it is strangely appropriate that it should become Leo's home. In one generation the estate is restored to the Penroses. The course of its history will barely have changed. Why, even the contents remain much as they were in his uncle's time."

Adam Penrose had been so wild to exorcise the memory of his profligate brother that he had sold Silvercragg and all its treasures to the earliest bidder. Angus Stewart, a canny fellow, as aware of the vendor's reputation for thrift as of his fraternal antipathy, had been astonished when his first tongue-in-cheek offer had been pounced upon. There was a streak of fatalism in it. That was years ago, of course, when George was a pupil of Charterhouse and Mr Pitt's iron-handed taxes on tea and brandy, silver and glass, houses with more than five windows, were biting hard. He remembered his father gleefully rubbing his hands together, not with outstretched palms as most people did, but with the knuckles bunched, as if they were palsied and would not open.

The mood of self-congratulation was short lived. At every turn his attempts to restore the house and improve the running of the estate met with fierce resistance. There were many things he overlooked about the dalesfolk and their lore. Closed off from the outside world, they were deeply entrenched in their own ways, evolved from generations of pitting themselves against a rugged terrain and an often inhospitable climate. Tales abounded of ships come over from the Isle of Man. They lay at anchor off the coast near Ravenglass in the dead of night, laden with French silk and lace, tobacco, tea and wine, which were traded for consignments of 'black gold' or 'wadd' the precious plumbago mined exclusively around Keswick and in Borrowdale. Covered wagons rattled back and forth in the darkness, following perilous routes over the mountains to elude the excise men who blocked off the passes. It was a highly organised racket as Matthieu, Madeleine's husband, knew in his heyday, and eyes were blind and lips sealed on pain of death. The last thing they wanted was an 'offcomer' landlord stumbling across their coverts. Mark Penrose was a wise man. He had chosen to look the other way and not interfere. Indeed many an unsolicited gift appeared on his doorstep, or in his barns and outhouses, in payment for his silence. Ever a man to appreciate a good cognac, it was remarkable how fine a savour it had when his cellars were thus replenished!

But that was only half the story. Deeper still, bred in the local people through centuries of affinity with the earth and landscape, was a mythology all their own. Moons waxed and waned, the seasons turned, and strange superstitions arose in the blood. Rites were faithfully observed each Candlemas and Lammastide, each Harvest Home and Hallowe'en. There was the drawing of the first water on New Year's day, the Flower of the Well, to bring good luck, to cleanse dairy utensils and increase the milk yield of cows. There was the blood-letting of horses and oxen on St Stephen's day to protect the animals from disease and increase their strength. Great store was set by these pagan customs. Portents were taken to heart. A good many folk, and not only those of the Quaker persuasion which was rife in the area, had seen the fire of Silvercragg as the hand of judgement on Mark Penrose for his wickedness. The castle was surrounded by legend. Stories were woven about its mist-wreathed towers, its elevations where some said no creeper would climb and its fastnesses where no bird would roost save that bird of omen, the raven. The misfortunes of the builders assigned to restore the West Wing proved that a sinister force was at work. The housekeeper and maids were convinced of it. And now that section of the castle was shut up and seldom visited, for it was gloomy and supernaturally chill and no amount of fuel, they said, could keep it warm since Meg McCullough let the winter in.

"It is almost as though the spirit of the old place were asserting itself," Lady Diana observed in a distant voice.

Her husband was fairly conversant with the beliefs of the Cumberland peasantry, but they could have no place in the philosophy of a hard-headed landowner.

"Do you listen to that heathen cant? I had thought better of you, Di!"

"I keep an open mind."

"Well, then, consider this! I suggest that the late Penrose's disaffection with Leo was not solely on account of his prodigal ways."

"Why?"

"As an elder son born the wrong side of the blanket and cheated of his expectations, it is a fine way to settle the score, acquiring Silvercragg, is it not?"

"You mean he is...?" The breath snatched in Lady Diana's throat.

"A bastard? Aye, I do! And that puts his motives in quite another league."

"George! I am shocked, nay, outraged!"

"I knew you would be."

"To think you could employ that vulgar expression in the hearing of your wife! I shall go directly and wash out my ears!"

In an instant she was up from the sofa, but before she had gained the door, found her progress impeded. "Pray, do not detain me! Were you to supplicate on bended knee, I should not stay!"

Sir George made no move to step aside so she began to pummel his sturdy breast with her fists, pitting all her gamine beauty against his ruggedness. "You are the most odious, obdurate, foul-tempered man I ever knew! I ought to have taken Mama's advice years ago and married the Canon!"

He gave her a fierce kiss so that his beard tickled and rasped against her skin. "I engage to insult your modesty no more."

"Then do, I beg you, stop this vilification of Leo. He is astute, yes. An opportunist, perhaps. He is not, however, the cold-blooded rogue you make him out to be. I cannot believe that he sought to hoodwink Cassandra. And you must agree, my dear, that whether your theory about his origins be right or no, Viscountess Penrose has a charming ring to it. It is infinitely preferable to plain Mrs McBride."

"How eloquently you plead his cause. I am sure the cursed fellow does not deserve such an advocate."

"Nor you such a longsuffering wife! Now what will you have? A fondant fancy?"

"A Pax Cake, is it?" Stewart asked with a rueful grin.

'There are more things in heaven and earth, Horatio, than are dreamt of in your philosophy.'

Fiona stuffed her tongue between her teeth, her freshly sharpened quill adventuring the pages of a new exercise book she had pledged to keep spotless from beginning to end. Her coarse, crinkly hair, though braided and severely coiled, created a fiery nimbus about her head. Apart from a pair of gull's wing brows, a denser version of her mother's, her physical attributes owed everything to her Scottish strain and caused her to appear more robust than she was. She had lively brown eyes fixed in a pale face, freckled as a wren's egg. When overtired or in the throes of a relapse, a ruby patch stained either cheek and alarmed those around her. It was a good thing that her father was heftily built, for often she had to be carried up and down stairs and must conserve her energies for outings in the carriage or short sallies on foot or in her Bath chair to the Parks, or to the shops in Bond Street.

Kate took her charge to heart at once and had the wisdom not to treat her as infirm, but found it exacting when the girl's appetite for life was so much stronger than her capabilities. Kate liked her parents, too. Despite the master's blustering, the household was a happy one. She was pleased when, passing the half-open door of the drawing room, she chanced to hear Sir George declare: "Not lax, old Attwood, in the prosecution of his duties. Capital fellow for all he stings me every quarter! I think we've struck gold with Miss What's-Her-Name? up there!"

Kate gathered that her predecessor, an elderly spinster by

the name of Miss Peppercorn, had died after eating cockles and mussels at Bartholomew's Fair. "Snuffed out like a candle!" Sir George would recount. "And her first taste of the world's wicked delights! The game old bird was out hobnobbing with that literary hack, Charles Lamb, and his lunatic sister. She wouldn't have gone but for them."

The boom and bark of his voice in the rooms below penetrated the unfurnished boards in the schoolroom. Fiona winced. She was of a stoical disposition and conveyed an air of being much wearied by the responsibility of rearing her elders.

"I wish Papa would not rave so. He will do himself a mischief. No doubt he will calm down presently and we can all be comfortable again." She let out a melodramatic sigh and stroked her snub nose with the goose feather.

"Now," Kate said, eager to concentrate on the matter in hand, "a *précis* of the plot, I think."

"He is forever taking pets over nothing."

"You do not believe his consternation justified?"

"Oh, but Lord Penrose is the kindest, most adorable man in the world, and exceedingly handsome. I swear, Miss Hanslope, my heart was quite broken in two for three days together when we learnt of the elopement. It was all a devious plot of Aunt Cassandra's to snatch him from me. She is as plain as the devil and often out of humour."

"Fiona, I beg you will take up your pencil and apply yourself to your notebook. You are forbidden to speak of your aunt in those terms."

Lord, what a schoolma'am I am becoming already, Kate thought. Prim and priggish and I don't want to be. The swing from governess to companion and back again did pose its challenges, the gap between their ages, teacher and pupil, being considerably narrower than was usual.

"Lord Penrose was our guest down in Brighton, you know, and we formed a strong attachment, he and I. Do you know

Brighton, Miss Hanslope?"

Kate's heart lurched. She glanced outside. "I have been there, yes."

"It is a splendid place, is it not? Everyone is in holiday mood and I don't have to practise my music because the pianoforte is always out of tune. The sea air damages the strings. Papa says he will have it attended to, but he never does. That's really because he's no taste for music himself and would rather pass his time playing cards or exchanging bawdy anecdotes with his cronies."

"Indeed. You should know nothing of such things, Miss."

"I once saw Harriette Wilson," Fiona said in accents of intrigue. "She was riding along Marine Parade in a scarlet habit made to imitate the uniform of the 10th Hussars, the Prince of Wales' own regiment."

"I don't believe I ever heard of the lady."

"You never heard of the notorious Harriette! Why, Miss Hanslope, where have you been? Papa deemed it a very apt colour for her to wear and said he'd heard tell how she belonged to the regiment!"

"That will do," Kate scolded. "I am sure your parents would wish me to curb such immodesty. We will have no more. Is that understood?"

"Yes, Miss Hanslope," replied the impenitent pupil dully and directly veered off on another tack. "I bet you never saw the 'Green Man' of Brighton either? His name is Henry Cope. He paints himself green and wears green clothes and eats only green foods, they say. His rooms are decorated entirely in green. Imagine it! I almost split my sides laughing when I saw him. Mama bade me not to stare, but he don't give a button for that. He's as mad as a march hare, but quite harmless."

"The reputation of eccentrics does lend itself to distortion."

"But I saw him! I give you my word!"

"That may be so, but could we please return to William Shakespeare?"

"Must we, Kate? It's such a glorious day. The sky is… that Mediterranean blue, like a Canaletto painting. Oh, how I yearn to travel! Papa says we might spend this winter in Italy. Won't that be wonderful?"

Kate overlooked the liberty with her Christian name and let out an exasperated breath. The child's butterfly mind flitted from one topic to another. Her illness seemed to divert her energy so that it poured into her imagination.

Over the rooftops, the pinnacle of a white poplar glistered. "Very well. We'll go to the Gardens. You shall take your sketch book and pastels and we'll sit under the mulberry tree and watch the swallows skim."

"How kind you are, dear Miss Hanslope! I knew you'd take pity on me."

"First you must rest, you must not overtax yourself. Tomorrow is the day of the Jubilee, don't forget."

"Yes, a holiday for the whole city! I wonder whether that agreeable Mr Grey from The Ark will join us."

Kate neatly sidestepped this piece of mischief and betrayed no surprise that her pupil was so disconcertingly well informed. "The Ark?"

"That is what Papa calls old Atty's establishment. A fitting epithet when you think of that crabby old stickler. Atty, I mean, not Papa! Only dear Mr Grey is not in the least antediluvian, is he?" Fiona affected a languishing sigh and peered slyly at Kate from beneath auburn lashes. "Mrs Butterfield says he's your beau and has been paying you his addresses."

"The good woman would do well to hold her tongue. Edward Grey is… is a faithful friend."

"Faithful friends prove faithless lovers," lamented Fiona, dwelling enviously on how Lord Penrose was cavorting in Paris with her Aunt Cassandra. She supposed she would have to call him 'Uncle' now.

Monday, August 1st, 1814 dawned with fingers of pale light chasing away the mist. The sun gathered gold as it rose behind leafy boughs and made the grass a twinkling carpet of gems. It dazzled the panes of town house and tavern and tinselled the finials of St Mary-le-Bow. Like a great giant, the city stirred from slumber. Early riders emerged for a brisk canter along the Row. Tradesmen's carts and wagons went trundling along the streets to set up stalls in the Parks. Beggars shuffled, rheumy-eyed, out of alleys, wincing against the cruel daylight; drunkards lolled in doorways. There had been much carousing the previous night. Some were glad of a respite from their labour and some a respite from the lack of it.

And then the bells commenced, swinging and cartwheeling high in their towers. First, St Paul's Cathedral and then Westminster Abbey. St Clement Danes took up the theme, then St George's, St John's, St Martin-in-the-Fields, and all the beautiful wedding-cake churches of London pealed in joyous dissonance.

"Hark! Oh, do listen!" cried Fiona, stumbling towards the window and gazing upwards as if the sound emanated from the very heavens. "Is it not wonderful to be alive, Nell?"

Nell, Lady Diana's personal maid, was left stroking thin air with the silver-backed brush. She had attended to her mistress and was in the frustrating process of trying to achieve a Psyche knot on the daughter's bushy hair. When Kate entered, Fiona hastened to embrace her.

"Peace, Kate! You and I have known nothing but our country at war. Thank God for Wellington who has ground the enemy under his heel!"

"Aye, long live the Duke of Wellington," Nell endorsed. "The Czar of Russia, too, and all the brave lads who helped 'em lick Boney. Our Jack died, God rest his soul, at Austerlitz, with a sabre in his belly, so they said. He was a fine man, my brother, with shoulders as broad as a lion and muscles like vices. He were a match for Tom Cribb any day of the week."

"The carriage will be at the door in fifteen minutes," Lady Diana called from below. "Don't keep your father waiting, Fiona!"

"But I am only half-coiffed and neither perfumed nor shod!" wailed her daughter. "I think I shall take my Paisley shawl."

Five minutes later they heard the baronet pounding up the stairs. The female chatter subsided as his great bulk filled the doorway. Nell dropped a curtsy and fled.

"Papa, I thank you, but I do not require to be carried downstairs. I am perfectly strong today. Look, I shall take Kate's arm and you shall see how ably I contrive."

"That's my lass! What say you, Miss Hanslope?"

"She's a plucky girl, sir."

"She has her father's spirit, eh?"

Kate smiled and tilted her head a fraction in a refined gesture of assent. By Jove, thought the baronet, his eye fixing hers warmly, she has the presence of a woman twice her age, one used to moving in exalted circles at that. There'd be better fry than young Grey trailing at her heels before long, dowry or not. He slapped his thigh resolutely. "Remind me, Miss Hanslope, to speak with you soon about your remuneration. I believe we may have arranged things a trifle on the… er… lean side."

All the world and his wife were making for the Royal Parks that morning. Piccadilly and Park Lane were blocked with vehicles. By the time they reached Hyde Park, a shower had begun to dampen everyone's enthusiasm. Nevertheless, Fiona fairly skipped down from the carriage to inhale the rain-scented air. "Why, I do believe that's Mr Grey!" she cried.

The figure hovering beneath a cedar tree just inside the entrance advanced towards them with a somewhat contrite grin and swept off his hat. "Ladies! Sir George! How pleasant this is!"

"You're welcome to join us, Grey, if you've a mind," the

baronet informed him magnanimously. "And I'll wager a pony you have! I could do with some support! Fancy a spot of faro in one of the booths, later?"

"Not my style, sir."

"Wise fellow. But one needs some remission from duty. The prospect of playing escort to a gaggle of women for the rest of the day is not one to be viewed with unmixed delight!"

"Surly brute! Ungallant toad!" retaliated his wife.

"Mrs Butterfield has packed a feast of a picnic," Fiona said.

"Say no more, Miss Fiona. I need no further persuasion."

"I misdoubt you ever did," came the arch rejoinder as Fiona glanced meaningfully at her companion. Kate was tracing imaginary patterns on the ground with the ferrule of her parasol.

"You are very quiet, Miss Hanslope," Grey said.

She was amused that he should address her so formally in the presence of her employer. "I was simply reflecting, Mr Grey, what a coincidence it was that we should run into you."

Lady Diana claimed her husband's arm and the two of them walked ahead, out of earshot.

"Not entirely accidental, I own."

"Indeed?"

"I took the liberty of making discreet enquiries of the good Butterfield when Sir George summoned me to South Audley Street yesterday."

"And I knew! I knew!" Fiona chimed in. "You can wheedle anything out of old Butterface if you know how!"

Presently they joined the crowd assembled to watch the battle-in-miniature on the Serpentine. The action took place between puffs of dense blue smoke, showers of sparks and volleys from the numerous toy cannon. A three-decker frigate burst into flames and yielded gracefully to the deep, whilst sailors in shirt sleeves floundered around in the water. The poor swans screeched and flapped their great wings, taking off for more peaceful preserves. No one was in the least danger of forgetting that this was Hyde Park and not the land of the ancient pharaohs. Despite the gloomy predictions of the Press, the people were well-behaved and not at all inclined to insurrection. The balloon ascent staged in front of Buckingham House went off without a hitch. The bloated orb sporting royal crests lifted off its platform and sailed upwards into a firmament by now of Dresden blue.

As the day wore on and a scorching sun sank behind the trees, the sky turned a twilight indigo, making a perfect backdrop for the clusters of rockets which gushed up, shimmered into brilliance and expired over the streets of Westminster. "I wouldn't have missed this for anything on earth!" Fiona cried.

Moments later, there was a deafening blast and the Castle of Discord, a fortress made of canvas and wood, disintegrated. The jabbering, smutty-faced Frenchmen overrunning its battlements were thrown into confusion. No one could discern what was happening behind the murky veil of smoke until, suddenly, it thinned and the Temple of Peace, blazing with lamps all the colours of the spectrum, illumined the night. Springs spurted from the throats of carved lions into golden basins. It was breathtaking. The crowds were in raptures. The Royal Standard was raised high and a detachment of Foot Guards gave three jubilant cheers.

The Corsican Monster was bound for ever on the Isle of Elba.

Fiona was understandably exhausted next day and did not arouse from sleep at the usual hour. Dressed for a trip to the Royal Academy , Kate duly tripped downstairs to join the others in the hall but stopped midway in her descent.

"What on earth is amiss, Kate? Have you seen a ghost?" queried Lady Diana.

"I… I was merely admiring your ladyship's gown." For it was of aquamarine and ivory stripes with an overskirt that was caught up into tiny posies above a rouleau hem. Kate knew every stitch of that garment and the anxiety the inset of the sleeves had caused! It was Essie who had taken the measurements.

"Yes, it is a trifle original, is it not? I've a wonderful French dressmaker down in Brighton who runs them up in a trice! Her work is quite equal to anything Bond Street has to offer."

"I can readily believe it, ma'am."

"Madeleine Matthieu. I doubt you'll have heard of her. Shall we go, then?"

It had been one of Kate's dreads that the Stewarts would require her to go down to Brighton with them. Until now, she had considered it unlikely that they would patronise Madeleine's establishment. She would be most unlucky to bump into someone who had known her in her former incarnation. Now her fears were given real foundation by the discovery that not only was Madeleine her ladyship's favourite couturier, but that she, Kate, had actually made those clothes. She stood to lose both position and reputation if she were recognised. When it was mooted that the family spend the early weeks of autumn there, her alarm increased. Lady Diana wanted a riding habit and some smart costumes for a proposed trip to Umbria.

But to Kate's profound relief, events took an unexpected turn.

One morning in the middle of September, when there was a slight nip in the air and some of the leaves on the London planes were hanging by threads, a letter arrived. Sir George, who was bemoaning the weight of affairs which kept him in Town, scowled at the frank and slit the seal with his butter knife. The communication was from Cumberland and he told his wife and daughter so.

"From Aunt Cassandra? Oh, what does she say?"

"From your uncle," the baronet grunted. He scanned the contents testily. "So the scoundrel thinks to mend matters now, does he?"

"George…!" warned his wife.

"Well...?" pressed his daughter.

He tossed the close-written pages aside and addressed himself to kidneys and bacon. "He is minded to bury the hatchet, if you please. Most generous! Will we do them the honour of spending Yuletide at Silvercragg? He bids us, moreover, come early next month before the winter sets in and the roads are impassable."

Fiona shrieked in delight. "That's bang-up news, is it not, Mama?"

Her father spluttered upon his food at this cant expression. "Curb your tongue, wench. I don't employ Miss What's-Her-Name to improve your thieves' Latin!"

The problem of semantic niceties was far from his wife's mind. She reached for the letter, prepared to mediate. "It shows goodwill," she said. "We ought at least to say that we are flattered."

"Flattered! I'd as soon wring his neck!"

"You mean, Papa, that we shall not go?"

"Of course we shall not go! Do you think to make me responsible for taking someone of your delicate constitution to that hell-hole at the nether end of the year?"

"But do reconsider, I implore you. I am so much improved of late."

"And I do not propose to be the undoing of it. We're bound for Italy, my lass, to get some sunshine into your bones. That's where!"

Fiona wretchedly fingered the enamelled bracelet Lord Penrose had given her. Her throat ached. She jumped up from the table and flung down her napkin. "Oh! And I had thought you the kindest, most understanding Papa in England!"

"Fudge!" he rejoined, unmoved by such tender blackmail.

"Finish your coffee, Fee," said her mother impartially, "and go up to the schoolroom. I wish to speak with your father alone."

Fiona withdrew self-consciously, closing the door behind her without a sound. She dared to hope that Mama was on her side.

The baronet's jaw was thrust forward at a stubborn angle. "I'll not be swayed. Tis vain to try your feminine arts on me."

"George, won't you allow the elopement to be a thing of the past? Maybe it was not the best form, but do let us do the honourable thing and be gracious. Leo is one of us now. Do let us go to Silvercragg. Let it be as it once was, when we were on the best of terms. For Fiona's sake, my dear. We may not always have her with us, remember."

"If you wish to expedite your daughter's end, madam, that is the way to set about it!"

"Wretch! You are at pains to confound me but you shall not succeed. There is no doubt that the Italian climate would do her infinite good, but the journey is long and could prove an ordeal."

Sir George had deliberated all summer over the wisdom of the plan and admitted that what his wife said was true. "I dislike the unseemly way she refers to Penrose," he decided.

"Fee? She's but a child. Tis nothing untoward. Only a heart of stone could resist a handsome cavalry officer who has bestowed so many kindnesses."

"Former officer!"

"As you wish," sighed her ladyship. She cast her eyes up to the Empire chandelier overhanging the table. "I fancy the green-eyed monster is on the prowl!"

"I don't care for the tenor of his letter, either. It smacks of... I do not know. There is something amiss between those two."

"Never say so! That's not a pretty notion when they have only been married these two months."

Her husband retrieved the letter and opened it out, anchoring the corner under his cup and saucer whilst he made short work of his breakfast. 'Cassandra enjoins me to bid you come soon,' he quoted. 'All the travelling has left her fatigued and somewhat out of spirits. The society hereabouts, such as it is, affords *scant diversion and we are in grievous want of congenial company. The dalesfolk assert that it bids fair to be a harsh winter, so I recommend you not to delay too long...'* "That does not exactly conjure a picture of post-nuptial felicity. I dare swear there's a good deal more space in the love-nest than she engaged for!"

"All the more reason to extend the olive branch. Your sister needs us."

"He holds his head high, I'll say that for him."

"Do let us go. I shall not need to spend half so much on my wardrobe this season if we went north."

"The devil, woman! Why did you not say so till now? We shall leave forthwith, if not before!"

Fiona was cock-a-hoop at her mother's victory and that very day arrangements were put in hand for the winter sojourn. Lady Diana sat down at her writing desk and penned a letter to Madeleine Matthieu, outlining their intentions. *'By the by, do you recollect my mentioning how urgently Fiona was in need of a governess? Well, we have found one! A perfect bijou! Her name is Kate Hanslope and she's a cleric's daughter. Only fancy! Grey, our man of business, chanced to meet her on the coach from Brighton. What a lucky find!'*

When La Belle Madeleine, resplendent among pillows of marshmallow pink satin and frills and furbelows of duty-free lace, received her post the next morning, she little anticipated news of Katrine.

First, she singled out the accounts, as was her custom, screwed them up and aimed them in the general direction of the hearth. Having disposed of this chore, she felt at liberty to settle down with her cosier billets. There was nothing so depressing, at the start of the day, as being reminded of all that one owed! With her gold-rimmed spectacles poised over the script, she skimmed the contents of each page, eager for titillating gossip.

The letter from Diana Stewart made her gasp and sit erect in astonishment. "So! Our little Katrine becomes a virtuous schoolma'am, does she? *Quel horreur!*"

Travers had set about clearing up the papers and was kneeling before the grate armed with a tinderbox.

"You've news of Miss Kate, mum?"

"She is gone for a governess of all things! To Diana Stewart!"

"Well, if you'll pardon me for saying so, mum, I never did think she belonged here. Wasn't one of us."

Madeleine viewed Kate's flight with more than a touch of Gallic chagrin. Had not every attention been lavished on the silly Miss? And for what? A governess! She was ready to forget she had once resorted to an identical post herself. Times had been different then. Kate had been offered the stuff of dreams. "They are two a penny, these sour spinsters crammed with learning," she grumbled. "Such a waste! Why, I think she is deserving that sullen young man who treads mud all over my carpets!" Malice glinted in the olive eyes and Travers could see that Madame was ripe for mischief.

For, soon after Kate's disappearance, the relative calm of 7, Vanbrugh Square had been shattered when an irate Anthony March gained admission and paced about the salons, brandishing his riding-crop in a most threatening fashion and demanding to know where Kate Hanslope was hidden. Madeleine had denied all knowledge of the lady and had quickly summoned those of her retainers renowned for their muscle and brawn to have him slung out. He had left his card but had not dared to return. There had been a couple of unpleasant letters but, lacking proof for his allegations, it was of no moment whether he believed Madame or not. She doubted she had heard the last of him.

Pondering the situation, with the tip of her spectacles between her teeth, Madeleine reasoned that she was committing no perjury in putting him on the girl's scent. She was doing the pair of them a favour.

So the summer passed and autumn came in. The rejoicing died down and the Royal Parks were left denuded of grass. Swallows took wing for sunnier shores. Lord Castlereagh and the allies repaired to Vienna to hammer out between them the future of Europe.

In South Audley Street, books were closed and restored to the schoolroom shelves, and Cary's matched globes, terrestrial and celestial, abandoned. Holland covers draped the furniture once more and the door knocker was tied up. One windy Thursday in October, the baronet's black landau with japanned panels drew up at the door and was loaded with trunks and bandboxes and the paraphernalia of travel. The ladies took up their positions inside the coach and smoothed their skirts. Kate sat stiffly, listening to the jingling of the fidgeting team. She had bidden Edward Grey a fond farewell and had promised to write.

One last glance at the house reminded her that this was where she had found shelter and security, the home of strangers marking a happy change in her circumstances. And now they were about to head north, to a part of England she had never seen.

Sir George heaved himself on to the quilted seat. The door was slammed and the footplates taken up. He gave two smart taps on the small pane of glass above his head.

"Drive on, coachman!"

Five

At last, after days of wearisome travel, the fells and meadows of Westmorland hove into view.

Far away to the north west, purple crags stood proud beneath a sky of tarnished pewter. Their names might have been culled from a fairytale. Glaramara, Helvellyn, Great Gable, Skiddaw, the Old Man of Coniston. Fiona knew them by heart and pointed them out. Massive stretches of softwood covered the foothills, chevron-textured like the weave of a warm and intricate tweed. Against this dense green, the turned beeches made burning splashes of colour. The birches were wispy and spangled with wafers of quivering gold. Weather-worn walls bounding the farmland crept up, up, over the slate-capped fells to prevent footloose sheep from roaming too far. The farmsteads, huddled in the leeside of the landscape, away from the wild north winds, were built of the same rough-hewn stone. Webs gleamed on the hawthorns, on brambles and bryony, yellow osier twigs and rosehips bright as lacquered beads.

Kate could hardly contain her emotion at the beauty of it, wanted to shout at the sky and hear the echo of her voice ring among the hills. She wanted to steep herself in the earthy tang of the woods, peer at her reflection in the glassy tarns and listen forever to the sibilant music of the little becks which ran among rocky slopes and filled the coach with a mysterious guttural harmony as it rolled precariously over bridges, listing from side to side. She felt, she could not have explained why or how, that she was coming home after a long period of exile.

The road, riddled with potholes, went winding through farmyards where painted haywains lay idle by the byres, their duty done. Geese and hens scattered in a fluster at the approach of the Stewarts' mud-splashed vehicle. At one prosperous-looking farm, a burly yeoman beckoned them to stop and step down. "A glass of wine with ye, sir!" The baronet, needing no further inducement, threw the reins into the hands of his coachman and swung himself down to shake the good fellow's hand. "That's uncommon civil of you, Squire. I swear my gullet's parched. Come ladies!"

You had to bend your head to enter the kitchen by the back door. Its flagstones were worn uneven by a dozen generations of feet. The farmer's wife, herself as plump as a dumpling, gave the guests the time of day and watched them file into the parlour. It was nothing unusual to share their rustic plenty with strangers. Up to her elbows in flour, she stirred up the maids and ran about to find goblets for her best parsnip wine and a platter of scones still warm from the griddle.

"This northern hospitality takes some beating!" the baronet proclaimed, munching avidly.

By way of acknowledgement, the mistress of the house dropped an ungainly curtsy, eyeing the fine merino and soft velvet in which the travellers were clad. "And where be you going, good sir?" enquired she. "Be it Carrel?"

"No, madam, not Carlisle, I'm thankful to say. Our destination is nearer. We're bound for Silvercragg Castle at the head of Lake Mereswater."

On receipt of this information, she darted her husband an ominous glance and unable to bridle her curiosity, piped up in awed tones. "Be you his lordship, then?"

"Nay, Bessie, tis not he," hissed the farmer, to whom Sir George had already introduced himself and his entourage.

"They do say herraboots that there's new folks in residence. A gen'leman come doon from Lunnon with his young bride and he's a Penrose reet an' true, a gey canny fellah. After aw these yerrs!"

Sir George flicked crumbs from his superfine coat. "You are

singularly well briefed, madam. Silvercragg must be - what? - twenty miles hence. A good couple of hours' journey. The Viscount is my brother-in-law. George Stewart's the name, Bart, that is, and this is my wife and daughter, and Miss Hanslope, her companion."

His hostess nodded courteously but seemed preoccupied with her own troubled thoughts and muttered: "Nivver say tis happening agin. Tis same as t'olden days when the last Lord Penrose brought home his bride, that Christmastide of the fyer."

It was uncanny how, once Silvercragg was touched upon, every other topic of conversation misfired. Mrs Mossop was on edge. Fiona distinctly saw the woman cross herself when she slipped out to fetch buttershags and further tots of the brew with which her husband insisted on regaling his visitors.

"How queerly that woman behaved," Fiona said, back in the coach and smothered in blankets. "Did you not think so, Mama?"

"It is a wonder to me these foolish tales should persist for so long. Good heavens, the grapevine here is more powerful than in Mayfair!"

Outside, there was a nip in the air, an insidious dampness that carried the vague scent of smouldering brushwood. The day had turned dull. Kate shuddered at the sudden remembrance of a dream.

Last night at a wayside inn, where shadows slithered across the beams of her room from the lantern-lit yard below and the murmur of voices went on long into the night, she had slipped into a fitful sleep inhabited by disquieting images. There was a pele tower with lancet windows. Ravens wheeled overhead in disorganised flight, harbingers of death. When she awoke, the dream had faded. What had been logical and compelling during its sequences slid into oblivion. But some scenes lingered which, in the calm light of day, still held undercurrents of menace. She had a vivid impression of a dark expanse of water, its surface broken by a shallow hump which revealed itself to be the corpse of a woman floating, Ophelia-like, to the shore, her pale tresses rippling out like waterweeds. Kate had tossed and moaned, a scream binding in her throat. She wanted to run but her feet were rooted to the earth. When she steeled herself to look again, the corpse had vanished. It was her own reflected form she saw, her own golden hair, unbraided as when she slept, shimmering on the face of the deep.

The coach bumped and skidded along the twisting fell road, all shale and mud compacted together, and, while eerie nightfall stole over the countryside and the dim cottage lamps glimmered bravely, Fiona told the strange tale of the last Viscount Penrose, the swaggering Mark and his ambitious paramour, Meg McCullough, the blacksmith of Wrydale's lovely daughter who, crossed in love, rained curses upon him and set fire to Silvercragg in revenge, killing her lover and his bride.

"There is a portrait of her on the staircase, by Sir Joshua Reynolds. He was paid a hundred guineas for the commission. I suppose," Fiona reflected, "that artists must learn to be discreet."

"What became of her? Do you know?"

"Oh, she died. She drowned herself in the lake, didn't she, Mama?"

"So the story goes. I've a strong notion she was a little 'to let in the attic'!"

Kate's blood ran cold. The dream swam up before her with the intensity of *déjà-vu*. Luckily, Fiona was absorbed by her theme and the light too feeble to betray Kate's ghostly pallor. "Meg was buried in a wood on the estate."

"In a wood?"

"They couldn't lay her to rest in consecrated ground, you see. She took her own life."

Lady Diana was relieved when the chatter ran dry. This passage of Penrose history had inspired an extraordinary degree of fear in the local populace, working like yeast in their minds so that the shadow and substance became fused together.

But, though Fiona grew subdued, the subject still exercised her thoughts. Presently, she blurted out: "Wasn't there a child, Mama? Hadn't Meg a daughter?"

"Yes, I believe she had. Wasn't that why she felt doubly outraged by what she regarded as the Viscount's perfidy? But really! Expecting him to wed her! The veriest nobody!"

"I wonder where she is now," Fiona mused. "Why, she'd be a grown woman, older than I!"

"No doubt some Wrydale family took her in."

"Perhaps she is unaware of her noble half."

"More than likely."

"But if she does know," Fiona persisted, "she may not take kindly to the new Lord Penrose."

"Let us hope," said her Mama, "that she is not of her mother's vengeful disposition. Nevertheless, I'm quite persuaded, Fee, that your uncle would contrive to disarm her."

At length they reached a fork in the road. The vehicle lurched and began to descend a gentle gradient. This was the Silvercragg estate and, although the lane was narrow and seldom used, the going was smoother. Old Benger, the steward, knew his business and had seen to it that all the ruts and hollows were filled in with cartloads of stones gathered off crop and pasture. The peasants collected the stones by the basketful and were paid fourpence a bushel for their trouble. The path meandered down in an elongated zig-zag to a ramshackle gatehouse overgrown with brambles and bleached, dead grasses, unearthly pale in the darkness. Soon they were rolling along the sweeping curves of a wide gravel drive that led nowhere, it seemed. There was not a building, not another sign of life, in sight.

And now a tumultuous racing of the blood swept over Kate, a tingling of every nerve. She was besieged by the perplexing conviction that she had been here before, knew the jagged outline of those mountains against the jewel-dark night. She craned and strained for the journey's end. Silvercragg! Silvercragg! But it refused to come forth, take on shape, whatever it was that stirred in the precincts of memory.

The coach rounded a bend to reveal the black sheen of Lake Mereswater and the silhouetted towers of the castle straight ahead. Hurricane lamps were ablaze at either side of the main entrance, enhancing the green granite of the front elevation.

Servants leapt to their duties. Doors were thrown open. The Viscountess appeared. Fond greetings and embraces ensued. Negus was called for to warm the travellers.

In a daze, Kate alighted from the coach, the wearying journey forgotten, and ascended the steps to the door.

The young mistress of Silvercragg was not by conventional standards a beauty. Her freckled countenance verged upon gauntness and her mouth was too wide, but she possessed in her favour a fine pair of jade-green eyes and a luxuriant mass of cinnamon waves, drawn off her brow by means of an ivory fillet and left to fall at random below her small bony shoulders. She looked like a famished waif of Whitechapel and had about her the distrait air of one anticipating bad news. Of her husband, there was no sign. When her brother commented upon this, she said: "Yes, I am sorry he is not here to receive you. He left early this morning for Sir Miles Middleham's house over the Raise. They were going on a shoot. I expected him back before this." Cassandra flashed an importunate, almost frantic glance towards her audience. "They are fast friends, he and Miles, and spend long hours together. Then, of course, his lordship is in and out of the farms. But I do not fret. There is plenty to occupy me. When a castle stands mostly unoccupied for two decades, its retainers tend to lapse into hapless ways. Were it not for Benger and Peggy Wagstaff, the cook, and her husband who chops wood and does his best with the garden, I cannot conceive how I should manage. They have been here since our Prince Regent was knee-high."

"My dear," said her sister-in-law soothingly, "you must not expect to set all in order overnight. Do take care of yourself. Get out and about."

"But you have no notion how dreadfully lonely it can be, Diana," Cassandra burst out. "Few people of consequence live in the neighbourhood. Sir Miles dines with us once a week and we take tea with Mrs Perrott at the Abbey on occasion. I once thought Cumberland a veritable Garden of Eden. Now I think it a wilderness." She peered out into the gloom as though from prison bars, alert for the figure of an approaching horseman, the white blaze of her husband's bay gelding. All she could see were the twinkling reflections of the interior printed upon the panes with increased precision as darkness thickened outside. "I wish we might go to London, but Penrose will not hear of it. He is determined to be a good landlord and desires to become familiar with the running of the estate. The tenants have been sadly neglected and he is anxious to reverse their opinion of the lords of Silvercragg."

"Most commendable," offered Sir George, eluding his wife's eye.

"You'd scarce credit how deeply ingrained are their beliefs about this place."

"Pagan rot!"

"It isn't easy to make light of it when you yourself are an object of suspicion." Cassandra laid an apprehensive hand upon her brother's sleeve. "George, you won't stir up a dust when Leo returns, will you? He is so eager to resume the old cordial relations. It...it was at my ardent request," she confessed, "that he kept our marriage secret. I knew that to begin with you would disapprove but that when you had had leisure to reflect, you would see what a happy arrangement it is."

"You do me an injustice, Cass. Do you suppose me so lacking in courtesy that I would call a man to account in his own house? No, all shall be sweetness! My oath upon it! There now, does that please you? Let me see you smile."

Cassandra could not help brightening at this. "Oh, but I am a shocking hostess. I do not mean to visit my concerns upon you. I hope you will indeed be comfortable here, though it is a gloomy castle at the best of times."

"We'll cheer the old place up, won't we Miss Hanslope?" volunteered Fiona.

Ever since she had crossed the threshold, Cassandra had regarded her contemporary with interest, possibly seeing her as an ally, more ready to console than to dispense advice. "Miss Hanslope, pray do make yourself at home among us. I don't know what arrangements you have in my brother's home, but whilst you are here, consider yourself as one of the family and do, I beg you, take your meals with us."

"Your ladyship is extremely generous," Kate said with a brief curtsy.

Cassandra turned her attention to her niece. "Fee, my darling, you look fairly worn out."

"A nursery supper for you, child, and then bed," decreed her mother.

"But Mama! May I not wait up until uncle returns?"

Cassandra threw the longcase clock a nervous glance. It was well after seven. "He is an unconscionably long time. What a good thing I instructed Wagstaff to delay dinner until eight. In truth, I had no idea when to expect you."

Fenwick, the butler, appeared with a tray of steaming negus. Much heartened by the sight, the ladies removed their bonnets and drew closer to the lukewarm fire, settling upon damp-stained tapestry couches in a curious state of transition. All were sensitive of the absence of their host. Kate's early elation at seeing Silvercragg had not abated and the spicy potations which were pressed upon her deepened her suspenseful flush. A melting depth of colour had come into her eyes as she stared about her, a little mistily. The reception rooms were half-panelled in rich mahogany. Torches flared on the upper stonework making light dance and glimmer on the gold-leaf frames of the portraits.

High above her head, at the summit of the staircase, Miss McCullough of Wrydale stared out with the same molten blue gaze. And if the painted lady smiled, and if the shadow of a smile passed over her cherry lips, no one was any the wiser.

"Can Penrose have met with an accident?" Cassandra queried in agitation.

"Shouldn't think so," said the baronet. "Punctuality never was one of his virtues. Not that he has many, mind you!"

Up in her chamber, where Kate had retired to refresh herself before dinner, she washed and splashed elderflower water over her flushed complexion and decided she had taken a chill. She ached from top to toe. Her scant belongings had been unpacked and put away by a chamber maid. She was putting her boots outside the door for cleaning, when she heard the clatter of hooves in the stable yard below. Peering between the drapes, she descried, in a wedge of lamplight, a gentleman in a riding-cape and curly-brimmed beaver dismount and call to one of the grooms. He strode across the yard, into the shadows, tugging off his gauntlets as he went.

Immediately, the castle was aroused from its torpor and the noise of rejoicing rose up the stairwell, Fiona's excited, fluting tones, the baronet at his most ebullient, and then the gentle resonance of the newcomer's voice. So the Viscount Penrose had come home at last.

Kate's heart began to palpitate foolishly. She was vexed to be in so great a taking about meeting a stranger. Everyone followed the Viscount into his library where Fenwick had set out goblets of sherry. The voices became muffled. Kate donned her shoes and, taking a deep breath, descended the stairs. She hesitated at the open door. At the centre of the group a tall gentleman in a maroon cutaway coat and biscuit-coloured breeches stood with his back to her.

The gale-severed boughs, the prunings and parings of autumn burned fiercely in the basket-grate. It was the cosiest room in the castle. Perhaps her pulse skipped a beat at the sight of tossed fronds of tobacco-brown hair. It all happened in an instant.

"Come in, my dear girl," invited Sir George. "Don't skulk in the shadows. Penrose, let me introduce you to the latest member of the household: Miss Kate Hanslope from Sussex."

The stranger turned. His jaw dropped open. His eyes widened in amazement. "You...!" he uttered in total disbelief.

He rapidly recovered himself. "... are the new governess, I take it." He was aware that a hush had fallen. The others were watching, baffled by a subtle contact between the two.

Kate advanced towards him and held out her hand, her limbs weak from shock. "I am pleased to make your lordship's acquaintance," said she.

Lord Penrose bestowed a feather-light kiss upon her knuckles. It was imperative to tread cautiously, but he fixed Kate's eye a fraction longer than he ought. "Kate," he murmured, in spite of himself.

"Today she is Kate," Fiona told him firmly, "but I suppose that directly we start upon Mr Pope's verse and the principal rivers of Europe, she will have to become Miss Hanslope again."

"I'd say you were a lucky young lady, Fee, to have Miss Hanslope for your tutor and companion."

"Yes," agreed Fee wickedly, "old Peppercorn would never have permitted me to devour *Tom Jones*!"

The baronet coughed upon his sherry and, mindful of his paternal responsibilities, deemed the situation to warrant a specious oath. "Aye, and you'll have taken a wee keek at *Moll Flanders* too, I dare swear.!"

"Miss Hanslope," said Fiona with a disdainful bat of her lashes, "does know where to draw the line, Papa. We shall graduate to that in due course!"

Kate was a little put out by this exchange but Sir George, grinning hugely, thrust a glass into her hand. "You'll do!" he approved. "What say you, Penrose?"

The Viscount, encouraged to pronounce upon Miss Hanslope as though she were a sweet-going filly from Tatt's, nicely skirted the issue. "A thousand times rather cultivate a taste for the full-blooded prose of Fielding and Defoe," he maintained, "than this damnable vogue for the Gothic. There is enough fear of the supernatural abroad without seeking it as a means of entertainment." He avoided looking at his wife who had spent the summer with her nose buried deep in *Vathek* and *The Castle of Otranto*.

"You said that with feeling," Diana observed.

"My dear, Diana, I have had the dubious pleasure of spending the last seven or eight weeks among the rustics of Cumberland. Whilst I am prepared to believe them the soul of humanity, their tenacious belief in some strange, not to say evil, superstitions renders the life of any sane person going about his business exceedingly trying."

"They do not want us," mourned Cassandra in a disembodied voice. "The servants are intriguing to get rid of us. They whisper behind closed doors. They are not, I am sure, above lacing our food with poison."

"Heaven forfend!" cried the baronet, half in jest and familiar with the excesses of his sister's imagination. "You do nought to whet a guest's appetite for his dinner!"

"Cassandra, you are being overly dramatic. This is Regency England, not Renaissance Italy."

Lord Penrose appeared grateful for the cool-headed intervention of his sister-in-law. He could not refute that there was some foundation for his wife's allegations. The servants were shifty and sly. They did gather in corners muttering darkly with their heads together and dispersing the second they heard the master's or mistress' tread. Those born and bred in the dale resented the ones who had come down from London. They would go about their work with a kind of shambling insolence. Poor Cassandra was not equal to handling mutiny below stairs. She had been used to the suave attentions of her brother's devoted retainers and was inexperienced in running a household. Twice she had scolded the dairymaids for their unhygienic ways, and Bella Larkin, the stillroom maid, for burning wax candles in her quarters instead of tallow. Cassandra knew they mocked and mimicked behind her back.

The occasions when the Stewarts had stayed at Silvercragg on their way to Argyll had been of short duration. They would always be 'foreigners', neither feared nor yet truly accepted. Now 'young madam', whom they regarded as little more than a gawky schoolgirl, had perpetrated the unforgivable in marrying a Penrose and restoring their dreaded rule.

Inwardly, Cassandra quailed before their sullen faces and began to forgo her daily tours of inspection, electing to keep to her bedchamber overlooking the lake and water meadows, where toadflax and bulrushes ran riot and where, in early summer, one might glimpse a swan's or moorhen's nest hidden among the reeds. Now the high water mark showed halfway up the bleached stems. Mereswater was smooth as silver oil and so deep that it seldom changed. Only the north wind, when it came funnelling down the valley, lashed it into a frenzy. The bright plane of water inverted the furrowed faces of the encircling fells, bereft of vegetation. Cassandra imagined the silent underwater with its soothing refraction of light in that peaceful abode. She would immerse herself for hours in tales of the Borgias, of Lancelot and Guinevere, and Tristan and Isolde.

Kate had taken advantage of this chilling digression to down her sherry, unperceived, in one draught. It would help to bolster her courage! Cheerfully, she resigned herself to the unexpected and unexplained. Not for an instant had she dreamed that the unprincipled and charming Lord Penrose whose cause Fiona had vehemently championed, was none other than Leo Quinn. He looked careworn and weary. His eyes were a mesh of fine creases and the sadness behind them was more evident than before. And still he studied her in that heartbreaking way so that she did not care what he had done. Maybe he was no saint, but she could not believe him capable of craftiness or meanness of spirit. Her secret would be safe with him.

Fenwick appeared in the doorway to inform the Viscountess that dinner was served. Fiona rebelled against being packed off to bed with poached fish and bread and milk, putting her arm through Leo's and beseeching him to intercede for her. He mollified her with assurances that she should join them on days when her stamina was strongest, if her Mama agreed. "For," he said, "I've a fine harpsichord, Miss Tuppence, a Kirkman, you know, and I shall expect you to play me some airs of an evening."

So Fiona was despatched to the care of Nanny Foster, a worthy soul from Penrith, appointed by the Viscount to ensure his niece's comfort during her stay. Then, as courtesy dictated, he offered his arm to her mother, obliging Sir George to link up with Kate and Cassandra on either side. Devil take him, the baronet declared jovially, if these lopsided arrangements weren't just the ticket!

Kate dared drink no more wine until she had eaten. Throughout dinner, she felt ill at ease and barely noticed what was put in front of her. At the centre of the table was a huge crystal cornucopia of fruits. What a benison it was, the Viscount told them, that the kitchen garden, the orchard and hothouses had not gone to rack and ruin. "I have nothing but praise for the industry of the gardeners." He was watching Cassandra edgily. She was in a reticent mood and picked listlessly at her food. "Eat up your dinner, my dear," he said kindly, as though cajoling a sick infant.

"Excuse me, I have a headache. I think I shall take to my bed."

The gentlemen raised themselves awkwardly as she got up to go. Lady Stewart, thinking that feminine ministrations were called for, made to follow her, but his lordship intervened. "Let her go, Diana. Let her sleep if she can. It's the best way."

When the Viscountess passed, Kate saw in the fullness of the light, the inert blackness of her eyes which earlier had appeared limpid green. Her pupils were so distended that the hollow core had almost obliterated the outer rim of the iris.

"She is not quite herself at present. The peculiar problems of the new environment have taken their toll, I think."

"She is not..." Diana began.

"No," denied his lordship firmly, "she is not with child."

He tactfully shifted the emphasis and indicated to a footman that his guests' glasses be topped up. "Miss Hanslope, another slice of lamb? More marrow?"

"Indeed, no, my lord, thank you. You must forgive me for doing less than justice to this excellent meal. The journey has left me a trifle fatigued."

"The bracing air of Cumberland will soon revive you."

"Indoors and out," added the baronet in an aside.

"Tell me, do you ride?"

Kate glanced at her host with a hint of reproach. You know that I do, she wanted to say. "Passably well, I fancy."

"Splendid! Regrettably, we cannot invite you to come riding to hounds. Hunting in Cumberland is performed on foot."

When they had finished eating and the baronet's garments strained at the seams, lavender water and hand towels were brought to the ladies and staff withdrew. "Perhaps you will pay us the compliment of not lingering too long over your port," suggested Lady Stewart. "I swear we shall faint from exhaustion if we don't get to bed soon."

"Away with you woman! We'll come when we've a mind!"

"Wild horses wouldn't keep us away," smiled the Viscount, but it was not upon her ladyship that his attention rested.

"Darn good port might, though," added his companion when the coast was clear. He reached for the decanter. "Have to keep the petticoat sex in line, Penrose. You'll learn! Lord knows, if you can get the measure of my sister, you're a cleverer fellow than I am."

Leo was about to reply but thought better of it. With George halfway stoned and in one of his obtuse moods, this was no time to discuss Cassandra. Life with her had been no honeymoon. Now that they were alone together, her company oppressed him unbearably. His own view of reality took on a certain warp. He could see that it was so and he could not control it. Cassandra was not as others were. The melancholia came upon her without warning. She would lock herself away and accuse all who crossed her of being traitors. Her heart was a storehouse of bitterness, of imagined slights and betrayals engraved as on tablets of stone. Her doctors dissembled, looked solemn, spoke of the likelihood of an incurable blood disease but seemed reluctant to form any fixed opinion. Unnerved and shaken in a way he had never been when facing the enemy in the bloody hills of Spain, Leo took himself off to seek sanctuary with Middleham. This insidious madness made Peggy Wagstaff's cretinous kitchen wench a source of light relief! Cassandra was intelligent. And plausible. She would come out of the darkness without any recollection of having been in it and would conduct herself as amiably as the next person.

In foul moods and fair, the Viscountess insisted there was a malign influence at Silvercragg. She dared not sleep, and had developed a habit of drugging herself with Kendal Black Drop. As fast as Leo disposed of it, she cunningly obtained further supplies, hiding the fluted brown bottles beneath a floor panel in her room. If it dowsed her fears and sent her to sleep, it made her nightmares worse and brought on delusions. There was nowhere she could take refuge from herself.

Only the knowledge that he had married to extricate himself from debt saved Leo from gall. It was Cassandra herself who had proposed the solution to him, obliquely at first, and then outright, so that at no time had he deceived her. He could not have brought himself to profess a spurious passion. She had observed his generous indulgence of her niece and recognised him as someone who would bear with her humours. He would not cast her aside the minute he had his hands upon her inheritance. For his part, he had not disliked her and was persuaded they would rub along together as well as any other couple united for temporal reasons. She had seemed, if slightly prosaic, companionable. Once or twice, George had referred to her 'vapours' but his friend had thought nothing of it. The moods had been neither frequent nor extreme and had been ridden out in seclusion. It was since they came to Silvercragg, this thrice-cursed seat of Leo's so-called ancestors where the shadows closed ranks and the Black Drop was easily come by, that her affliction was manifest.

Leo crossed to the ancient dresser to fetch brandy, placing the decanter squarely on the table. "You may think what you choose, George, but you'll find me a fair husband. I married with the intention of starting afresh. I mean that this estate shall be prosperous and the name of Penrose honourable."

"Noble stuff," said the baronet who was inclined to leave such inscrutables in the hands of professionals. He selected a cigar from the open box and bit off the end, leaning forward with a daring disregard of his whiskers to light it at a branch of candles. "Wish you the devil's own luck, boy! You'll need better success than you had with your former career, that's for sure!"

"At the tables?"

George drew on his cigar and settled back, squinting astutely. It was good to be enjoying the old comradeship again. "Your old man would have clapped you on the back at any rate."

The other raised an ironic brow. "It's deuced odd, but by some perverse law, I no longer feel the compulsion to court disaster now that he is gone. I've quite lost the taste for running on the red! Have no fear, I shall not be tempted to stake the roof over your sister's head!"

"Dare say you feel mightily at home with your antecedents strung about the walls."

"Firewater?" Leo asked. He began to suspect that George had an inkling of the truth. "I feel no particular affinity with Silvercragg. Wrydale, however, is beautiful. It's the inhabitants who spoil it. But enough of my affairs," said his lordship, itching to change the subject. "What of Fiona? Does she continue to mend? She looked tired tonight but that is only to be expected after the journey."

"It has been a good summer. I own I'm not easy about the Cumbrian climate at this time of year."

"We shall do all in our power to prevent a relapse. Her governess…"

"Ah, the delectable Miss Hanslope. Thought she'd be on the agenda!"

Leo nursed his brandy and schooled himself to respond coolly. "Oh?"

"Knew you'd taken a shine to her the moment she set foot in the library. Plain as a packsaddle."

"Fiona appears to be fond of her."

"Very proprietorial. So beware!"

"Not at all like the starched females one usually encounters in the schoolroom. Where on earth did you find her?"

"Attwood engaged her. One of his minions discovered her on the London coach going up from Brighton. Remember that pale-faced chub, Grey? Came down to discuss business with me in the summer."

"Good Lord!" breathed the startled Viscount. "On a public conveyance bound for the capital! Unchaperoned!"

"Sharp as knives, I'll say that for him."

"It does not bear thinking about."

"Not one to let matters hang fire."

"What! Er, no! No, indeed!"

"Been maundering at her heels ever since."

"Has he, by Jove?" The Viscount grappled with the full import of this intelligence, a keen light in his eye which did not escape his brother-in-law.

"Now, see here, Penrose! If you imagine I'll stand by whilst you play my sister false and ruin an innocent maid, a parson's daughter to boot, you must be foxed. For I won't. I'll draw your cork first, guest under your roof or no! Take a bit o' muslin if you must, but for pity's sake do it discreetly, well away from here."

His lordship was stultified. "Miss Hanslope's father is a cleric?" he said. "You know, George, that's odd. Confoundedly odd. The other day, I had a long talk with Canon Stackpole, the incumbent here, and said I desired to quell the fearful rumours about this place. He told me he came to Wrydale in '97 and referred to his predecessor, a fellow by the name of James Hanslope…"

"Before my time, old boy. Before my father's time, too. Never ones to foster relations with the Cloth anyway. Rum culls the lot of 'em. 'S no wonder Miss Thingummy slipped her reins."

"How remarkable, though. The name is uncommon, you'll agree."

Mereswater lapped against the shore. Kate could not sleep. A low wind moaned between cracks in the woodwork, made the bristle tips of a Scots pine chafe against the mullioned glass. Somewhere behind the castle, a beck splashed and tumbled down to the lake, echoing in rocky gullies. All was strange and yet tormentingly familiar. She could not get to grips with the ferment of her emotions since she arrived here. And Leo! How had he erupted on to the scene, just when she supposed she had shaken off the past?

The wine at dinner had given her a raging thirst and, scrabbling to rekindle a night-light, she went to the washstand and tilted the ewer to pour water into a tumbler, drinking it down in deep draughts. Outside, an owl hooted, a chill, low note, almost human. And then, another sound. A soft click. She held her breath: she had neglected to lock her door. The brass handle rotated and in slipped none other than the Viscount himself, still fully clad in his ruffles and gleaming buttons and buckles, and it was Brighton all over again. Kate gave a soft cry and found herself in his crushing embrace. The tension within her began to resolve and dissolve as she yielded to the eloquent pressure of his mouth. "I had to come. I had to speak with you away from them all. To have you so close and yet out of reach… Kate, my darling, I searched high and low…"

"I ran away," she said foolishly.

"George told me of your encounter with Attwood's man!"

"I did not understand the nature of Madame's house."

"You were lucky that Diana never saw you in Brighton."

"Consider my utter confusion, the violation of all I believed in… I have led a sheltered life."

"Truly, I don't know what I intended except to warn you, for you did not seem to fit. I could not gauge precisely how much you were aware…"

"And then," Kate said, "when it was too late, I realised I didn't care about your motives. I missed you abominably, out of all reason."

Leo rocked her to and fro and rested his cheek against her crown, his fingers stirring the blonde tousled strands. "What a coil!"

"Your marriage…was sudden, was it not?"

"It was expedient, I'll make no bones about that."

"I see." Her voice quavered.

"But you, you do not see. How could you?" He held her at arm's length, his countenance an amalgam of tenderness and regret. He could not explain that he had married so precipitately not merely as a means of discharging his obligations, but to cover the poverty of his father's bequests. Tongues would wag, ribald conjecture would be rife. He had to do what he could to protect his mother's good name. He had also to contend with a complete loss of creditworthiness. The duns would have started to harass him with a vengeance once word got around.

"How capricious fate is," he went on. "Tonight I was riding back over the Raise through fallen leaves. It was dusk and the presage of winter was in the air. Then I saw a pair of wild geese winging across the sky, straight as arrows and so marvellously free, and I was overwhelmed by a powerful and pervasive sense of you, as though you breathed through me..."

"And here I was, all the time, under your very own roof!"

"Safe and sound. Oh, you were like sunshine tonight in your yellow gown. I cannot tell you what I felt."

"But tell me that you are not unhappy." Whatever it was, that disconsolate thing behind his expression, provoked a searing ache under her ribs.

"Is there any lasting contentment upon this earth? Even if one should chance upon the Garden, there is always the serpent coiled in the undergrowth. Promise me you won't run away."

"How can I stay, feeling as I do? To have you near me..."

"Hush," he said, tightening his embrace, acutely conscious of the tantalising softness of her under the thin nightgown. "Come, you are shivering. Let me put your shawl around you. Sit by me on the bed and it shall be as it was in Brighton. I was happy then."

In the half-light, Leo was stunned by a flashing vision of another face, superimposing hers, the face of the woman in the portrait on the staircase. Already it had evoked many poignant reminders of the vanished girl from Brighton. The dreariness of succeeding events had conferred a dreamlike quality upon her. He was not at all sure that he had not invented her.

"Won't you be missed?"

"My wife, I assure you, is sound asleep....in her own bedchamber. She has dosed herself with laudanum and will not stir until well into the day."

He spoke with resignation, even a touch of rancour. In her mind's eye, Kate saw her ladyship's pale, quivering hands, the dark, blank stare. "She is not well, I think."

Leo did not answer. His jaw muscle tensed. "She... Cassandra and I... are joined in name only. The natural concomitants of marriage are distasteful to her."

Kate gave his hand a long sympathetic squeeze. She was wiser, far wiser than she had been when they last met. Whilst other men might seek their pleasures where they could, whilst Leo himself might have sowed his wild oats, she knew in her heart that he would not be content to pass the rest of his life consorting with women of Essie's stamp, or dallying with the bored wives of diplomats. "I guessed it was so."

"Did you? Why, I wonder?"

She spread her hands in a gesture of inadequacy. "Because... Oh, because there is no cement between you and the Viscountess. You do not conspire against the world. For all your bonhomie, I saw in off guard moments a kind of sadness, an exhaustion, as though you were being consumed by an inner fire."

"You are indeed perceptive."

"I love you," she whispered. "Downstairs I wanted to put my arms around you and kiss you and tell you that all would be well. The long quest for whatever it was that you wanted was at an end."

He took her chin in his hand and pressed restrained kisses around her mouth. A wild upsurge of joy such as he had felt riding home under a lone star combined with intense desire to undo his determination not to involve her in his troubles. He had not reckoned with the fact that she might feel deeply about him. "I want nothing so much as to be in this bed with you."

She slid her arms about his neck, one hand under the collar of his shirt. His flesh burned beneath the silk shirt. "So, then..."

She tugged the ribbons at her throat and, without coyness or immodesty, allowed her nightgown to slip to the floor in a pool of linen. Hers was a joyous body that invited trust and tenderness. It was soft and sweet and supple, made for love. He was utterly patient, utterly indulgent. Overcome by so profound and salutary an experience, she began to sob helplessly whilst he smiled down at her, glad, exultant, inspired. She seemed to unfold like blossom in the sun. Soon she stumbled upon reserves she did not know she possessed, the power to sustain him and deliver him from an inner bondage, scaling the peaks around this land-locked place so that the rush and clamour of her blood was drowned in the singing waters of the beck cascading to the shore.

Kate bound her hair tightly next morning and reverted to her serviceable merino. Above the prim white collar, her eyes glowed with a softened light. Stowing away her sunflower gown, she sighed. She must not covet what she could not have, for that was a very grave sin.

She knelt in the window embrasure and gazed out. The sky was blue, the maples shone a bright citrus yellow. Steam rose off the roofs of the farm cottages along the valley and the slate hovels at the entrance to the Pass. A vague odour of musty leaves and dying, dew-drenched bracken hung on the air. I must have dreamt this place, Kate thought. I have the strangest sensation that I am fulfilling a plan. I almost think I was meant to come here.

She went off to enquire after Fiona and had just left her room when Leo appeared on the opposite side of the landing and caught up with her.

160

"I trust you slept soundly," he enquired in an intimate undertone.

A soft blush crept up to her temples. "I love you," she said in a stricken whisper. She was not cut out for a double role. His hand moved towards hers and was about to imprison it when he snatched it away. A door opened behind them and Nanny Foster emerged, straightening her cap. She acknowledged them and stalked off towards the Stewarts' suite.

"That, Miss Hanslope," Leo said hastily, indicating a portrait on the left of a long casement window, "is Meg McCullough, the local blacksmith's fated daughter."

"Oh, so that is she," said Kate in accents of discovery.

In the searching daylight falling slantwise through the glass dome above, Leo was startled anew by this seeming facsimile of the woman beside him. "You've heard of her?"

"Oh, yes. Fiona regaled me with the whole macabre story on our way here. Meg has quite captured her imagination."

"Young ladies of that age are inclined to be susceptible."

Kate's nerve-ends tingled. She might have been confronting her own reflection. She knew that woman under the skin. Sir Joshua Reynolds had captured exquisitely the translucent folds of her muslin fichu which was tied with provocative negligence on her straining bodice. It was a querying pose, half sideways on. She presented a challenge. On her lap rested a small ivory casket, inlaid with mother-of-pearl. The lid was lifted a fraction and Meg's fingers spread in teasing defiance of all counsel to keep it closed. You could tell she was mercurial and altogether ungovernable.

"What do you suppose is concealed in the box? A necklace of emeralds. A rope of fine pearls?"

"Oh no, not gems."

"How can you be sure?"

"Because that box is here at Silvercragg, in a glass case in the Italian Room. It is a musical box and bears the legend of

Pandora."

"She who let loose all the evils flesh is heir to?"

The Viscount nodded. "It is not wholly inappropriate, you'll agree. Mark Penrose brought it back from his travels. I will show it to you later, when we have breakfasted."

There had not been a sound, not the softest footfall or susurration of silk, but the two of them became aware of a third presence. Lady Penrose stood silent and watchful in a shabby dressing-robe she had not bothered to fasten. Her hair was unkempt. Bafflement creased her brow. The eyes in her vixen face were wild. Gone was the veneer of graciousness. "Where is Tilly?" she demanded in shrill tones. "I ring the bell and she does not answer."

Kate dropped a curtsy. "Go back to bed, Cassandra," said the Viscount. "I will have Wagstaff find your maid and send her to you."

Leo led Kate to the Breakfast Room and excused himself from her company. If the servants were malingering, they must be chastened. The heat of the kitchen and its medley of odours wafted over him as he ventured into unaccustomed regions.

The servants, both upper and lower, were assembled at a refectory table over bowls of porridge. From the range, Peggy Wagstaff carried a serving dish laden with fried potatoes and thick rolls of Cumberland sausage which she set down by a stack of plates. The chatter died. One by one, the faces turned towards the door. Fenwick cleared his throat. He rose and the others followed suit. "Mrs Wagstaff, where is the girl Tilly?"

"Why, I dunno, my lord, if she's not upstairs waitin' on her ladyship."

"Find her, if you please. And send her to attend Lady Penrose without delay."

"Yes, sir."

"That bell, Fenwick," his lordship rapped.

"Bell, my lord?" All eyes swung up to the system of

communication fixed high on the wall now running with condensation.

"Why has it no hammer?"

Nudges and sidelong glances were exchanged among a small clique at the lower end of the table. Even as he spoke, the bell linked to Cassandra's bedchamber agitated mutely. He was glad he could not hear the invective at the other end.

Fenwick seemed genuinely bewildered. "My lord, I do not know how such a circumstance… Maybe it has chanced to fall behind the dresser."

A faint snigger was stifled.

"I fancy there are those here who do not share your ignorance," glowered the Viscount. "Winkle out the culprits and see that they are relieved of their duties."

With that he turned and went. There was little likelihood of establishing the truth, but he had delivered his warning and trusted that Fenwick's embarrassment would do the rest. This insubordination below stairs must be stamped out. Cassandra's lunatic fantasies needed no stoking.

Sir George Stewart surveyed his daughter's companion across the breakfast table with peculiar interest. He was in a fragile and lacklustre mood after the excesses of the previous night and had taken the precaution of bracing himself with a stiff tot of whisky at the ungodly intrusion of daylight. The sight of the girl, fresh and blooming, brought a lift to his spirits and a searing pain to his head.

"Fine thing," he muttered.

"Did you say something, George?" asked his wife. "Or were you chewing the cud?"

"A fine thing. The full flush of youth," he elucidated.

"And what prompts this feat of memory, we ask?"

"Miss Hanslope, here. Ability to shrug off the rigours of

travel. Nights spent in *improbable* beds."

Kate's countenance burned. She did not dare glance at Leo. Was the change in her this morning so conspicuous?

"My dear, you have weathered the journey better than any of us," Lady Stewart declared with a polite yawn.

"A brisk ride on the fells is what you need, George," recommended the Viscount. "I shall not permit you to squander such a day in maudlin reflection. Why don't we invite the ladies? Miss Hanslope, you'd care to sample the North Country air, would you not?"

"Pray excuse me on this occasion, my lord. I have promised to read Fiona some passages from Gilbert White's diaries."

"The tiresome fellow shan't always take precedence," he teased with a familiarity bordering on the rash. As it was, his brother-in-law's perceptions were too blunted to register the hint of flirtation and his sister-in-law was engrossed in her own thoughts.

"It is Cassandra who stands in need of an outing."

"Diana, if you can persuade her, then she shall come. She won't listen to me."

"Ought not to isolate herself," mumbled George. "T'ain't natural in a young, new-married woman."

"This exasperating situation with the servants has preyed on her mind overmuch," Diana said impatiently. "Why does she let them gain the upper hand? She must be mistress in her own house."

"I've given a good deal of thought as to how best to promote goodwill all round," his lordship told her. "One tradition I am set upon reviving is the Christmas ball for the tenants."

"Does Cassandra agree?"

"We have not discussed it. Heaven knows we have a responsibility towards them."

"Noblesse oblige?" Lady Diana quizzed, tilting the coffee pot interrogatively over his cup.

"It is no bad thing. I've no time for reactionaries like Mr Paine who stir up discontent and leave the people wanting. The government was wise to post agents up and down the land seeing his books and pamphlets burned. The British establishment is the best in the world. We were the envy of the Allies when they came here in the summer, yet we have only narrowly averted a crisis on the French scale."

"I quite agree. But how serious you are, dear Leo. You used to be so carefree."

"And impecunious!" he said sheepishly. "What are your views on the subject, Miss Hanslope?"

"If I presume to have an opinion, my lord, it is that Mr Paine has perhaps helped to redress a balance. There are those, less liberal than yourself, who take their position for granted and do not scruple to exploit the poor and those dependent upon them."

"Yes, the way we order things does have its abuses. That does not make it wrong, however."

"At all events," Diana said, "we can feel easier now that Boney's hands are tied."

"I should feel safer were he confined below ground!" Leo said.

"Surely he will not attempt to escape?"

"He is not a man to take defeat lightly. Anything is possible. So we shall have our ball and make merry whilst we may and you shall see that I am not as glum as I am painted!"

As it turned out, the ladies stayed at home. Diana spent the morning closeted with Cassandra. Fiona fell asleep over her breakfast tray and Nanny Foster would allow no one past the door. Kate was left to her own devices.

Throwing a cape about her, she decided to explore the grounds of Silvercragg. The gardens had long lost their Arcadian charm. Only a minimum of work had been done to retard the despoliations of nature. The formal layout of lawns and beds and arbours surrounding the castle gave upon a rambling wilderness which shelved steeply down to the lake. Rocky outcrops poked through the thick carpet of leaves swirling and cartwheeling in gusts of wind. There was a gentler descent to the water on the western side of the castle. It was a pleasant aspect and a shame that it should possess such a derelict air. Someone else evidently thought so, too, because a semi-circle of rowan saplings had been planted in the unscythed grass, recently, by the look of the freshly-turned earth. How strange that it was otherwise untended. The portico and façade were overrun with ruddy creepers.

Kate scorned to let superstition rule her and, picking her way to a window, shielded her eyes and boldly peeped in.

The room had a faded elegance and was all but unfurnished. Oil paintings, dark and cracked with age, were propped against the walls; some chipped gilt chairs were stacked in a corner beside a gutted spinet. She was captured in the atmosphere of another age and was suddenly struck by a conviction that she was not alone. She span round, as though tapped on the shoulder, but saw no one, merely caught the flickering gleam of a timeless breeze among the glossy leaves.

After passing through the kitchen garden where she paused to admire the orderly rows of winter vegetables and herbs, she went indoors and settled down to prepare some lessons on the Tudors, the while longing to be cantering through the bracken with Leo. He had encouraged her to use his library for her morning sessions with Fiona and she felt soothed and at home among his books and his Girtin watercolours.

In an hour and a half, he returned by himself. She heard his voice, Fenwick's answer; the measure of his stride on the oaken floor. The door was thrust open and in he came. He stopped short, disbelieving his good fortune at finding her solitary. Without a word, she flew into his embrace, returning his kisses

166

with a fervour that left her shaken.

"How agreeable it is to be missed," he laughed.

"Did you have a pleasant ride?"

"I thought I should die if I could not have my arms about you before long."

"Upon your honour?"

"Upon my honour!" He nuzzled her neck, groaning softly. "Kate, Kate, you try a man's patience sore."

Her eyes were liquid and magnified. "Come soon."

"Yes, yes, yes," he promised hoarsely. "Oh, you are so warm and sane and responsive. You bring me such joy, such strength, such a possibility of living…!"

Kate wished devoutly she had the courage to dissuade him from visiting her room again. But the vision of Cassandra's icy, demented stare caused her resolution to perish.

"Where is Sir George?"

"He stopped at the gates to parley with Benger. And you? Why are you so studious and alone?"

"Fiona is sleeping. Under Nanny's orders, I suspect! Their ladyships have been shut away any time since breakfast."

"If anyone can do Cassandra good, it is Diana. Well, then, now's our opportunity to go to the Italian Room and see Meg's music box."

"Oh, do let's!"

It was a forgotten room, facing south, and hexagonal in shape. It proclaimed Mark Penrose's dilettante interest in classical history. He had been a man of many parts but few disciplines. Six scagliola columns supported the frescoed ceiling; the walls were of watered silk in a diluted blue resembling Mr Wedgwood's famous jasper ware. Busts of long-buried emperors haunted the recesses in an atmosphere of benign antiquity. Tall French windows opened on to a terrace which in turn led, via a series of elliptical steps, to a mossy stretch of law intersected with parterre paths and hedged about with box.

From a hidden drawer in the bureau, Leo produced a small key. Before he'd unlocked the cabinet, Kate spotted among the enamelled urns and chunks of mineral, the Pandora's Box. Its ivory carvings were strongly suggestive of Flaxman's designs on Wedgwood's Etruria pottery. Leo lifted it down for Kate and handed it to her. A frisson of excitement and fear ran along her spine. Gingerly, she raised the lid and set in motion the delicate mechanism. The strains of another age rose up in the space between herself and Leo. She gave a constricted little cry, her heart hammering. "But it's the same. Exactly the same."

"What do you mean?"

"At home...in my father's house, there is a music box which plays this very air. I cannot describe what I feel when I hear it. Often I wake in the night and hear it ringing in my head."

Less than two hours ago, she had walked in the garden, stung by the same pungent emotion. To have come within a hair's breadth of revelation twice in one morning...

"Come, we will shut the box," Leo said uneasily.

"No! Do not!"

"But it is evident that it pains you."

"Pray, let it wind down. Let it...her...have her way." Bewildered, Kate stared through space, unconfined by the limits of the room. "The Enchantress of Wrydale!"

The box whirred. The melody faltered and died. Leo pressed down the lid firmly and fastened the gilt clasp, restoring the piece to its shelf once more. The peremptory click of the lock brought Kate out of her reverie. All at once she felt drained.

It was Florrie McGee, the third chambermaid, who heard the poignant little harmony float up behind closed doors. She paused outside the Italian Room and cocked an ear, her stumpy arms straining to girdle a bundle of linen. Could it be the Pandora's Box? Saints alive! Mrs Wagstaff had warned the maids not to touch it. When it needed dusting she would do it herself with a feather duster.

In terror, Florrie dropped the sweet-smelling laundry in the middle of the hall and fled to the kitchen, blurting out her tale to the housekeeper. "Tis true, Mrs Wagstaff! Tis true as I stand here!"

Peggy Wagstaff girded her bosom with folded arms and snorted as she was wont to do when panic prevailed. "Hold thy peace, child! Thee've a face as white as a sark!"

"Twere his lordship and her ladyship. I heard them speakin' together, all secret-like. Didst thou not warn them aboot the box?"

"Dost think tis my place to warn the likes o' them! They fancy themselves above such things with their London airs and gey clever cant. They come down here meddlin' where they've no business to meddle, disturbing things that are best left to rest. The master's well enough, mebbe, but I'll nivver make out that quair wife of his..." She broke off, gaping at Florrie under the delayed impact of what the girl had reported.

"Nay, couldn've been Lady Penrose in that room. Cissy went up with a bowl of broth not ten minutes since."

"Twere a lady's chat, that's all I ken," whimpered Florrie who could not see that it mattered.

Peggy Wagstaff squinted bleakly, slowly nodding her head. She had been at Silvercragg before Florrie McGee was as big as a sark button and knew things that Florrie did not know. "Aye, twere that fancy governess, if I ken owt."

"Miss 'Anslope?"

"She's bad tidings, that one. They let in a burden o' trouble last night when she darkened the door, mark what I'm telling thee, Florrie McGee. I wondered then..."

"Wondered what, Mrs Wagstaff?"

"...but when I spied her out yon this morning, it fair took my breath. Twere Meg McCullough stepped out of the grave."

"Meg!" squeaked Florrie.

"Dost not ken, child, who yon fine lass be? Why, she's Meg McCullough's daughter, his lordship's cousin no less!"

And Peggy told Wagstaff and Fenwick and Benger. And Florrie told Bella who told Cissy who told the grooms. The news spread like wildfire below stairs in the castle. The harlot of Wrydale's daughter had come to avenge her dead mother and woe to the valley that this day should dawn.

Six

Each night of the following week, Leo sought Kate's room. The household would retire into its shell and he would listen for the last footfall on the landing, the last soft screech of a doorknob. He would leave his bedcovers in disarray and his drugged wife dead to the world in the communicating room.

The pleasure and solace of one another's arms was not an end in itself. They fell as naturally as breathing into a fond and trusting partnership. Leo confided his hopes for the estate, the extent of his predicament with Cassandra. It was easier to bear now that he had Kate. "What is to become of her," he brooded, "if she will not assert herself? She is playing into the servants' hands."

He lounged beside a heartening fire, still clothed, his long legs stretched out to the Dutch-tiled hearth. The sadness and overstrained stoicism had gone out of him and a new endearing mellowness had crept into his voice. Kate knelt against his knee, her hair unbound. "I cannot but sympathise with Cassandra," she said. "The servants are forbidding."

"But it has become an obsession with her."

"They do stare at one so."

"My love, they are unlearned and inbred northerners. They fear outsiders. Kendal town is their antipodes!"

"Sometimes, I think they…know."

"About us? How could they when we have practised such prudence? The rooms in this quarter are unoccupied. We are quite alone."

"Then why do I suffer those slighting glances? Of what am I accused?"

"You?"

"At first I thought I had imagined it. But I have watched them with others, seen the hatred, the suspicion kindle in their eyes when they turn to me."

Cassandra's malaise, it seemed, was infectious! "These are unwholesome fancies fostered by the Viscountess. I adjure you not to refine upon them."

"I begin to feel guilty." She took his hand and interlaced her fingers with his, squeezing them to communicate remorse. "I care for you so much, my will is so bound up with yours, I am afraid that at any moment the axe will fall."

"These Puritan conceits of punishment and damnation! I cannot abide to see you torn apart by them."

"My father once said that we ought to be careful of our deepest desires, for God would surely grant them."

"Amen to that," said Leo and bent to kiss her hand. "Incidentally, is there a clerical tradition in your family?"

"What makes you ask?"

"The other day, I happened to learn that the vicar here before Canon Stackpole was someone called James Hanslope."

"But that is Papa's name!"

"I recalled mention of your Papa's accent. That it was like William Wordsworth's..."

Kate's brows suddenly drew together. "Do you know, yesterday when the Canon was here paying his addresses to Lady Penrose, he observed my likeness to that painting of Meg. He regarded me so particularly and then said: 'I collect, Miss Hanslope, that your Papa is also a gentleman of the Cloth.' Did you inform him of that?"

"I don't believe so. Cassandra may have mentioned it. Does it signify?"

"Well, do you think he inferred that I might be related to his predecessor? How singular that he should have been a Hanslope, a James Hanslope, too."

"Could he not have asked you directly?"

"I don't know."

"You did inspire a keen interest at the church door on Sunday, that I do recall! My profound jealousy was tempered only by the discovery that Stackpole was mortal like the rest of us!"

Later, when he was about to drift into languorous sleep, Kate said: "Leo?"

"Hmm."

"Why have they planted those rowan trees around the West Wing when it is otherwise forgotten?"

"What on earth has that to do with anything?"

"I was walking in the garden the other day and had the strangest impression I was not alone."

"Ah, that is Meg's province. The staff maintain that she haunts those groves."

"You're quizzing."

"No, indeed, I am not. It is widely held among country folk that the mountain ash has the power to drive away evil spirits. Wagstaff saw those trees planted. I didn't forbid it. If it keeps the peace, well and good."

Kate shuddered, savouring Leo's palpable warmth. It was good to bask in the love of another human being. It is all a dream, she thought. One day I shall awake in my lonely narrow bed in the cramped room under the eves of Merrowdene vicarage.

"Such a stir among the servants! You'll never guess what they are saying!"

Kate's small feet froze upon the library steps as Fiona burst into the room, flushed and dishevelled. She struggled to suppress a coughing fit, her soft brown eyes bright with excitement.

"I beg you will calm yourself," Kate said, a little more severely than she intended.

"Well, but Kate, do listen!"

"Miss Hanslope today, if you please."

"Miss Hanslope, then. Oh, but how can I address you thus when I have this morning made the most extraordinary and astounding discovery? Dearest Kate, you will not believe it but you are my own dear cousin. By marriage, that is," she appended, somewhat reluctantly.

Kate frowned in bewilderment. "What...what are you saying?" Clumsily, she stepped down from the ladder, of the strong opinion that the child was ailing.

"Do sit down, my dear," Fiona commanded, enjoying the reversal of roles. "Would you like a brandy or a nip of rum. I know Uncle Leo keeps some in his cabinet."

"That won't be necessary, thank you. Do please explain yourself."

"They are saying below stairs that you are Meg McCullough's daughter, the love-child of the infamous Mark Penrose!"

"What nonsense! It is all because some have fancied a resemblance between myself and that work of Sir Joshua Reynolds."

"It is more than that."

"What can you mean?"

"Peggy Wagstaff says that after Meg's death, old McCullough, your grandfather, the blacksmith, was ostracised from the dale. He upped and went and you were adopted by the Reverend Mr Hanslope and taken away to the South of England where no taint of scandal could touch you."

Kate sank on to the sofa. Blindly, she fingered the snagged brocade. She was trembling from head to foot. The clock in the hall chimed twelve, dealing vibrant blows. "It cannot be true." But even as she stammered out the words, some inner tension snapped. It *was* true. Had she not known in every nerve the reverberations of an old association with Silvercragg? Had she not felt the twitch on the unseen thread drawing her back to where she belonged? Those slighting looks! The Canon's discreet inquisition! It flashed across her mind that not only had he been interested in her father's profession, but had enquired whether she had brothers or sisters. She told him she had two sisters, Ruth and Sarah. "Ah," he approved, "fine biblical names. And are you the elder Miss Hanslope?"

"No, sir," she replied. "Ruth is the elder and Sarah the younger."

"Indeed?" The cleric nodded and stroked his beard in a sapient manner, then bade her good-day.

"You can verify it if you wish," Fiona pursued, faintly aware that she was intruding, but seeing the situation from a youthful and romantic standpoint.

"What?"

"You can ascertain the truth for yourself."

"How?"

"Desire Canon Stackpole to show you the Parish Register. There will be a record of your baptism."

"Yes, of course. I will go presently, when I have spoken with his lordship. Thank you."

"How ironic it is! How fantastic! You realise what it means, do you not?"

"No."

"Why, that you are Uncle Leo's first cousin! Even though," Fiona added mischievously, "you were born the wrong side of the blanket!"

It was a dreary November day. Fog hung about the valley and effaced the mountains. The last tired leaves clung to the trees. Mereswater was dark and sheer, but for the triangular imprint made by paddling shelduck. Now and then a full-throated shindy broke out and echoed up between the pines and the tangled red osiers.

In silence, Kate and Leo walked through the beechwood. She was grateful that he had insisted on coming. He guided her by the elbow through the lych-gate and they proceeded up the church path, scuffling the mulch of wet leaves. Canon Stackpole had been primed to expect them and waited in the porch. He received them in a fatherly, elegiac mood and motioned them to follow him to the vestry.

Under the ancient buttresses, the ashen-haired clergyman, garbed in the robes of his office, inserted a key into the brass-plated lock of an oaken drawer and took out the Parish Register. Diocese of Carlisle. Carefully, he turned back the musty annals of time, to the year 1796 and the first month when Kate would have been six or seven weeks old. There, on the sallow parchment, in her father's own hand, a more confident hand than he had been able to master since his sight had deteriorated, she read a fulsome entry of her own baptism.

Kate Genevieve, adopted daughter of James Edward Drew Hanslope, Vicar of the Parish of Wrydale-with-Holtleap, and his wife Priscilla Elizabeth, baptised this twenty-first day of January in the Year of Our Lord, Seventeen Hundred and Ninety-Six.

The script swam out of focus. Kate did not move. Mere words could not have described the tumult of her mind at that moment. She was meeting herself for the first time. "Thank you, Mr Stackpole," she managed to say. "And were my sisters also christened in this church?"

"The baptism of the elder Miss Hanslope is recorded, if you care to see, two years prior to your own. Your younger sister, I presume, was born in the south."

"The south. Ah, yes. It sounds like another hemisphere, does it not?"

"Miss Hanslope, this is a shattering blow. To have had no inkling of the circumstances of your birth! To have chanced upon the harsh truth in this fashion is so beyond the limits of credibility that we must infer some Divine Purpose..."

"You misapprehend, sir," Kate cut in, choked. "My whole life begins to make sense!"

At a sign from the Viscount, Stackpole made a token bow and withdrew. The book lay open on the table against the hoary grain. Inside the church was doubly chill, dispersing human breath.

Brokenly, Kate sat in a pew, drawing her cloak closer about her. She could not cry. She had been betrayed. She wanted to rail against those who had kept her in ignorance. No longer could she cast Meg as the villain. Meg had been wicked, but Meg had been wronged, used, discarded at will. Poor, deluded Meg. There was no one in Wrydale, nor the length and breadth of Cumberland who would take her part.

Leo took her hand and chafed it between his own. At his touch, her anger evaporated. "Dearest cousin," she whispered. "Was it the bonds of kinship that drew us together that evening in Brighton?"

He fixed his eye on the beryl-studded crucifix, then on the slate tombstone with its worn inscription beneath his feet. "Kate..." he faltered. "Dear Kate, I am not your cousin. Mark Penrose was not my uncle. There are no ties of blood between us. In truth, if blood connection be the sole qualification for my title, I have no right to it."

She listened without interruption and with astonishment and compassion while he poured out the story which had been dammed up within him for so long. How his mother had loved Herr Neumann of Hanover and had suffered for it for the rest of her days, how inexorable the old Viscount had been, and how he himself, when penury threatened, had resorted to marriage with Cassandra Stewart. "You must understand," he said, "that I fully intended to forsake those ways."

"Had it not been for your wife's indisposition... You are

more justified in feeling aggrieved than I."

"I am not aggrieved, not now. I ceased to feel that when the Viscount died. Somehow death squares all accounts. Cassandra goads me, oppresses me, taxes my patience to the extreme, but I chose this course. Therefore I can bear it without acrimony. Does that sound perverse?"

Kate rose and shook out her cloak. Her hood had fallen back and the coil of fair hair had worked loose so that many strands escaped about her neck. She went to the Register and clamped the stained covers together in an act of finality. When she had lowered it into the drawer, she turned the key in the lock, dropping it into Leo's palm and dusting her fingers. To have learnt that she was someone else, to have gained and lost a cousin in so short a space, was too much to grasp. She made off while Leo sought the Canon.

Soon he caught up with her on the woodland path. She scarcely heard him striding through the damp litter of autumn behind her. The bare trees exposed a desolate sky. "Tell me," she said when he drew level, "where is she? What have they done with my… my mother?"

He turned to her and held her gently by the wrists. "Kate, this anguish serves no purpose. She was a malicious woman. You are well rid of her."

Tears sprang to her eyes. "Do you think that helps?" she cried.

"You would despise me for distorting the truth. She is not worthy of your pity. Forget her! You have another destiny, a whole tissue of antecedents that she did not."

"I am like her. Others say that I am. My father, Mr Hanslope, you know," Kate said with a touch of hysteria, "had me down for a wanton! I have a terrible foreboding that history is repeating itself. The Lord of Silvercragg is my lover, too."

"You are distraught. Banish these wild imaginings. Our situation cannot be compared to theirs. For as God is my witness,

I would marry you if I were free. Would that I were! Come now," he soothed, "don't fight me. Take my arm and we will walk in unison."

"Do you know where she is buried?"

The Viscount hesitated. "Yes. I will show you if you wish."

He led her back over the path they had just trodden and through a mass of thorny undergrowth. He picked up a stick and beat out a clearing. Broken boughs frosted with lichens crackled underfoot. A lone heron passed way above the treetops, trailing ungainly legs. Kate lifted her skirts and stepped warily between the barbed stems. Brown pine needles were strewn on the spongy ground, driven by wind and rain into the texture of a coarse fur pelt. The further they digressed from the path, the darker the wood became. "Is it much further?" Kate asked. She felt as though they were making an excursion, out of time, into a sphere of Stygian shade forgotten by the living.

"A few yards more."

They stepped over a rivulet glimmering darkly between outgrowths of roots and started down a gentle slope. Several feet below, where the water curved and spilled into a tiny gorge underneath the turf, the spindly frame of a rowan tree could be distinguished. No others of its kind grew in that part of the wood, though it had not been planted by nature, by a hapless breeze or visiting bird. Its uptilted branches leaned motionless to one side and, close by, a chipped fragment of green slate, half-interred, inclined in the opposite direction in a state of mute antipathy. Minute yellow fungi thrived about its base. The initials M.M. followed by R.I.P. could still be discerned crudely engraved in the moss-soured headstone. A pauper's grave. The burial place of someone outcast and dispossessed. Kate ran to it, half-stumbling, in an access of violent emotion. She knelt down and wept bitterly, wept for her dead mother, for herself. I am entirely alone in this world, she thought. There is no one.

The Viscount gave the lie to that by clasping her hand so

tightly it momentarily wrung pain. "She was wicked," Kate said. "I can bear that. But how shall I forgive him."

"Mark? He was a firebrand, a philanderer, but no worse than many of his kind."

"No, not him. My father. My adoptive father."

"The Reverend James?"

"He deceived me. All these years he and my mother have practised the most abominable deceit!"

"For your protection, you can be sure."

"I cannot forgive him when he set so much store by absolute honesty."

Christmas approached. The weather turned acidly cold. Snow capped Glaramara and the Scafell Pikes, first thinly lining the crags, then obliterating them with a stealthy persistence.

Fiona was causing concern. She seldom spent more than an hour or two out of her bed. At night she slept with the pillows plumped behind her shoulders. Lying down brought on a paroxysm of coughing which left her exhausted and the linen flecked with blood. Her father was generous enough to refrain from observing that his misgivings had been justified and called in the best physician in Keswick. The advice of this gentleman, however, proved no more efficacious than that of Dr Knott from Ravenglass way, a stuffy old gamecock who could do no better than prescribe mild doses of laudanum and a tincture heavily laced with garlic. Kate passed long mornings in the parched and airless room, doing her best to amuse the patient who had not the spirit to lament her confinement let alone play chess or solitaire. The pitted glass marbles she had had since infancy rolled about the covers, eluding her listless efforts to gather them and drop them back in their slots.

The conviction that she ought to write to her father and hazard the consequences plagued Kate, but she could not face doing so until she had ordered her thoughts. The foundations had been pulled from under her. He was still her legal guardian and could require her obedience. She saw how untenable her position was as the Viscount's mistress. Then there was the delicate question of conscience. How could she blame Hanslope for deception when she herself could not be acquitted?

"I have looked long and hard at that portrait of Mark Penrose in the Gallery," she told Leo, "but I feel no rapport with him. It gives me no insight into him or myself. But with Meg... I am unnerved."

The fiction that she was Leo's cousin had to be preserved for his sake. Upon record, it was true. The exposure of her origins had thrown into relief a close connection with him which conspired to cover any fleeting suggestion of intimacy. No one had reason to suspect them lovers. No one save Cassandra. Her ladyship had a finely tuned instinct about such things, as those of unsound mind often do, and she allowed her fancy to dwell upon it. The lack of material evidence did not deter her. It was a way of putting herself in the right, of excusing her attitude towards Leo. Upon being first introduced, she had seen Miss Hanslope as an ally. The notion was quickly dispelled that evening in the library when her husband stepped forward to greet his niece's companion. There was an intimacy between them that excluded all others.

In the privacy of their chambers, Leo bore the brunt of his wife's razor-edged tongue. Day by day, she had grown less accessible and was prostrate with fits of depression in which she uttered trance-like warnings.

"Do you suppose that I am a fool?" she railed at him. "Anyone with an atom of intelligence can see how it is between you and that...that woman! She has proved what kind she is, walking unchaperoned with you in the woods and coming back with her skirts smothered in mud."

"You test my patience, madam! I would not stoop to defend

myself, but you shall not vilify Miss Hanslope."

"What! Do you attest her good name, your baseborn little coz!"

A flint-hard anger gleamed in his hazel eyes. "You are beneath contempt!"

Suddenly, an anguished cry broke from her. She clutched her temples, wrenching at the roots of her hair. "Oh God! I wish I were dead!"

"You are not alone in that!" he flung at her and stormed off, abandoning her to her misery.

This was unforgivable, but she had driven him to it. He feared the white-hot reactions she aroused. Shaking, he went to his library and swallowed brandy and wondered what was to be done with her. Neither doctor nor cleric seemed able to help. He was beginning to think an asylum was the only answer.

So December was bleak, the days fraught. The Viscountess was not to be seen at table or in the main rooms. She haunted the upper chambers, a sinister shadow, eating the merest morsels of food and complaining that it was tainted. She assumed in the minds of the servants and the neighbourhood in general, the kind of dimension that hitherto had been Meg McCullough's. Cassandra Penrose was now the *bête-noire* so that Meg was robbed of her chilling sway. The shades were claiming her at last.

Thus 1814 drew towards its close. The year which had fizzed and crackled in celebration of peace sank into a trough of anti-climax and irresolution. The Viennese Congress dragged its feet over its business, if not over its social life. Whilst the new map of Europe remained undrawn, its crowned heads and luminaries waltzed until dawn, or gave themselves up to the coruscating diversions of opera and ballet.

All Leo could do to cheer that dark Cumbrian winter was to promise his staff a Grand Ball in the old style on Christmas Eve. The younger servants brightened with pleasure, the older ones looked askance and hoped for the best. The last time a Lord of

Silvercragg had come home with his bride and had given a ball for his neighbours, there had been the devil to pay.

Thursday the twenty-fourth of December saw Silvercragg come alive as it had not done since way back in the last century.

"Ee, lass, there's not been such a to-do for yerrs," declared Peggy Wagstaff to Bella Larkin. Despite her earlier presentiments, she was looking forward to it. The old trestle tables brought out of the barns as extra work surfaces were about to buckle under the weight of creams and trifles, cinnamon cakes, roast hog and fowls and sausages, great hams, malt loaves, sweet and savoury pastries. It had taken skill and ingenuity to organise and she was now able to toast her feet at the fender over a mug of hot chocolate and view the result with a just pride. "Hast seen the like? Mr Fenwick I reckon this deserves a nip o' that nice mellow rum, though I says it myself."

Fenwick sketched a mock-polite bow. "Indeed it does, Mrs W. I believe we've a keg or two laid by in the cellar!"

Upstairs in the hall, the floor had been sprinkled with French chalk. Chandeliers had been polished and mirrors hung to increase the light and create an illusion of space. Candles were planted in their sconces and discreet sprigs of mistletoe pinned above doorways. The fireplaces were flanked by holly boughs and the staircase garlanded with gold ribbon and paper chains.

Wrydale was upholstered in fleecy whiteness. The snow glittered suggesting shadows of soft blue and mauve. Ice rimmed the lake in frozen ripples and the ducks huddled together and tucked their beaks under their wings. Conjecture was rife as to who among the gentry would manage the journey and who would not. As the light faded and the sky turned fondant green streaked with pink, the anticipation mounted indoors.

At six o' clock, the fiddlers and pipers from Cockermouth tapped on the kitchen door. They were a motley group used to performing in inns and barns and would spruce themselves up and hope to multiply their gratuities when summoned to the halls of the Quality. They came with empty bellies and would leave with their poacher's pockets crammed to bursting.

When Fenwick opened the door to the first arrivals, snow was tumbling steadily in the porch light. Melting flakes glistened upon capes and cloaks and glossy beaver hats. Like a magnet, the roaring fire drew the guests. Fiona was carried downstairs and tucked up on a couch close to the fire. She was adamant that she should miss nothing and had been given special dispensation for this night's festivities against Nanny Foster's better judgement. The child's eyes gleamed from deep within their sockets, as though composed of some dark, spiritual liquid. Bright patches burned in her pallid cheeks. "Uncle Leo, promise me one thing..." she asked, catching his sleeve.

"Anything in my power, Miss Tuppence."

"Promise me that when you take your partner and twirl about the room, you will imagine I am she."

His smiling eyes were full of compassion. "That will be no irksome task," he said kindly. "And when I have opened the ball with her Grace of Kendal, who then shall my partner be? Your aunt will not consent to appear."

"My aunt is not sensible of her own good fortune," Fiona presumed. "I abhor the way she treats you, Uncle Leo."

Leo squatted down beside her. "Try to forgive her, Fee. She is sick and cannot help herself. And I am a worthless rogue, you know, when all's said and done."

"I cannot forgive her," Fiona said, and he was dismayed to see tears filming her eyes. "But you shall dance, Uncle Leo!" she cried, gasping for breath. "Dance for me the whole night through. Why, here is a partner for you! See! At the top of the stairs!"

He turned and rose to his feet, bewitched. Descending towards him was Kate in burgundy lutestring upon which she had been stitching away since her birthday. Diana had made her a present of it. Leo wished wholeheartedly he could have presented her as mistress of Silvercragg.

By and by, guests from far and near thronged the old hall, done up in gaudy finery and their Sunday best garb. Shrivelled old squires, harking back to former days, donned powdered wigs and moth-eaten frockcoats of every hue. Musky odours blended with chypre and Hungary Water, the scent of pinewood bubbling and flaring up the great chimney, the appetising whiff of white soup. The accents of merrymaking, stilled for a generation, soared among the beams, stirring faded memories of how things used to be. Presently, Fiona, tired out, was compelled to seek her room.

The evening gathered momentum and was in no danger of flagging. The occasion was all that Lord Penrose had hoped for, except that it manifestly failed to recommend his wife to the good folk of Wrydale, or them to her. Lady Diana stepped into the breach. She was known and respected among them and did much to prosper Leo's cause.

But her ladyship was not the prime object of interest. It was Meg McCullough's daughter they pressed to see. She aroused in them a startled curiosity, for her fame had spread through the mountains and dales. Nor were they hostile. A festive mood was upon them: a sense of being attuned to fate. It was as if they were cognisant of a deep-rooted blood bond and were ready to celebrate the return of their own. Kate was taken aback, but was soon treading on air. The role of hostess was thrust upon her inadvertently and she met the challenge with spirit, glad of her Brighton training. She had not realised it before, but this was what she had waited and yearned for. This was where she belonged.

She had come home.

Far beyond the warm lights and music and the rugged walls of Silvercragg, the north wind mourned over the ghostly fells and whipped snow into blinding flurries. The wayfarer cursed his luck. Swaddled in a thick greatcoat, in thigh-boots and moleskins, he lowered his head and tugged down the brim of his hat, refusing to slacken his pace. Having put up at an inn, he had struck out into the darkness on foot, bent on closing the last stages of his mission and deaf to the landlord's warnings. Offcomers were 'nobbut blithering fools'. Lives had been lost in less treacherous weather. Tomorrow the road would be impassable.

No moon rode the sky, not tonight. There would be no spectre abroad. And perhaps she need lament her lost daughter no more. Only an otherworldly whiteness invented a dim light to guide him on his way. The driving snow-flakes clung to his left side so that he moved, half-shadow, along the deserted road. His feet kicked a brave trail, ploughing a swathe where the carriage-way should have been. But for the fact that it was slung between parallel stone walls, it would have been impossible to see which way it threaded.

At length, panting, he reached Moss Ghyll and looked down upon Mereswater. Above the blizzard, carried on a howling wind, he thought he heard music. He trudged on, rewarded when the castle loomed into view, many of its windows radiant. He paused again for breath. His goal was in sight. The long months of pursuit were at an end. As he drew close, the foot-tapping rhythm of a country reel became plainer coupled with the sound of revelry. He could see figures now, moving about on the inside. Fear swept over him, chilled him to the marrow.

Was it, after all, an hallucination that would fade and vanish, leaving him in outer darkness?

The waltzes and minuets had been few. Tirelessly, the fiddlers played on and the tripping feet kept pace. The frenetic folk music hummed and thrummed in the blood, Christmas day came and nobody heard the witching hour chime. Nobody saw the figure in white materialise at the balcony above.

The next instant the music was riven by a nerve-shattering scream. The churchwarden's wife fainted and had to be carried out by a footman. Aghast, everyone looked up to see what had caused it. A magnetic hush prevailed. There, on the staircase, passing under the nose of Meg McCullough, was the spectacle of a female draped in white muslin. The ravaged countenance was half-concealed in a Medusa's head of untamed hair. Her stare was wild and penetrating. But this was no apparition to pour curses on the scions of Silvercragg, no visitation from the grave. It was the Viscountess. She had been incarcerated these three weeks and Kate was appalled by her physical degeneration. Could this be the same young mistress of Silvercragg whose behaviour, though a little distrait, had been so welcoming several weeks ago?

Leo squared his shoulders. "The devil is in her tonight," he murmured. "Be brave, my love."

Quick to perceive the collusion between her husband and his partner, Lady Penrose glared at Kate. She raised her bony hand and stabbed the air with a talon-like forefinger. "You!" she spat. "Woman in red! Why did you come here to torment me? Seize her! Cut off her hair!"

A rumour had gone the rounds that the Viscountess was brainsick: her guests wanted no further evidence.

"You rave, madam! Go to your room! Violins, a gavotte if you please. On with the dance!"

Haltingly, the musicians obeyed. The dancing was resumed but without the same spirit. Leo strode up the stairs and took his wife firmly by the arm. "I implore you to conduct yourself in a seemly fashion," he hissed in her ear, "for I do not propose to strive with you here. You have outraged every tenet of decency tonight."

Kate steadied herself against a pier-table and took the glass of rum punch proffered by the baronet who patted her hand consolingly. "What am I to say, Miss Hanslope? A thousand apologies."

At the earliest opportunity, she made a polite excuse and disappeared.

"Be assured, Cassandra, you shall be repaid in good coin for this! I mean to have you put away!"

In a lightning motion, Cassandra wrenched herself free and clamped her hands over her ears. Rushing across the landing to her room, she attempted to slam the door upon her captor, but he overtook her. She crumpled into a heap upon the floor, her face twisted with an agony close to abject remorse. "Why, why did you bring me here?"

It took Leo a moment to become accustomed to the gloom after the well-illuminated hall. A single lamp with a cranberry glass reservoir burned on top of a pedestal. Its wick needed trimming and the flame ran dangerously high.

"But it was you who said there was nowhere on earth for you but Cumberland. You were wretched in Paris."

"The city reeked of blood. There was an odour of death everywhere."

"Determine to cast these shadows from you. The Revolution is long over. Now, get up! I will send a maid to attend you."

He avoided touching her again. Contact was repugnant. She smelled of a strange bitter chemistry, antipathetic to his own, not strong, but distinct, which her rose-perfumed bedlinen failed to disguise. It was futile to reason with her. He did so solely to defuse the situation.

"Shadows… I am dogged by shadows. This house is full of them." The sentences were fey and pregnant with foreboding.

"When I turn to confront them, they vanish. But I know they are there, taunting, mocking, inciting me. Why do you conspire with that woman? Do you imagine I am blind?"

"I take it you refer to Miss Hanslope."

"She who has come to supplant me."

"Don't be absurd, Cassandra. There is not a more peaceable soul alive than your niece's governess."

"Then what has brought her here, tell me that?"

He could offer no satisfactory answer. She leapt at him and grabbed him by his velvet lapels, a mere inch from his nose. All his energies were engaged against his will in a desperate battle beyond the scope of the conversation. A cold sweat broke out across his back. Grasping her forearms, he flung her from him and with a prodigious effort remained calm. Like a soul banished from the realms of the living, she fled to the far side of the room and stood with her back compressed against the wall, shivering, emitting a thin mewing cry, her hands spread.

"You were unhappy here long before Miss Hanslope's arrival. It was on that account that I sent for your brother and family in the first place."

"It was different in the old days," Cassandra said. "When I came here as the Viscountess Penrose, all the dark forces of the castle were unleashed. I have seen her, out there on the shore, the wraith whom they say pines for her lost child." She pressed an arm to her forehead. "How hot these rooms are tonight. How cool the lake must be."

Leo swallowed hard. "Come, lie down, Cassandra, quietly on the bed. You need a physician…"

"No!" she cried as he strode towards the door. "I need no one!" Her eyes were as stark as a terrified mare's. "They come and peer at me. The breath wheezes through their teeth. They do not understand. They think my wits are diseased. They want to shut me away, pretend I do not exist…!"

"You have chosen to do that for yourself," were Leo's

parting words.

"I hear them whispering behind the screens...the voices."

She was alone. The wind seethed about the casement, piping an unearthly air. Behind the curtains, a battery of snow dashed against the panes. Yet nothing diminished the commotion of the driven breakers crashing upon a rocky inlet over which the oriel window projected. In a flash of craven inspiration, Cassandra knew what she must do. She fumbled to undo the catch, scraping the paintwork with her nails. An icy whirlwind flushed through the interior and knocked the breath out of her, sent the framed silhouettes awry on the walls and the lamp crashing over. In a trice she was gone. The foaming waves closed over her head and Cassandra, Viscountess Penrose, was received into the dark silence she had yearned for.

It was as Wagstaff had predicted, Wagstaff, his wife, and those sage old crones down in the dale, prophesying over their spinning and weaving, measuring out their days to the rhythm of the treadle, watching circles turn and return with an unerring regularity, divining patterns in the warp and weft of destiny. They knew little of science and mathematics, but they understood that equations had to be satisfied. No good would ever come of tempting the spirit of Meg McCullough to wrath, least of all by heedless newcomers out of the south, beyond the mountains and the mist.

A spurt of flame licked up the whale-oil oozing over the marble surface of the washstand. It leapt high to scorch the old Provençal tapestry whose rotting fabric curled into glowing tatters, communicated to the bedhangings and the tester, seared across the cornices, gathered muster and set the whole room ablaze.

In the respite between dances, the company below had

frozen to hear another harrowing scream from the mistress. The master was at the bottom of the stairs by then, ordering a servant, a hardy young fellow, to go with all despatch and alert Dr Knott who had kept his own fireside and not come to the junketings at the castle. He turned rigid with alarm. Some hideous intuition informed him what Cassandra had done. That same instant a panic-stricken Kate appeared on the landing. "Fire! Fire! Her ladyship's room is on fire!"

An unholy turmoil broke out. Nanny Foster rushed about hysterically, afraid for the life of her charge. Leo bounded up the stairs but by that time a choking black heat was billowing around Cassandra's door. "She is trapped!" Kate sobbed. The torrid crackling from within grew louder: there was a thunderous crack and flaming rafters came toppling down.

"George! Diana!" the Viscount bellowed. "Evacuate the lower rooms! Wagstaff, find pails, ewers! Fill them with snow!" He turned swiftly to Kate who had marshalled her senses enough to smother Fiona in a quilt. "Cassandra is elsewhere. Now flee, my love. We shall bring Fiona to safety, Nanny and I. Flee for your life!"

Coughing, clutching at the handrail, the spreading heat at her heels, Kate hurried down the stairs. The walls began to slant and swerve. Flee for your life! All the weeks bedevilled by conflict and indecision were subsumed in the crisis. Kate groped for support at empty air.

A sable darkness closed about her.

What happened thereafter was never clear to her. She had a half-delirious recollection of being swept up and carried and set upon a horse amid pandemonium. Flickering sensations of heat and light, a raucous din of ravens put to untimely flight, the mare whinnying, the mare controlled, of galloping through the driving weather. Then there was the stranger, come out of nowhere to save her, whose voice was familiar. A voice from afar.

At noon she came to in a white-washed room, sparsely arranged with cottage furniture. Her head was hot and throbbed violently. Beyond the tiny window, with the curtains half-drawn, the country was placid and white. "Where am I?"

A blurred presence crossed from the fireside and stood over her. "Anthony," she frowned. "Anthony March."

"I found you," he said, "after searching so long. How do you feel?"

"Odd. Light of limb."

"I fear you've a fever." He hesitated to continue. For the present she seemed to accept her circumstances. "The innkeeper's daughter was good enough to put you to bed. You have on a borrowed shift." He blushed mildly at the lawn items slung over a three-cornered chair. The red silk was torn across its smocked bosom and one of Kate's shoes had been lost. Last night he had stretched his own coat to envelop them both.

"Inn?" Shadows of a nightmare disturbed her. A nerve-tingling fear brought the events of the dark hours reeling back. She started up, at once clasping a hand to her swimming head. "But what of Silvercragg? Leo? Did everyone escape?"

"Yes, by the greatest good fortune! Now don't alarm yourself," he exhorted her. Whether this happy conjecture was right did not at present matter.

Kate's lids met in deep relief. Her head found the pillows again. "Thank God! I thought her ladyship was trapped in her room, but Leo assured me that she was not."

Anthony wandered over to the window so that his masculine frame blotted out most of the daylight. He regarded her sideways. "Leo? Who is he?"

"Lord Penrose."

"Lord Penrose, no less," he muttered sarcastically.

"It is over," Kate said in a barely audible voice. Tears were sliding down her temples. Leo would do well to forget her. She could give him no comfort without an equal measure of pain. God had meted out punishment for loving too dearly where love was forbidden. She must contrive to forget them all, dear Fiona and her parents, the haunting beauty of Cumberland.

Hearing this, Anthony was inclined to believe that his altruistic lie had been divinely inspired. More than ever he desired that Kate should have no further contact with Silvercragg. In the light of her admission, the full facts were best unproven. The life of the Viscountess may not, after all, have been spared. "You must realise," he said, drawing up a rickety chair to the truckle bed and sitting astride it, "that I came to Cumberland to entreat with you, not to abduct you against your will."

"How did you find me?"

"You have Miss Polly Pringle to thank for that. Then that Brighton harpy, under whose dubious protection you were, advised me, after much inducement, to make enquiries at an address in Mayfair."

"South Audley Street?"

"The infamous Jezebel amused herself by dangling me on a hook for weeks. When I learnt that it was to Silvercragg you were gone, I could scarcely believe it!"

She seemed puzzled, then she said: "So you know about my birth?"

"It was your father's wish that you should not remain in the dark. He enjoined upon me the task of breaking the news to you gently, to prepare for your homecoming."

"How is he? And Mama and my sisters?"

"They bear up with immense courage." The scent of tobacco impregnating Anthony's clothes was an oppressive reminder of former days. "As soon as you are well and the weather permits, we shall journey south. I mean to take you back to the home where you truly belong, to live among those whose chief concern is your happiness."

At that point, for all her indebtedness, Kate could not help hating him. He had meant to be gracious and that made it worse.

A pang of longing for the life she had left behind smote her. She had found what she was seeking, and lost it.

"Now won't you take a little food?" Anthony urged. "A bowl of chicken broth? A boiled egg?"

Thenceforward, Anthony took matters into his own hands. He returned the horse he had appropriated from the Silvercragg stables, but did not consider it necessary to address himself to the lordship Kate held in such high esteem. Nevertheless, he wrote to Sir George Stewart, explaining her disappearance. Mr Hanslope was seriously ill and his daughter would not therefore be returning to her post.

The high-handed tone of this letter conveyed nothing of Kate's warm gratitude to the Stewarts for their kindness, nor of her regret at letting them down. Had she read it, she would have burned with shame.

Anthony's next missive was to Merrowdene rectory, detailing what had taken place, a rather turgid version of the facts in which he figured as the hero. They were holed up on the borders of Westmorland, he told Hanslope. He hoped the mail would not be delayed unduly. At the first sign of a change in the climate, he would be returning the poor renegade to the bosom of her family which news, he trusted, would bring unalloyed joy.

Kate rallied. A week later, on a crisp and sparkling New Year's Day, they set off for Sussex. There had been no fresh snow and the main turnpikes were navigable with caution. Anthony had purchased for her a thick cloak, half-boots, a muff and a heavy serge gown to keep out the cold.

1815. Kate wondered what it would bring.

She was resigned to her future and tried to be companionable. At least Anthony had expressed no renewed hopes of her hand. Pale and in sober mood, she climbed into the carriage and waved farewell to her host, farewell to the dear northern fells she would never see again. Soon the mountains and moors had given way to the lowering mill towns of Lancashire and the rolling plains of Staffordshire where the smoky sky was reddened by the ember glow of furnaces. The places ran together, nights spent in poky taverns and days of rattling motion, across bridges, past toll-gates, through pastoral scenes untouched by snow, all the signposts pointing south, and finally to Lewes and Merrowdene and the gates of home.

"Drive up to the door, Josh," Anthony instructed his driver who had met them at Lewes. "

"No, no," Kate countered, "pray set me down here, if you please." She turned to Anthony. "Grant me a little time to walk the drive at my own pace. I must compose my thoughts."

"As you wish." He consulted the repeater tucked in his pocket. "I'll bring up the rearguard in ten minutes or so."

Shaking, she found her legs, heard her own boots crunching over the shingle. How small her home seemed after so long an absence, how lost in a world of its own. The breath caught in her throat. On the porch, she espied a white-haired man, bent and altered and defeated by life. Last spring the hair had been grey. He was thinner. He was cupping a hand over his ear, craning for sounds. He did not start forward and, as she drew nearer with mounting anxiety, she saw why. Much moved, she paused several yards away from him.

"Kate? Is it Kate? Forgive me, I do not perceive the world too well."

In a blinding onrush of tears, she ran to him and fell on his neck and kissed him. "Papa! Papa! My own dearest Papa!"

For he had reared her and loved her and wanted to spare her. True kinship was born of the spirit, more precious than the bondage of flesh and blood.

His brittle frame shook as he clung to her. The poor glaucous eyes turned fluid. "My child, my child," he crooned. "I have waited, listened, every day since you went. Ah, but you are changed. Your voice is the tender voice of a woman."

She wanted to tell him that she had fallen in love, that it was safe out there in spite of the perils. For her part, she could bear the consequences of her follies. But his life was a monument to other lights, other beliefs, and he had none of the resilience of youth with which to shoulder his afflictions.

Her mother became visible in the shadows of the doorway. "What have you been about, child? How you distressed us!" she chivvied, as though Kate had dawdled over an errand.

"Mama! How well you look!" Kate hugged her.

Just then, her sisters came into view. Ruth, tight-lipped with no ring on her finger, embraced her solemnly but gave her no kiss. Sarah regarded her with a kind of envious awe and then sobbed out an incoherent welcome. Meanwhile little Polly Pringle who had retained her position, sniffed behind the parlour door, her mobcap askew and peeped through the crack to see the goings-on. In the kitchen, at her much-grazed chopping board, cook dabbed an apron to her eye and swore the Reverend's onions were powerful strong that season.

That night, back in her narrow bed, Kate grieved for the plight of those back in Cumberland and for the yawning gulf between herself and Leo.

The weeks ambled by. Tom Wakefield breathed his last and was buried alongside his wife. The first snowdrops appeared in the spinney behind the house, hazel catkins drooped from the hedgerows. February was sombre and nothing had changed. Nothing and everything. Life resumed its old course. Kate bound up her hair and presented those around her with a clean-scrubbed face. Village folk had no used for powder and salve, albeit modestly applied. She went about her chores prepared to be cheerful, but her big luminous eyes were sad. When she read to her father nowadays, long episodes from the Law and the Prophets, or the hectoring letters of St Paul, he was apt to lose attention and doze, and she would lay down the bible and go to the window and remember that there was a world out there, way beyond Merrowdene. He would come to with a jerk, unsettled by the silence. "Kate? Are you still there?"

"Yes, Papa, I'm still here," she would say. "Shall I make you some peppermint tea?"

Her patience was unfaltering. But he knew she was unhappy.

As for her engagement to Anthony March, Hanslope did not recur to the subject. Anthony himself, whilst he treated her with a pleasing respect, did not press his suit. An intangible barrier had come between them. If anything, he was disposed to favour her elder sister. Ruth had sadly been jilted. Her doctor had been found wanting in valour when called upon to unite himself with a family dishonoured by scandal. Kate was deeply sorry to have been the cause of this, but was secretly of the opinion that Ruth was well rid of the fellow if he lacked the mettle to outface the gossip. Ruth, however, could not forgive her. Half a man was better than none at all and she sought balm for her mortification in Anthony's presence.

So the days slipped into the old, uneventful groove. Had it not been for the lively society of Robert and Anne Vernon who welcomed Kate back with unreserved pleasure, there would have been no break in the monotony.

But even Merrowdene, hidden away on the Sussex Weald, was not an island, and further afield the storm clouds were gathering.

On March 7th, the endless deliberations in Vienna were abruptly terminated by the news that Bonaparte had escaped from Elba and was rampaging up through France gathering about him the remnant of his old army with all the furious force of the fanatic he was. The Bourbons were unpopular, the wine-bibbing Louis inspired no loyalty and the indefatigable little General had heard that there was already a plot afoot to overthrow him. This was the moment to rebuild his empire and conquer the 'wooden walls' of his most obdurate enemy across the Channel. The Old Guard was willing to march to his tune. Soon the whole nation was in a fever for war. The Imperial Eagle was flying the full length of France and the strains of the Marseillaise rang out. Even the fiery Marshal Ney, 'the bravest of the brave', who had called for Napoleon's abdication only eleven months earlier and had promised the King he would bring the Corsican to Paris in an iron cage, shrank like a whipped cur before his old mentor and re-avowed allegiance to him.

Thus, after centuries of relative complacency, Britain prepared to defend her Crown with a staunchness untapped since the Norman Conquest.

By the second week of April, feelings were running high. Bluebells misted the woods of Sussex and the martello towers along the coast were manned once more. In the garden, whither his wife had gone to inspect the primroses, Hanslope imparted the astonishing news that young Vernon proposed to buy a pair of colours.

"He is going to Belgium?" exclaimed she, aghast. That he should make this rash decision at so delicate a stage of his relations with Kate did not recommend him for his gallantry one wit! Thank heaven Anthony March was not moved to such folly!

"His Uncle Peachum, the General, you know, has taken an apartment in Brussels for himself and his good lady. He has invited Robert to join them."

"When does he leave?"

"On the twenty-second, I understand. His sister is to accompany him."

"Anne!"

The outdoor light suffused the lens of Hanslope's eye with a paler opacity against which the form of his wife was greyly rendered. He put out his hand and touched her arm. "They desire that Kate shall go with them," he said.

"But you will not hear of such a thing! A foreign country on the brink of war!"

"Kate is very agreeable," he informed her calmly.

"What! Are you run mad! I wish you will not provoke me so!"

"My dear, I think we must yield gracefully."

"Well, but Mr Hanslope, you have changed your tune, I must say!"

"Perhaps I am wiser than I used to be," he observed gravely. "I am put strongly in mind of our Lord's promise that the sown seed is not quickened, except it die."

Swayed less by this theological insight than by allowing her mind to run on the advantages of keeping The Honourable Mr Vernon within range, she clasped her hands together in excitement and lamented the impoverished state of Kate's wardrobe. Scurrying indoors and upstairs as nimbly as any young girl, she delved into the linen chest and produced a bag of crown-pieces she kept salted away for a rainy day. This she pressed upon the dumbfounded Kate, exhorting her to buy some new bonnets and gowns. "For you will go to balls and fêtes and reviews," said she, "and outshine all the ladies of rank and fashion."

"Mama," Kate whispered and kissed her cheek, her heart bursting with shame at having taken so long to recognise true charity.

And so it was that after many tearful farewells, with the wind set fair, Kate boarded a steam packet bound for Ostend and watched the shores of her homeland recede.

Many days after her departure, Jem Potter came whistling up the drive carrying an envelope addressed to Miss Kate. It bore the Penrose frank.

"We must forward it to Brussels," Hanslope said. "Depend upon it, she will not return this side of midsummer."

Seven

Never was the enchanting city of Brussels bursting with so much effervescent gaiety as in that spring of 1815 on the eve of war.

There were picnics and receptions, the military dashing hither and thither, drilling in the Squares, escorting pretty partners to the Opera House where La Catalani herself was engaged to sing. It seemed that the flower of English society had set up camp over the Channel, eager to savour the unique poignancy of those eleventh hour celebrations.

Emerging from the Custom House at Ostend, Robert Vernon and the ladies transferred to the more tranquil waters of the canal and travelled to Bruges and from thence to Ghent, medieval gems of cities both, mirrored in a network of waterways, the Flemish step-gables and needlepoint towers stippled with pink and foam-white blossoms. The French court had taken the precaution of removing to Ghent well behind the first lines of defence and within easy reach of the Channel ports. The Vernons' carriage had been consigned to the care of a couple of grooms. "Let them negotiate the baggage-wagons and ammunition carts," Vernon declared. "We shall proceed in a civilised fashion."

And so they did, drinking claret and eating succulent lamb and the *mille-feuille* pastries along the way, gliding through the congenial Flanders countryside where a fairytale château might be glimpsed among the trees and where peasants toiled with oxen and plough and the green rye was knee-high.

General Henry Peachum, his wife Pamela and her brother, Mr Fitzroy Fenton, occupied an upper storey of a fine cream-washed house in the *Rue Ducale* overlooking the Park. The General's lady, a plump, good-looking woman ten years in excess of the two score she admitted to, warmly welcomed the travellers and bade them refresh themselves with China tea and chicken sandwiches and a variety of other dainties.

"Now that the Duke has arrived, I own I shall rest easier in my bed," she said, handing round the cups. "He was in no haste to return from Vienna."

"Orange is keen to test his combative skills and don't know what all the commotion's about," the General, who was on the Duke's staff, enlarged. "Reckons he could account for Bonaparte single-handed if need be. He's an impetuous blade, plenty of backbone, but no mind for tactics."

"Ain't qualified for leadership, is he, Henry?" put in Mr Fenton. Unlike his sister, this foppish bachelor was of thin build. His girlish hands were blanched and his countenance made swarthy with walnut juice.

"By Jove, no. He's well enough pulling his own troops together, acquitted himself very creditably out in the Peninsula, but wants experience."

"He took it on the chin like a gentleman when the Princess Charlotte gave him his *congé* last year," Anne said. "That's a valour of sorts, I think."

"Or profound relief," quipped her brother. "For my part, I'm deuced glad he's not in charge of operations. We need a man of Wellington's stature and cool calculation. The troops do not love him, but they trust him to a fault. They would follow him into the jaws of Hell."

"And is it true," Kate asked, "that we are heavily outnumbered by the French?"

"It appears so," Robert told her. "We're ill-equipped as well. Many of our veterans are still in America. We've had to stiffen our regiments with the unemployed."

"Scum of the earth," his Grace calls 'em, don't he, Henry?" drawled Mr Fenton in a high-pitched voice.

"He's in the right of it, too. They're criminals, many of them, fleeing retribution. Your common soldier is possessed of a wonderful patriotism with cash in his pocket and free gin inside him!"

The conversation ran on in the cream and gold salon with the sun flashing a wild copper light as it went down behind the trees. Darkness was encroaching. Amid all the *joie de vivre*, there were moments of sombre reflection. Nobody knew what tomorrow would bring, what dynasties would founder, whose arms be left comfortless.

May passed for Kate in a whirl of magical pleasure. There were outings to the *Forêt de Soignes*, to galleries, to a fête at the *Hôtel de Ville*, to the flower market, to the milliners' and mantuamakers' shops. There was always something novel to see. Here a wrinkled old lacemaker at her bobbins out on the pavement, there a sprightly troupe of Flemish dancers in traditional costume. Everywhere the air sparkled with martial music. The regimental reviews were a splendid sight. Robert had been appointed a Captain in Sir John Colborne's fighting 52nd. In his coat of scarlet and buff with silver lace and a silver epaulette swinging on his right shoulder, he marched off to his duties in purposeful mood, confident that the Light Division would have the enemy squealing for quarter at their first engagement. Although not an unduly vain man, he enjoyed the admiration of the ladies and had acquired the knack of clicking his heels to Miss Hanslope in chivalrous fashion. He was fond of relating how Mr Creevey, that busybody who kept journals and knew everybody's business better than his own, had run across the Duke in the *Place Royale* and had demanded to know how confident his Grace was of putting the Corsican down. The Duke had pointed to a young infantryman intrigued by the statues. "It all depends upon that article there," he averred. "Give me enough of it and I am sure."

Meanwhile, out along the Belgian frontier, the Prussian allies commanded by Blücher were posted from Charleroi to the

Ardennes, their lines of supply going eastwards. Throughout the towns and villages of the west, a third of the Anglo-Allied army protected Wellington's lines of communication from the North Sea to his headquarters in Brussels. After his experiences in the Peninsula, he was morbidly alert to the dangers of being cut off and had figured that Napoleon would make this his first objective. There was a rumour abroad that the French General, Count d'Erlon and the whole of his corps, were approaching the frontier. He was not yet within striking distance but at night, in the second week of June, the telling reflection of numerous camp fires was to be seen in the clouds of the southern sky.

A thrill of fear ran through the city of Brussels. No fighting had been anticipated for at least a month. As the tension mounted, so did the desperate jollity

On Thursday June 15th, the revelry reached its zenith. For weeks, the Duchess of Richmond's forthcoming ball had been the chief topic of conversation. Many prayers were offered up, many arts employed, to obtain tickets for this dazzling occasion. Through the mediation of General Peachum, the Vernons were allotted four tickets. The General did not care to go. Neither did his lady feel her chaperonage was essential if her nephew and brother were to attend.

"There'll be dancing enough when the Frenchies come," the General warned. "You go, Bob. Take your sister and Miss Hanslope. Shall you go, Fitz?"

Mr Fitzroy Fenton took a pinch of snuff of rare and clandestine blend, a ritual not to be hurried. He sniffed deeply. "Gad's life Henry, I believe I shall! Twill be a capital diversion!"

On the morning of the ball, General Peachum left the *Rue Ducale* early to breakfast with the Duke at headquarters. Reports of further movement along the frontier had everyone on tenterhooks.

That afternoon the ladies returned in high spirits from a strawberry picnic at Enghien where Lord Edward Somerset's 1st and 2nd Life Guards and the Blues had paraded for inspection. The girls went straight up to bathe and pamper their sunburnt complexions with Denmark Lotion in preparation for the evening ahead.

Mrs Peachum lingered in the reception hall to sift through a handful of mail. News from England was often delayed and doubly welcome when it came. "Kate, my dear, there's a letter for you."

"That will be from Mama," Kate said breathlessly, tripping downstairs again to take it from her.

But when she saw that an earlier address had been crossed out and the letter was merely forwarded from Sussex, her heart skipped a beat. It was from Cumberland! She fled to her room, closed the door smartly, and tore open the seal. She devoured the contents, her pulse racing.

Dearest Love, (it ran)

I was mad with anxiety when you were nowhere to be found. I thought you were lost in the fire, but Fenwick informed me that a stranger had come through the snowstorm to ask for you and had given his name as Anthony March. Apparently, he arrived just prior to your raising the alarm. Imagine what a stir he would have caused had we all been abed like honest folks! Fenwick reported that you were seen riding away with the gentleman. I knew then what you had decided and that I was unworthy of you. I scarcely wanted the confirmation of his letter to George. Pray tell him I am much obliged for the return of my horse!

These months have been the most melancholy of my existence. What you will not know is that Cassandra took her own life on that ill-omened night. She cast herself into the lake, as I believe she had been tempted to do on other occasions. Few know the truth. It is widely assumed that she died in the fire and I shall not enlighten the world. I owe her that. Our marriage was short and spent in seclusion; her decline into insanity, rapid. People remember her for a quiet, if cryptic, soul and that is how it shall remain.

No lives were lost as a direct consequence of the fire, thank God, but to compound the tragedy, poor little Fee contracted a convulsive fever and died three days later at the Mereswater Inn where we had taken shelter. She is laid to rest in Wrydale churchyard under her favourite lilac tree which blossoms copiously in May, they say. I loved her dearly and never knew anyone unmoved by her courage. George and Diana are heartsick at so grievous a blow. Cassandra, too, is buried a stone's throw away, for Stackpole himself is ignorant of the circumstances of her death and I did not see fit to disabuse him of his natural assumptions. Of all the sins which may be laid to my charge on the Day of Reckoning, I cannot think that Cassandra's interment in consecrated earth will account for much.

Fortunately, by a miracle, the damage done to Silvercragg is not too extensive. A large part of the building is habitable and repairs are in hand. Since Monday, I have been closeted with my lawyers tidying up some affairs, having re-applied for an Army Commission in view of the developments in France. This beautiful island of ours must be defended. I cherish the hope that Old Hookey will not look too unfavourably upon a Peninsula veteran and expect to leave for the Netherlands within a month. When this sanguinary affair is over, I beg leave to call upon you (whatever your present status!) Should I fail to return – and perhaps I am tangling with fate in this – Silvercragg is settled upon you alone. The property bears no entail.

Au Revoir then, my dear one. Au Revoir and Adieu. God bless and keep you safe.

Your devoted,
Leo.

The parchment slipped from Kate's hand. The Park shimmered before her gaze. Silvercragg hers! It was too overwhelming a token of love. But he must not die! Leo! Fiona!

206

Pain lanced under her ribs and nostalgic echoes of Cumberland stole over her, so incongruous in the present setting.

"Why, Kate! Is it bad news?" Anne asked, coming through from the connecting room to seek advice upon a pair of silk tights.

Instantly, Kate retrieved the letter and folded it. "It is from Lord Penrose."

"Lord Penrose?"

"Whom I met in Cumberland."

"Ah."

The tumult of Kate's heart found release in a peal of mirth. "Dearest Anne, do not look at me so!" she cried, kissing her friend's cheek.

"I suspected someone had engaged your affections while you were away," the other remarked, slightly peeved at not having been taken into Kate's confidence.

"Did you so? Well, he has bought a commission. Only think, he will be here by now! In all likelihood in this very city!"

"He is quartered here? Which regiment has be joined?"

"He does not say. The thing was not settled when he wrote. The letter was addressed to me in Sussex and has been long in coming."

"Then he has no notion you are here!" Kate's features were invested with a softened beauty Anne had not witnessed in her before. "I perceive you are much taken with this lord."

"I love him," Kate whispered.

"Then must I relinquish all hope of your becoming my sister some day?"

"Anne, you are a most dear and faithful friend. I am exceedingly fond of Robert, of you both, and will always be sensible of your goodness to me…"

Anne smiled. "You are too generous to trifle with Robert and he won't come up to scratch while you hold him at arm's length."

"If I did but know where to find Leo."

"Supposing he goes to Her Grace's ball...! There are to be nigh on three hundred guests and you can wager half of them will be officers!"

"Oh, if only it were possible that I might see him tonight! I dare not think of it!"

"No doubt Robert could be persuaded to make enquiries on your behalf. Uncle Henry might know your Leo."

Kate glanced at her friend in mute entreaty. "At least your beau has a ticket for the ball," she chuckled.

"My beau?"

"That dashing Captain Mottram of the Blues."

"Yes," Anne said with a speculative gleam, "I own he was uncommon civil today. I am greatly exercised as to what strategy to employ to fix him!"

Around seven o' clock General Peachum crossed the Park from the Duke of Wellington's headquarters and came in looking grave and haggard. He was giving his hat to Camille, his Belgian servant, when Robert accosted him.

"What news, Uncle? It is a hum?"

"No, the rumours are true, lad. Orange came in from Braine-le-Comte to dine with the Duke this afternoon. No sooner had we sat down at table than a despatch came for the Prince from General Behr at Mons to the effect that the Prussians had been engaged since dawn. Thuin has fallen. Ziethen's 1st Corps got a bloody nose and the alarm guns sounded all along the line."

The General's wife joined them, ghastly pale. "Merciful God! Then we are at war!"

"A later report from Ziethen himself confirmed it. He thinks there is to be an assault upon Charleroi and wants the Duke to concentrate at Nivelles."

"Then why, by all that's famous, have we no orders?" Robert expostulated.

The tired General shook his head. "Stubborn fellow, Wellington. Insists it's a feint. Won't leave his right exposed. The whole day he has waited for intelligence from Grant, our man at Mons, and having received none refuses to budge."

"But we're losing valuable time!"

There were times when the General was mightily glad the future of Europe did nor rest on the zeal of the younger element who knew little of the exigencies of war. Nevertheless, he could not help deploring Wellington's caution. "I left him twenty minutes ago issuing stand-by instructions. We shall march tomorrow, have no fear."

"Then the ball is cancelled," concluded Mrs Peachum. "How disappointed the girls will be!"

"No, no, the ball goes forward. The Duke is anxious that there shall be no panic. He is all for his officers enjoying themselves to the last and proposes to be there himself if he can."

As twilight closed in, the Vernons' barouche turned into the *Rue de la Blanchisserie* to find it congested with the vehicles of Her Grace of Richmond's guests. They could not but be aware how honoured they were to be attending. It was the crowning event of Kate's life.

Mr Fitzroy Fenton offered Anne his arm and swept up the steps in a flamboyant opera-clock lined with purple tissue. Clutching her silver reticule and the posy of lilies Robert had bought for her in the flower market, Kate rested her hand upon his scarlet sleeve, heart in mouth.

Once through the elegant portals, their capes were numbered and whisked away by a footman who directed them to a large hall on the left where the Master of Ceremonies announced them in booming voice. A waltz was already in progress and the atmosphere was one of intense vivacity. The house had been hired from a coach builder and the ballroom, once used to keep carriages in, was papered with a pattern of trellises and roses. It was a stifling night and the French windows had been flung open. Sweat gleamed on the overclad officers' brows who trod the paces of the dance with unflagging chivalry.

The Duchess, a slightly angular, but not ungraceful matron, sailed forth to receive them and respectfully enquired after the absent Peachums. "As you see, everyone is on the tiptoe of expectation!"

"Uncle seems to think we shall be on the move tomorrow, Your Grace," Robert told her.

His enthusiasm was ill-concealed. She sighed sadly. "The Prince is here and Uxbridge and Lord Hill, but all remain maddeningly tight-lipped."

Sir Thomas Picton, commander of the 5th Division, shambled up behind her. He was a garrulous Welshman approaching sixty, stout in the beam, who made few concessions to the social graces. "Look you, boy, none of Perponcher's officers is here. Tis my belief the Dutch-Belgian Brigade have defied orders and advanced."

With the merest suggestion of distaste, his hostess detached from the hand clasped upon her shoulder. "I dare say Wellington will clarify matters when he arrives."

They took glasses of champagne offered by a waiter. Eagerly, Kate scanned the room but saw no familiar face among the mosaic of bright uniforms. On the spur of the moment, she turned to Robert. "By the by," she said, "do you happen to know Viscount Penrose?"

To her utter amazement, he nodded. "Devilish odd you should mention him. Ran into him only yesterday at Lady Conyngham's. Cavalry man. King's Dragoons. Have you met him?"

Faint with joy, she modestly lowered her gaze, "I...I was a governess to his niece when I made my infamous disappearance."

"I see."

"How did he strike you?"

"Decent sort of fellow."

"Was he...in good spirits?"

It required no special perspicacity to know that she was struggling to keep her voice level. "In excellent spirits, I'd say, judging by the way he paid court to all the ladies."

Kate choked back the lump in her throat and promptly switched tack. "Is the young gentleman talking to Georgiana Lennox not one of General Maitland's aides?"

"Ensign Lord Hay, yes."

"How youthful he looks to be fighting for his country."

"Shall we dance?" was Robert's only reply.

His sister was circling the room with her Guards officer. Captain Mottram had been quick to single her out. Mr Fenton took out his quizzing-glass in quest of a fine pair of male calves, but presently left off and established himself in a corner of the orangery to play cards. A group of privates from the Royal Highlanders were about to entertain the company with reels and sword-dances to the music of their own pipes. Fleet of foot in their tartan hose, the brawny soldiers displayed such infectious zest that they called forth loud cheers and encores. One daring damsel plucked a flower from her bosom and threw it to the tallest. Immediately others followed her example. Grinning with pleasure, the clansmen executed neat twirls for their benefit.

Shortly after midnight, the Commander-in-Chief made his entrance. The orchestra stuck up Handel's *Conquering Hero*. He waved the accolade aside. Picton broke the deadly hush which had settled upon the room.

"What's afoot, Duke? Is it war?"

"Yes, it is war. We leave tomorrow."

The ladies cast anxious eyes upon their beaux, husbands, fathers, sons, nephews. Elation shone in the men's faces. "By God!" cried Hay, "we'll show Boney he's no match for the 1st

Foot!"

"Let the ball proceed," said the Duke to his hostess. "I won't have it said that my officers are disobliging to their ladies. Let the Corsican's informants in this city think we have been taken unawares."

Robert seized Kate and gave her a triumphant kiss. It was hard; impersonal. Her heart was too full to speak. For the dancers, fear found expression in high-strung merriment. One by one, officers paid their final tributes and left for their respective regiments. The music continued as though victory depended upon it.

In the midst of it all, few noticed the harassed despatch rider, red of face, stride into the ballroom in mud-spattered jackboots. The long awaited intelligence from Mons had arrived. Wellington's Generals converged upon him, seeing his fiery consternation. "Napoleon has humbugged me, by God! He is striking north instead of west. He means to cut me adrift from Blücher."

Uxbridge gave a low whistle. "So that's his cunning game, is it? He drives a wedge between us and the Prussians and aims to defeat each in turn."

"Charleroi has fallen. He has crossed the Sambre. He has stolen a march on us of twenty-four hours." The Iron Duke turned to his host. "Have you a good map, Richmond?"

"Come into my study, gentlemen. We shall not be disturbed there."

All the military brains of the Anglo-Allied powers pored over the linen-backed map spread out on His Grace of Richmond's desk. De Lancey, the young American Chief of Staff, sank into despair. He had exhausted himself sending out Wellington's concentration orders that afternoon and knew full well that they would do more to promote Napoleon's advance than impede it.

The Duke, however, remained unruffled. Coolly, he placed a

well-manicured forefinger on the crossroads marked *Quatre Bras*. "We are too late to halt him here," he speculated. "If it comes to the worst, we will allow him to drive us back and trap him *here*. I have studied the terrain and know it well. There is a wide ridge called *Mont St Jean* and we shall take full advantage of it. If the Prussians are beat, which I think very probable, that is the spot where we must lick those fellows."

Everyone's attention was riveted on the village of Waterloo.

"Uxbridge, alert the cavalry! Picton, rouse your Division! We march in three hours!"

Eight

Lavender-grey dawn spread over a city in ferment.

Assembly bugles sounded the clarion-call. Drums beat a tattoo that throbbed in the blood and brain. All over Brussels, soldiers tumbled out of billets, half-dressed, steeped in sleep, their knapsacks thrust over their shoulders. Officers scurried from the *Rue de la Blanchisserie* in their dancing pumps. Sobbing wives, clutching round-eyed infants, others clinging to their skirts, thronged the *Place Royale* where the regiments were forming. Sweethearts pressed amulets into the hands of their lovers. The Square was ablaze with infantry uniforms, contrasting the Blue of the Horse Guards and Light Dragoons, the dark green of the Riflemen, the black of the Brunswickers. The Scots Greys, far from ben and burn, rallied to the pipes of their homeland. Privates bustled about loading up baggage-wagons and supply carts with sacks of corn, nosebags, horseshoes, bandages, gun carriages with arms, canteens with fresh water, gin for the privates and brandy for the officers and a modicum of port wine for the Duke. Unlike Napoleon, whose soldiers had to fend for themselves, Wellington held the view that his army marched on its stomach and he took good care to feed it. The penalties for foraging were severe.

Entangled in the mêlée were the market stallholders whose carts always came jogging into town before civilised folk were abroad. Old Flemish women in black shawls and skirts leaned on great baskets of potatoes and turnips, strawberries and lettuces, and gaped at the noisy incursion this Friday morning, causing some colourful vernacular among the troops.

General Peachum rose at four-thirty and partook of light pastries and strong coffee before he left. "Lock up the stables.

Keep a guard on the horses, m'dear," he said cheerfully. "If we don't make short work of Frog, you'll need 'em."

Robert had no time to say good-bye to his aunt. Leaving the ball, he made straightway for the *Place Royale* in search of Colborne. Anne, Kate and Mr Fenton, caught up in the drama, rode with him in the carriage, jostling its way through the beleaguered streets. Residents waved and cheered from wide-open windows.

"Only fancy," Anne said, "a year ago we were all rejoicing over the Peace. Uncle Henry described scenes such as this when the Sovereigns came."

Kate thought of London last August, with Edward Grey and the Stewarts. How long ago and far away it seemed. She was so fretted by emotion and lack of sleep that detachment engulfed her. Yet everything appeared to her in explicit detail. Today would be forever graven upon her memory.

Reaching the Square, they alighted and took their leave of Robert. He hardly belonged to them now. Fenton shook hands with him and wished him in clover; the girls hugged him. They watched him thread his way through the crowd and join ranks with his comrades. Some of the regiments had already marched away, others were poised to commence.

The English cavalry was finely caparisoned and mounted on the purest bred horses in the world, Lord Edward Somerset's Guards in burnished helmets sporting curved plumes.

"There are the Blues!" Anne burst out, eyes peeled for the gallant Captain Mottram. "Come, let us move closer."

Kate followed her. In the multitude it was hard to keep in contact. "Tell me," she said, panting for breath, "which are the King's Dragoons? Are they here?"

The answer came from an unexpected quarter. "Indeed, ma'am, they are!" affirmed a debonair officer against whose back Kate had brushed. He had on a crested helmet. Two gold epaulettes stood proud upon his shoulders. His crimson coat was heavily braided and bore a crown badge of rank. A white sash, breeches and spatterdashes, black boots with brass spurs and a gleaming scabbard completed the regalia.

Touching the peak of his headgear, he turned to confront her and great was his stupefaction. Her heart sang for joy.

It was Leo!

Lieutenant-Colonel Penrose, 1st Dragoon Guards, was speechless. Afterwards he could not be sure that something in Kate's voice had not registered subconsciously. The next moment she was being squeezed against a colonnade of bright buttons. "Kate! My life! What in the name of all that's sacred are you doing here?"

"I'm staying with friends at General Peachum's house," she gabbled excitedly. "Your letter did not reach me until yesterday. Oh Leo!"

"To think you've been here in Brussels and I didn't know!" He took in the significance of her evening gown, the train which had been draped over her wrist now slithering down to the cobblestones. "You have been to some splendid romp by the look of you!"

"I've been to the Duchess of Richmond's ball!"

"Have you, by Jove! I wish I'd been there!"

He sought her left hand and satisfied himself that the fingers were unadorned. "So I still have the pleasure of addressing *Miss Hanslope*."

She became suddenly serious. "Leo, you remember our first night in Brighton?"

"I had rather remember your first night at Silvercragg," he teased in an undertone. "Yes, I recall it perfectly."

"You told me that when you returned from the Peninsula, you had no one in England... No one to care..."

"It is no longer so," he said earnestly, tilting her face

upwards. Clasping her tightly, he gave her a desperate farewell kiss.

A bawdy cheer went up from some of the cavalry mounted behind him. An audacious sergeant yelled: "Give her one from me, Penny!" which had the company within earshot in an uproar. Lieutenant-Colonel Penrose wished them at the deuce and told Kate he must leave or there would be a breach of discipline in the ranks. He planted another kiss upon her brow. "Keep your spirits high." Then, receiving the reins from a groom, he swung himself into the saddle of his charger and hailed a hopeful young cornet. "Horner!"

"Sir?"

"See that you capture an Eagle for this lady!"

"Yes, sir! Begging your pardon, sir, would it be worth a captaincy?"

His lordship grinned. "Damn your impudence, boy! You'll go far!"

The stragglers had been whipped into line and the cavalcade was on the verge of departure. On an impulse and in defiance of the proprieties, Miss Hanslope proceeded to lift her skirts a fraction and rip a length of white lace-edged ribbon from her petticoat which she tossed to her lover amid a chorus of whistles. It was decorously contrived. "Farewell, soldier. Farewell! Put Boney to rout and come back safely."

Leo touched the fluttering lace to his lips and looped it through a buttonhole. "My oath upon it, lady."

"I'll marry you, sir, if you do!"

Leo let out an unashamed whoop of delight. The line lurched into motion as he snapped out his commands. "Au revoir, then, Kate. Au Revoir, not Adieu!"

So, setting his face towards combat with that impatience for action which women never understand, he moved off and did not look back. Kate stood stock still while the regiment filed past, harnesses jingling, accoutrements flashing, in the background the thrilling beat of the drums, the shrilling of fifes. Down the *Rue de Namur* the cavalry went, through the Namur Gate and out into the pastoral countryside of Flanders where the sun was rising. Larks sang high in the celestial blue and all thought of war was remote.

Throughout Friday, Brussels waited in suspense. At intervals the thunder of distant cannonading brought the nervous citizens rushing into the streets to confer with one another. The partisans of Bonaparte, of whom there were a fair number, maintained that Wellington's forces had been massacred and were in retreat. The Emperor had promised his soldiers the sack of the city and Brussels would be in enemy hands by nightfall.

The squeamish fled. Old Louis in Ghent put his horses into harness and prepared to make himself scarce. The hard-driven landaus of retreating civilians met with a train of artillery caissons and supply wagons coming up from the seaports. Between Ostend and Brussels and Brussels and Antwerp, the *chausées* were in chaos and many vehicles overturned.

At number *49, Rue Ducale*, the deserted womenfolk paced about the salon in a dismal state of apprehension, walked in the Park, received a steady stream of callers, all come to air the latest conjectures which soon took on the authenticity of facts, and made endless depredations on the teapoy. Mr Fitzroy Fenton's vanity was boosted by being constantly applied to by the female visitors for his opinion, and presently, after a hearty dinner and three glasses of port, he rode down to the Namur Gate and along the Charleroi road to see what information could be gleaned.

Two hours later he returned. A courier had come into the city from the scenes of battle and posted up placards announcing that the Duke of Wellington had halted General Ney's forces at the *Quatre Bras* crossroads.

What the placards did not say was that the Baron de

Perponcher, whose officers had failed to turn up at the Richmond ball, had disregarded his Chief's concentration orders and had advanced with his Netherlands force to meet Ney on the previous night, thus regaining some of the precious time which had been lost.

What the placards also did not admit was that although Blücher had fought valiantly at Ligny all day against Napoleon himself, his army had been, in Wellington's own words, 'damnably mauled' and was now retreating in considerable disorder.

Early on Saturday morning, the muted reverberations of the firing started again. As the day passed and the heat became intense, a steady band of wounded soldiers staggered back to the city, many falling exhausted to die by the wayside. At the Namur and Louvain gates, tents were erected to treat them, blankets and pillows requisitioned and any old linen that could be torn up for bandages. The good burghers of Brussels threw open their homes to all and sundry and the apothecaries' shops supplied dressings free of charge. Society ladies rolled up their gauzy sleeves, donned pinafores and toiled alongside their *femmes de chambre* to bring relief to the suffering.

Every so often a contingent of cavalrymen, Germans or Netherlanders, would come charging into the town on foam-flecked steeds, scattering whatever lay in their path and crying that the French were at their heels.

Panic grew. Everything on wheels and hooves was sought out by the timorous whose ranks were hourly multiplying to add to the same confusion as the day before.

It transpired that the British were withdrawing, still fighting, to the valley south of Waterloo. Unknown to the defeatists, it was exactly what Wellington had planned.

The heat was suffocating. Not a breath of wind stirred the

air. By late afternoon, anvil-shaped clouds the colour of bruises, darkened the sky.

Huge drops of rain began to rebound off the dusty, blood-stained cobbles.

The heavens opened.

All night, water cascaded down as though from great vats to drench just and unjust. Sulphurous streaks of lightning forked the darkness. Both armies slept out in a quagmire, under cloaks if they were lucky and amidst the flattened rye. Seasoned campaigners smeared themselves in clay and spent the night in relative comfort.

At the village inn at Waterloo, which Wellington had made his base, he was disturbed at two in the morning with a message from Blücher. The intrepid old Marshal, so beloved of Londoners the previous summer, instead of fleeing east along his lines of communication, as Napoleon had supposed, had marched north to Wavre. He told the Duke that he was prepared to join him as soon as possible with what forces he could muster.

"Then we shall do the business today," Wellington informed Lieutenant-Colonel Gordon, his aide, with martial resolution. "We shall stand and fight."

Mist wreathed the valley when the first trumpet sounded. The shivering troops stirred to a cheerless morning and tried to restore the circulation to stiff and aching limbs.

It was the last day many of them would see dawn.

As the clouds lifted and a brassy sun showed through, their clothes started to steam. Camp fires were coaxed into flame and a breakfast of porridge and thick slabs of bacon sizzled and boiled. Afterwards, upon officers' instructions, the men cleaned their weapons, roughly honing swords to inflict the deadliest damage.

Cannon, rifle and muskets had to be thoroughly dried.

Soon the tapering black shakos of the infantry, the red wide-topped shakos of the Dragoons, the bearskins of the Highlanders, the crested helmets of the Guards, the cocked hats of the field officers, all the mighty array of headgear denoting rank and regiment, was deployed in fine rows.

Presently, the familiar gentleman with the aquiline profile, in plain dark blue coat and hat minus cockade, came cantering down from the elm tree under which had had stationed himself at an unsteady baize table brought out from the inn. Accompanied by his staff, he rode up and down inspecting his lines and appeared quite as at ease as if he were riding to a Meet in the Shires of England. Now and then he raised his Dollond telescope to peer at the opposition across the valley. They were in no haste to attack.

Light flashed off the cuirassiers' steel and the formidable tines of the lancers as they manoeuvred, pennons fluttering. The wily Corsican warrior was indulging himself in a brilliant exhibition of his power and might in an attempt to undermine his adversary. Shouts of *'Vive L'Empereur!'* carried in a triumphant crescendo across to the Allied lines.

"A pretty parade," commented the Duke drily. "What say you, Hay?"

A terrible awe suffused the lad's countenance. He marvelled that his Chief could remain so impassive. "It's magnificent, Your Grace."

"Flatters himself he can daunt us," grunted Picton. "John Bull don't quake at a mere piece of theatre. Boldness in action's the thing!"

Wellington said nothing. He was soberly estimating the strength of the foe and had to concede that it would be no runaway victory. The slaughter would be extensive.

"I reckon we can put up a damned good fight," claimed Maitland with cautious optimism.

De Lancey came riding up on his blue roan. "Any sign of Bulow?" enquired the Duke, anticipating that the Prussian reinforcements would soon arrive.

The newcomer's brow was furrowed. "Nothing, Your Grace. Last night's storm has turned the roads to soup."

Wellington grimaced and offered de Lancey the use of his telescope. "See how Napoleon whips up the blood of his men. Tis a mighty fine spectacle, to be sure."

De Lancey peered hard down the barrel, panning from left to right. "The mud in the valley's still pretty thick. Do you think he means to hold off until it's drier?"

"I imagine so. This delay is not his usual style, however," mused the Duke, wondering whether his opponent's reluctance signified a state of mind that might be turned to advantage later.

"Our men are chafing for action."

"But we shall keep our powder dry, de Lancey. We shall not provoke an attack. Whilst the Eagle displays his plumage, we are gaining time."

A kestrel, suspended on tremulous wings for what seemed an eternity, plummeted like a stone to capture some small furry creature scuttling out of the rye.

Earlier that morning at *Le Caillou*, the farmhouse the French Generals had commandeered for their quarters, Napoleon raged and fretted about the murderous state of the ground and would not listen to the opinions of his staff who were all for slashing a swathe through the Allied lines and dining in Brussels that evening. His sudden frustrating mood of indecision perturbed them at so crucial a stage when *La Gloire* was within an ace of their grasp.

But Napoleon was febrile and in pain with a re-occurrence of his old complaint, cystitis, brought on by cold and damp, the bugbear of his long campaigns. He realised that in the heat of triumph over Blücher at Ligny, he had made the vital error of letting the Prussians out of his sight and had since despatched Marshal Grouchy to tail them. It was not impossible that they intended to rendezvous with Wellington and that must be prevented at all costs.

He glared at the ever-changing sky, rays of sun playing hide-and-seek between hillocks of cloud.

"We will mount an attack on the left at noon," he decided at last. He drove his fist into his palm and turned sullen eyes upon Ney. "I shall hammer them with my infantry, charge them with my cavalry to make them show themselves and when I am quite sure where the actual English are, I shall go straight at them with my Old Guard!"

For Wellington, superb at the art of defence, did not possess Napoleon's Gallic ostentation and the little Emperor had no idea what forces were drawn up on the reverse slope of *Mont St Jean*.

Leo had had the good fortune to pass the night in a shared tent with straw for a pillow and a blanket to cover him. Against the din of thunder and driving rain, the murmurous sounds of coupling infiltrated his shallow sleep, the tender attentions of those redoubtable wives and sweethearts who had followed the drum and knew not what the morrow would bring.

He awoke at the first hint of dawn, braced in every sinew and nerve and obscurely elated. Three hours earlier, he had received a message from Uxbridge who headed the whole of the British cavalry, that the Prussians were on the way and Wellington was making a stand.

Sunday June 18th, 1815. Today the world's future and his own would be decided. He had a reckless urge to tempt fate or God, or whatever it was out there that presided over the destinies of men, to arbitrate in the question of his own worth. His past had been dogged by a deep-seated conviction of moral inequality which hitherto had brought all his best endeavours at close relationships to nought.

When the camp fires were lit, his batman brought hot water for shaving. Leo snatched a clean shirt from his saddle-bag, singing snatches of airs from *The Marriage of Figaro* in a tuneful tenor voice.

Swirling mist dissolved over the battered fields of barley, wheat and rye, grown nearly as tall as a man. An opal light shone about the horizon, tinting the walls of the *Château Hougoumont* to the west of the valley with violet, rose and gold. The building was garrisoned by British Guards, Hanoverians and Nassauers. He could see them moving about the woods and blossom-bereft orchards making ready for the day.

And while he stood in contemplation, savouring the rare sweetness of the air, soon to be corrupted by the stench of sulphur, blood and smoke, he was filled with a certainty that the fortress would hold, come what may.

Across the chequered plains behind him, the Waterloo church bell chimed for Mass.

At quarter past eleven, Napoleon, fired with a fatalistic courage, clapped on his bicorne and grasped the reins of his grey charger, Marengo.

Slowly he rode down from the French lines with a marvellous show of bravado and traversed the hollow towards *Hougoumont*. Every muscle in the Allied camp tensed. During those moments he was an easy target but honour forbade them to exploit the opportunity. Suddenly a volley of cheering broke the stillness. Infantry began to pour down the slopes, batteries of cannon were drawn up at his rear.

"Gentlemen," the Duke cordially addressed his staff under the elm tree, "it is about to commence. If the Prussians come up in time, we shall have a long peace. And if they don't, please God the result will be the same."

The almighty rumble of discharging cannon heralded the opening of the battle which would spare mankind from tyranny.

By half past one, all the legions of hell had broken loose and still the Prussians did not come. Explosions of rocket fire, highly inaccurate, lit up the field. Palls of acrid smoke stung the sinuses and parched the throat. Dying men fell down upon dead, impaled upon lances, butchered by sabres, their screams lost in the whine of shot and bursting shell.

Napoleon's prime objective had been to engage the extreme right and left of Wellington's lines, turn them, and open a breach in the centre. Now the thinning columns showed that he had every chance of succeeding.

It was then that Picton's division, supported by the cavalry, came into its own. Wellington had directed them to retire well back from the ridge to avoid the worst of the barrage of French artillery as shot ricocheted up the bank. Concealing themselves behind hedges, they awaited the onslaught. They could no longer see the enemy's progress but they could hear it. Half an hour slipped by. Then, abruptly, the firing ceased. The sound of drums beating the relentless slow march increased in volume. Shouts of *Vive L'Empereur!* rent the air. Coming over a mound on the right, the foremost ranks met with a hail of shot from the Rifle Brigade and fell back, every dazzling man jack of them. Those behind were thrown into disarray and hastily tried to reform. Seizing his advantage, Picton urged the Scottish infantry forward: "Rise up! Fire!" They burst through the hedges, three thousand men conjured out of the brimstone mists, bayonets poised, muskets discharging. "Charge! Charge! Hurrah!" cried Picton in an apotheosis of zeal. His moment of glory was his final one. No sooner had he given the command than a bullet in the skull sent him toppling off his horse.

Some distance away, the Earl of Uxbridge saw what was happening and immediately ordered his waiting cavalry, tightly packed to charge. "Now! In with you, my lads!" The Household Brigade, the Blues, the Lifeguards and the King's Dragoon Guards took the hedges like steeplechasers and in a vast rolling wave of red and blue and flashing steel bore down on the astonished French, many of whom, sooner than fight hopelessly, lay down and feigned death. Matchless in courage, if not always in discipline, the rum in the veins of the British cavalry and the corporate pounding of hoofbeats intoxicated them to a pitch of ecstasy so that, rising up in their stirrups, they milled through the French infantry, sabres flailing, driving them back, fighting hand to hand as they went, and did not hear the trumpet's recall. On they pursued, right up the opposite slope and past the enemy lines to be set upon and scattered in turn by a savage horde of lancers and Kellermann's famed cuirassiers.

Galloping down from *Mont St Jean* and sweeping through the valley, the reedy wind upon his face and an edge to his sword and his senses, Leo knew a timeless moment of apperception. Scenes from the past shimmered up before him and were gone. He knew the transience of pleasure and pain, of life itself, and the tarnished vault of heaven unfurling in a soft iridescence to disclose the resolution of all conflict. Eternal peace.

His terrified mount reared. There was the grinding clash of steel upon steel, the searing fulgence of a cuirass splattered with blood, a quintessence of pain, fading, ebbing away. An Armageddon of brute legs and hooves.

Lieutenant-Colonel Penrose slumped into the mire.

All afternoon fugitives from the embattled plains beyond the *Forêt de Soignes* flocked into Brussels, bewildered peasants, panic-stricken hussars fresh from the unimagined horrors of Waterloo. As fast as they came, civilians fled. Chaos piled upon chaos and many knew not where to turn.

In the *Rue Ducale*, they passed a third day in suspense. Mr Fenton strongly favoured leaving for Ostend. Mrs Peachum might have acquiesced had it not been for the younger women who would not countenance so base a betrayal of their loved ones. Kate could not eat. Tense and listless, she sat down at the General's escritoire and composed a letter to the Stewarts in London, telling of her sorrow at their dual bereavement and how fond she had been of Fiona. She thanked them for their goodness and said how happy her term with them had been. She supposed she ought to have written earlier, but it had seemed prudent not to open up that chapter of her life. She mentioned that she had seen Lord Penrose in the Place Royale riding off with his regiment, "as though," she said, "he had some score to settle with life."

She folded the page firmly and decided not to commit it to the post until matters were resolved.

Around two o' clock, when the party came in from an airing along the Allée Verte, Kate went to her room to change her footwear. Her red morocco shoes were soaked from the drenched grass. Far away, the sporadic rumbling of cannon could be heard. Wringing her hands, she went to the window and sighed wretchedly for all the prayers she could not articulate. The little pink and white Louis Quinze clock chimed the quarter hour. Suddenly, something smote at the core of her being. She was steeped in black and bitter melancholy. Dear Lord, do not say his hour has come! Instantly, she was down on her knees in impassioned supplication. She prayed as she had never prayed before, unclenching her body in the most positive act she could perform.

When a degree of calm had been achieved, she went into the salon and tried to persuade her hostess that Anne and herself ought to be doing their patriotic duty by tending the injured rather than filling their time with pointless tasks. "For," said she,

"I have never in my life been so unoccupied and never so in desperate want of occupation. What is stitchery when men are giving life and limb for us!"

The General's lady was horrified. "My dear, how full of restless energy you are! The tents of the wounded are no fit place for a lady of delicate sensibilities."

"Dear ma'am," Kate implored, "often I have waited upon the sick in my father's parish. I may suppose that many a lady of rank is less qualified than I…"

"Child, child, you allow your heart to govern your head. Are the sick of your father's parish to be compared with the horrendous casualties of a battlefield?"

Kate glanced towards Anne in a plea for support.

"Tis very pretty in you, Miss Hanslope, to be sure," interjected Mr Fenton, "but Pammie's in the right of it. Saw a fellow once, had his claret tapped at a meeting of the Four-in-Hand Club. Devilish business!"

His sister scowled at this crass comment and turned to her niece's impetuous friend. "Pray forgive the admonition, but…"

"Aunt, you underestimate our courage," Anne said. "I should dearly like to help."

"Well!" breathed Mrs Peachum on a shuddering note of outrage. "It seems that I must yield to pressure. Fitzroy, oblige me by pouring a generous measure of the General's sherry wine!"

Nothing could have prepared either Kate or Anne for the hours of harrowing toil which followed. Again and again, they had to brace themselves to continue. They vowed they would not prove to be vapourish females. What was their suffering beside the gruesome afflictions of the soldiers stumbling past the Namur Gate with bandaged heads, contused eyes and lacerated limbs, ragged uniforms hanging about them caked in mud and congealing blood? The girls ran back and forth to the chemist for supplies of lint, hartshorn, smelling bottles, witch hazel, emollients, anything which might bring relief to the ailing men. They listened to the last incoherent messages of the dying, received tokens destined for loved ones back in England. They knelt in the dust and sponged and dressed wounds, seeing bowl after bowl of clear water incarnadined. Kate hated with a passionate hatred, the tyrant who had done this to her countrymen, who had slain myriads in a ruthless pursuit of his own grandiose ideals. Fighting for composure, she prayed for grace. Her chest ached with a fiercely repressed desire to weep. Would she ever eradicate the primeval stench of blood from her nostrils?

As nimbly as they worked, more victims arrived. Tilt-carts of wounded constantly rattled into the city, jarring the agonised men aboard them, prostrated on straw and swigging dregs of gin and rum to deaden their pain. Word that Napoleon was on the doorstep spread fast. In the face of such devastation, it was hard to disbelieve it, despite the testimony of a courageous young Rifleman who described how he and his comrades had stood their ground when Count d'Erlon's troops came at them and how the Household and Union Brigades had launched a simultaneous counter-attack and swept across the valley in a thundering diagonal. "Slashed 'em to ribbons," he boasted. "Cut 'em down to a man!"

As evening approached, Kate's own troubles vanished. She became inured to the sights around her. She was numb through and through.

She was ministering to a lancer who had had a musket ball and a good deal of splintered bone removed from his ribs, when she was jolted out of her absorption. Straining to support the man while he took languid sips of water, she chanced to look up as two harassed orderlies passed by, a stretcher between them. The soldier upon it, covered in a horse blanket, would not have merited a second glance had it not been for the remnant of filthy scalloped lace dangling from the tattered coat across the foot of the stretcher.

"My petticoat! Oh...! It is Leo!"

Forsaking the poor lancer, she hurried to the stretcher-bearers and nervously pulled back the cover. The iron went out of her.

Recognition flickered over the cadaverous face. He gazed up at her through narrowed lids, gazed but barely focused. His shirt was gashed. His shoulders and chest were swaddled in red-stained bandages. She saw to her horror that his right arm had gone.

"Been to the sawbones, ma'am," explained one of the men, not without sympathy, "in the farm cottage at *Mont St Jean*. Poor devils are queueing for the blade."

"Where... are you going?"

"To the *Hôtel de Ville*, ma'am. That's where the Colonel was quartered."

Kate's hands flew to her trembling mouth. She could stem the tide of tears no longer. He was alive! Leo was alive! "T-take him," she stammered, "please take him to number *49, Rue Ducale,* General Peachum's apartments. Ask them to send for his valet. I will come presently."

At Waterloo, the inferno still raged and there was no telling which way it would go.

At long last, around five o' clock, some of the tardy Prussians made their appearance. Bulow's corps emerged from Paris Wood to the left of Wellington's line and augmented the repulse from the crest of the hill. Having attempted to throw Grouchy off their scent, they had come through fire and water to assist the Duke, dragging cannon axle-deep through slurry and negotiating an outbreak of fire in the narrow streets of Wavre which had hindered them considerably.

Napoleon was having a tough time trying to break the

British squares. Over and over again, his horsemen would encircle the formations, stiff with bayonets, and find no means of pitching in. As Wellington observed to the ubiquitous Mr Creevey, everything depended upon his infantry.

Two hours later, when Ziethen's Prussians came up in support, Napoleon had to concede the possibility of defeat. His only hope was to make a daring bid for victory. He decided to risk all and throw in his Middle and Old Guard, the cream of his troops, and drive the immovable British off their pedestal.

"*À Bruxelles, mes enfants! À Bruxelles!*" he roared, fling wide his greatcoat and flashing his row of medals at them.

"*Vive L'Empereur!*" they chorused yet again, and began to whistle the Marseillaise as they trod in unison to the swelling beat of drums.

Nearer they advanced, pressing up the slope. Whatever Wellington's feelings were, he did not betray them, standing in readiness beside the 1st Footguards. "Now Maitland! Now's your time!"

"Stand up, Guards!" shouted Maitland. "Show them what you're made of!"

Up they sprang, out of the corn, and loosed off a volley of shots at point-blank range. Confounded, the rival guards were forced to give ground but rallied with all speed.

It was at this juncture that Sir John Colborne unexpectedly delivered the coup de grâce, stepping in with his invincible Fighting 52nd, one of the few battalions that was up to strength on that fateful day and one of the few which had remained so throughout the feud. On his own initiative, he took the 52nd out of line and when the French drew level, cried: "Right shoulders forward!" and wheeled his columns round against the enemy's flank. It was a brilliant tactic but fraught with risk. Taken off guard, the French began to discharge their weapons in panic – Colborne lost one hundred and forty men – but the sacrifice was slight in comparison to the casualties caused by his battalion's reply.

The Imperial Guard broke rank and fled. Their terror spread like an epidemic. Soon the whole French Army was throwing down arms to make a rapid exodus from the corpse-strewn plain. Never had the British Generals seen anything like it. Down the Charleroi *chausée* the enemy swarmed towards France, all notion of glory vanquished.

For Wellington, the weary campaign was over. The battle fought against tremendous odds with his 'infamous army' was won.

The last of the smoke thinned and vanished. The gilded edges of the clouds died. Dusk and sober reflection set in. Outside the aptly named inn of *La Belle Alliance*, a jubilant Blücher embraced the English Commander, not a demonstrative man himself, exclaiming: *"Mein lieber Kamerad,"* and adding for good measure. *"Quelle Affaire!"* which, according to Wellington, was about all the French the old warrior knew.

But later, when a hoary mist descended to screen the moonlight, the Duke rode alone through the lugubrious valley, the runnels of tears upon his cheeks unseen. So many of his confederates were gone. Picton, Ponsonby of the Union Brigade, Gordon, his aide, whose death he felt most sorely of all, young Lord Hay, but seventeen years old. The Earl of Uxbridge had had his leg shattered by shell and subsequently amputated. The Duke's demeanour was seldom an index of his emotions. He himself had neither flirted with danger nor avoided it. During eight or nine hours of unremitting conflict, he had been present among those troops about to go into action, encouraging them with his level-headed appraisal of the situation. In the teeth of failure, he had been conscious that the finger of God was upon him.

Now the groans of the injured, who lay forgotten where they fell, were all about him. Looters armed with knives moved shiftily among them. The ditches around *Hougoumont* which had borne the heat of the day and had been stoutly defended by Coldstreamers, were choked with the bodies of six thousand men. Running water for miles around was the colour of claret and no use for slaking thirst. In one place, the slain described a perfect square. The East Lancashire Regiment had been completely wiped out, not one of them lived to beget a new generation that would learn of his father's valour in securing the freedom of the 'sceptr'd isle'.

"Except a defeat," Wellington said afterwards, "a victory is the greatest tragedy in the world."

Immediately he learned of the Viscount's predicament, Wardle, his faithful valet, refused to wait for horses to be put into harness and came galloping up from the *Grand Place* on a borrowed mount. He had with him a bundle of clean clothes and effects such as a gentleman might need in the circumstances. These included a flask of the best vintage cognac. A dishevelled Kate met him upon the stairs. She was clearly tired and overwrought. "Oh Wardle, how good it is to see you!" she hailed him, grasping both his hands warmly, the formality of their Silvercragg days forgotten. "I am so glad you are come."

"Miss Hanslope, tis a fine sight you are, though the bloom be gone from your cheeks," he responded, his Celtic origins coming to the fore as was often the case in moments of stress or pleasure. "God be praised that his lordship's life has been spared." He crossed himself and enquired after the master.

"He is in agony, to be sure. Not aware of his surroundings at all. We have sent for a physician, but as you can imagine, they are hard-pressed. I can only pray that Lord Penrose will come through."

"I understand tis his right arm that's gone?"

Kate nodded woefully. "Would it had been his left."

Wardle was eager to look on the bright side. He tugged at his chin. "Twas his Bayonne shoulder, the site of a previous wound. He'd a vast deal of pain from that at times, though he'd have died sooner than admit it."

A vision of those scars she had once tenderly traced with lips and fingertips in the voluptuous softness of a shared feather bed brought a raking sadness to Kate's heart. "Fate does have a wicked propensity for dealing blows in the same spot," she sighed. She led Wardle up to the Peachums' quarters. Through the finely parted doors of Robert's room, the sick man could be glimpsed, crazed with fever. Kate hesitated on the threshold. "He is in a grave condition, I warn you."

Lord Penrose was in the throes of delirium, his glistening head wrenching from side to side. The texture of his grey-tinged skin looked as artificial as wax. When his lids parted, he seemed to peer through burning mists, unseeing. Blood was soaking through the sheets. Camille, mastering his Continental excitability, had had the good sense to remove milord's hessians by slitting the seams with a pocket knife in order to spare him further torture.

"Ah, Camille, merci, merci. Vous êtes très gentil. Ce gentilhomme est ici vous assister."

Kate had to grit her teeth, watching Leo writhe. She wrung out a cloth at the washstand and pressed the cool dampness upon his brow. "Form on me, Guards," he moaned. "It's Jacquinot's men! Left, limber up and as fast as you can!"

"He is consumed with heat," Kate said, shoving back her disordered hair.

Wardle patted her hand kindly. "Away wid you now, Miss Kate. I engage to take good care of him for you. Forty winks is what you need."

She consented gratefully. "Send for me, won't you, if there's any change?"

"He's a lusty fellow, his lordship. He'll come about," Wardle said.

The *bonne* was scuttling to and fro with canisters of hot water for the bathtub. Kate stripped off her soiled clothes and asked her to burn them. Would she ever rid her system of the smell of blood and humanity? The luxury of warm water and scented soap, thick soft towels and dusting powder, was bliss beyond imagining. She climbed into bed and tried to compose herself, but sleep eluded her.

At twenty minutes to nine, a sharp rap on the street door put an end to her striving. She leapt out of bed and peeped through the window. A chaise was drawn up outside. Let it be Dr Redfern or one of his assistants, she prayed. Deftly, she pulled on starched petticoats and the cotton dress the maid had left out for her.

Washed and hauled back between the sheets, Leo tossed restively. Wardle, stationed in a chair by the bed, jumped to attention when the doctor strode in. He was a brusque, heavy-set man whose own equanimity was frayed by two nights of missed sleep and the harrowing needs of so many patients. He took one look at the Viscount and pronounced that he must be bled expeditiously.

"For the love of God, sir," Kate cried, "has he not spilled enough blood?"

Redfern dealt her a withering sidelong glance. "Madam, if you've no stomach for the procedure, kindly leave the room." He took out his pocket watch and felt Leo's pulse. "When I have bled him and changed the dressings, I will give you a febrifuge to administer every three hours. Be good enough to continue with the cold compresses."

Redfern took out his lancet and demanded a bowl, performing the task in silence. "And now," he said, collecting his instruments together and snapping shut his leather bag, "we can only await the dictates of Providence."

"Oh, sir, please say that he will live," Kate entreated him, unable to stop herself.

The doctor regarded her less severely than at first. "Depend upon it, madam, you need not call for the Sacrament yet! A very good night to you."

Beams of faded gold filled the oncoming dusk and brushed the room with a sanguine lustre.

Wagon-loads of dead in transport to the charnel-house rumbled through the darkness.

But there was a great commotion, great rejoicing in the streets of Brussels that night. Soon the glorious tidings that Boney was beaten reached the *Rue Ducale*. General Peachum was unscathed, and so was Robert Vernon. The General's brigade of Light Dragoons had acquitted itself with honour in a dashing defence of *La Haye Sainte*, the farmhouse close to the Charleroi road below *Mont St Jean*, and Robert's proud boast that his regiment would be Old Hookey's salvation had been vindicated. Tomorrow they were off to Paris to make a triumphant entry into that troubled capital.

Of Captain Mottram there was no news, but in the general exultation, Anne chose to believe the best and fervently hoped that her happiness would not be short-lived.

"Then your noble Colonel did not lose an arm in vain," she consoled Kate.

Of all the bedsides over which Kate had watched, her vigil over Leo's was most thankfully kept.

Vainly did Mrs Peachum appeal to her: "When his lordship returns to full consciousness, then you will wish to be restored and refreshed. I do counsel you, my love, to get some rest. My brother and I can take turns at sitting with him." She sailed into the room in a wrap and a nightcap over her gunmetal grey hair, wielding a branch of candles like Britannia's trident.

"That is exceeding kind of you, ma'am, but I am perfectly content to stay. Wardle is in the passage-way should I need him."

When her hostess had gone, Kate slipped her hand into Leo's and willed him to recover. He tossed and moaned, though not so violently now, muttering a feverish litany. "The château. The château will not hold. The barns are on fire… the roof… *Hougoumont!*"

Dabbing his wet hair, Kate's instinct was to answer him, whether he heard her or not. "The château is safe. Quite safe. There now. According to General Halkett's brother who was here this evening, the Coldstreamers defended it gallantly. The whole of Bonaparte's army is in retreat. Listen to them outside. Listen, my love! The city rejoices tonight. The tyrant was beaten at Waterloo."

The Viscount's body jerked more vigorously. Kate wrestled to keep him from turning on to his right side. It seemed that her crooning could do nothing to quieten him. Presently, he grew alarmingly still. She sought his pulse and then put an ear to his chest. In a wave of sweet and overwhelming relief, she heard the strong, steady rhythm of his heart. Her eyes closed. An uprush of tears squeezed between her lashes. He was at peace. The fever was waning, the crisis past.

It was just before four, as a new day and a new era dawned, that Leo awoke. In the feeble candlelight, the unfamiliar room slowly impinged upon him. Incomprehension was displaced by a hazy remembrance. With the ghost of a smile, he uttered Kate's name.

"My dear love," she said. "Welcome back to the world."

"You look exhausted."

She smiled uncertainly. Whether he should be gentled into knowledge of his handicap or whether he had taken it for granted, she could not tell. "You kept your promise."

"Promise?"

"You sent Boney packing."

"He's beaten?" Leo started up from the pillows and, wincing, slumped back in a welter of pain. "Thank God. Oh thank God. I… I did not dream it, then?" His brows contracted in puzzlement. "There were crowds…in the street… Did I dream that?"

She shook her head. "The château is safe," she ventured softly, "although it is in want of repair."

"The château? *Hougoumont*? They…they set fire to it, the French."

"General Halkett's brother called here last night. He described how the battle had gone. *Hougoumont*, he said, had been under siege all day. It was of paramount importance for the defence of the west .You spoke of it much in your sleep.

"Did I so?" Leo appeared to have no recollection of this. The old keen intelligence was back in his eyes and the drawn visage wanted only his usual spry humour to reanimate it. On his cheeks and chin, the stubble had grown rapidly in the hours of high fever. "What day is it?"

"Monday. Monday, the nineteenth of June."

"Monday?"

"Shall I open the drapes for you?" Kate doused the candle stubs and flung wide the convoluted folds of percale. In its first magic flush, the sky was milky bright with soft curdling clouds.

"Yesterday - can it only be twenty-four hours ago? – I watched the dawn break over Genappe." He turned his head towards her and her heart lurched at the miracle of having him close. She could see that he was frustrated. There was something he urgently wanted to convey, but the right words would not come. "During the morning, as it got lighter, the sky changed. There were hints of rainbows... The château appeared to be made of some pearly, shell-like substance, ethereally frail yet durable… It was unspeakably lovely. And I saw the trampled rye, the camp fires, the weapons scattered about, and thought: In years to come, long after they have finished exhuming our bones and our brass, the land will be tilled and harvested again, the poppies will blow. The blacksmiths will take up our swords and beat them into ploughshares. There will be peace. The soldier's frail thread of energy snapped. He fought for breath. "Hell, I've a raging thirst," he said hoarsely.

"I'll fetch some fresh water for you. What's in the ewer will be stale."

When Kate returned, he half-raised himself upon his left side. Tilting the tumbler, she supported him as best she could. He sank down on the hastily plumped pillow. "How is it possible," he demanded with a resurgence of the old spirit, "to derive such acute sensation in a member that does not exist?"

Turning to place the glass on a console table, Kate breathed a long sigh. The tension slackened in her limbs. All at once she felt exhausted to the utmost degree. Willpower had sustained her during the night. Now, a corner had been turned. Leo was his own man, on the road to recovery. "Dr Redfern left a potion for you," she said. "Do drink some now and I will make you a little gruel."

"No. You have done enough. If I engage to be a model patient and take my medicine, shall you go and lie down?"

Half-reluctantly, she assented. "The girl shall make the gruel. Wardle is outside the door. I roused him a few minutes ago to tell him you were much improved."

"Wardle! Then, pray, ask the good fellow to come in and shave me! I'm certain I am no fit sight for a lady!"

"Leo, dear Leo," she said, smiling through misted eyes and clasping his hand to her cheek. "I am so profoundly relieved."

"You...meant what you said out there in the Square, did you not? Shall Meg have her way?"

"I should be extremely proud," Kate replied, "to be your Lady Penrose."

Thereafter, Leo's recovery was accelerated by the prospect of new horizons. Wellington wrote to him the morning after the battle, a terse but not unaffectionate missive, expressing the desire to see him join his regiment in Paris as soon as he was able. The Viscount grinned ruefully. "Remorseless ogre!"

"Tis not everyone receives the favour of an acknowledgement from Himself," Wardle submitted, for whom the Great Man, a Dubliner born and bred, could do no wrong.

"A couple of days and I shall be ready to travel."

"Holy Mudder! *Why the delay?*"

"We Guards are made of sterling stuff! Not ones to desert the colours! And after Paris, I've matters to settle in England. A visit to Rundell's in Bond Street, I think, for the ring. Then I must seek both the sanction and the good offices of a certain Reverend gentleman in Sussex if I am to be married. Then there is the question of an abigail, extra grooms, a smart carriage..."

"Married, my lord!"

"Yes, and to a clergyman's daughter! Refrain, if you please, from waving the razor about in that perilous fashion. Do have some regard for those faculties I still possess!"

Wardle cast his eyes heavenwards and vowed that Miss Hanslope, for he surmised she must be the lady in the case, did not deserve her misfortune. Leo, rendered mute by the proximity of the blade and the snowy lather applied to the nether half of his countenance, could only scowl and wish his knave of a valet in perdition.

Just then, Mrs Peachum, all brisk and bright, introduced herself and spoon-fed him some gruel.

"I am indebted to you for your hospitality, ma'am, and must beg forgiveness for this imposition."

"Nonsense, young man. It is the least we can do. The General and I were not blessed with sons of our own, you know. You shall stay until you are perfectly mended. Redfern says it will take you a good fortnight!"

"But I am for Paris, ma'am. My regiment rides south this very day."

The full impact of his limitations was borne in upon him. He would probably never sit on a horse again, would never ride to hounds over the dew-flecked heather. Could not fasten Kate so firmly against his heart. Damn! He could! And would!

The gruel was uncommonly palatable and when he had drained the bowl, to Mrs Peachum's immense satisfaction, she asked if anything further might be done to make him comfortable.

"Yes, if you'd be so kind, I'd like a pencil and notepaper."

"Pray, do not exert yourself. I will gladly take dictation for you," she offered. "Heaven forbid that you should suffer a relapse when you are improving by the hour."

"You're the soul of kindness, ma'am, but I shan't need to put you to so much trouble. I intend merely to practise. The sooner I acquire a legible hand, the better."

By the end of the week, nothing would do but that he set out for Paris. Brussels had become a place of sobriety and mourning after the flush of excitement at Napoleon's downfall. The air was as malodorous as the Smithfield shambles on a summer afternoon. Leo was homesick for England, for the velvet Downs of the south and the clean scent of the Cumbrian forests, even for the dusty pavements of London simmering in the heat, and the sugar-loaf white crescents built by Mr Nash. Wardle spruced up his spare uniform, smeared his hessians with a compound of black treacle and best dairy butter, and polished them to an immaculate sheen. He rubbed the brass plate on Leo's shako vigorously upon his cuff. "There now! Sure, tis a turnout fit for a hero!"

Kate surveyed him proudly, a catch in her throat at the limp sleeve hanging by his side. "Soldier, you look fine," she said. "Fine."

Easing on the close-fitting coat over his shirt and bandages had taxed his forbearance somewhat, but he put on a brave face, bone-pale though he was, and stepped smartly out to the waiting vehicle with many avowals of gratitude to the household. It had been their intention to go to Paris themselves, but the General had written advising against it. The city would be hot and overcrowded, barely more salubrious than Brussels. There might be riots when Louis was installed at the Tuileries once again, you never knew with the volatile French.

Kate followed Leo out of doors. There was a taciturn but emotional parting, more fierce and intense than before Waterloo. The expression in his eyes, darkened with love, said everything she could have wished to hear.

"Godspeed, my love," she said under her breath. "Take care of him, Wardle."

"And now, go back to England, to that fine country we fought for, and I will come out of France and fetch you as soon as may be. At a jerk of the reins from Samson, the groom, the horses surged forward, dragging the wheels of the chaise into faster and faster revolutions. Down the street it went, out of sight, towards the *Place du Trône* and past the Gothic fortifications of the *Porte de Hal.*

As they left the city behind and took to the wide open highway, Leo felt that the whole of his past was rolling away. The scars were healing. A new life was about to begin.

Ever After...

They were married one golden Sunday afternoon in late September at the quaint little Saxon church in Merrowdene which was tainted with damp even in the driest summer.

Stellar clusters of Michaelmas daisies winked in the cottage garden; hollyhocks stood high against the wattle walls, lanterns of soft colour. Swallows skimmed around the chimneys, massing for flight.

The sun drenched through the stained windows, dappling the ancient stonework like an open treasure chest. Anthony March gave Kate away. Her father officiated, fumbling for the bright circlet of gold laid upon the freckled pages of the Good Book, centuries old, by Sir George Stewart who had come over from Brighton with his wife to do honours as best man. The Vernons attended and did their utmost to be delighted. It was a quiet and simple affair.

Mrs Hanslope sniffed audibly in the background. Sarah clung to her arm in much the same state. Ruth held herself erect and stared stony-faced ahead of her, of the fixed opinion that Kate did not deserve such happiness. Anthony evinced no particular emotion, but consulted his repeater more often than was polite. Cook and Polly were in transports of delight and Jem Potter grinned wickedly that he'd be the next poor devil to have his neck in the noose. The villagers came to the church door to gape and those who'd foretold that no good would come to Merrowdene's prodigal daughter, swallowed their words and let goodwill prevail when she appeared, radiant, after the ceremony on the arm of her soldier come back from the wars. Children showered them with rose-petals, crushed from hot little fists.

Rosy apple, lemon and pear,
A bunch of roses she shall wear,
Gold and silver by her side,
I know who'll take her as his bride;
Take her by her lily-white hand
And lead her to the altar;
Give her kisses, one, two, three,
Mrs Hanslope's daughter.

Laughing, Leo tossed them the shiniest coins in his pocket and obligingly kissed his bride.

After the wedding breakfast, the couple took their leave, spending and receiving kisses and counsel, tears and pledges.

For the present, they did not plan to return to Cumberland. Although Leo saw no occasion to extend the period of mourning for Cassandra, he did not consider it politic at this stage to parade his new wife before the world. Besides, he wanted her to himself for a while. Instead, he took her to Angell Place, the Richmond home he had inherited at his majority seven years ago and nearly lost. They reached their destination by nightfall, tired out, but ineffably content and in tune with one another, ready to chuckle at the slightest provocation.

Angell Place was a picturesque Palladian mansion in fifty acres of ground, a herd of shy fallow deer creeping through the woodlands at sunset. Kate fell in love with it straight away.

That night, in the down-soft, muslin-draped bed, after the long aching wastes of separation in which war and death, anxiety, doubt and longing had intervened, they basked in the sheer pleasure of their liberation to love one another. She put her arms about him and pressed healing kisses upon the funny puckered hollow where his arm should have been. And it was as it had never been at Silvercragg. Their chastening experiences had added a deeper dimension to their lovemaking so that the moments of blissful empathy were prolonged.

The honeyed interlude slipped away. Christmas came and with it thoughts of Silvercragg. The inevitability of their return loomed over them and they procrastinated, not wishing to break the spell, only half persuaded that the propitious beginning to their marriage would not be overset by the ghosts of Silvercragg.

In due course, however, on a gusty day in March, they set out on the long journey north, back to the county both of them loved and the castle they had good reason to fear. The servants were waiting to greet them, lined up on the gravel sweep before the front entrance. Leo alighted and handed his wife down from the carriage, giving her his arm with a slight air of ceremony. Bashfully, she took her first steps towards Silvercragg as its mistress and, in an access of relief, realised that her audience was not hostile. Kate acknowledged each one by name as she passed them. They curtsied and bowed, called her 'my lady, and by the time she and Leo had reached the door, a cheer had broken out.

"My lord," ventured Fenwick in his usual stentorian key, "may I make so bold as to carry her ladyship over the threshold for you?"

"Certainly you may not!" retorted the Viscount, taking off his beaver hat and the glove he had to pull on and off with his teeth. "I'll do the thing myself! I may be wanting in dexterity, but should any steal my privileges, I'll not answer for the consequences!"

And a fine show he made of it, while Kate clung to his neck and the servants cried: "Bravo! Bravo!"

Peggy Wagstaff stepped forward, her eyes shining with moisture. "Welcome home, my lord! Welcome home, my lady! We're that glad to have you back where you belong."

That autumn, Wrydale rejoiced when her ladyship's first child, a son, was born at Silvercragg and christened Leonard Mark William at the font where his mother had been baptised two decades ago.

And so, after a generation of strife, Silvercragg was at peace. The Penrose line was restored and of all the wild tales bequeathed to posterity, none would mention the humble Herr Neumann of Hanover whose passion for the Incomparable Betsy Chadwyck had had such a signal influence upon the chain of circumstances which brought it about.

The charred smell in the rafters faded away and the shades no longer stirred. It was as if, by her death, Cassandra had redeemed an outstanding debt created when Meg McCullough gave vent to her almighty wrath. "It is strange," Kate mused, "that I never glimpsed her here as others claim to have done. Perhaps it was because she lived in me and breathed through me and would give me no rest."

"While we are all unique," Leo said, "perhaps we are not as singular as we are inclined to think."

Now, when Kate opened the music box and let the melody fly, the sound was sweet. The anguish had gone. The future lay ahead, an open book.

Leo took her chin in his hand and gazed at her with tender pride. "Kate, run away no more. Our love has quelled the spirit of the past. For one thing failed to escape Pandora's Box when all the evils were let loose…"

"…and that was Hope," she whispered, and smiling, closed the lid."

Royal Crown Derby
Imari Wares

Royal Crown Derby
IMARI WARES

by Ian Cox

ROYAL CROWN DERBY

194 Osmaston Road · Derby DE23 8JZ
ISBN 1 85894 075 3

Front cover illustration:
10-inch dinner plate decorated in pattern number 1128 ('Old Imari'), 1988
Back cover illustration:
Selection of Royal Crown Derby wares
decorated in various Imari patterns, *ca.* 1890 to the present
Frontispiece:
Royal Crown Derby vase hand-painted in the 'Witches' pattern, 1916

Photography by Mark Duckett ABIPP
at Nigel Taylor Photography

The image on page 17 is reproduced courtesy of the Bridgeman Art Library,
London/New York
The images on pages 18 (bottom) and 19
are reproduced courtesy of the V&A Picture Library
The image on page 18 (top) is reproduced courtesy of the Staatsarchiv, Dresden

Designed by Dalrymple
Laid out by Matthew Hervey
Typeset in Caslon

Produced by Merrell Holberton Publishers
Willcox House, 42 Southwark Street
London SE1 1UN
Printed and bound in Italy

CONTENTS

Foreword

Derby porcelain and Imari have been constant partners since the late eighteenth century. Although most of the other pottery- and porcelain-makers of Europe have also experimented with the style at one time or another, none of them has done so with such artistic and commercial success as Derby.

Perhaps the most innovative and brilliant example of the use of the style by Royal Crown Derby's designers has been the range of so called paperweights introduced in 1981, and now a very substantial part of the present factory's total production. In 1997 we asked Ian Cox to write a book about these highly colourful animal sculptures. The result was so well written and produced, and so popular with collectors, that we decided to ask him to produce this companion volume.

I am equally delighted with the result, and I am sure readers and collectors will be, too. Most writers tend to divorce the history of ceramics from the story of modern wares. In this book, however, Ian shows how the English tradition of Imari started, how it developed as two centuries passed, how the designs changed as the technology changed, and brings the story seamlessly to the present day. As time went by, the patterns came to acquire their own distinctively English character, quite different from their ancient Japanese origins. This is a highly original study of an important strand in the history of world ceramics, as well as a valuable guide for the collector of both antique and modern Royal Crown Derby Imari wares.

Hugh Gibson
Managing Director, Royal Crown Derby
September 1998

opposite
Urn and cover designed by Tien
Manh Dinh, 1997

9

CHAPTER I

Birth of a New Firm – Revival of an Old Tradition

The Royal Crown Derby Porcelain Company has long been known for its manufacture of dinner, tea and dessert services and ornamental wares decorated with rich patterns inspired by porcelain made in Japan and exported to the West in the late seventeenth and early eighteenth centuries. Production of these wares dates back to the establishment of the factory on the site of the former Derby workhouse in the 1870s and since then they have been produced continuously, in one form or another, through to the present day. In the early days, reviews of the manufacturing capability of the recently established firm appeared in the local, national and international press; in these much importance was attached to wares decorated in patterns dominated by the colours of dark blue, iron red and gold, the so called 'Imari' palette now ubiquitously associated with the company.

"It is impossible to go into detail into the exhibits, but in referring to the principal objects we may say that in the Crown Derby

The Osmaston Road factory, Derby, in the late 19th century

opposite
Group of objects from the Derby Crown Period, *ca.* 1890

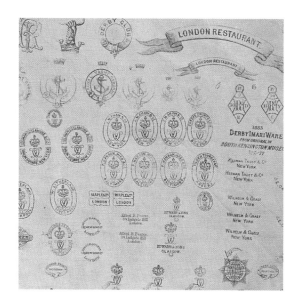

left
Page from a sales ledger dated
January 1880

right
Late 19th-century backstamps

china, lent by the Derby Crown Porcelain Company, Osmaston Road, Derby, we see the splendour of the colouring and gilding of the well-known Derby Japannes most successfully revived, and nothing can be more brilliant than the decoration in blue, gold and red of this firm. The deep blue against the gold is most effective and when lit up by the artificial light it is quite Oriental in magnificence."

This quotation appeared on 14 February 1883 in *The Sheffield Telegraph*, which reported a *conversazione* held by the Sheffield Literary and Philosophical Society. One of the main sources of conversation at the meeting was a case of fine china supplied by the Derby Crown Porcelain Company, and the richly patterned Japan or Imari wares merited, as we have seen, special attention. This was not an isolated event, as other press cuttings from the period concerning showroom displays of wares make it clear that special mention of these richly decorated, orientally inspired products was widespread. How and why these wares came to feature so strongly in the early production of the factory is an interesting story, one that is closely bound up with the establishment of the new china works in Derby in 1876.

The driving force behind the setting up of the new china-making factory at Osmaston Road was Edward Phillips, former joint managing director of the prestigious Royal Worcester Company. Phillips had had a highly successful sixteen-year career at Worcester, but following a long series of disagreements with co-director Richard

Binns concerning the future direction of the firm, he was, in effect, sacked by the Board of Directors in 1875. He was fifty-eight years old. There can be little doubt that Phillips had always had a burning desire to lead a ceramic firm that had a reputation for excellence, supplying customers at the top end of the market. It is perhaps not surprising, therefore, that his ambitions were to lead to a new initiative. In partnership with William Litherland, a china retailer from Liverpool and customer of Royal Worcester, Phillips took the momentous decision, in 1876, to establish a brand new factory in Derby.

The provisonal prospectus, dated 1877, for the new firm, which was to be known as "The Derby Crown Porcelain Company", indicated that a considerable amount of capital was involved in setting it up. An issue of 160 shares at a value of £500 each and totalling £80,000 was proposed in the prospectus with the expectation that 75% would be called up. The document listed the directors as Edward Phillips, William Litherland and William Bemrose, a local printer, author and china collector. The prospectus also provided clues concerning the motivation behind the establishment of the factory and the choice of Derby for the factory site:

"The great demand for Porcelain manufactures which exists in the European and American markets, the excellent site of the Works, and the favourable terms on which it has been bought, the name of the Town, which is known as a household word in connection with China Manufacture, and the practical knowledge, long experience, and established business connexion which Mr Phillips is enabled to bring to the Company's affairs, conduce to the belief that the operations of the Company will be commenced with every prospect of success."

The market opportunities for manufacturing high-quality wares for a discerning clientele were certainly judged correctly when Messrs Phillips, Bemrose and Litherland decided to set up business in Derby. The British economy was doing well and the middle classes were expanding and enjoying unprecedented levels of prosperity; there was plenty of disposable income available to spend on quality porcelain. The sales ledgers of the newly established firm show that, within a short space of time, the company was supplying prestige china retailers in most parts of Britain, including several of the most important retailers in the West End of London. The United States was also correctly perceived to be a great potential market, as that economy was undergoing massive expansion and development; the renowned firms of Tiffany & Co. of New York and Bailey & Banks of Philadelphia were just two important china retailers to be supplied with wares from the Derby Crown Porcelain Company.

The town of Derby was selected as a suitable place to site a porcelain factory because of its association with a tradition of fine china-making that had been established there since about 1750, when Andre Planche set up the first factory at a site on Nottingham Road.

"This factory is formed for the purpose of re-establishing the manufacture of Porcelain and Opaque Crown China, for which Derby was formerly so celebrated .... It is intended to produce a manufacture of a quality which shall take rank with the first houses in the trade for perfection of composition and high artistic finish."

Hugh Gibson, Managing Director of Royal Crown Derby today, in his highly readable account of the history of the early factory, notes that Edward Phillips and his partners quickly established a substantial, modern factory that by necessity had to produce wares that would sell in the prevailing market conditions. The production of high-quality, expensive, artistic decorative items, which was to be achieved by "employing the finest artists and craftsmen", was a major priority, but at the same time utilitarian wares such as dinner services and tea sets, made in quantity, were going to be important to the firm's early profitability.

A Derby Crown Porcelain Company sales ledger provides detailed information of items sold to china retailers during the early years of production. Written in beautiful copperplate, these entries reveal that Japan patterned dinner and tea wares were a significant part of production and sales at this time. The well known firm of A.P. Daniell & Son of London, for example, purchased "12 Dessert Plates, Gadroon No. 1 Japan" and William Litherland's Liverpool-based shop purchased "6 Cans and Saucers 374 Japan." Almost all the entries in the ledger, many of them relating to repeat orders, include listings that concern the purchase of wares with Japan patterns. Sales brochures from this early period of production also indicate the importance of the Japan patterns. An undated catalogue from the 1880s shows some of the designs available to retailers at this time: the page depicting "China Dessert Patterns" shows several in the well known colour combination of cobalt blue, iron red and gold. On a subsequent page, similar patterns are applied to earthenware bodies for "dinner patterns".

Where, then, did the inspiration come from for the so called Japan patterns that formed the basis of an important part of the Derby Crown Porcelain Company's early product ranges? To answer that question we must turn to the origin of porcelain making in Japan in the late seventeenth century.

Page from a Derby Crown Porcelain Company brochure, *ca.* 1885

Made in the East –
Used in the West

During the late seventeenth and early eighteenth centuries the collecting of oriental porcelain was a fashionable pastime for many
European aristocrats, a phenomenon that was part of a broader taste
for oriental artefacts that had resulted from increased trade with the
East. Porcelain was considered a fascinating and mystical commodity and collections of oriental wares were often displayed in elaborate arrangements in important palaces and houses in many
European countries. At the end of the seventeenth century Queen
Mary endorsed the already well established Continental taste in
England when she amassed a collection of more than eight hundred
pieces of Chinese and Japanese porcelain at Kensington Palace. On
the Continent in the early eighteenth century, Augustus the Strong,
King of Poland and Elector of Saxony, put together a collection of
oriental porcelain that was to become so large that a special palace
was acquired and eventually rebuilt to house it. This also involved
the production of detailed drawings for wall structures that were

Portrait of John Verney, 14th
Baron Willoughby de Broke and
his family, 1766, by Johann
Zoffany (1733–1810),
The J. Paul Getty Museum,
Los Angeles
Japanese and Chinese Imari
porcelain stands on the table

opposite
Group of objects from the Bloor
period of the Nottingham Road
factory, Derby, *ca.* 1835

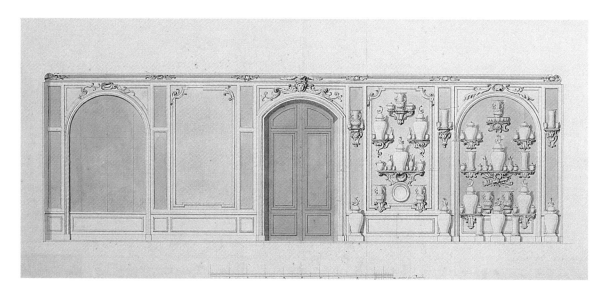

Drawing for a gallery in the Japanese Palace, Dresden, by Z. Longelune, 1735, Staatsarchiv, Dresden (SächsHStA, OHMA, Cap. II, Nr. 15ᴵᴵᵇ)

to be specially commissioned to display the collection (illustrated above). Augustus was especially fond of Japanese porcelain and his collection contained a large number of impressive pieces, many of them in the so called Imari style. Illustrated below is a large Imari dish from about 1700 that was originally part of his hoard, inscribed on the base with the inventory mark of the Royal Saxon collection.

The dish, measuring 46.7 cm in diameter, has a central well with an asymmetric composition depicting a woman and her attendants in a garden, and a wide border decorated with a repeating pattern of fruits and flowers among foliage. Although the figurative design itself is slightly unusual for a piece of Imari ware of this date, the palette, the rich and elaborate decoration, and the stylization of the botanical elements are all typical of the Imari polychrome wares

Imari dish showing a design with a woman with attendants in a garden, 1700–25, inscribed with the inventory mark of the Royal Saxon Collection on the base, Victoria and Albert Museum, London

being imported into Europe from Japan in the early decades of the eighteenth century.

Another large object made in Japan at a similar time to the dish is illustrated above. Standing 76 cm tall, the vase (with cover) was part of a five-piece garniture of vases designed to be displayed as a set. Richly decorated in the same palette as the dish, the vase depicts flowers, foliage and landscapes within reserved panels surrounded by a dark-blue ground decorated with leaves and flowerheads in red and gold. It is easy to see why Augustus the Strong and other aristocratic porcelain collectors were fascinated and impressed by these richly decorated wares, for they made splendid display pieces. They were often shown on mantlepieces and shelves, on and under cabinets and even in fireplaces during the summer. But how did the wares originate and arrive in the West?

Porcelain was first made in Japan in the early years of the seventeenth century following the discovery of suitable supplies of china

Map of Japan and the island of
Kyushu

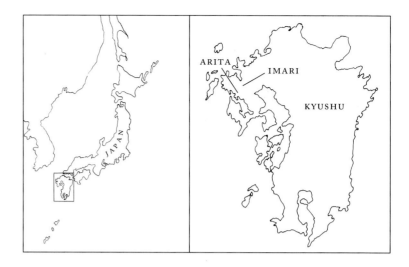

clay and china stone, the raw materials essential for making the
commodity, near the town of Arita on the south-western island of
Kyushu. The wares were fired using kiln technology imported from
China and Korea and they were destined largely for the domestic
market. Most pieces were decorated in underglaze blue with patterns heavily influenced by Chinese designs, but a few were also
decorated with green glazes. Following the collapse of China's
export trade with the West after the fall of the Ming dynasty in 1644,
Japan replaced China as a major exporter of porcelain from the
second half of the seventeenth century until well into the eighteenth
century. Demand for porcelain from the East was not suppressed by
the demise of the Chinese industry and the relatively new industry
established in the area round Arita was well placed to benefit from
the new market opportunities.

The new porcelain export trade was established and promoted by
the Dutch East India Company, which had established exclusive
rights to trade with Japan following the withdrawal of the English
from Japan in 1632 and the expulsion of the Portuguese in 1639. Even
the Dutch, however, were restricted to a base on the small island of
Deshima situated in the bay opposite the port of Imari (now
Nagasaki). The traders were prevented from travelling onwards
from Deshima by the isolationist Tokugawa Shogun government, a
situation that led the Dutch to believe that the porcelain was made
in the hinterland of Imari rather than in the Arita district. They
gave the generic name 'Imari' to the porcelain they exported from
Japan and the name has stuck through to the present day, although
the term 'Imari' is now generally associated with the heavily decorated polychromatic wares and the term 'Arita' is used for the blue-

and-white export porcelains. In reality, all the wares were made in the Arita area in the same kilns.

Evidence suggests that the Dutch were purchasing small quantities of porcelain from the Japanese as early as the 1630s, long before the collapse of the China porcelain trade; this must have been the porcelain that was being made for the domestic market. The first well documented large order for porcelain, however, dates from 1659, when 64,866 pieces were purchased for export, most of them of the blue-and-white variety. Not all of them were destined for western Europe, as the Dutch were also trading in porcelain with a number of eastern countries, including India. A small proportion of the order does, however, appear to have been decorated with coloured enamels and surviving documents note there were "100 white sided cups decorated with red and green decoration". In 1660, a year later, 11,530 pieces of porcelain were shipped to Holland and 57,173 pieces to Malacca, both orders including wares decorated in combinations of colours including blue and red and red, blue, green, black and gold. During the 1660s there was a continued expansion of the export trade characterized by the introduction of new shapes, many of them influenced by European taste, and much of the production enamelled.

Imari wares were made in at least eleven kiln sites in the Arita district at the height of production in the first half of the eighteenth century. During the early history of manufacture there were considerable differences in the appearance of wares, and styles, colours and quality of production varied considerably. After the turn of the

left
Saucer-shaped dish with a design based on fruiting pomegranates and the 'Buddha's hand' and with a small monogram 'VOC' (Vereenigde Oostindische Compagnie) in the centre, Arita kilns, *ca.* 1670, British Museum, London

right
Large dish with 'VOC' monogram surrounded by two phoenixes, fruiting peach and camilia, with bamboo and peonies on the rim, Arita kilns, *ca.* 1670, Ashmolean Museum, Oxford

century, however, most of the polychromatic wares were decorated in underglaze blue, iron red and gold, although the Imari palette could often still include other colours, including yellows, greens, aubergine and black. As we have already seen, wares made after the 1690s were characterized by rich decoration and often the entire surface of a piece of porcelain would be decorated. A variety of objects were made, ranging from teawares, dishes, jars and vases (the last often of considerable size) to small 'toy' pieces made for dolls' houses. Many of them were based on European shapes.

Designs could be patterned or pictorial and it was not uncommon to find several scenes, in cartouches, on one object. Decorators made use of flowers and foliage, and bird, human and landscape elements. Many of the designs cleverly captured the essence of a particular type of flower or plant in abstract form and certain motifs were used over and over again in the development of patterns. A number of the motifs have a long history of usage and have symbolic associations deriving from Chinese culture. Given Japan's proximity to the mainland and the close historical interrelationship between the two cultures, this is not surprising. A few examples of motifs associated with Imari compositions are:

BAMBOO   This plant originated from China and was cultivated in the gardens of the Japanese nobility. It was used for making a variety of objects, including fences, lattices and writing brushes. Along with the pine and the plum blossom it was known as one of the three 'companions of the deep cold' in Chinese legend, given its ability to survive in low temperatures. Chinese legend also associates bamboo with the mythical phoenix, which was said to feed only on bamboo seeds. Bamboo was also traditionally associated with the virtues of constancy, integrity and honour.

CHERRY BLOSSOM   Originally found wild in the foothills of the Nara and Kyoto mountains, cherry blossom was admired for its aesthetic properties from as early as the tenth century, when it became Japan's national flower. It was planted in formal gardens, and annual blossom-viewing ceremonies were held by courtly and religious establishments.

CHRYSANTHEMUM   This flower was introduced to Japan from Tang China and many of the legends and supserstitions associated with it there persisted in Japanese culture. It was known as one of the four 'princes' (along with plum blossom, bamboo and orchids) because of its association with 'nobility' and 'purity'. It was also associated with longevity, as mountain hermits, who lived to a great age, were said to subsist on a diet of this flower. From the early thirteenth century chrysanthemums were associated with the Japanese imperial line and motifs were often incorporated into courtly costume and engraved as motifs on sword blades.

PEONY   Another import to Japan from China, the peony was admired for its beauty and medicinal properties. It ranked almost as highly as the chrysanthemum in prestige and was widely used as a decorative motif and as a family crest.

PINE   An evergreen tree, the pine, along with the tortoise and the crane, was considered a symbol of longevity – a thousand years of life. Another of the Chinese 'companions of the deep cold', pine was often used to decorate doorways of Japanese houses at New Year.

PLUM BLOSSOM   The third of the 'companions of the deep cold', plum blossom had religous connotations in Japanese society. It was appreciated aesthetically for many centuries before the advent of Imari wares and plum-blossom viewing parties were held as early as the eighth century. It was widely used as a motif in the design of textiles, furnishings, carriages and even on the backs of mirrors. It was a popular heraldic motif.

BUTTERFLY   Japanese aristocrats admired the elegance of the butterfly, and warriors used it as a decorative motif on their armour.

CRANE   This bird was considered a symbol of longevity – a thousand years of life. It was used as a decorative element during the Heian period and adopted by some Japanese families as a crest.

Part of the richness of Imari designs comes from the use of underglaze cobalt blue applied to the surface of the pot before the initial glazing and firing. The colour was resistant to the high temperatures characteristic of the first firing, which produced a consistently good, deep blue colour. The iron red and the other polychromatic colours were applied on the surface of the glaze and fired again at a lower temperature, partly because they were more sensitive to heat. The gold decoration was applied last and, being the most temperature-sensitive material of all, was fired at an even lower temperature – the third firing in the process. Enamelling and gilding were done by skilled decorators, following initial designs developed on the pot in underglaze blue. Reserved areas were often built in to the underglaze design, in which enamel and gilt decoration was placed. This suggests that there must have been close cooperation between the two sets of workers. When looking at Imari porcelain wares it is often easy to discern the three stages of production as the blue areas tend to have smudgy, blurred edges. These

are normally covered by the enamel and gilt decoration, but on poor-quality pieces the enamelling fails to cover the blue edges completely.

A second type of enamelled ware was produced in the kilns around Arita at the same time that Imari wares were being made, and was also a significant part of the export trade to the West. 'Kakiemon' porcelain, although made in the Arita district, was different from Imari wares in a number of ways. The Kakiemon family of potters developed a technique of overglaze enamel decoration on a milky-white opaque glaze, which was easily distinguishable from Imari porcelains. Influenced by Chinese decorative patterns, the distinctive coloured enamels were painted on the opaque glaze sparingly, with only touches of gilding, and without the use of underglaze blue, producing refined, witty designs in both patterned and pictorial forms.

Imari and Kakiemon porcelains both found favour with collectors in Europe and both were comparatively expensive. It should therefore come as no surprise that ceramic manufacturers in Europe tried to imitate these desirable wares. Initially this was done by attempting to use ceramic techniques native to Europe. The Dutch, for example, who were skilled in the manufacture of tin-glazed earthenwares in such towns as Delft, tried to make objects that looked like the Japanese wares. First, blue-and-white articles imitating Japanese designs were made but, when multi-coloured enamelled wares became popular in the early eighteenth century, items with a characteristic Imari palette of blue, red and gilt were also pro-

duced. In reality, although the products looked superficially similar to the oriental originals, they were never really rivals to the genuine article. More formidable competition, however, came from the European porcelain factories.

On the Continent the porcelain factory at Meissen, established by Augustus the Strong in about 1708, soon began to imitate the wares imported from the East. They produced fine copies of Kakiemon porcelain pieces and also made many items with Imari-inspired patterns in the 1730s and 1740s. Many of the Imari patterns could be found on practical objects such as teapots, tea and coffee sets and other tablewares. Other European producers, including the Vienna factories, imitated Imari patterns on their wares, but the French and Italian factories seem to have been less enthusiastic and Imari-patterned pieces from these centres are rarer.

In England, porcelain production was slower to get off the ground than in mainland Europe and the major centres of production did not establish themselves until the second quarter of the eighteenth century. The London factories of Chelsea and Bow both produced wares with Imari-inspired patterns and sometimes the patterns were copied almost exactly from Japanese pieces. In 1769 William Duesbury acquired the Chelsea factory and when, in 1783, he moved all production to Nottingham Road in Derby, the Chelsea Imari patterns may have inspired him to introduce similar designs there. We know that Imari patterns were in production at Nottingham Road by 1776, as records show that Queen Charlotte purchased a salad bowl with an Imari pattern in that year for

left
Lobed saucer dish, Meissen, *ca.* 1720, painted in direct imitation of a Japanese Imari original, British Museum, London

right
Chelsea porcelain fluted dish, England, *ca.* 1760, British Museum, London

£1 11s. 6d. By the early 1800s Imari patterns were an important part of the Derby firm's stock in trade. The richness of the blue, red and gold designs was ideally suited to Regency tastes for opulent, orientally inspired patterns, and must have looked magnificent in candlelit interiors. Imari-patterned wares were also being produced by other factories, including Spode and Coalport, but Derby seems to have established itself firmly in this market by the 1820s. The firm had been taken over by Robert Bloor in 1811 and it is known that he actively promoted the production of Imari-patterned wares to enable him to raise capital to finance other aspects of production. It was under his leadership that the factory took on extra workers to cope with increased production of this type of ware. A handbill issued throughout the Staffordshire potteries in 1817 stated:

"To Enamel Painters – WANTED IMMEDIATELY – About twenty good enamel painters who can paint different Japan patterns, Borders etc. Any person of the above description may have constant employ by applying to Robert Bloor, china manufactory, Derby."

We know from surviving pieces that dinner services, tea services, breakfast services and dessert services, as well as vases and other ornaments, were all produced at this time with patterns inspired by Imari designs. Patterns had interesting names such as 'Witches', 'Grecian', 'Rose', 'Duck' and 'Partridge', to name but a few, and the Royal Crown Derby Museum has a fine collection of coffee cans (see illustration) which shows the variety of hand-painted Imari designs made at the factory during the Duesbury and Bloor periods. The popularity of the Japanese imports had had a major impact on the design and production of porcelain in England and no more so than at the first of the Derby factories on Nottingham Road.

9595

9595　Tea Saucer
Sefton

9596. Tea Saucer, Talbot only

9596
as
9595

inside cup

9596
Talbot only

CHAPTER 3

Imari Patterns at Royal Crown Derby

Tracking the history and development of Imari wares at Royal Crown Derby was a fascinating experience and involved many visits by the author to the works to carry out research. The firm's distinguished history is immediately apparent when one arrives at the factory in Osmaston Road, as the original Derby workhouse which provided the focal point for Phillips's grand plan is still very much intact and fully used. The factory proudly displays the Royal Warrant, granted by Queen Victoria in 1890, to the left of the front entrance, and it was in that year, too, that the firm changed its name from Derby Crown Porcelain Company to Royal Crown Derby Porcelain Company. Upstairs from the entrance hall the firm further reveals its rich heritage in a splendid museum established by the company in the 1970s in what used to be the old factory showroom. It houses a representative collection of wares made by the three factories involved in the making of porcelain in Derby since 1750. There are fine examples of figures and dessert services from the old Nottingham Road works and an important collection of coffee cans which shows some of the Imari patterns made by the firm in the late eighteenth and early nineteenth centuries. There is also a section devoted to the King Street factory, which was established by six workers from Nottingham Road when it closed in 1848. This factory was taken over by Royal Crown Derby in 1935, directly linking the Osmaston Road factory with the porcelain-making traditions that had begun in Derby almost two hundred years previously.

The museum displays its collections of Imari pieces alongside the fine eggshell wares and raised-gold items associated with innovations at the factory in the late nineteenth century, but it is the surviving Imari-patterned objects made at all three factories that enabled the first-hand investigation of the story of these wares to begin. Direct observation of the objects themselves, however, was only part of the enquiry. Housed in an archive behind the museum is a wonderful repository of papers and documents relating to the firm's history. It includes sales ledgers, inventories of stock, costing

opposite
Artwork for pattern number 9595

29

books and, perhaps most important of all, a unique set of pattern books which record the introduction of designs from the early days of production through to the 1930s. Using all of these sources it was possible to piece together an interesting picture of the history of production of Imari wares at the Osmaston Road factory.

There are twenty-nine pattern books in the Royal Crown Derby archive. The first twenty-five cover the period August 1878 to July 1926 and the last four, the A books, extend the range to an unclear date in the 1930s. Each covers a specific period and contains a detailed record of all the new tableware designs introduced and mostly put into production during that time. When a new pattern was introduced it was allocated a number and the design was recorded in pen and colour washes. Certain Imari patterns made at the factory today date from its earliest years – for example, 1128, known as 'Old Imari', which was introduced and given its number in 1880. Complex Imari patterns on holloware shapes such as teacups were sometimes recorded as if unfolded from the outside of the cup and, if the pattern extended to the inside, further detail of that part of the pattern was also given. For a plate or saucer, either the whole design was given, or part of it with details of how many times the pattern had to repeat around the surface of the item. Sometimes details were given in writing regarding the use of particular colours and in most cases the name of the 'shape' on to which the pattern was to be applied is recorded.

Between the start of production in 1878 and the end of the nineteenth century 6069 patterns overall were developed, of which 559 –

below left
Pattern number 8689 shown on an Elgin teacup and saucer

below right
Pattern number 41, a forerunner of pattern numbers 879 and 2451 ('Traditional Imari')

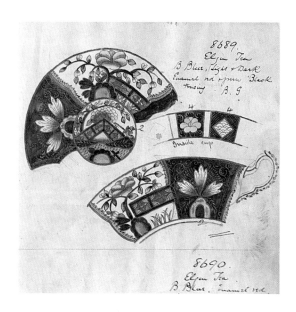

Pattern number A1283 showing the artist's design and a coffee can and saucer made at the factory today

or 9.2% – were Imari or Imari-inspired in character. Between the beginning of the twentieth century and July 1926 the number of new patterns developed was two thirds what it had been in the first twenty or so years of production. Of the 3929 designs developed, only 244 were Imari or Imari-inspired – the number had fallen to approximately 6% of the total number of designs produced. This is not perhaps surprising given the market opportunities that existed in the early years of the firm's development and the fact that some of the designs continued in production in one form or another for many years. The early twentieth century was also significantly marked by World War I, which had a considerable impact on production and the development of designs at the factory in Derby, as it did on the ceramics industry generally. Unfortunately, the records do not tell us when designs were withdrawn, so it has been difficult to establish the life of many of the designs. Interestingly, however, Margaret Sargeant, Curator of the Royal Crown Derby Museum, who has had many years' experience of looking at objects brought into the museum by the general public, has come to the opinion that many of the nineteenth-century designs had been withdrawn by the years immediately following World War I. New Imari patterns, or adaptations of old ones, were still being introduced, however, in the 1920s. In the range of patterns 9000–9999, developed between 1911 and 1930, around 10% were inspired by Imari designs and the Imari palette. This is approximately the same percentage achieved for Imari designs in the 1890s. Certain patterns do appear to have sold well, however, and the fact that some of them are still made today is testimony to their continuing popularity.

What form did the pattern development take at the factory and how did it evolve in the first few decades of production? New Imari-related patterns were developed at Osmaston Road in a variety of ways. One of the oldest and best known of the Imari patterns is pattern 383 – the 'King's Pattern' – which was introduced at the start of manufacture and which continued in production until just a few years ago. Pattern number 1 in the very first pattern book was a fore-

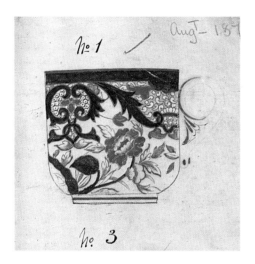

left
Pattern number 1, a forerunner of pattern 383 which became known as the 'King's Pattern'

right
Teacup and saucer showing a modern version of the 'King's Pattern'

runner of the 383 pattern applied to a tankard-shaped cup. It is a direct copy of a pattern which had originally been developed at Nottingham Road, and the illustration of items made at that factory during the Bloor period shown on page 16 includes a butter dish and cover using this original design. The pattern as developed at Osmaston Road was used on Crown earthenware-pottery table-wares during the Derby Crown period and many pieces surviving through to the present day date from 1878–90. They bear an impressed crown as an identifying mark and the design provides a good example of Phillips's original objective of reviving old Derby designs being put into practice.

In his book *Royal Crown Derby*, John Twitchett, former Curator of the Royal Crown Derby Museum, records details of designs connected with particular named artists who worked at the factory, but within this list there are very few examples which relate to Imari designs. Only in one or two cases are particular Imari designs related to named individuals. An interesting example is afforded by pattern number 1145, where the design is attributed to Richard Lunn, a former art director at Osmaston Road from 1882. Lunn enjoyed the distinction of designing an important pair of vases for Queen Victoria and the glorious Gladstone dessert service decorated with hand-painted scenes of Derbyshire presented to Prime Minister Gladstone in December 1883. The costing book indicates that the pattern was derived from a design found on an old vase at "SKM". These are the initials of the South Kensington Museum (now the Victoria and Albert Museum), which had been established in London from the profits of the Great Exhibition in 1851 to help foster industrial design.

 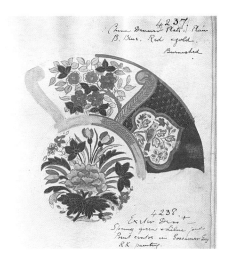

Another example of objects from earlier periods inspiring Derby designers turned up in a survey of the costing books in the Osmaston Road archive. Pattern number 4237, developed for application to a 10-inch dinner plate, is a typically rich Imari-inspired pattern with an underglaze-blue border with reserved panels containing sprays of flowers and foliage and a central roundel with an elaborate arrangement of flowers; the design is highlighted with areas of burnished gold. The costing book notes against this pattern "Plate – Old Derby Japan. Blued and enamelled by women; gilt by men. Copied from a plate sold June 1894 at Nottingham and bought by A Daniells and Son who sent it here." The plate almost certainly provided the design studio with another example of a Nottingham Road idea thought suitable for reproduction at Osmaston Road in the late nineteenth century. Interestingly, the name Daniells refers

left
Pattern number 1146, designed by Mr Lunn, appointed art director at Osmaston Road in 1882

right
Pattern number 4237, "to be enamelled by women and gilded by men"

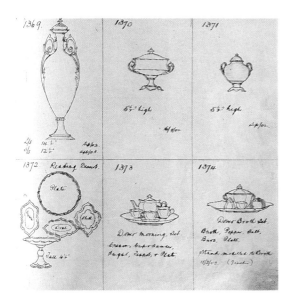

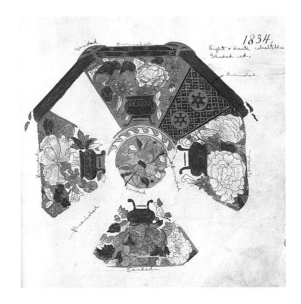

to a china retailing firm that was a customer of the Osmaston Road factory. Perhaps even more noteworthy is the reference to the method of decoration and to the division of labour between men and women on the factory floor. Gilding, which was seen as a more demanding skill, was considered the prerogative of men, the more mundane part of the decoration being assigned to women.

All ceramic factories producing tablewares produced tea and dinner services with particular shapes. The shape of a plate or teacup could be varied almost infinitely to cater for new fashions and tastes, and varying shapes was a typical device used in the development of products by all nineteenth-century ceramic firms. Some of the teaware shapes developed and manufactured by the Derby Crown Porcelain Company are shown in the illustration from one of their early brochures shown on page 15. When a new shape was introduced, new designs were sometimes developed that were specific to that shape. Pattern number 1834 was developed for a hexagonal dessert plate, and it is interesting to observe the close relationship that exists between the shape of the plate and the design composition. When an established pattern was applied to a newly developed shape it was often given a new number and the design in the pattern book would show how the existing pattern was to be adapted to the new object. There are many examples of this adaptation process in the pattern books, and sometimes a pattern later becomes known by a number given to an adaptation of an original design with a lower pattern number. 'Traditional Imari', a pattern which is made at Osmaston Road today, is universally acknowledged to be pattern

number 2451, but it originates much earlier in the form of pattern number 877, 'Japan Derby'. The number 2451 comes from its adaptation to a new shape introduced in 1888, several years after the design had originally been developed. Pattern number 1128, 'Old Imari', the pattern most often associated with Royal Crown Derby today, is closely related to the design found on a scent bottle known by the pattern number 876. When the Brighton dessert plate was first introduced in the early 1890s, old patterns were employed: pattern number 383, the 'King's Pattern', was applied to it as pattern number 4500, and 2451, 'Traditional Imari', was applied to it as number 4568.

Another way in which new designs were developed was by enriching an earlier pattern. This more often than not involved the use and application of more gold than on the earlier design. For example, pattern number 1911 was a more luxurious and expensive version of pattern 1721. The costing book notes "China Table Plate – as 1721 but richly gilt", and it is interesting to look at the figures recorded against the two patterns in the ledger:

	Pattern 1721	Pattern 1911
Gold	8/-	13/-
Gilding	3/6	5/-
Burnishing	2/-	2/6
Enamelling	2/-	1/-
Grounding	1/6	2/-
Printing	2/-	2/-

The extra costs derived from the use of additional raw materials, *i.e.* gold, and the extra time taken to apply it during the gilding and burnishing stages. It is interesting to see, too, that as more gold decoration is applied, there is less need for enamelled decoration, and the cost for this falls in the 1911 example.

A more extreme example of this type of development is seen when traditional Imari-inspired designs are given a type of decorative treatment different from the usual one of underglaze blue, iron red and gold. During the late nineteenth century the Derby factory developed amazing decorative techniques for the luxury porcelain market; this had been another of Phillips's objectives. The technique of raised goldwork involved the careful application of a special paste to specified areas on the surface of a pot. This almost took on the form of a type of sculptural bas-relief decoration, often in the form of delicate arabesque scrolls, which could then be gilded. The eventual result was both attractive and exclusive. Derby craftsmen became extraordinarily adept at applying this type of decoration, and it was only a matter of time before the technique was applied to Imari-inspired designs.

Pattern number 1879 provides a good example of a traditional all-over Imari pattern in underglaze blue, iron red and gold that was converted to a raised gold design. The cost variation is given below:

	Pattern 1879	Pattern 1981
Gold	12/-	48/-
Gilding	8/-	51/-
Burnishing	2/6	3/-
Enamelling	5/-	0/-
Grounding	2/6	4/-
Printing	1/-	1/-

Not only are the costs of the raw materials considerably higher in the raised gold example, but also the labour costs at 51/- are more than six times the cost involved in gilding the basic Imari example. Interestingly but perhaps not surprisingly, in the period 1878–1900 only 3% of the Imari-inspired designs are of this type, and after 1900 this type of design must have fallen out of fashion or become too expensive, as no new designs of this type are introduced between 1900 and 1925.

New designs were often developed by combining elements from earlier patterns to make new ones. Again, 'Old Imari', pattern number 1128, was in fact not an original pattern or even a direct

Royal Crown Derby jar and cover decorated in pattern number 1128 ('Old Imari'), made and hand-decorated in 1913, Royal Crown Derby Museum

reproduction of an old Nottingham Road one; it was made up from a combination of two earlier patterns. The easily recognized central roundel containing the six kite-shaped panels, each with a white ground and containing the underglaze-blue flowerheads surrounded by iron-red and gilt flowers and foliage, was taken from the design on the scent bottle, pattern number 876; the famous 'Old Imari' border of alternating panels, one set with iron-red peony flowerheads on a dark-blue and gilt ground, the other with lozenges filled with a scale pattern, was derived from the border design of pattern 919. Again, this method of combining existing elements to make new designs is one which occurs over and over again in the pattern books.

A good many of the Imari designs that were developed were hand-painted in the decorating shops, just as they had been in the Nottingham Road factory. Smoke outlines from tissue prints were applied to the surface of wares to give the decorators an outline to work to at the underglaze-blue stage, and the 'bluers', as they were known, filled in the appropriate areas with cobalt blue before the first firing. After firing the enamelling was applied by hand and the pot was again fired, but at a lower temperature. Finally, the gilding was done at a third stage and the pot was then fired for the last time. In many respects the process was similar to the one that the Japanese craftsmen had used in Arita in the late seventeenth and early eighteenth centuries. The richly hand-painted designs are shown with their pattern-book sources in the illustrations below.

Such wares were expensive to produce and the firm therefore developed a whole range of Imari-inspired designs that were produced using transfer printing, which was of course cheaper than hand-painting. A transfer print was used for the iron-red part of pattern number 383, the 'King's Pattern', which, in the early days, was developed on Crown earthenware dinner services. Pattern number 3679 was one such transfer-print design, developed on a Surrey 10-inch china plate that had a crinkly edge (shown against a completed plate in the illustration on page 41). The instructions at the top read "print in smoke, blue, reprint in red, burnished gold".

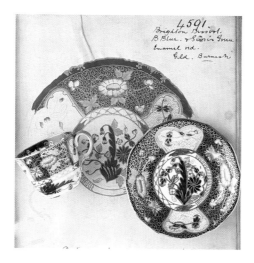 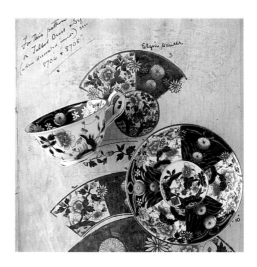

left
Pattern number 4591 and a cup and saucer made in the same pattern

right
Pattern number 8683 and a cup and saucer made in the same pattern

The smoke outline provided the template for the underglaze blue, and the second print transferred the design to the plate in red; the gilding was finished by hand. These designs are often referred to as 'semi-Imaris' and the printed elements are usually easily distinguishable. Transfer-printing was used extensively to develop a whole range of designs which were only loosely based on Imari sources. They often related to the production of cheaper tewares, and the number of design options could easily be increased by altering the tints and colours of the prints, in effect increasing the choice available to the customer. These designs lack the richness of traditional Imari patterns and make only limited use of gilding.

It will have become apparent that many different methods were used by the Derby design studio to develop the Imari-based product

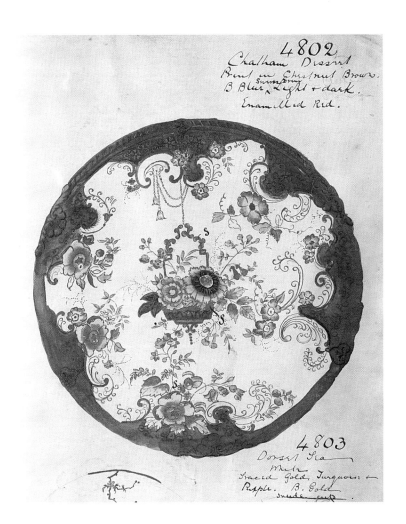

4802

Chatham Dessert
Print in Chestnut Brown.
B Blue, Light + dark.
Enamelled Red.

4803

Dorset Sea
White
Traced Gold, Turquois +
Purple. B. Gold

Pattern number 4802 – a
particularly English interpretation
of an Imari design

ranges in the late nineteenth and early twentieth centuries. Some designs were based on Imari patterns developed at Nottingham Road, or on earlier pieces studied by the workers in the studio. As time passed, however, the Imari language became a familiar one and it was used in a variety of more unorthodox ways in order to develop new patterns. One interesting trend noticeable in the development of patterns at Osmaston Road is the way in which they became progressively less Japanese in character and more and more English as time passed. The English obsession with balance and harmony ensured that many of the Derby designs adhered to strict rules of symmetry in the arrangement of elements on a surface. Pattern number 1128 is a good example of how these preoccupations affected the end result. The designs also became increasingly eclectic as time went by. Eclecticism was, of course, a feature of much Victorian design in the late nineteenth century, but is interesting to see how this phenomenon manifested itself at Derby. Designers, who after

Goblet decorated with pattern number A8686 ('Asian Rose')

all were also working on designs other than Imari ones at the same time, tended to use the Imari palette, which was popular with customers, and combine it with elements of French Rococo design, which was also very popular. The end result was an essentially English rendering of two or more design traditions, which were combined to produce something that satisfied the demand for chintzy patterns. Pattern number 4802 (see previous page), developed on a Chatham dessert plate, provides a good example of this phenomenon.

During the late nineteenth century, to be successful the firm had to compete in the marketplace by offering customers a wide choice of goods. The Imari wares were one option within a range of decorative themes. Within that option customers were increasingly offered a greater variety from which to choose. The number of new and original designs was less than one might have expected, however, given the number of Imari-inspired designs in the pattern books. The combination and re-combination of motifs, often applied to a wide range of shapes, together with the use of both hand-painting and transfer printing as decorative techniques, widened the number of design options in subtle ways that gave the impression of vast choice. After World War I, the number of options was reduced and many patterns were withdrawn. Just four seem to have become classic patterns that have remained in production through to the modern period. They are: pattern number 383, 'King's Pattern', withdrawn in 1987; pattern number 1128, 'Old Imari', still very much in production today; pattern 2451, 'Traditional Imari', still in production today; and pattern number A8686, 'Asian Rose', withdrawn just a few years ago.

The archive and factory museum together embody the history of the Royal Crown Derby factory from its inception in 1876 to the present day. Additionally, they function as a valuable resource for designers developing the Imari tradition at the factory today, a theme that is fully explored in the next chapter.

opposite
Pattern number 3679 with corresponding plate from the Royal Crown Derby Museum

3679
Surrey 10" China
Print in smoke. B Blue
+ print in red.
Burnished gold

CHAPTER 4

Modern Times

The tradition of making Imari and Imari-inspired wares at the Royal Crown Derby factory continues to thrive today in an environment that is both heritage-conscious and forward-looking. Some of the rich Imari patterns introduced at the factory in the late nineteenth century, such as 'Old Imari' and 'Traditional Imari', are still made today, but the factory does not rest on its laurels – it continues to look for new ways in which the rich Imari tradition can be adapted to develop new and exciting products which will suit old and new customers alike. The factory has also responded to changing economic circumstances in a highly positive way, and the developments that took place in the design and technical studios in the 1960s and 1970s have had a dramatic impact on the production of Imari-patterned wares.

NEW TECHNOLOGY

In the early 1960s Royal Crown Derby was acquired by Allied English Potteries, and a management review of production methods at the factory led to the conclusion that some new ways of achieving the decoration found on the Imari-based wares would have to be introduced to improve efficiency. The all-over, complex patterns characteristic of such designs as 'Old Imari' involved an amazing amount of handwork at the enamelling and gilding stages and production costs were consequently high. Brian Branscombe, the Art Director, came up with an inspired method of adapting lithograph transfer technology, which was by then being widely used in the ceramics industry, to Derby wares. The success of Branscombe's initiative relied on the fact that it was possible to develop high-quality lithograph transfers which could be applied to the surface of Derby bone-china wares and produce an excellent result without compromising the high standards associated with the factory. The aim, in the conversion of these patterns, was to choose the very best standards of decoration available in the decorating shops and apply these to the new process. Wares with the traditional Royal Crown Derby 'Posie' pattern were already being made on the basis of artwork developed in the Derby studio, but with lithographs

opposite
Vase made to commemorate the Royal Crown Derby Stakes in 1981, Royal Crown Derby Museum

commissioned from an independent printing firm called Harding & Howell. Branscombe's aim was to develop and apply a similar technology to the Imari patterns in-house.

In June 1965 Avis and May Garton, sixteen-year-old identical twins, joined the staff of the studio to assist Branscombe with the development of lithograph decoration. Avis, who is now Head of the Technical Studio at Royal Crown Derby, can remember conditions being primitive, with little in the way of modern equipment and piles of plates everywhere. On starting work the twins immediately began 'on-the-job' training to acquire the skills that would enable them to develop silk-screen transfers for the Imari patterns. Both girls became involved with the development of lithographs for pattern 1128 – 'Old Imari'. Initially, lithographs were developed for the underglaze-blue parts of the decoration, this being the least complex part of the design, requiring flat areas of dark-blue colour with areas reserved for the on-glaze parts of the pattern. Developing lithographs for the on-glaze parts of the decoration was a much more complex process.

It took a full five years to develop the skills necessary to develop lithographs which would accurately and effectively reproduce the feathery iron-red leaves and berries that infill the white areas surrounding the underglaze flowerheads in each of the six kite-shaped panels. Separate screens had to be developed for the iron-red line work, the delicate colour washes that fill the leaves and the tiny areas of green used to depict the berries. Avis's workbook, which she started in the 1960s, notes "31st June 1967 – trials for half tones re berries in red", and again, later on in the same book, "24th March 1972 – half tones for berries". This five-year duration is revealing in that it shows the dedication and skill required to produce the required effect.

Finally, the 22ct gold patterns were tackled, and again many experiments were required to achieve the characteristics of Derby gilding that were such an integral part of the design. This time Avis can remember working with expert gilder Betty Bailey, who 'gilded' pieces of acetate sheet so that she would have something to work from in the studio at the experimental stage. Drawings for every part of an 1128 pattern were produced, as the production of 'segments', which could then be repeated around a plate, was not considered conducive to the production of lithos that would accurately reproduce the hand-crafted all-over decoration found on Derby designs. The results were impressive, and enthusiastically welcomed by the Derby management, who knew that the success of this

Bloor-period coffee can and saucer, *ca.* 1835 (left), King Street plate, *ca.* 1900, and an Osmaston Road coffee can and saucer, *ca.* 1998. All are decorated in the same Imari pattern, known now and at its introduction as 'Derby Garden' but as 'Old Derby Garden' during production at King Street

process guaranteed the viable and continuing production of Imari patterns at the factory. Gradually, over a ten-year period, other traditional Japan patterns were shifted over to this form of decoration. The designs had not been simplified at all to accommodate the new technology and the quality of the resulting products was excellent. If one examines a piece of 'Old Imari'-patterned ware made at the factory today, the 22ct gold decoration is an amazing reproduction of the best work of Derby's gilders of the 1970s, and the accurate re-creation of their brushwork in the trellis decoration found on the border and in the characteristic scrolled decoration in the central area is technically brilliant.

The illustration above is interesting because it shows three items, decorated in the same pattern, made at the three Derby factories. The coffee can and saucer on the left were made at Nottingham Road in the early nineteenth century. The large plate was made at the King Street factory in the late nineteenth century. Both of these items were produced using traditional hand-crafted methods of decoration. The coffee can and saucer on the right were made in 1998 and decorated with lithographs based on the wonderfully skilled work carried out in the Technical Studio.

Even today, however, many of the Imari-patterned pieces require elements of hand gilding. On the factory floor today it is still possible to see gilders exercising their traditional skills when providing the final touches to 1128-patterned pieces.

'Old Imari' – Pattern Number 1128

The development of new products is a high priority for the Royal Crown Derby factory today, for the management recognize that it is only by renewing and innovating that the company will continue to flourish. There are many different ways in which the Imari tradition is being used imaginatively to create designs for new wares which keep the old traditions going, but which, at the same time, produce new, contemporary designs that appeal to old and new customers alike.

The popular ranges such as 'Old Imari' are still a very important dimension of present-day production and, although it has been estimated that in excess of ten million items have been made in this pattern since production of it started in about 1880, both dinner wares and ornamental items continue to be made in this hallmark pattern. New items are regularly added to the range and the pattern has often been adapted to new shapes. May Garton has become an expert in applying the 1128 pattern to new objects in the Technical Studio, and her considerable expertise means that she can readily adapt the pattern to suit any shape. May was responsible for the majority of the 1128 giftware designs introduced in 1995, for example, which included a table-lamp, a photograph-frame, a mantel-

Miniature Duesbury-shaped tea set and tray decorated in pattern number 1128, *ca.* 1998

opposite
Selection of wares decorated in pattern number 1128 and made at the Royal Crown Derby factory today

clock and the Ram three-piece tea service with matching cup and saucer. In 1998 two new vases were added to the 1128 range, called 'Sudbury' and 'Tissington'. Both are named after Derbyshire villages; the former is a reproduction of a vase shape recorded in one of the early shape books in the Derby archive, but the latter is an entirely new shape. The pattern found on both vases is a May Garton adaptation of the pattern found on the scent bottle, pattern 876, already mentioned in Chapter 3 (see page 35). Dinnerware patterns have also been developed from the basic form of pattern 1128: for example, the 'Derby Border' and 'Ambassador' patterns, which both have plain centres, show the versatile 1128 pattern being used in an imaginative way.

For many years, the 1128 pattern has provided inspiration for the design of special objects made to commemorate significant events. The impressive vase and cover made to mark the Royal Crown Derby Stakes in 1981 was hand-painted with a scene of the racecourse between bands made up of an 1128 border (see page. 42). The hand-painted 1128 plate made to commemorate Derby County's achievement in the final of the FA Cup in 1946 is popular with visitors to the factory museum, as is the Derby Mansion House Dwarf, made to commemorate Margaret Thatcher's election victory in 1983. In the eighteenth century dwarves paraded up and down the streets of London telling the news of the day by way of sheets of paper fastened to their broad-brimmed hats. Ceramic dwarves of this kind were made at Nottingham Road and are still made to special order at Osmaston Road today. Fastened to the 1128-bordered hat of this figure is a note that reads "Margaret Thatcher – Re-elected with Record Majority, 9th June 1983". Most poignant of

this page left
Plate decorated in pattern number 1128 and made to commemorate Derby County's victory in the FA Cup Final in 1946

this page right
Derby dwarf, decorated in pattern number 1128, with hat

opposite
Derby border-patterned dinnerware

Signature of Diana, Princess of Wales on a candlestick decorated in pattern number 1128, 1987; candlestick illustrated on page 66

Coffee can and saucer decorated in 'Acanthus' from the Curator's Collection

opposite
Items from the Curator's Collection of coffee cans and saucers with complementary coffeepot, sugar and cream

all the 'Old Imari' items made to commemorate special events is the large 1128 candlestick which Diana, Princess of Wales signed in gold when she visited the factory to open the Ronald William Raven Room in 1987; the candlestick is displayed in the factory museum alongside the palette and brush that she used to make her mark.

Curatorial Imari

The museum collections continue to provide a valuable resource for Derby designers. On a number of occasions in recent years, largely because of continuing interest in historical aspects of Derby Imari patterns, the decision has been taken accurately to reproduce designs made in earlier periods. The Curator's Collection of coffee cans provides an excellent example of this concept being put into practice. John Twitchett, the Curator of the Royal Crown Derby Museum in the 1980s, scoured auction houses, antique shops and markets to put together, over a period of seventeen years, a splendid collection of Nottingham Road coffee cans decorated with designs developed at that factory. A small selection from the collection of over seventy-five designs is illustrated on page 27. In 1991 a selection of six designs were reproduced as the Curator's Collection. The six

Selection of Royal Crown Derby
thimbles with Imari-inspired
patterns

designs shown on page 51 are, from back to front, 'Tree of Life',
'Acanthus', 'Pardoe', 'Derby Garden', 'Rich Japan' and 'Derby Old
Japan' (now known as the 'King's Pattern'). In 1991 elements from all
six designs were combined to produce an entirely new design for a
coffeepot, sugar and cream, which was applied to the traditional
Wishbone shape.

The Twitchett coffee-can collection has also been used for the
development of a series of designs by June Branscombe for thimbles,
which began in the 1970s; she is still working on the collection today.
Many of the designs found on the thimbles are miniature reproduc-
tions of original patterns.

The Paperweight Range

The introduction of the paperweight range with just six models in
1981 marked the beginning of one of the most important design ini-
tiatives in the firm's history. Jo Ledger, a talented and experienced
designer and art director, who first came into contact with Royal
Crown Derby when the firm became part of the Royal Doulton
Group of potteries in 1972, became aware during the 1970s that the
firm needed to branch out further into the giftware market. He
came up with the idea of a range of paperweights that would have an
animal theme and be distinctively Derby in character. The hall-
marks of the new range were to be a stylishness which would appeal
to contemporary tastes and an appearance which would continue
Derby traditions of rich decoration.

Ledger had shrewdly and quickly spotted the wealth of talent
that lay in the hands of the technicians working in the studio at

opposite
Royal Crown Derby paperweights
decorated with 1128 ('Old Imari')
patterns

Royal Crown Derby. In developing lithographs for Imari-patterned dinnerwares they had become extraordinarily adept at solving the problems of adapting highly complex graphics with all-over patterns to three-dimensional surfaces. Ledger knew that these talents could be adapted to porcelain animal forms in a pleasing and practical way. The first six paperweights were launched in 1981 and comprised a rabbit, an owl, a duck, a quail, a wren and a penguin. Interestingly, in the first instance, none of the patterns was directly derived from exisiting Imari patterns. Indeed, June Branscombe recalls that the wish was to create new and interesting patterns that worked well with the abstract shapes of the animal sculptures; fur and feathers were suggested rather than directly represented through appropriate use of motifs, but the colouring was always based on the traditional Imari palette of cobalt blue, iron red and gold.

Gradually, the range gained in popularity and, as demand rose, more and more models were added in an ever increasing spectrum of subject matter, form and size. Today, collectors can indulge their interests in everything from native British animals to domestic cats or even to an exciting range of exotic animals. In fact there is no one aesthetic that dominates the entire paperweight range, and Louise Adams, the Art Director at Royal Crown Derby today, is keen for this trend to continue. Individual artists are encouraged to develop their own particular ideas about the adaptation of Imari traditions to the models on which they work. Paperweights are now being designed that reflect Imari traditions in different ways, including models decorated in 1128 'Old Imari' patterns and others which reflect a more avantgarde interpretation of the Imari use of pattern and colour. Both kinds are proving equally popular with customers, and paperweights now count for more than a quarter of production at the factory. Additionally, as new models have been introduced, so old models have been withdrawn, and there is a thriving secondary market for out-of-production paperweights.

opposite
Selection of Royal Crown Derby paperweights with surface designs inspired by Imari patterns

Sue Rowe develops artwork for a
plate in the second series of
Christmas plates

Festive Imari

Sue Rowe, the Senior Designer at Royal Crown Derby, has become
an expert over an eight-year period in developing Imari-inspired
designs for tableware and giftware ranges. At the beginning of the
1990s a new series of plates based on the theme of Christmas was
proposed and in 1991 the first plate in a set of six was issued. The
designs all have an 1128 'Old Imari' border, and the patterns were
made to fit on to Duesbury 8-inch plates. Sue chose a Christmas-
tree bauble with traditional 1128-pattern Imari gilding as the main
element of the design for the first plate. The decoration incorporates
a blue diamond motif to echo the diamond pattern found in the
border, and within this a Christmas tree stands on a ground pattern
based on the scale pattern found in the border diamond lozenges.
The decoration is surrounded by a wreath made up of poinsettias,
Christmas roses, pine cones, yew-tree leaves, berried holly and
mistletoe, all set on a soft-green ground. All the flowers and leaves
are edged delicately in gold.

The second plate, 'Partridge in a Pear Tree', incorporates elements of the first design in the form of Christmas-rose motifs and
the circular band of interlocking diamonds, which in this case contain snowflake motifs. This idea of incorporating elements of a
design into the subsequent one is carried through to the end of the
series, so that plate 6 (1996), 'The Sleigh', contains elements taken
from Christmas trees, poinsettias and Christmas roses from plate 1
(1991), pears in trees and repeating snowflake patterns from plate 2
(1992), a background hillside from the 'Robin' plate (1993), the blue
pattern on the Christmas baubles from plate 4 (1994) and the paired
bells from plate 5 (1995). The set is thus united by subject matter, by
incorporating elements from one plate on to the next, by the use of
the distinctive 1128 border and by the subtle use of small design elements from the 1128 'Old Imari' pattern. Sue has cleverly merged her

interest in painting and design by combining subjects from nature with her thorough understanding of the Imari pattern.

The success of the first set has inspired Sue to develop a further set of four plates, which are currently being issued on an annual basis up to the year 2000. This time the borders vary, although each is based on Sue's own interpretation of traditional Derby Imari patterns. She has chosen elements and design motifs from borders shown in the pattern books, and below one can see the 'Plum Pudding' plate alongside Sue's meticulously executed artwork. It is also possible to see a copy of the original border pattern that she developed for this plate, the first in the set of four.

The 1997 Christmas plate, corresponding artwork and designs from pattern books used by Sue Rowe when working on the second series of plates

Selection of hand-painted Imari-patterned minatures: cauldron, 1911; coal scuttle, 1909; jug and bowl, 1908

A Miniature Revival

In 1996 a new range of miniature ornamental items was introduced, which is being gradually extended each year. It re-establishes a Royal Crown Derby tradition which began in 1904 with the introduction of what were called a series of 'toy' shapes, many of them decorated with Imari patterns. The majority of the miniature items are 3 inches or less in height, conforming to the strict definition of a 'toy' shape. Most take the form of common household objects such as coal-buckets, cauldrons, tea-kettles, matching jugs and bowls, fish-kettles, tea- and coffeepots, cups and saucers and milk churns. One of the most interesting shapes was a tiny flat-iron and stand measuring only 1½ inches, which is now highly sought after, commanding a price on the second-hand market in excess of £1200! The Imari patterns most commonly found on miniature items from the period 1904–40 were 1128 'Old Imari', 2451 'Traditional Imari', 6299 'Derby Witches', and semi-Imari patterns including numbers 2643 and 2649. With the exception of the semi-Imaris the patterns were hand-painted and gilded and the designs were accurate, smaller versions of the normal-sized patterns. The following list of 'toy' shapes (listed by shape number) has been compiled by Margaret Sargeant, Curator of the Royal Crown Derby Museum:

1455	Cup, saucer, plate, sugar and cream; 'Greek' shape.
1476	Helmet-shaped coal scuttle, pattern number 6299, 2¾ in.
1477	Coal-bucket, pattern number 6299, 2½ in.
1478	Watering can, pattern number 6299, 2½ in.
1479	Kettle, pattern number 6299, 2½ in.
1480	Cauldron, pattern number 6299, 2¾ in.
1491	Teapot, 2½ in.
1494	Mug, pattern number 6299, 1½ in.
1495	Tea caddy, pattern number 6299, 1½ in.
1496	Teapot, sugar and cream; 'Dublin' shape.
1497	Vase, globe shape, pattern numbers 6299 and 1128, 2¼ in.
1499	Vase, as above with wider neck, pattern numbers 6299 and 1128, 1½ in.
1502	Spill vase, 4 small feet, pattern numbers 6299 and 1128, 2½ in.
1672	Milk churn, 2½ in.
1673	Saucepan, 2 in.
1674	Fish-kettle, 1¼ in.
1675	Coffeepot, 3 in.
1678	Basket, 1½ in.
1679	Basket, 1¼ in.
1680	Tray, 2½ in.
1681	Iron and stand, 1¼ in.
1688	Teapot, sugar and cream; 'Greek' shape.

The new series of miniatures was modelled by freelance Derby sculptor Mark Delf, working in association with the Derby Art Director, Louise Adams. Once again, the patterns found on the Curator's Collection of coffee cans provided the inspiration for three of the four patterns found on the first four models, which were the milk churn – 'Tree of Life'; the kettle – Derby 'Old Japan'; and the watering can – 'Rich Japan'. The one-piece iron on a stand was decorated in a miniature version of the 'Traditional Imari' pattern. Recent additions to the range have included a wheelbarrow, garden seat and garden roller.

Royal Crown Derby miniatures from the range introduced in 1996

CHELSEA GARDEN

Birth of a New Pattern

'Chelsea Garden' is the name given to a recently introduced range of tableware on the Ely/Chelsea shape, the design of which draws its inspiration from Imari sources. The final part of this chapter looks at the way in which this design was conceived and translated into a form that enabled it to be produced on the factory floor. The intricately patterned border design was the work of Louise Adams, the Art Director at Royal Crown Derby.

Louise was keen to develop a dinnerware pattern that used Imari traditions for rich decoration, but in a more restrained way than pattern 1128; she wanted to design something with a more contemporary feel. The idea for the pattern came from two coffee cans which she chose from the museum's Nottingham Road collection. Initially, she chose to work with a gold flower motif emerging from blue 'rock'-work on the green-ground coffee can, and from the other more traditionally decorated can she chose a motif of blue leaves with an emerging red flower. Louise's style of working led her to arrange two collages of colour and pattern on the drawing board, one based on the more traditonal palette of blue, red and gilt, the other based on creams, blues, pinks, black and gold. Two separate designs options were developed and a discussion group involving Hugh Gibson, Managing Director, and Simon Willis, Marketing Director, was formed to consider them. The group decided that the introduction of panels into the borders would help to emphasize the Imari aspect of the pattern, although everyone also agreed that the lighter, creamy-ground version would look good from a distance and would blend well with natural fabrics, which are popular in the late 1990s for dining room interiors. It was also felt that the goldwork would help to harmonize the pattern overall. Louise went back to the drawing board to refine the chosen design and to prepare artwork for the technical studio. She was happy with the decision to go for the slightly more adventurous pattern, arguing that the Imari language was versatile enough to be developed in interesting, new directions, in the same way that it has been adapted with increasing freedom in the paperweight range.

Louise Adams develops ideas for the new 'Chelsea Garden' pattern

Bloor-period coffee can and corresponding artwork used in the 'Chelsea Garden' pattern

Bloor-period coffee can and corresponding artwork used in the 'Chelsea Garden' pattern

opposite
'Chelsea Garden'-patterned dinnerware

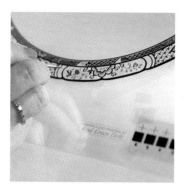

Three stages in the development of the 'Chelsea Garden' pattern in the Technical Studio

Once Louise Adams had completed the artwork it was passed to the Technical Studio for the next stage of development. The Technical Studio is the main bridgehead between the art studio and the factory-floor decorating shops, and its main purpose is to convert an artist's designs into a form which will enable the decoration of a ware to take place smoothly, efficiently and with consistent results. The studio aims accurately to reproduce the artist's work down to the subtlest shades of colouring and even to the nuances of individual brushstrokes. The skills of the technicians working in the studio are formidable, heightened and refined by the years of work spent converting Imari patterns to lithograph decoration in the 1960s and 1970s. In this instance, May Garton, with thirty-four years' experience of working in the Technical Studio, took overall responsibility for the 'Chelsea Garden' dinnerware.

To make a lithographic transfer which can be applied to a bone-china body, a screen-printing method is used whereby layers of colour and gold are laid down on special paper, one on top of the other, with drying stages between each one until the final design is complete. In the print shop, densitometers are used to reproduce an artist's selected colours accurately, and polyester screens are used to achieve the reproduction of fine detail. It is the work carried out in the Technical Studio that translates an artist's designs into a set of screens that will print the lithographs used to decorated the dinnerware items.

May's first stage was to develop the shape and form of transfers that would be needed to decorate the various pieces in the dinnerware range. This process is called fitting, and the technician attaches printer's tissue over the surface of the different areas to be decorated to determine the precise shapes needed for the transfers. This is done by drawing the shapes of the transfer on to the tissue, which can then act as a template for the design of the lithographs. It is vital that the eventual lithographs fit properly when they are laid down on the piece of porcelain, especially over curved surfaces; correct fitting ensures that this is the case.

The 'Chelsea Garden' pattern involved three in-glaze colours – cream, blue and green – and six on-glaze colours – green, black, crimson wash, crimson line, blue and gold. Two sets of transfers were thus needed to effect the decoration, and, for each set, separate screens had to be developed for each colour. For each colour, a line drawing on an acetate sheet was produced, exactly reproducing the lines on the original artwork. When this had been done, all the transfers were laid out on one sheet, which was photographed to produce a contact negative. From the negatives, positive contact sheets could then be produced. After registration checks had been carried out and the sheets had been examined for any flaws, they were sent down to the print shop for printing. Screens were developed for each separation from the contact positives, and the lithographs needed to decorate the wares were then produced in quantity.

Preparing clay for plate-making

From Clay to Glost

The plates and other items needed to make up the dinnerware range are manufactured using a well tried technology that has been in use at the factory for many years. The clay used at Derby to produce the fine white bone-china bodies is made from a mixture of china clay (25%) and china stone (25%), both obtained from Cornwall, and bone ash (50%), imported from Holland. Plates for the service are made using a semi-automatic technology involving the use of a jigger. A measured amount of clay is thrown over a revolving template, which then has a profile brought down over it to shape the base of the plate. Each plate is then fettled, a process which removes rough edges from the rim and bottom of the item, before the first firing takes place. Firing takes twenty-four hours in all and involves eleven-and-a-half hours building up to the desired temperature of 1250°c, two-and-a-half hours 'soak' at this temperature, then a ten-hour cooling-down period. When items are removed from the kiln they are white and translucent but matt in texture, and very strong.

Plate-making using a jigger

When further quality checks have been carried out and any substandard items have been discarded, the bone-china plates are passed on to the glazing shop. They are placed on moving spikes and sprayed with a solution of water and frit (ground glass). The plates are then fired again in a glost kiln at a temperature of 1100°c for about an hour in a firing cycle of approximately twelve hours. The firing process causes vitrification to take place so that the glaze fuses with the china bodies of the plates. When they emerge from the glost kiln they have a clear, glassy appearance, and after further quality checks they are ready for decorating.

Kiln trolleys stacked with plates

Glazing cups to be decorated with the 'Chelsea Garden' pattern

Making lithographs in the print shop

Application of underglaze transfers

The Decorating Shop

Lithograph transfers are made in the print shop and carefully printed on a thick paper with a waxy coating; they are gradually built up with layers of colour and the 22ct gold is applied as a liquid brown paste with the consistency of melted chocolate – giving little indication of the wonderfully lustrous colour it will have after firing and burnishing. After printing, stocks of transfers are moved to the decorating-shop storeroom, where they remain until production of the dinnerware range is put into operation.

Where in-glaze lithographs are to be used, these are done first and applied directly to the surface of the glazed item. Transfers are soaked off the sheets of waxy paper and applied with consummate skill to the pieces after they have been warmed in an oven beneath the decorator's workstation. The fit and disposition of the lithographs has to be exactly right, or correct registration will not occur when the next set is applied. The transfers were, of course, printed to a precise specification correlated to the size of the pieces emerging from the biscuit kilns. After the in-glaze prints have been applied, the pieces are placed on a conveyor belt to be fired for a third time, and this causes the colours to sink into the clear layer of glaze and produce the rich, even hue that characterizes Royal Crown Derby wares which have been decorated in this way. The pieces then return to the decorating shop to have the on-glaze transfers applied in the same way as before. This time the decorator lays them down over the in-glaze colours, and, as these transfers contain gold, which is heat sensitive, the fourth firing takes place at an even lower temperature than the last one. When pieces emerge from the enamelling kiln they are passed to the gilding department for hand-finishing. At this point the pieces are fired for a fifth time at 805°c. When the pieces emerge from the kiln they are passed to the burnishers, whose job it is to buff the gold areas to develop a rich lustrous shine.

Finally, the completed items are subjected to rigorous checking in the quality-control department and flawed items are discarded or retained for sale as seconds in the factory shop.

The production of Chelsea Garden dinnerware involves numerous departments and a range of artistic, technical and craft skills, resulting in wares of very high quality. Many of the craft skills are rooted in ceramic-making traditions that go right back to the beginning of porcelain making in Derby, but at the same time they are integrated with the more modern technologies that characterize a forward-looking firm. The Chelsea Garden range of dinnerware epitomizes the continuing development of the Imari tradition, in which the artistic intentions of the designer are clearly carried through to the final product by the brilliant work carried out by the technicians working in the studio and by the highly skilled production staff on the factory floor. The service is the product of the close working relationship developed between artists, technicians, printers and production staff at Royal Crown Derby – testimony to a modern-day factory proud of its heritage, but at the same time determined to maintain its position as one of the foremost ceramic factories producing quality wares in Britain today.

from left to right
Application of overglaze transfers

Final stages in the application of overglaze transfers before firing

Final inspection of completed wares

CHAPTER 5

Identifying Imari Wares

All three Derby factories – Nottingham Road, King Street and Royal Crown Derby at Osmaston Road – have manufactured wares with Imari and Imari-inspired patterns. A selection of the most common marks from all three factories is shown here to aid identification of individual pieces.

By using a magnifying glass it should be possible to identify the Derby factory which manufactured a particular piece and, in the case of the Royal Crown Derby works, it is usually possible to determine the year of production.

STEPS IN IDENTIFICATION OF DERBY WARES

1 Identify the factory that made a particular piece.

2 If a piece was made at Royal Crown Derby, check the date of manufacture by looking up the year cypher.

3 Look up further information about a particular pattern by identifying the pattern number and checking it against the table at the end of this chapter.

The Curator of the Royal Crown Derby Museum inspects marks on a candlestick decorated in pattern number 1128

opposite
1128 'Old Imari' candlestick, 1987

The distinguishing mark of Royal Crown Derby was and is applied to all pieces originating from the factory, usually to the base of the object. The original Derby Crown Porcelain Company mark consisted of a cypher surmounted by a crown, a mark that had its origins in those used by William Duesbury to signify wares made at Nottingham Road from 1775, after George III granted the factory the rare honour of being able to incorporate a crown into a back-stamp. Sometimes it appears as a black underglaze mark without a year cypher. In 1890 the mark was changed to incorporate the new name of the factory, "Royal Crown Derby". Mark number 2 from 1891 has the word *England* in a vertical position at the side, and from approximately 1921 to 1964 *Made in England* horizontally beneath it. Normally, the marks are in overglaze red but occasionally they may appear in different colours. There have been several subsequent changes, which are shown below. The mark used today is based on the one first used by the Osmaston Road works. The mark © denotes design copyright; the date that follows is the year the design was registered, not the year of production

Nottingham Road (1756–1848)

ca. 1782–1825, painted marks in various colours: blue and puce ca. 1782–1800; red ca. 1806–1825

ca. 1806–1825, painted in red

ca. 1820s, poorly painted mark in red

ca. 1825–1848, the earliest Bloor mark

ca. 1825–1848, variant of the Bloor mark

King Street (1848–1935)

ca. 1849–1859,
printed mark

1863–1866,
Stevenson and
Hancock

1916–1935,
William
Larcombe

1917–1934,
Larcombe and
Paget

ca. 1934,
Paget

ca. 1934–1935,
later Paget mark

Osmaston Road (1877 to the present)

1877–1890

1891–*ca.* 1940

ca. 1921–*ca.* 1965

ca. 1921–*ca.* 1965

1940–1945

ca. 1950

ca. 1921–*ca.* 1965
(XVIII = 1955)

ca. 1921–*ca.* 1965
(XX = 1957)

ca. 1921–*ca.* 1965
(XXIV = 1961)

1964–1975
(XXXI = 1968)

1964–1970
(XXXIII = 1968)

1976 to the
present

2 DATE MARKS

Royal Crown Derby Year Cyphers

Several of the marks illustrated on pages 68-69 carry a cypher as well as the backstamp, which signifies the year in which a piece was decorated. It is thus possible to determine when a piece was made.

John Twitchett has noted that the V mark of 1904 is accompanied by the word *England*, and that the mark of 1942 is accompanied by the words *Made in England*. Similarly in respect of the X marks of 1901 and 1947.

1880	1881	1882	1883	1884	1885
1886	1887	1888	1889	1890	1891
1892	1893	1894	1895	1896	1897
1898	1899	1900	1901	1902	1903
1904	1905	1906	1907	1908	1909
1910	1911	1912	1913	1914	1915
1916	1917	1918	1919	1920	1921
1922	1923	1924	1925	1926	1927
1928	1929	1930	1931	1932	1933

1934	1935	1936	1937	1938	1939
⊤̣↓̣	↓	⇩	⬦	I	II
1940	1941	1942	1943	1944	1945
III	IV	V	VI	VII	VIII
1946	1947	1948	1949	1950	1951
IX	X	XI	XII	XIII	XIV
1952	1953	1954	1955	1956	1957
XV	XVI	XVII	XVIII	XIX	XX
1958	1959	1960	1961	1962	1963
XXI	XXII	XXIII	XXIV	XXV	XXVI
1964	1965	1966	1967	1968	1969
XXVII	XXVIII	XXIX	XXX	XXXI	XXXII
1970	1971	1972	1973	1974	1975
XXXIII	XXXIV	XXXV	XXXVI	XXXVII	XXXVIII
1976	1977	1978	1979	1980	1981
XXXIX	XL	XLI	XLII	XLIII	XLIV
1982	1983	1984	1985	1986	1987
XLV	XLVI	XLVII	XLVIII	XLIX	L
1988	1989	1990	1991	1992	1993
LI	LII	LIII	LIV	LV	LVI
1994	1995	1996	1997	1998	1999
LVII	LVIII	LIX	LX	LXI	LXII
2000	2001	2002	2003	2004	2005
LXIII	LXIV	LXV	LXVI	LXVII	LXVIII

A number of other marks are found on the bases of Royal Crown Derby pieces. Small letters may indicate the name of an enameller, or, in the case of pieces made since the late 1970s, the names of either in-glaze or on-glaze lithographers. Other letters, often in gold, indicate the name of a gilder. Such a system enables the quality control department to identify the work of a particular decorator or gilder. This system is still used today, but the marks are of little use for identification as letters are reissued to new workers when old ones leave.

More important are the pattern numbers that appear on the bases of Royal Crown Derby objects. These numbers can be checked against the pattern books to obtain further information about a piece. It is impractical to reproduce all the information contained in the pattern books, or to illustrate every single pattern. An important step, however, has been to categorize all the Imari patterns into five basic groups. Using the table below it is possible to determine in which general group the pattern on a particular piece belongs, and also the date when the pattern was first introduced. Combining this information with the cypher mark on an object enables the investigator to determine whether a piece was made towards the beginning of the life of a pattern or some years afterwards. In many cases, some additional interesting information about a pattern has also been provided, such as its relationship to other particular patterns.

The basic descriptions of the five categories of pattern are:

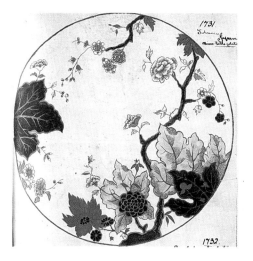

GROUP A
Patterns based on a traditional Imari palette of underglaze blue, iron red and gold. Patterns take the form of an all-over design but have no distinctive border at the edge.
Example of Group A: Pattern 1731

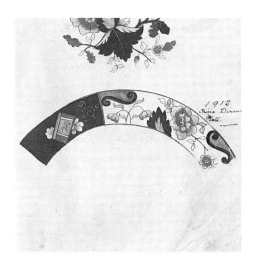

GROUP B

These patterns are based on the traditional Imari palette, but the designs incorporate distinctive borders as part of the compositions. This is the group containing the largest number of patterns.
Example of Group B: Pattern 1717

GROUP C

Again there is a distinctive Imari palette, but the designs are developed as borders only, the centres being left plain.
Example of Group C: Pattern 1912

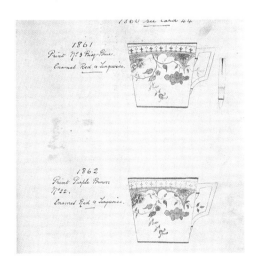

GROUP D

Patterns in this group have a range of colours inspired by the traditional Imari palette, but the overall effect is one lacking the richness of the designs found in the patterns allocated to groups A to C. Additionally, they often make use of printed decoration and seem only loosely inspired by traditional Imari designs.
Example of Group D: Patterns 1861–62

GROUP E

These patterns are inspired by those allocated to groups A and B, but the palette is not an Imari one. The designs show adaptations of other techniques of decoration used at Royal Crown Derby and often use large quantities of gold and extensive use of raised gold on an ivory ground. They were expensive to produce and this is therefore the smallest group in terms of the number of designs.
Example of Group E: Pattern 1981

THE INFORMATION IN THIS TABLE IS GIVEN IN THE FORM:

PATTERN NUMBER	PATTERN BOOK	YEAR OF INTRODUCTION	PATTERN CATEGORY
1145	2	1882	B

394

876

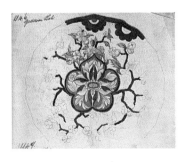

1146

opposite 1130

1	1	1880	B	Antecedent of well known Derby pattern originally developed at Nottingham Road and which later became known as the 'King's Pattern'.
2	1	1880	B	As previous.
6	1	1880	B	Design incorporates a peacock among foliage.
198	1	1880	B	Design has a narrow border incorporating butterfly motifs.
367	1	1880	B	As pattern 1 but in blue and gilt only – no red enamel.
383	1	1880	B	This is the pattern number normally associated with this well known design.
394	1	1880	B	On a dessert plate the pattern book notes "rich gilt & enamel japan ornament".
395	1	1880	B	A variant of 394 with less gold – "printed in blue and red, gilt & enamelled".
396	1	1880	B	Another variant of 394.
477	1	1880	A	Related to pattern 383 but with no border.
486	1	1880	B	Derived from pattern 198 but without panels.
491	1	1880	D	All-over pattern in shades of pale-blue and turquoise.
495	1	1880	B	Similar to pattern 486.
524	1	1880	B	Pattern book notes "as pattern 495 with less gilt".
788	1	1880	B	As pattern 383 but "all blue and gilt".
876	1	1880	B	On a scent bottle, this design is a forerunner of pattern number 1128, 'Old Imari'.
877	1	1880	B	Pattern book designates this design as 'Japan Derby'; it is a forerunner of pattern 2451, 'Traditional Imari'.
893	2	1882	A	
919	2	1882	B	Pattern book notes indicate "Royal Gadroon Dessert Plate showing finish at edge. For Tiffany, July 1914".
953	2	1882	B	Design is shown on a teacup and saucer and Stanhope dessert plate.
971	2	1882	B	Pattern book notes "Japan border".
972	2	1882	B	Border as for 971.
973	2	1882	B	Design is shown on a Crown table plate with a narrow border.
1009	2	1882	A	
1018	2	1882	C	Based on a pattern 919 but with a plain centre.
1075	2	1882	B	Pattern book notes this as a "Japan" pattern.
1124	2	1882	B	As previous.
1125	2	1882	B	Border derived from 919, centre from 876 and large centrally placed floral motif also from 919.
1126	2	1882	B	Border derived from 919, centre from 876 and centrally placed flower in dark blue. Pattern book notes – "pattern repeats six times round the plate".
1127	2	1882	B	Based on a design that the pattern book refers to as "lime leaf", this pattern is treated as a 'Japan' in terms of palette.
1128	2	1882	B	The classic Royal Crown Derby pattern, which is still made today. It was eventually called 'Old Imari' and is based on a border from pattern 919 and a centre from 876.
1130	2	1882	B	
1131	2	1882	B	
1132	2	1882	A	Based on pattern 1127 'lime leaf Japan' with one large spray of foliage.
1137	2	1882	A	As previous.
1138	2	1882	A	Based on pattern 1127 'lime leaf Japan' with three sprays of foliage.
1143	2	1882	D	With a "rustic border in blue and red", the design incorporates birds on branches "painted with gilt etching".
1145	2	1882	B	Pattern book notes "design from an old vase in the S.K.M. – the South Kensington Museum."
1146	2	1882	B	Pattern book notes design was done by Mr Lunn, former Art Director at Osmaston Road.
1147	2	1882	B	Design by Mr Lunn.
1148	2	1882	A	Design by Mr Lunn – "blue ground Japan plate in gold and red".

1129. Four red and blue Stars
on Cup five on Saucer.

1130.
Pattern repeats twice on Cup
and Saucer.
Print in Smoke

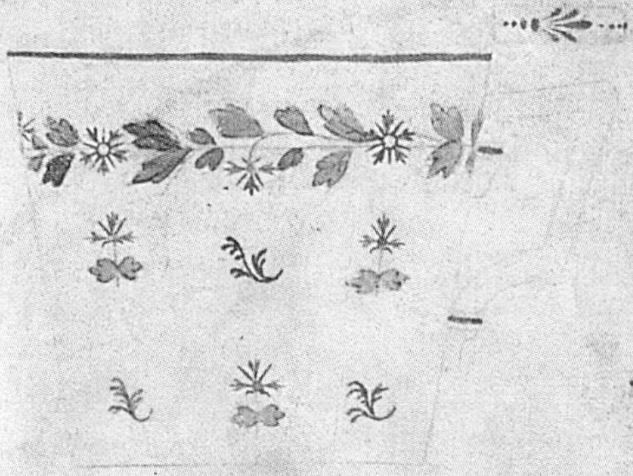

1130
China Table plate
Pattern repeats 3 times

this pattern on
Abbot Derost pa
8736

1153

1382

1627

1149	2	1882	A	Design by Mr Lunn – "Japan pattern in blue, red and gold".
1151	2	1882	C	
1152	2	1882	A	Design incorporates a pot with flowers.
1153	2	1882	A	Design incorporates oak leaves and acorns.
1154	2	1882	A	Variation on 1152.
1159	2	1882	A	Variation on 1152.
1161	2	1882	A	Variation on 1152.
1162	2	1882	B	Related to the 1128 group of designs.
1163	2	1882	B	Variation on 1162 with cobalt-blue ground.
1202	2	1882	C	Related to 1153 and incorporating a border with oak leaves and acorns.
1211	2	1882	C	Related to 1153; border of oak leaves and acorns on a cobalt-blue ground.
1216	2	1882	C	Border pattern derived from pattern 1145.
1224–8	2	1882	D	Designs are shown on Regal plates.
1230	2	1882	D	Design is shown on a Regal plate.
1248	2	1882	D	Dessert plate – 'Persian Japan'.
1253	2	1882	A	Pattern book notes "as 919 slight gilt".
1270	2	1882	C	As 383 but red replaced with aubergine.
1296	3	1883	C	As 1151 but with a cobalt-blue band to the rim and border.
1305	3	1883	B	Design based on pattern 1162.
1317	3	1883	B	Based on patterns 1162 and 1305.
1318–20	3	1883	D	Printed designs all variations on pattern 1318.
1323	3	1883	D	Closely related to 1318–20.
1332	3	1883	B	
1366	3	1883	B	Design shown on a Bute dessert plate.
1380	3	1883	B	Design shown on a Pinxton cup and saucer "in red, green and gold".
1381	3	1883	B	Variation on 1380 in "blue, red and gold".
1382	3	1883	B	Design shown on a tankard cup.
1383	3	1883	B	
1384	3	1883	B	
1392	3	1883	B	
1436	3	1883	B	As 198 but enamelled by hand.
1437	3	1883	B	Variation on 1436, also enamelled by hand.
1513	3	1883	B	Pot and flowers design.
1514	3	1883	B	
1516	3	1883	B	
1517	3	1883	B	
1518	3	1883	B	Design shown on china table plate and Gadroon dessert plate.
1519	3	1883	B	Design shown on Bute teacup and saucer and china table plate.
1523	3	1883	B	
1533	3	1883	B	
1559	4	1884	B	Pot and flowers design based on 1513 but with "slighter enamelling".
1587	4	1884	A	
1627	4	1884	B	Border of design has three panels, one with cranes, another with a buttefly and the third with a Chinese lion.
1646	4	1884	B	Centre of design includes a pagoda within a cartouche.
1648	4	1884	B	Design has a dark cobalt-blue ground.
1656	4	1884	B	Notes indicate "3 panels in Hancock's Chinese Red".
1658	4	1884	B	
1659	4	1884	B	Same border as 1658 with a different centre.
1660	4	1884	B	Border panels as 1658 but white instead of pink; centre as 1659.
1670	4	1884	D	Design shown on Bristol cup.
1671	4	1884	D	Variation on 1670 with additional gold decoration..
1673	4	1884	D	Variation on 1671.
1674	4	1884	D	Variation on 1670 with ivory ground.
1675	4	1884	D	Variation on 1671 with raised gold decoration.
1676	4	1884	D	Variation on 1671.
1677	4	1884	D	Variation on 1671 on a Derby flute cup.
1679	4	1884	D	Design shown on a Regal plate and printed in red enamel and turquoise.
1680	4	1884	D	Variation on 1679.
1688	4	1884	D	Variation on 1679
1690	4	1884	D	Variation on 1679.
1691	4	1884	D	Variation on 1126 with gilt on bronze ground instead of red enamel.

1694	4	1884	D	
1704	4	1884	C	One of several designs consisting of trailing foliage with flowers; this one in Imari colours.
1707	4	1884	C	Similar to 1704 with slight colour variation.
1717	4	1884	B	Border incorporates a fence design.
1718	4	1884	D	
1719	4	1884	D	
1721	4	1884	B	Design shown on Crown table plate.
1723	4	1884	D	
1724	4	1884	B	Pot-and-flowers printed design.
1725	4	1884	B	As 1724 but with a Turkish blue background print.
1726	4	1884	B	AS 172 but with a red background print.
1727	4	1884	B	As 1724 but with an Emery's mixed brown background print.
1728	4	1884	D	
1729	4	1884	D	
1731	4	1884	A	Design based on tobacco plant.
1761	4	1884	D	As 1677 but with a plain edge.
1762	4	1884	B	Based on the 1126–28 set of designs. Centre ground colour is a bronze rather than a red enamel.
1763	4	1884	D	
1766	4	1884	B	
1767	4	1884	B	Variant of patterns 1659 and 1660.
1774	4	1884	B	Variant of patterns 1659 and 1660 in cobalt blue and gold only.
1775	4	1884	B	Variant of patterns 1659 and 1660 in "blue and chinese red".
1804–7	4	1884	D	Print and tint designs loosely inspired by Imari patterns.
1812	4	1884	D	Design shown on Derby flute cup.
1813	4	1884	B	
1814	4	1884	D	
1833	4	1884	D	
1834	4	1884	D	Design shown on a Bamboo dessert plate and has a raised border design.
1845	4	1884	B	
1850	4	1884	B	Stork and bamboo design and showing an unusually wide range of colours, including greens and yellows.
1856	4	1884	B	Based on pattern 1834.
1857	4	1884	D	A 'Japan' design with an unorthodox colour treatment.
1858	4	1884	D	As previous.
1861–2	4	1884	D	Print and tint design.
1866	4	1884	D	As previous.
1868	4	1884	D	Notes indicate "in no. 90 red and gilt with no cobalt blue."
1872	4	1884	A	Design shown on Gadroon dessert plate.
1873	4	1884	D	Design shown on Cavendish flute dessert plate.
1874	4	1884	D	Design shown on Derby flute teacup.
1875	4	1884	D	
1876	4	1884	C	Based on pattern 1829.
1877	4	1884	C	As 1876 but with different colour ways.
1878	4	1884	B	
1879	4	1884	B	Pot and flowers design.
1888	4	1884	B	Pot and flowers design.
1891	4	1884	B	Design derived from pattern 1660.
1900	4	1884	B	Design incorporates a central arrangment of flowers on an ivory ground.
1902	4	1884	B	
1911	4	1884	B	As pattern 1721 but richly gilt.
1912	4	1884	B	
1913	4	1884	B	Design shown on Gadroon dessert plate.
1914	4	1884	C	
1919	4	1884	B	Central roundel has a design incorporating trees and a fence.
1922	4	1884	B	Design incorporates a pagoda with a tree beside it.
1924	4	1884	B	Design shown on Gadroon dessert plate.
1925	4	1884	B	
1932	4	1884	B	
1937	4	1884	B	Design shown on Victoria dessert plate.
1942	4	1884	B	As previous.
1945	5	1885/6	D	Design incorporates hanging lanterns.
1958	5	1885/6	D	

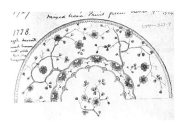

1728

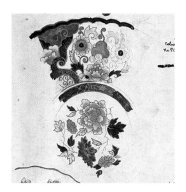

1873

1902

1966

2024

2173

1962	5	1885/6	E	Based on pattern 1659, which was in Imari colours. This time the design has an ivory ground with "centre in raised gold, cut up in red".
1963	5	1885/6	E	Based on pattern 1659 and with raised gold decoration.
1966	5	1885/6	E	Raised gold decoration on an ivory ground.
1968	5	1885/6	B	Based on pattern 1659; as 1963 but with a dark and light cobalt border.
1969	5	1885/6	B	As 1963 but with a dark and light cobalt border and light cobalt centre.
1981	5	1885/6	E	Based on pattern 1879. Notes indicate "dessert gadroon japan in 2 ivories; raised gold cut up in red".
1982	5	1885/6	E	Based on an Imari pattern but decoration is in raised gold on an ivory ground.
1983	5	1885/6	B	Based on pattern 1721.
1984	5	1885/6	B	
1985	5	1885/6	B	Based on pattern 1813.
1986	5	1885/6	B	
2008	5	1885/6	E	Notes indicate "raised gold Japan cut up in red with two ivories".
2015	5	1885/6	D	Brown print enamelled in blue and turquoise.
2024	5	1885/6	B	
2025	5	1885/6	E	Based on an Imari pattern but with decoration in raised gold on ivory ground.
2026.	5	1885/6	E	As 2025 but with less raised gold decoration.
2029	5	1885/6	E	Notes indicate "Dessert Devon Japan, in two ivories, raised gold, no red".
2034–8	5	1885/6	D	Designs with the background print in different colours and then enamelled in dark and light red and turquoise.
2039–44	5	1885/6	D	As previous.
2045–7	5	1885/6	D	As previous.
2048–9	5	1885/6	D	As previous.
2050	5	1885/6	C	"light and dark blue rich gilt".
2051	5	1885/6	C	As previous.
2052	5	1885/6	D	Design attributed to Wale.
2055	5	1885/6	D	Based on pattern 1813.
2063	5	1885/6	D	
2064	5	1885/6	D	
2066	5	1885/6	E	Raised gold decoration on an ivory ground.
2070	5	1885/6	E	As previous.
2076	5	1885/6	D	Print and tint decoration.
2082	5	1885/6	E	Raised gold decoration on an ivory ground.
2084	5	1885/6	B	Traditional Imari pattern.
2105	5	1885/6	B	1721 border in red and gold.
2106	5	1885/6	A	919 border in red and gold with plain centre.
2107	5	1885/6	B	1721 border in red and gold with design in the centre.
2108	5	1885/6	B	As previous.
2109	5	1885/6	A	919 border in red and gold, plain in the centre.
2111	5	1885/6	B	383 border, centre based on pattern 1873.
2113	5	1885/6	B	As 1270 but with a red central design.
2114	5	1885/6	B	As 1721 but all red.
2148	5	1885/6	D	
2149	5	1885/6	B	Design shown on Crown dinner plate.
2150	5	1885/6	B	As previous.
2151	5	1885/6	C	As previous.
2159–61	5	1885/6	D	Printed 'Chandos' border design.
2162	5	1885/6	D	'Chandos' border, printed vase and flowers design to centre.
2163	5	1885/6	D	'Chandos' border, different centre design to 2162.
2164	5	1885/6	D	Variant on 2162.
2173	5	1885/6	B	'Traditional Imari' design.
2174	5	1885/6	B	As previous.
2175	5	1885/6	C	'Traditional Imari' border design.
2177	5	1885/6	B	Notes indicate "as 1721, more blue".
2179	5	1885/6	D	Print and tint design.
2180	5	1885/6	D	As previous.
2181	5	1885/6	D	As previous.
2189	5	1885/6	B	Based on pattern 1721.
2190	5	1885/6	B	As previous.
2192	5	1885/6	D	Based on pattern 2148.

2197	5	1885/6	D	Print and tint design.
2198–99	5	1885/6	D	Variant of 2197.
2201–2	5	1885/6	D	As previous.
2206	5	1885/6	D	As previous.
2208	5	1885/6	D	As previous.
2216	5	1885/6	D	As previous.
2224	5	1885/6	B	Notes indicate "printed, cobalt and gilt burnished".
2229–30	5	1885/6	D	Variations on 2197.
2230–35	5	1885/6	D	As previous.
2236–41	5	1885/6	D	As previous.
2298	5	1885/6	B	Notes indicate "china table plate – as 1911 but blued as 2224".
2312	5	1885/6	D	
2313	5	1885/6	D	Notes indicate "Osborne as a Japan".
2317	5	1885/6	D	Notes indicate "Windsor as a Japan".
2320	5	1885/6	D	Pattern has an ivory ground with gilt decoration.
2406	5	1885/6	D	Chatsworth pattern "blued and printed".
2415	5	1885/6	D	Design attributed to Lunn.
2416	5	1885/6	B	Design derived from pattern 1721 – "heavily gilt".
2419	5	1885/6	B	'Traditional Imari' pattern.
2420	5	1885/6	B	As previous.
2424	5	1885/6	D	
2425–7	5	1885/7	B	Print and tint design.
2434	5	1885/7	B	Variant of 225.
2443	6	1887	B	Notes indicate "as 1533 but slighter gilt enamelled in black".
2444	6	1887	B	
2447	6	1887	B	Design attributed to Lambert.
2451	6	1887	B	Based on pattern 877; this is one of Royal Crown Derby's best known patterns, 'Traditional Imari', which is still made today.
2472	6	1887	B	
2497	6	1887	D	Printed design.
2539	6	1887	B	Notes indicate "as 2444 but finished all in red".
2551	6	1887	E	Notes indicate "as 2444, two grounds, ivory, gold raised and cut up in red".
2583	6	1887	B	Notes indicate "as 2444 but cobalt and antwerp blue in lieu of red".
2646	6	1887	B	Chatsworth pattern in Imari colours.
2651	6	1887	B	Traditional Imari pattern.
2654	6	1887	B	As previous.
2684	6	1887	B	
2712	6	1887	B	1721 border in blue and red with a central pattern of four fern sprays.
2713	6	1887	A	Notes indicate "Melton print in underglaze brown; blued, enamelled in red, black and green, gilt and burnished".
2716	6	1887	D	Pattern incorporates a jug and bowl.
2727	6	1887	D	Variant of 2716.
2731	6	1887	B	As 876 (and 1126 and 1128) but with a gadroon edge.
2732	6	1887	A	Notes indicate "Print in underglaze brown enamelled in red, gilt and burnished".
2733	6	1887	A	Variant of 2732.
2775	6	1887	A	As previous.
2776	6	1887	B	Pot and flowers design; border incorporates moth motifs.
2781	6	1887	A	Border incorporates pineapple motifs.
2782	6	1887	B	Pot and flowers design.
2783	6	1887	D	Variant of 2781 with no underglaze blue and little gold.
2784	6	1887	B	Pot and flowers design; variant of 2782.
2791	6	1887	B	Variant of 2781.
2795	6	1887	B	Notes indicate "blue and pale apple-green underglaze; enamelled in red; gilt and burnished."
2810	6	1889	A	A printed design in underglaze brown.
2823	6	1889	A	
2825	6	1889	A	Design relates closely to 2451, 'Traditional Imari'.
2836	6	1889	A	
2840	6	1889	A	
2869	6	1889	B	Notes indicate "Pattern 198. Print in biscuit blue Sèvres; green leaves underglaze; enamelled in red and black; gilt & burnished".
2889	7	1889	B	
2897	7	1889	B	

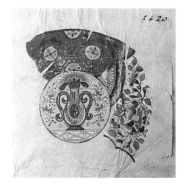

2420

2451

2712

2917

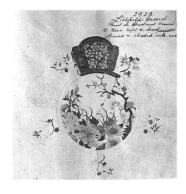

2928

3171

2898	7	1889	B	
2899	7	1889	A	
2917	7	1889	B	Pot and flowers design with butterfly motifs incorporated into the border. Royal Crown Derby Museum has a plate featuring this design.
2918	7	1889	B	
2920	7	1889	B	
2921	7	1889	B	
2924	7	1889	B	
2926	7	1889	B	
2928	7	1889	B	Design shown on Lichfield dessert plate with scalloped edge.
2930	7	1889	B	Basket and flowers design.
2931	7	1889	B	Trough, pot and flowers design.
2932	7	1889	B	Design shown on Rugby dessert plate; centre as 2931.
2937	7	1889	B	Pot and flowers design.
2938	7	1889	B	Pot and flowers design.
2953	7	1889	B	Chatsworth pattern in Imari colours.
2954	7	1889	D	Melton print.
2997	7	1889	D	Based on pattern 1659.
2998	7	1889	D	Same design as 2997 with a different background print colour.
3004	7	1889	D	Pot, basket and flowers design based on an earlier pattern; some raised gold decoration.
3013	7	1889	D	Similar to 3004 but with a rich border in biscuit blue and the raised gold decoration cut up with colours.
3016	7	1889	D	Based on pattern 2712.
3017	7	1889	D	As 2997 but with a pink underglaze print.
3019–21	7	1889	D	Printed designs, "all gold burnished".
3023	7	1889	E	Shown on a Rugby dessert plate, this design has raised gold decoration to the central basket and border.
3024	7	1889	D	Variant of 2997.
3033–36	7	1889	D	Variants of 3019.
3037	7	1889	D	Variant of 3004.
3038	7	1889	B	Notes indicate "As 2823 but solid gold background with diaper pattern traced over in red".
3048	7	1889	B	
3058	7	1889	B	As 2444 but without the red colour.
3066	7	1889	C	Notes indicate "rich gold border cut up in colour on a dark blue background".
3068	7	1889	D	Variant of 3019.
3083	7	1889	E	
3091	7	1889	B	Variant of pattern 383.
3092	7	1889	C	
3097	7	1889	C	Closely related to 2937.
3119	7	1889	E	As 3083 but on Gadroon dinner plate.
3124	7	1889	D	
3131	7	1889	B	Design shown on Carlton teacup.
3142	7	1889	B	
3143	7	1889	A	
3144	7	1889	A	
3147	7	1889	B	
3148	7	1889	C	Design shown on Surrey teacup.
3154	7	1889	B	Notes indicate "as 2444 with design cut up in raised gold".
3155	7	1889	B	
3156	7	1889	B	
3170	7	1889	B	Variant of 3156.
3171	7	1889	B	"Lichfield dessert Japan".
3246	7	1889	C	
3247	7	1889	C	
3266	7	1889	B	
3267	7	1889	B	
3268	7	1889	B	Design shown on Clarence dessert plate.
3270	7	1889	C	
3271	7	1889	B	
3272	7	1889	C	
3276	7	1889	B	Design shown on Lichfield dessert plate.
3290	7	1889	D	
3336	8	1889	C	
3396	8	1891	D	

3397	8	1891	D	Based on pattern 1659.
3400	8	1891	B	Based on pattern 383 and introduced on Clarence dessert plate.
3402	8	1891	A	
3404	8	1891	B	Centre as pattern 2931.
3461–65	8	1891	D	Printed designs based on 3461 and shown on Bristol teacups.
3501	8	1891	B	Based on pattern 383 and introduced on Surrey table plate.
3502	8	1891	B	Pattern shown on a cocoa jug.
3503	8	1891	B	Pattern shown on a toby jug.
3504	8	1891	A	
3505	8	1891	B	
3506	8	1891	B	
3508	8	1891	C	
3567	8	1891	D	
3568	8	1891	D	Variant of 3567.
3577	8	1891	D	
3578	8	1891	D	
3579	8	1891	D	
3580	8	1891	D	
3590	8	1891	B	Variant of 383.
3594	8	1891	D	
3596	8	1891	C	
3614	8	1891	B	Variant of 383.
3615	8	1891	C	Variant of 383; border only.
3635	8	1891	D	
3653	8	1891	D	Variant of 3635 with an additional band of decoration.
3657	8	1891	C	Notes indicate "Old Spode Japan".
3670	9	1892	D	
3678–79	9	1892	D	Variants of 3670
3685	9	1892	B	
3686	9	1892	C	
3687	9	1892	C	Design shown on tankard cup.
3688	9	1892	D	
3689	9	1892	D	
3698	9	1892	C	Design shown on Carlton teacup.
3701	9	1892	B	
3714	9	1892	B	Closely resembles well-known Derby pattern 'Asian Rose'.
3729	9	1892	D	
3778	9	1892	D	Closely related to 3396.
3844	9	1892	D	Variant of 383.
3866–67	9	1892	D	Variants of 3670.
3956	9	1892	D	Design shown on Brighton dessert plate.
3957	9	1892	D	
3973	9	1892	C	
3991	9	1892	D	
3992	9	1892	D	
3993	9	1892	D	
4237	10	1894	B	Notes indicate "plate in Old Derby Japan blued and enamelled by women; gilt by men".
4249	10	1894	B	'Traditional Imari' design.
4253	10	1894	C	
4353	10	1894	B	Variant of 383.
4358	10	1894	B	
4359	10	1894	B	Variant of 383; introduced on Sefton teacup.
4360	10	1894	B	
4363	10	1894	B	Variant of 383.
4371	10	1894	D	
4382	10	1894	B	Based on an earlier Imari pattern; decorated in blue and gold.
4391	10	1894	B	Variant of 383.
4394	10	1894	B	Based on an earlier Imari design.
4441	10	1894	C	Pot and flowers design.
4442	10	1894	C	Variant of 4441.
4459	10	1894	B	
4493	10	1894	B	
4494	10	1894	B	
4500	10	1894	B	Variant of 383.
4542	11	1895	D	Printed design.
4568	11	1895	B	Pattern number 2451, 'Traditional Imari', introduced on Brighton dessert plate.

3506

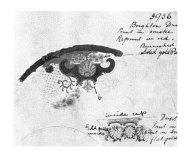

3956

4394

4646

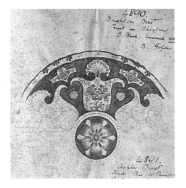

4890

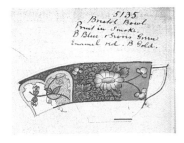

5135

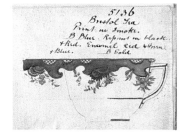

5136

4571	II	1895	C	
4583	II	1895	C	
4585	II	1895	D	
4591	II	1895	B	Variant of 2795.
4618	II	1895	D	Variant of 4371.
4643	II	1895	C	
4644	II	1895	B	Variant of 1130.
4645	II	1895	B	'Traditional Imari' pattern.
4646	II	1895	B	Pot and flowers design.
4649	II	1895	B	Developed from 4646.
4650	II	1895	B	'Traditonal Imari' design.
4652	II	1895	B	As previous.
4653	II	1895	B	
4655	II	1895	B	Notes indicate that this is a "rich Japan" pattern. Based on an earlier pattern incorporating vase and bamboo.
4656	II	1895	B	Same border as 4655 but different centre.
4657	II	1895	B	Based on an earlier pattern.
4658	II	1895	B	Centre finished as 4656.
4671	II	1895	B	
4674	II	1895	B	Notes indicate "Rich Japan".
4676	II	1895	C	Notes indicate "Japan".
4678	II	1895	B	As previous.
4692	II	1895	B	Variant of 3794.
4693	II	1895	C	Notes indicate "Rich Japan".
4738	II	1895	C	
4739	II	1895	C	Variant of 4738.
4740	II	1895	D	
4741	II	1895	D	
4799	II	1895	B	Notes indicate "Rich Japan".
4802	II	1895	B	Notes indicate "Japan".
4809	II	1895	B	As previous.
4818	II	1895	B	
4835	II	1895	B	
4840	II	1895	C	Notes indicate "Japan".
4842	II	1895	C	
4843	II	1895	B	
4846	II	1895	C	Notes indicate "Japan".
4850	II	1895	C	As previous.
4855	II	1895	D	Variant of 'Old Chelsea' pattern.
4875	II	1895	B	Traditional Imari design.
4889	II	1895	B	
4890	12	1896	B	Traditonal Imari design.
4946	12	1896	C	Variant of 1128 on Chatham dessert plate.
4947	12	1896	C	Again on the Chatham dessert plate, the design incorporates a 919 border, edged as 4946.
4963	12	1896	B	Based on an earlier pattern.
4970	12	1896	B	As 4591 but Sèvres green used instead of red.
4971	12	1896	B	
4982	12	1896	C	1128 border on a Clarence 10-inch plate.
5021	12	1896	C	Notes indicate "Rich Japan".
5022	12	1896	B	As previous.
5023	12	1896	C	As 5022 but border only.
5024	12	1896	B	Derived from pattern 1128 on Clarence plate.
5120	12	1896	C	Closely related to pattern 4651.
5121	12	1896	C	Closely related to pattern 3973.
5122	12	1896	C	Derived from pattern 2649 but edge from 5120.
5123	12	1896	C	Derived from pattern 1270 but edge from 5120.
5124	12	1896	C	Derived from pattern 563 but edge from 5120.
5125	12	1896	C	Derived from pattern 383 but edge from 5120.
5126	12	1896	C	Derived from pattern 3653 but edge from 5120.
5127	12	1896	C	Derived from pattern 3714.
5128	12	1896	C	Derived from pattern 2442.
5129	12	1896	C	Derived from pattern 3985.
5130	12	1896	C	Derived from pattern 3788.
5131	12	1896	C	Derived from pattern 2444.
5132	12	1896	C	Derived from pattern 4640.
5133	12	1896	C	Derived from pattern 2649.
5134	12	1896	C	Border taken from pattern 2451.

5135	12	1896	C	
5136	12	1896	C	Pattern similar to 4506.
5193	12	1896	B	
5232	12	1896	C	Notes indicate "Lowestoft treated as a Japan".
5239	12	1896	C	Referred to as a "Japan" in the cost-book notes.
5243	12	1896	B	Pot and flowers design.
5244	12	1896	C	
5245	12	1896	C	
5295	12	1896	B	
5376	13	1897	C	
5377	13	1897	C	
5378	13	1897	B	
5387	13	1897	C	
5388	13	1897	C	
5390	13	1897	B	
5391	13	1897	B	
5392	13	1897	B	
5396	13	1897	C	
5435	13	1897	C	
5439	13	1897	B	
5440	13	1897	C	
54441	13	1897	C	
5442	13	1897	B	
5459	13	1897	C	Variant of pattern 383.
5468	13	1897	C	
5470	13	1897	C	
5556	13	1897	C	
5560	13	1897	C	
5565	13	1897	C	
5607	13	1897	C	
5618	13	1897	C	
5619	13	1897	C	
5620	13	1897	C	
5621	13	1897	C	
56442	13	1897	B	
5657	13	1897	B	Based on pattern 1627, the design incorporates a pot between fences and the borders incorporate the cranes, lion and butterfly motifs. The design is for a Brighton dessert plate.
5671	13	1897	B	
5674	13	1897	C	
5675	13	1897	C	
5683	13	1897	C	Variant of 2451 'Traditional Imari'.
5714	14	1898	D	Border is Rococo in character although done in Imari colours; cost book refers to the design as "Japan".
5715	14	1898	D	As 5714 with more gold.
5721	14	1898	B	
5733	14	1898	B	Design incorporates a fence and shrub pattern in the centre.
5734	14	1898	B	Design includes a landscape containing islands with buildings, a ship and a flying crane.
5735	14	1898	D	Similar to pattern 4952.
5747	14	1898	C	Notes indicate a "rich Japan".
5748	14	1898	B	As previous; same border as 5747.
5771	14	1898	B	Pot and flowers design.
5789	14	1898	C	
5804	14	1898	C	Referred to in the cost book as "a slight semi-Japan".
5805	14	1898	C	Based on 5804, the design has additional elements. It is also referred to as a "semi-Japan".
5840	14	1898	C	'Traditional Imari' pattern.
5852	14	1898	D	Derived from pattern 2649.
5853	14	1898	D	Derived from pattern 3788.
5911	14	1898	C	
5922	14	1898	C	
5923	14	1898	C	
5958	14	1898	B	
5959	14	1898	B	
5960	14	1898	B	Design incorporates a pagoda beside a tree; described in the notes as a "Rich Japan".
5961	14	1898	B	Same as 5906 on a different-shaped cup.

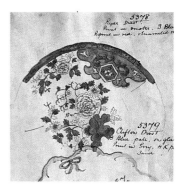

5378

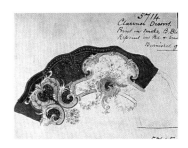

5714

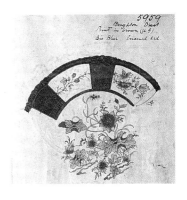

5959

6026

6217

6299

5962	14	1898	A	
5967	14	1898	B	Notes indicate a "Rich Japan".
5974	14	1898	B	Notes indicate "as 4160 (2553) but cobalt ground instead of ivory".
5975	14	1898	B	Based on pattern 5974.
6006	14	1898	B	Variant of pattern 383.
6007	14	1898	B	Based on pattern 6006 and on a cup and saucer instead of dessert plate.
6012	14	1898	B	Design attributed to Wale.
6016	14	1898	D	
6018	14	1898	B	
6019	14	1898	B	
6020	14	1898	B	
6026	14	1898	B	Variant of pattern 2451 but central design has a vase positioned on a table.
6041	14	1898	B	Based on pattern 2434.
6043	14	1898	B	Notes indicate "as 2654 in blue, red, pink, green, yellow and gold".
6095	15	1899	D	Cost book notes "Japan by Wales's people".
6096	15	1899	D	As previous.
6114	15	1899	D	As previous.
6137	15	1899	B	
6138	15	1899	B	Derived from pattern 6137.
6140	15	1899	C	
6151	15	1899	C	Based on pattern 4591.
6155	15	1899	B	
6157	15	1899	B	Variant of pattern 6007.
6206	15	1899	B	Pot and flowers design.
6207	15	1899	B	
6208	15	1899	B	
6209	15	1899	B	
6210	15	1899	C	
6211	15	1899	B	
6217	15	1899	B	Pot and flowers design.
6234	15	1899	C	
6235	15	1899	B	
6244	15	1899	D	Derived from pattern 2712; notes indicate a semi-Imari pattern in cobalt and pink only.
6276	15	1899	B	
6283	15	1899	B	Variant of pattern 383. Notes indicate "Japan similar to No. 1 but the red panels enamelled by hand".
6284	15	1899	B	Derived from pattern 3357.
6285	15	1899	B	Pot and flowers design.
6294	15	1899	B	Variant of pattern 4591.
6295	15	1899	B	As previous.
6297	15	1899	B	As 6041 but on a silver teacup.
6298	15	1899	B	This is the famous Derby 'Witches' pattern. Cost book notes "W.J. similar to 877 in red, blue, gree and gold".
6299	15	1899	B	On a Dover teacup. Cost book notes "Witches Japan (similar to 877) in red, blue, green and gold".
6300	15	1899	B	Pot, flowers and fence design.
6302	15	1899	D	Notes indicate "Semi-imari as 2649 (5842)".
6303	15	1899	D	Notes indicate "as 5590 border".
6304	15	1899	D	Notes indicate "as 5590 full pattern".
6305	15	1899	D	Notes indicate "as 2444".
6319	15	1899	B	Basket and flowers design.
6344	15	1899	C	
6433	16	1900	B	Derived from pattern 6299 and on an Edinburgh can. Notes indicate "panels in bronze".
6478	16	1900	B	
6479	16	1900	C	
6480	16	1900	B	Notes indicate "as 6478 but different edge".
6481	16	1900	B	Notes indicate "as 6479 but edges gilt as shown".
6519	16	1900	B	
6520	16	1900	B	
6530	16	1900	B	
6637	16	1900	C	Design based on border of pattern 4651.
6661	16	1900	B	Derived from pattern 6300.

6662	16	1900	B	
6663	16	1900	B	
6664	16	1900	B	Pot and flowers design.
6665	16	1900	B	
6675	16	1900	B	Cost-book notes indicate "New Valentia Japan".
6676–79	16	1900	D	Variants of 6675 with different colours for the background prints.
6680	16	1900	B	Based on pattern 6675. Notes indicate "Valentia treated as a Japan".
6682	16	1900	B	Based on pattern 6665.
6685	16	1900	B	Another 'Valentia Japan' pattern.
6686–88	16	1900	B	Variants of 6685.
6718	16	1900	B	
6779	17	1901	B	Another 'Valentia Japan' pattern.
6780	17	1901	D	As 6779 but with different colours.
6785	17	1901	B	Based on patterns 1533 and 2433.
6897	17	1901	C	
6898	17	1901	C	
6899	17	1901	D	Notes indicate "semi-imari in cobalt and pink only".
6901	17	1901	B	Similar to pattern 3714.
6902	17	1901	B	Pattern 2451 on a Cardiff teacup.
6903	17	1901	B	Pattern 2451 on a Brighton teacup; notes indicate "the top border omitted".
6947	17	1901	B	Notes indicate "as 2825 with edge and foot adaptation".
6948	17	1901	C	Notes indicate "as 2444 with edge and foot adaptation".
6949	17	1901	C	Notes indicate "as 1952 with edge and foot adaptation".
6950	17	1901	C	Notes indicate "as 4738 with edge and foot adaptation".
6951	17	1901	C	Notes indicate "as 3788 with edge and foot adaptation".
6952	17	1900	C	Notes indicate "as 5748 with edge and foot adaptation".
6953	17	1900	C	Notes indicate "as 5663 with edge and foot adaptation".
6954	17	1900	B	
6955	17	1900	C	Derived from pattern 4591.
6956	17	1900	D	
6957	17	1900	C	
6958	17	1900	B	
6970	17	1900	B	Pot and flowers design; border of 4493 combined with centre of pattern 2776.
7009	17	1902	B	Cost book notes "Done for A. Barker Esq. December 02".
7046	17	1902	D	Notes indicate "as 6779 but extra enamel only".
7057	17	1902	C	
7087	18	1903	B	
7097	18	1903	B	Based on pattern 7087.
7112	18	1903	C	Notes indicate "Valentia border as a Japan".
7121	18	1903	C	Notes indicate "Ashbourne treated as a Japan".
7164	18	1903	B	Design incorporates 7112 border.
7260	18	1903	C	Similar design to pattern 1952.
7261	18	1903	A	
7262	18	1903	B	
7263	18	1903	B	
7267	18	1903	C	
7463	19	1905	B	Derived from pattern 2712.
7469	19	1905	B	Derived from pattern 2649
7470	19	1905	B	Design incorporaates "Valentia Japan border".
7471	19	1905	B	As previous.
7472	19	1905	C	As previous.
7481	19	1905	C	Pot and flowers design.
7482	19	1905	B	Derived from pattern 1130.
7501	19	1905	B	Variant of 383
7523	19	1905	B	
7524	19	1905	B	
7760	19	1905	B	
7762	20	1906	B	
7763	20	1906	B	Derived from 7762.
7764	20	1906	B	
7765	20	1906	B	
7796	20	1906	B	
7797	20	1906	B	
7845	20	1906	B	
7913	20	1906	B	

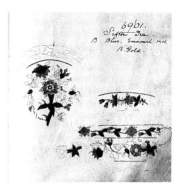

6901

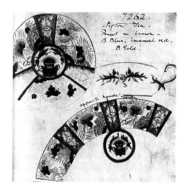

7262

7797

8607

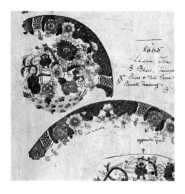

8665

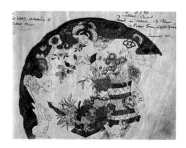

8738

7914	20	1906	C	Notes indicate "as No 1 Japan but edge as shown".
7991	20	1906	C	Notes indicate "as no 4591 but edge as shown".
8032	20	1906	B	
8044	21	1907	B	Notes indicate "as 6661 but centre altered as shown".
8145	21	1907	B	Variant of pattern 383.
8254	21	1907	B	Derived from pattern 2451 'Traditional Imari'.
8258	21	1907	C	Variant of pattern 383.
8259	21	1907	B	Related to pattern 563.
8304	21	1907	B	
8310	21	1907	B	Variant of pattern 383; notes indicate "printed from the number 1 coppers".
8330	21	1907	C	
8338	21	1907	C	Related to pattern 3788.
8439	22	1909	C	Based on pattern 2649.
8446	22	1909	B	
8450	22	1909	C	
8453	22	1909	C	
8496	22	1909	B	Variant of pattern 383.
8607	22	1909	B	Similar to pattern 8330.
8646	22	1909	B	
8647	22	1909	D	
8648	22	1909	D	
8649	22	1909	D	
8650	22	1909	B	Pot and flowers design.
8651	22	1909	B	
8652	22	1909	B	
8653	22	1909	B	
8654	22	1909	C	Related to pattern 8653.
8655	22	1909	C	Related to pattern 8654.
8656	22	1909	B	
8658	22	1909	B	
8659	22	1909	B	Related to pattern 8658.
8660	22	1909	B	
8661	22	1909	B	
8662	22	1909	B	
8663	22	1909	B	Related to pattern 8662.
8664	22	1909	B	
8665	22	1909	B	
8666	22	1909	B	Pot and flowers design.
8679	22	1909	B	
8682	22	1909	D	Notes indicate a "semi-Imari".
8683	22	1909	B	
8685	22	1909	B	
8687	22	1909	B	Related to pattern 8685. This is the well known Derby pattern which has become known as 'Asian Rose'.
8688	22	1909	C	Border pattern derived from 2553.
8689	22	1909	B	
8690	22	1909	B	Pot and flowers design.
8696	22	1909	B	Variant of pattern 383.
8703	22	1909	B	Variant of pattern 383.
8704	22	1909	B	Similar to pattern 8683.
8705	22	1909	B	As previous.
8706	22	1909	B	Variant of pattern 1128.
8729	22	1909	B	Variant of pattern 4591
8731	22	1909	B	Variant of 2451 'Traditional Imari'.
8735	22	1909	C	Variant of pattern 4591.
8736	22	1909	B	Variant of pattern 1130.
8737	22	1909	C	Variant of pattern 1952.
8738	22	1909	C	Pot and flowers design.
8742	22	1909	B	Similar to pattern 7796.
8785	23	1911	C	Based on pattern 1270 (383).
8956	23	1911	B	'Traditional Imari' design incorporating two birds beside a blossoming tree.
8977	23	1911	B	Variant of pattern 8906.
9011	23	1911	B	Based on pattern 8731 and border of 1128.
9013	23	1911	B	Similar to 8735.
9014	23	1911	B	
9015	23	1911	B	Variant of pattern 1128.

9021	23	1911	B	Variant of pattern 1128.
9022	23	1911	B	
9136	23	1911	B	Variant of pattern 2451 'Traditional Imari'.
9197	24	1914–16	C	
9259	24	1914–16	D	
9264	24	1916	D	Variant of pattern 6299.
9298	24	1917	D	Variant of pattern 919.
9309	24	1917	D	Variant of pattern 919.
9310	24	1917	D	Variant of pattern 9021
9332	24	1917	D	Variant of pattern 9137
9344	24	1917	D	Based on an earlier design.
9345	24	1917	D	Variant of pattern 8683.
9348	24	1918	D	
9351	24	1918	D	
9352	24	1918–25	D	
9402	24	1918–25	D	
9511	24	1918–25	C	Derived from pattern 2451.
9595	24	1918–25	B	Pot and flowers design.
9604	24	1918–25	C	Variant of 1128 border.
9665	25	1926–30	C	Variant of pattern 8450.
9666	25	1926–30	B	Variant of pattern 2451 'Traditional Imari'.
9667	25	1926–30	B	Variant of pattern 1128.
9673	25	1926–30	C	Based on pattern 1270 (383).
9674	25	1926–30	C	As previous.
9686	25	1926–30	B	Pot and flowers design.
9687	25	1926–30	C	Based on pattern 1270 (383)
9688	25	1926–30	C	As previous.
9695	25	1926–30	B	
9696	25	1926–30	B	Variant of pattern 383.
9697	25	1926–30	C	
9702	25	1926–30	C	Border of pattern 2451.
9710	25	1926–30	B	Similar to pattern 6299 (2451).
9711	25	1926–30	B	
9718	25	1926–30	B	Based on pattern 1128 with adaptation at the edge.
9729	25	1926–30	C	Based on pattern 383 with green panels.
9747	25	1926–30	B	As 6041, adapted at the edge.
9752	25	1926–30	B	Variant of pattern 383.
9755	25	1926–30	B	
9756	25	1926–30	B	Pot and flowers design.
9781	25	1926–30	B	Variant of 9756.
9810	25	1926–30	B	Variant of 6041
9811	25	1926–30	B	Variant of 6041.
9812	25	1926–30	D	Based on pattern 8978.
9815–16	25	1926–30	D	Based on pattern 8978.
9259	25	1926–30	B	
9820	25	1926–30	D	Another 'Valentia Japan' pattern.
9826	25	1926–30	B	Variant of pattern 383.
9832	25	1926–30	B	Vase and flower pattern.
9833	25	1926–30	D	
9834	25	1926–30	D	Vase and flower pattern.
9835	25	1926–30	C	Border of 9834.
9836	25	1926–30	B	
9849	25	1931		
9850	25	1931	C	Based on "number 1 Japan (383)".
9854	25	1931	B	
9855	25	1931	B	Bamboo and flowers design.
9856	25	1931	C	As 9571, adapted at the edge.
9857	25	1931	B	Vase and flowers design.
9865	25	1931	B	
9869	25	1931	C	
9870	25	1931	C	
9871	25	1931	B	
9872	25	1931	B	Pot and flowers design.
9966	25	1931	B	
A54	A1	nd	B	
A66	A1	nd	D	
A69	A1	nd	D	
A80	A1	nd	D	Printed design, "semi-imari".

9571

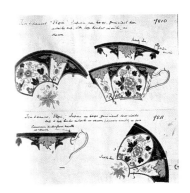

9810 and 9811

A254

A1283

A1295

A1298

opposite
Pattern number 1627 and a tea
plate decorated in the same
pattern, 1911

A93	A1	nd	D	As previous.
A128	A1	nd	B	
A240	A1	nd	A	
A254	A1	nd	B	
A291	A1	nd	B	Rich all-over pattern.
A337	A1	nd	C	
A345	A1	nd	D	Based on a non-Imari pattern – A336 – but given an Imari palette.
A365	A1	nd	A	
A367	A1	nd	D	Based on a non-Imari pattern – A366 – but given an Imari palette.
A382	A1	nd	A	
A383	A1	nd	C	
A384	A1	nd	C	
A385	A1	nd	A	
A398	A2	nd	C	
A399	A2	nd	C	
A402	A2	nd	D	
A403	A2	nd	D	
A419	A2	nd	B	
A443	A2	nd	C	
A444	A2	nd	C	
A445	A2	nd	B	
A446	A2	nd	C	
A447	A2	nd	B	
A480	A2	nd	C	
A481	A2	nd	C	
A482	A2	nd	B	As pattern 480 with the addition of a central design.
A525	A2	nd	C	
A546	A2	nd	D	Border design.
A560	A2	nd	C	
A561	A2	nd	B	As pattern 560 with the addition of a central design.
A562	A2	nd	B	Vase and flowers design.
A563	A2	nd	C	
A573	A2	nd	B	
A574	A2	nd	C	Deep border.
A575	A2	nd	B	
A576	A2	nd	B	Vase and flowers design.
A583	A2	nd	C	
A589	A2	nd	C	
A593	A2	nd	C	
A594	A2	nd	C	
A595	A2	nd	C	
A720	A2	nd	A	
A721	A2	nd	D	
A730	A2	nd	B	
A733	A2	nd	B	
A750	A2	nd	C	
A760	A2	nd	B	
A787	A2	nd	D	
A794	A2	nd	D	
A962	A3	nd	B	Notes indicate "as 8687 with extra gold around gadroon edge".
A1095	A3	nd	C	
A1253	A4	nd	C	Notes indicate "Derby border" pattern.
A1283	A4	nd	B	Design originally done for Tiffany & Co., *ca.* 1900.
A1292	A4	nd	C	
A1294	A4	nd	D	
A1295	A4	nd	B	
A1296	A4	nd	D	
A1297	A4	nd	B	
A1298	A4	nd	B	

1627. Dessert Plate.

Cobalt blue. red. Pale.

Blue Green on

Butterfly;

Pale rose
Color.

Birds
Traced
in
Black

Pale
rose
Color.

1628
346

16:

Author's Acknowledgements

I express my sincere thanks to all of those who have helped me complete the research for this book. I should particularly thank:

The Hon. Hugh Gibson, *Managing Director, Royal Crown Derby*

Sue Morecroft, *Product Development Co-cordinator, Royal Crown Derby*

Louise Adams, *Art Director, Royal Crown Derby*

Sue Rowe, *Senior Designer, Royal Crown Derby*

Tien Manh Dinh, *Designer, Royal Crown Derby*

Avis Garton, *Head of Technical Studio, Royal Crown Derby*

May Bottrill, *Design Technician, Royal Crown Derby*

Chris Bottrill, *Clay to Glost Manager, Royal Crown Derby*

Richard Birkin, *Decorating Shop Manager, Royal Crown Derby*

Elizabeth Parr, *Tours Organizer, Royal Crown Derby.*

I should particularly like to thank Margaret Sargeant, Curator of the Royal Crown Derby Museum, for providing valuable advice and assistance at all times and for checking details of marks on Derby wares. Also, Mark Duckett, whose patience was often tried during photographic sessions at the factory.

IAN COX 1998

Further Information

ROYAL CROWN DERBY COLLECTORS' GUILD

The Royal Crown Derby Collectors' Guild was established in 1994 to enable the company to develop closer relationships with collectors. Membership benefits include:

- A members' pack including an exclusive complimentary paperweight on payment of the annual subscription fee. A new guild complimentary paperweight is introduced each year.

- Subscription to *Gallery*, the quarterly Royal Doulton Group magazine, which regularly includes articles and information about Royal Crown Derby products, including Imari wares.

- Exclusive club offers, usually a special paperweight, available to members only. Guild exclusives are available only from Royal Crown Derby stockists on production of a membership card.

- Notification of special Royal Crown Derby and Royal Doulton Group events.

- Free entry to the Royal Crown Derby Visitor Centre including a factory tour.

- A free historical enquiry service.

Further details and application forms are available from:
Guild Headquarters, Minton House, London Road, Stoke-on-Trent, ST4 7QD, England. It is also possible to enrol as a Guild member at any Royal Crown Derby stockist registered as a Guild centre:

- UK Branch: Freepost (ST1624), Stoke-on-Trent ST4 7BR

- US Branch: PO BOX 6705, Somerset NJ 08873

- Canadian Branch: 850 Progress Avenue, Scarborough, Ontario, M1H 3C4

- Australian Branch: PO BOX 47, 17–23 Merriwa Street, Gordon, NSW 2072
- New Zealand Branch: PO BOX 2059, Auckland.

ROYAL CROWN DERBY ON THE INTERNET

The Royal Crown Derby website was created in 1996 to provide new opportunities for the company to develop contact with customers and collectors. The web pages include a short history of the company and its antecedents, details for those wishing to visit the company in Derby, details of the Royal Crown Derby Collectors' Guild and lists of stockists. Customers may e-mail the company directly for further information about Royal Crown Derby products or to ask questions about wares or even to make suggestions for new product ideas. In 1987 an internet discussion forum was set up for dedicated collectors or for those interested in discussing Royal Crown Derby products with other collectors.

ROYAL CROWN DERBY VISITORS' CENTRE

For many years Royal Crown Derby has welcomed visitors to the factory and 1998 saw the opening of a new Visitors' Centre, which further enhanced facilities and attractions for members of the public. The centre includes a demonstration area, the museum and a new restaurant. The Visitors' Centre is open 7 days a week, 9.30 am to 5.00 pm Monday to Saturday, 10.00 am to 5.00 pm Sunday.

Factory Tours

Experienced guides take small groups of visitors around the factory to see all the processes involved in the manufacture of Royal Crown Derby products, from the clay stage through to the final burnishing. A visit to the demonstration area and museum is also included in the factory tour.

Currently, tours take place at 10.30 am and 1.45 pm Monday to Thursday and 10.30 am and 1.15 pm Friday, and last about seventy minutes. It is necessary to book in advance. To reserve places phone the Tours Organizer on 01332 712841 or 01332 712800. There is a charge for each person. Reduced rates are available for pensioners and students. Please ask for details at the time of booking. Large, special-interest groups can also be accommodated. For safety reasons, tours are not suitable for babies, children under ten or disabled persons. Tours are not available during factory holidays.

Museum

The factory museum houses a fine collection of Derby porcelain, including pieces made at the Nottingham Road and King Street factories as well as pieces made from all periods of Osmaston Road's history. The cabinet displays are housed in a fine gallery on the first floor of the factory and are augmented by the Ronald Raven Room. A celebrated cancer surgeon, Mr Raven bequeathed his magnificent collection of Derby porcelain to Royal Crown Derby. It is now displayed in a reconstruction of Mr Raven's drawing room which includes original furnishings and pictures.

The museum is open seven days a week and is included in the factory tour together with a visit to the demonstration area.

The museum curator and staff are available to answer questions and provide advice and information, and members of the public may also write to the museum with particular queries concerning Derby products. The museum is open from 10.00 am to 12.00 noon and from 2.00 pm to 4.00 pm, except bank holidays; it is also open at weekends. Please contact the Museum Curator for further information.

Factory Shop

The factory shop sells clearance lines at advantageous prices as well as best-quality merchandise. Customers should check availability of products before travelling to Derby. Credit-card sales are also available over the phone. The factory shop may be contacted on 01332 712833. The shop is open daily througout the week and at weekends.

The Demonstration Area

Visitors to the demonstration area are able to see a variety of hand skills demonstrated by experienced craftsmen. These range from flower-making to lithography and gilding.

A programme of special events exploring other skills associated with porcelain manufacture is on offer throughout the year. The demonstration area is open seven days a week. For further information please contact the Tours Organizer on 01332 712841.

The Duesbury Restaurant

Open seven days a week, the Duesbury Restaurant offers a wide variety of snacks and hot meals served on the finest Royal Crown Derby Chatsworth bone china. The restaurant is available for corporate functions and private hire.

SUGGESTIONS FOR FURTHER READING

The Story of Royal Crown Derby
John Twitchett, FRSA
Published by Royal Doulton, 1976

Royal Crown Derby
John Twitchett, FRSA
Published by Antique Collectors' Club, 3rd edition 1988

Porcelain for Palaces: The Fashion for Japan in Europe, 1650–1750
John Ayers, Oliver Impey and J.V.G. Mallet
Published by the Oriental Ceramic Society, 1990

The Elements of Japanese Design
John W. Dower
Published by Weatherhill, 1990

"A Case of Fine China": The Story of the Founding of Royal Crown Derby, 1875–1890
Hugh Gibson, Managing Director, Royal Crown Derby
Published by Royal Crown Derby Porcelain Company, 1993
(Available from the Royal Crown Derby Museum)

Royal Crown Derby Paperweights: A Collectors' Guide
Ian Cox
Published by Royal Crown Derby Porcelain Company, 1997; revised edition 1998

The Arcanum: The Extraodinary Story of the Invention of European Porcelain
Janet Gleeson
Published by Bantam Press, 1998

ROYAL CROWN DERBY

194 Osmaston Road, Derby DE23 8JZ
Telephone 01332 712800
Fax 01332 712899